A DRESS
FOR THE
WICKED

AUTUMN KRAUSE

A DRESS
FOR THE
WICKED

HARPER TEEN
An Imprint of HarperCollinsPublishers

HarperTeen is an imprint of HarperCollins Publishers.

A Dress for the Wicked

Copyright © 2019 by Autumn Krause

www.epicreads.com

Library of Congress Control Number: 2019935785
ISBN 978-0-06-285733-0

Typography by Molly Fehr
19 20 21 22 23   PC/LSCH   10 9 8 7 6 5 4 3 2 1

❖

First Edition

To Leilani,
the Charlotte to my Emily

I want people to be afraid of the women I dress.
—Alexander McQueen

A DRESS
FOR THE
WICKED

PART I

CHAPTER ONE

WHEN I WAS GROWING UP, the rector of our parish told me, "Don't judge people by the way they dress. There can be angels in rags and demons in silk."

My mother encouraged me to listen to him in all things—except this. She had an entirely different opinion on the matter of people and dress. "Clothes tell you *everything* about a person, Emmy," she said.

If a man came into our pub, the Moon on the Square, with a patterned neckerchief or, God forbid, a colorful bow tie, she'd purse her lips and shake her head. She liked it when men's clothing bore evidence of their workday: dirt stains on their shirts, tears in the knees of their trousers, frayed shoelaces stringing through the holes on their boots. This meant they were one of our own, men who raised sheep in our countryside parish, far from Avon-upon-Kynt, the capital city. While everyone in our small country of Britannia Secunda appreciated fashion (after all, it was the national commerce that put bread in our mouths and roofs over our heads), people in my parish took a strange pride in their simplicity, even as the wool from our sheep and the threads from our cuttleworms went to the city to be turned into exquisite cashmeres and shiny silks. My mother, more than any other inhabitant of Shy, eschewed the national obsession with fashion.

I didn't dare think about what she—and the rector—would make of the man standing before me, his frame eclipsing the sun as I sat on a bench outside a large canvas tent.

Despite the heat, he was wearing a thick black coat with angular shoulders that rose high in sharp, rigid points. Three gold pocket watches hung from his tailored waistcoat. The first two were etched with the heads of horses, while the third was embellished with the face of a zebra with human lips and gigantic teeth. I didn't understand this man's appearance. It was asymmetrical and strange . . . yet beautiful.

"What is your name?" the man asked, bending forward to see me better and making his pocket watches sway in unison. As he came closer, I could see that his jacket was embroidered with silver thread that wound its way over the fabric in crooked swoops. If this was how people dressed at the Fashion House, then I belonged there—not in Shy, where one was often elbow-deep in dishwashing water or wielding an edging iron through the vegetable garden. My efforts at style—boots laced up the sides with black ribbons and bonnets trimmed with oversized flowers—always elicited whispers of "Does she think she's from the city?" from anyone I passed. With this man beside me, dressed from head to toe in couture, I didn't stand out at all in my wide-skirted purple gown.

"My name is Emmy Watkins. Well, Emmaline, actually," I

said, forcing myself to speak steadily.

I'd been waiting all morning to meet Madame Jolène, head of the Avon-upon-Kynt Fashion House, the most prestigious design institution in all of Europe. Earlier, when I'd first sat down on the bench outside her tent, nausea had needled my belly. But the hours of waiting in the heat had lulled me into a bit of a stupor. An ache had settled in my forehead, and heaviness pulled at my eyelids. I stared up at the man, my skin suddenly prickling beneath a layer of sweat as I realized it might finally be my turn. I took a deep breath, trying to calm myself. Hot air stung the back of my throat.

"I'm from Shy," I said, swallowing. I took another breath, slower this time as the man wrote my name on a list.

He consulted his zebra pocket watch and released a low, heavy sigh. He had been outside as long as I had, ushering girls into the ivory tent one at a time. "Blast this infernal heat!" he moaned, more to himself than to me. "She has to pick someone—she's turned away the last twenty girls."

My fingers tightened on the sketch. I'd been balancing it on my lap, trying to keep it safe from my moist palms. All hope of getting a position at the Fashion House rested on this single piece of paper and the image sketched within its perimeters.

Certainly, I wasn't the only one with such hopes. Any girl who wasn't royalty or born into a high-ranking titled family wanted to be a designer at the Fashion House. For a girl from an untitled family, it was the most prestigious job available and placed her amid the highest levels of society, all while giving her the chance to both wear and create couture. In Britannia

Secunda, where one was raised on fashion (unless, of course, one had the misfortune of being born in Shy), it was a dream come true. But getting that job was nearly impossible.

Every five years or so, Madame Jolène invited a few select girls to participate in what she called the Fashion House Interview. Those girls lived at the Fashion House for a full fashion season and underwent a variety of challenges that tested their design creativity and technical skills while also attending to the Fashion House's clients. At the end of the season, one or two became design apprentices. Even if one wasn't chosen at the end, the excessive pay and connections (never mind the wardrobe!) one received during that time were life-changing.

During the process, the papers reported heavily on the Fashion House Interview, and the entire country watched, often creating betting pools about which girls would make it furthest, and even putting up signs in their windows about who they wanted to win.

Ever since I could read, I'd followed the competition, daydreaming that I was one of the competitors. A silly notion, of course. The only girls invited to apply had always been culled from the city. Until now.

Two months earlier, Madame Jolène had announced that she was touring the countryside to seek a girl to join the Fashion House Interview. Unmarried girls ages seventeen to eighteen with a "sense for fashion" were encouraged to apply.

Despite coming from such a small country, Madame Jolène prided herself on being Europe's fashion muse. She had a right to be proud. While department stores like Whiteleys in London and Le Bon Marché in Paris now offered premade clothing, the Fashion House still created made-to-measure gowns from custom patterns. Madame Jolène's designs were so compelling that women from all over Europe traveled to the Fashion House for their spring and fall wardrobes. Customers who couldn't afford the trip—or the steep price of a Fashion House creation—purchased Madame Jolène–inspired clothing from the department stores or had copies made by dressmakers from illustrations in *La Mode Illustrée*.

In the ad, applicants had been instructed to bring just one sketch to the interview, no more. I had settled on a jade-colored jacquard gown. The pattern woven into the fabric was gold, and the design wrapped up the front panel like a seductive snake. Its neckline was low, with wisps of chiffon pulling horizontally across the bodice. The chiffon was light, whimsical, sheer, while the jacquard was heavy, the design chunky.

At home, I'd thought it was perfect. Yet now, under the unforgiving glare of the naked sun, I couldn't tell if the image in my mind—sumptuous folds of fabric with luminescent glimmers—had translated to the pencil and watercolor sketch. I fixated on the places my brush had strayed outside the pencil lines. I liked the resulting image, the effect of movement created by the flaws, but would Madame Jolène think they were mistakes?

"You're nearly the last one, thank all that's blessed!" The man pulled a fan out of his pocket and snapped it open with a flourish. It had foreign characters on one side of it and a painting of a black tree with delicate blossoms on the other. I'd never seen a man possess such an accessory before, much less one with pink flowers. "This heat is melting me. *Melting* me!"

It was true. His eyebrows, which had been darkened with charcoal, were starting to smear.

"Do you think she's ready for me now?" I asked, drawing his attention back to me and my sketch. I half hoped he would say no. I wasn't sure if I was ready to meet Madame Jolène. I tried not to think about how she might see me. If one considered my years of household duties and waitressing, one would think I was applying to be her scullery maid, not her design apprentice.

"Go, go." The man fluttered a dismissive hand at me, preoccupied with fanning his neck.

I forced my grip to relax around my sketch and noticed, for the first time, a dried stain in the top corner. Beer. Our new beer. The one we had just gotten on tap. I bit my lip, hard. How would I explain it to Madame Jolène? *Oh, never mind the pale ale on my sketch. I just wanted to personalize the couture gown with a little beer.*

"Good luck," the man said.

"Thank you," I managed, and rose to my feet. His eyes fastened on my dress and I fought the urge to pull at my skirts. Could he see where I had cut and re-sewn them? Three years and six Fashion House seasons had passed since I'd made the gown, and I'd redesigned it several times to accommodate the changing styles. Just this past month, I'd dropped the waist and added black bands of velvet to the skirt. But the dress's history and age could not be denied. The fabric was old, the skirt's cut dated. I'd done my best to update it based on illustrations from Avon-upon-Kynt's fashion pages, but by the time those pages reached Shy, the trends had already passed. At best, my gown was a copy of a copy.

I touched the yellow feather in my dark-blond hair for luck. That morning, I'd taken it out of my drawer of ribbons, feathers, and old broken brooches, and then hesitated, wondering if I should wear a black feather instead. My mother, who had been lurking in my doorway, holding a ledger, had asked, "Going somewhere?"

I hadn't answered because that would only lead to more questions. Ones meant to push and prod me into someone who could spend the rest of her life over a sink or pot of stew on the stove, ones like *Haven't you learned anything from my past?* and *How can you expect to feed yourself with sketches on paper?*

"Just running out to the store. I'll be back soon."

"Be sure you are. Mrs. Wells and Johnny are coming over later."

"Are they?" I tossed out the words easily, as though the thought of a visit with Johnny was the most delightful thing in the world.

"He's a nice boy, Emmy. Dependable."

He also has sweaty hands and an inability to maintain a conversation, I thought. The last time Johnny had been over, I'd found myself prattling on about the size of buttonholes while he'd downed cup after cup of tea.

"The black one is pretty," my mother said abruptly.

It had been strange for her to offer a suggestion. She rarely commented on my love of fashion, and whenever she did, her tone was so grim that one might think my passion was to prepare bodies for burial at the undertaker's home, not design and sew gowns.

"It is," I'd said. "But it's not quite right."

"The black one is best," she repeated, her voice tinged with agitation. "You should wear the black one."

By then, she had tucked the ledger under one arm and begun to bite her nails. It always made her seem young, as though she were my sister, not my mother. Sometimes she would resolve to stop. Inevitably, though, her hands would wander to her mouth and her nails would be reduced to stubs once again.

I didn't say anything else, and she waited, the silence building between us. Finally, she made a harsh sound under her breath—one single, angry *humph*—and left my doorway. The minute her footsteps had receded down the stairs, I grabbed my purple gown out of my closet and struggled into it. I slipped the yellow feather into my hair. Then I snuck out the back door of our pub and walked the two miles to Evert, the neighboring town where the interviews were being held.

The strange man was behind me now, nudging me through the tent. "Madame Jolène is waiting, darling. And let me tell you, Madame Jolène doesn't wait for anyone."

I glanced over my shoulder at him one last time as I slipped through the tent flaps, clutching my sketch and trying to conjure up some kind of prayer for my future. The last image I saw from the outside was the smiling, toothy zebra.

The minute I was inside, all thoughts vanished as I took in the tent's interior. Its canvas walls were striped teal and black. Huge fans, the blades painted with gargoyles wearing top hats and bowlers, hung from the ceiling, rotating in hissing swoops. A man in a gray suit controlled their direction and speed with a crank. Five fluffy Pomeranians attired in embroidered jackets padded around a bronze statue of a woman whose long streams of hair poured down over her voluptuous body in lieu of clothing. In the tent's center hulked a huge marble table with legs carved in the shape of horses' hooves.

And there, sitting behind the table like a queen, was Madame Jolène. Though I'd seen countless illustrations of her and read dozens of articles about her career, none of my research had prepared me for this moment.

At first, all I saw were her eyes, piercing and gray, like the pointy ends of sewing needles. She seemed to stare at me for a very long time, though it could only have been a moment before she directed her attention to the woman seated beside her. The woman was dressed in a green gown hemmed with extravagant layers of horsehair. As they whispered together, I suddenly realized I hadn't taken in Madame Jolène's attire. Her presence was even more captivating than her designs, though she was wearing a bloodred gown adorned with patches of lace.

"Where are you from?" I barely heard someone say.

No, not lace. Those were pieces of delicate metal arranged in sharp, neat rows across her bodice. But her gloves were lace. Black lace that wrapped around her palms and wrists, leaving her fingers bare.

"I said, where are you from?" The woman in green spoke harshly, clearly annoyed by my distraction.

"I'm sorry," I said, my voice strange and high. Somehow Madame Jolène made me feel as if I didn't belong in my own skin, much less in the gown I'd designed. "I'm from Shy."

"How . . . *adorable*." Madame Jolène cut off the ends of the words, as though they weren't worthy of her breath. The bracelets on her wrist clinked as she raised one hand to her forehead and pressed her fingers against her porcelain skin. A woman in a high-necked, lace-trimmed black dress came forward to set a cup of steaming tea in front of her. She wasn't outfitted like a maid, but she stepped back into the corner demurely, her hands folded.

"This," Madame Jolène said, "is a circus."

The woman in the horsehair gown touched her shoulder in a firm but sympathetic gesture.

"You need this," she said. She hesitated before saying, "You need one of them." Without looking, she gestured toward me.

One of them? Without meaning to, I peeked down at myself, trying to see what they were seeing. Scuffs on my shoes. Bits of dirt clinging to my hem, picked up on my long walk here, and painfully visible despite my efforts to brush them away. Pilling at my waist from where I carried trays for delivering dinner. I raised my sketch a little, as though I could somehow hide my inadequacies behind it.

Not that it mattered. Madame Jolène wasn't looking at me. Instead, she lifted her teacup to her lips. The steam from the tea drifted up around her face in thin streams.

"I don't design for the press," she said. "I don't design for anybody." She set the teacup down without ever sipping from it.

"Since when is beauty for everyone? If fashion does not inspire aspiration, then what, tell me, is the point?"

I noticed, for the first time, a newspaper on the ornate desk. It was turned to the fashion pages. Even at this distance, I saw the bold headline: "PARLIAMENT SLASHES CROWN'S ARTS BUDGET, PUSHES FOR TECHNOLOGICAL ADVANCE-MENTS AND FASHION FOR ALL."

I was aware it wasn't Madame Jolène's first choice to include a country girl in the Fashion House Interview. Country girls had never been included in the competition, and it was well known that she'd been encouraged to do so as a sign of progressiveness.

But this scene was not at all what I had imagined.

Madame Jolène was supposed to reach out for my sketch. She was supposed to understand that I didn't belong in Shy and that I belonged at the Fashion House. Even though the tent was cool and the artificial breeze from the fan wafted over my skin, my face burned hot.

"Madame Jolène," I said, trying to make her look at me. A fluffy white hairball of a dog started yipping, its high-pitched bark swallowing my words. "Madame Jolène!" I said again, loud enough to quiet the dog. "I think I could do very well in the Fashion House Interview. In fact, I know I could."

"My dear girl," she said. Her smile was full of pity. "The candidates for the Fashion House Interview are handpicked from hundreds of girls. Educated girls who understand not just fashion but high culture. Education is the cornerstone for creativity, and you are woefully lacking." She pushed her chair back, and it scraped across the wooden floor, making a dark, gruesome sound. "I have seen enough. I won't cater to this nonsense."

Her words sent my heart straight up into my throat and I stepped forward, still holding out my sketch. She was moving away, and I had to stop her—she hadn't even seen my work. She couldn't turn me down, not like this.

"You should go." The woman in the horsehair gown nodded at the maid. She came forward, ushering me out.

"Wait!" I said loudly, desperately. Yet it had no more effect than the yipping dogs. No one even glanced in my direction.

"Of course, we appreciate you coming," the horsehair woman said brusquely. I turned toward her, ready to entreat her to help me—anything to make it all stop so I could explain and show them I belonged. The maid's firm hand landed on my shoulder, and she shoved roughly.

And then, just like that, I was outside, stumbling over tufts of dead grass, my senses jolted from the blinding sunlight and drastic change in temperature. It happened so quickly that, for a moment, my lips were still parted as I tried to protest.

"Record time," the man with the three pocket watches said. "I was hoping you would rescue us from this godforsaken wasteland of a place." He turned his face to the cloudless blue sky. "I dream of . . . sorbet." He sighed longingly, sweat glimmering on his forehead.

I could barely hear him, much less reply. My breath was short, like I'd been running, and I started sweating again but not from the oppressive heat. I crumpled my sketch into a tight ball, the outline of the dress disappearing with the clutch of my hand and the crinkle of paper.

"Oh, honey." His face softened underneath its sheen of perspiration and smudged eyebrow charcoal. "Don't be so hard on yourself. It's not you. It's Madame Jolène. Let's see it." He held out his palm. Automatically, I placed the ball there, my movements dull, as though I wasn't the one making them.

The man propped his foot up on one of the tent stakes, spread the drawing across his knee, and stared at it in silence for several moments. The zebra on his pocket watch leered.

"It's good," he said. He ran his hand over it, smoothing out the wrinkles. "It's quite good."

"It doesn't matter. Madame Jolène didn't even see it." Talking sent nauseous waves through my stomach, and a disgusting, bitter taste rose on my tongue. Nothing made sense. Everything inside me had pulled me to this place and tricked me into believing my dreams were coming true. Despair, strong and thick like tea dregs, surged with the taste of bile. I glanced around, trying to determine the best place to vomit.

The man's charcoal-darkened eyebrows arched. "She didn't even see it?"

"No."

"Well." The man brushed his hand over the sketch one more time, but the creases still crisscrossed the paper. "That's a shame. It's lovely. The best I've seen all day, or my name isn't Francesco Mazinnati. I imagine you're the closest thing to style this place offers. The last thing I want is for Madame Jolène to hire a girl who only knows about dressing scarecrows."

He smiled at me. It was a strange sight, especially since the charcoal on his eyebrows had started to run down the sides of his face. He handed the sketch back to me, his movements careful, as though it was a fine painting or a drawing from Madame Jolène herself.

Somehow, his actions quelled my nausea. I stood there, gathering myself. I'd just been inside the coolness of the tent, but the heat of the day had already begun to reclaim me—as though the country was pulling me into itself again. I was surrounded by a barren wasteland of dead grass and sunbaked trees, the backdrop of my childhood and, if I kept standing there, my future.

I didn't give myself time to think; otherwise, I wouldn't have been able to move. I would have stayed rooted to the scorching ground forever. Without a single thought or word to the man, Francesco, I walked to the tent flaps and stepped through them to face Madame Jolène once again.

This time, she was standing in the middle of the tent, her little dogs and her servants revolving around her in chaotic circles.

"Madame Jolène!" My shrill voice cut through the commotion. Everyone froze, their eyes fixing disdainfully on me, as though I was a drunk stumbling into Sunday liturgy. Even the little dogs went still, like they knew I was breaking some sacred rule of etiquette and were quite appalled.

Only Madame Jolène remained in motion. She cast one glance at me and then threw an annoyed hand into the air, sending her bracelets spiraling down her wrists. "You again? What on earth do you want?"

My fingers clenched so tightly around my sketch that they added more wrinkles to the paper. The room's coolness swept across my skin. Still, I made myself speak.

"I think you should see my sketch."

"You think I should see your sketch?" Her words were razor sharp. I didn't say anything else. I simply held it out to her. The horsehair woman let out a scoff, but I remained where I was, arm extended into the air, sketch hanging in empty space.

Madame Jolène didn't take it. Instead, she pursed her lips, considering me. My face had to be flushed as red as Madame Jolène's dress.

Madame Jolène had looked at me before, but only in condescension. This time, her eyes ran from my worn, low-heeled shoes, over my old dress, and to the yellow feather in my hair. They stopped, lingering on the feather. Her gaze wasn't cruel or unkind. Instead, it was detached. I wanted to squirm under the weight of her attention, but I knew I shouldn't. I forced myself to remain still, chin up and shoulders straight.

"Interesting choice," she said. "Yellow feather and purple gown. Very interesting. Tell me, dear . . ." The word *dear* sounded neither affectionate nor playful from her lips. "How did that little idea pop into your head?"

She stepped back behind the table and the maid rushed forward to pull out her chair. Without even pausing, she sat down on it.

"'Fashion is the unexpected,'" I said, parroting Madame Jolène's own quote from a recent article.

A slight smile came to her tight lips, loosening the corners a bit. "And what is unexpected?"

"'The elements of an outfit that surprise—and sometimes even confuse—but delight,'" I continued, watching her face for any hint of approval.

Madame Jolène held out her hands, but not for my sketch. Wordlessly one of her ladies picked up one of the Pomeranians and handed it to her. She set it on her lap and slowly ran her fingers over its furry head and down to its beaded jacket. "You presume you have the capability to work for me?"

"I know I do."

"Bring your sketch here."

It was a ludicrous request—I had been holding it out to her for the past several minutes. I stepped forward, my limbs moving stiffly. A chill had settled into my bones, or maybe it was the disapproval of everyone around me, their disdain as paralyzing as any cold.

I held my breath as Madame Jolène took the drawing. Her eyes started at the top and then slowly worked their way down the page, in the same way she had observed my outfit. I held still, my breath caught in my throat, twin beats of my heart pulsing in my neck and chest.

"Well drawn," she said.

I gasped, the sound weak and whispery. I had been so certain she would hate it that her approval was more alarming than any rejection.

"Her choice of colors shows promise," the woman in the horsehair gown murmured, craning her neck forward to see the sketch for herself.

"It does." Madame Jolène sounded reluctant. "Where are you from?"

Obviously, she hadn't bothered to listen when I told her earlier.

"Shy. My mother owns a pub there. I've always loved fashion, ever since I can remember, and—"

"A pub? How primitive." The dog in Madame Jolène's lap began to yelp. She rose to her feet, pushed her chair back, and stepped around the table, not bothering to set the dog on the floor. It fell to the ground with a yelp.

"Listen to me well." She seemed to grow taller as she walked toward me. I could smell the chypre scent of her perfume and see the muscles in her face tighten under her skin. "You may be ambitious, but my critics necessitate your acceptance. They say my collections are extravagant and that I have no connection with the common man. Your inclusion in the Fashion House Interview will ease public pressure and appease those ridiculous members of Parliament, nothing more. Understood?"

Acceptance? Her tone was so taut I thought I'd misheard her. It sounded as if she was banishing me for all time, not admitting me to the Fashion House Interview. I was *accepted*? I would live at the Fashion House, create couture, compete to be an actual design apprentice? I glanced from Madame Jolène to the horsehair woman, trying to confirm this wasn't some cruel joke. The horsehair woman was staring at me as dourly as Madame Jolène.

"Understood?" Madame Jolène demanded again. One of her thinly tweezed eyebrows arched, but it didn't matter. I, Emmy

Watkins, was going to compete in the Fashion House Interview.

"Yes. Thank you," I said. I wanted to say more, to tell her how much this opportunity meant to me, that I'd do my very best to be chosen as an apprentice at the end, but she had already turned away. I didn't care. I could prove her wrong. Yes, it would be hard work, and I'd have to fight to be the best. But the one thing that every girl dreamed of—getting into the Fashion House Interview—had somehow happened for me.

"File away her sketch," Madame Jolène ordered, and the horsehair woman immediately slipped my sketch into an embroidered valise before rattling off traveling instructions for tomorrow morning to me. I listened, but it was hard to concentrate, and it wasn't because she was speaking quickly. From my peripheral vision, I saw the maid step forward to fold up the newspaper on the desk. The headline, in conjunction with Madame Jolène's contempt, spoke louder than the woman.

I'd gotten into the Fashion House Interview . . . but I was the only person who was happy about it.

Long shadows were crawling across the ground by the time I returned home. Since it was Sunday, our pub was closed. I'd heard that in Avon-upon-Kynt, places stayed open even on the Lord's day, but in Shy, everyone went to church and then to their houses for early dinners and bedtimes.

I walked through our vegetable garden, let myself in the back door, and made my way past the kitchen toward the staircase. The table was set with four place settings of our nice blue china. Crumbs dotted three of the plates, and half-finished tea sat in the matching cups. The fourth setting was untouched. Mrs. Wells and Johnny. I'd completely forgotten. Thinking of my mother trying to make small talk with the taciturn Wellses made me wince.

I made my way up the stairs. My room was directly at the top, right across from my mother's. Slowly, I eased my door open, trying to keep it from creaking, and stepped inside.

"You're back."

My mother was sitting on my bed, holding Madame Jolène's advert.

"I'm—" I started, and then stopped, trying to think of what to say. Suddenly, all I could see were the dark semicircles under her eyes and how, even though she normally stood straight and tall, her shoulders were drooping.

"So, you went to Evert to apply for the Fashion House Interview. Were you accepted?"

There it was. The question hung heavy between us. My mother had made it easy for me, summing up everything so all I had to do was admit that yes, I had been given a spot. Yet it was hard to nod, to confirm everything she'd said.

"Johnny was disappointed you weren't here." She changed the topic without any warning—but that was just like her. She was always saying things without saying them, leaving me to read her true feelings between the lines. Over the course of my lifetime, I'd gotten quite good at it.

"I'll make money at the Fashion House and send it back," I said. "Marriage isn't the only way to save the pub."

"How do you—?"

"I've seen the letters from the bank. I know we're behind on the mortgage."

A new anger flashed in my mother's eyes. She hated appearing weak, even to me, her only living relative.

"It isn't just the money, Emmy. It's a secure life with a good man who will take care of you. Do you think you can find that in the city?"

"That's not why I'm going to the city. I'm going to design. I'm going to do everything I can to be one of the apprentices."

I walked over to the far side of my bed. An old carpetbag was tucked against it. I crouched down and unlatched its mouth. The motion sent delicate dust particles spinning up into the air. I had never used the bag before. In fact, it had not been used since my mother had returned to Shy, pregnant with me.

When she'd been about my age, she'd gone to the city to work in a textile factory. Whatever had happened between her and my father remained a mystery to me. The only time I'd heard anything about him was when I was seven, when I'd walked into the kitchen to find my mother, a woman who was always in perpetual motion, sitting still at the table. She held a letter and said to me, "Your father died."

And that was it. She didn't cry, and she told me not to cry either. I obeyed. It wasn't difficult. I'd never known the man. It would've been hard to cry for someone I'd never met. I soon forgot about him, aside from occasionally wondering what parts of me belonged to him—my eyes? Or maybe my nose? My appreciation for whimsy and beauty, two things that I definitely had not inherited from my mother?

Others had not forgotten him. People in Shy had memories that stretched long into the past. Even while they gave us bags of hand-me-down clothing or did simple repairs to the pub, they always whispered about the single mother and her daughter.

"How did she look?" my mother asked after a long while.

"Who? Madame Jolène?"

"Yes."

"She looked . . ." I stopped. I wanted to tell her Madame Jolène was haughty, and that my stomach had been in knots ever since we met. I said, "She looked beautiful."

My mother winced, and I sat back on my heels. A shaft of fading daylight caught her face, illuminating the lines around her mouth and across her forehead. I suddenly wanted to hug her and tell her to trust me and everything would be all right. But then she spoke.

"I've worked hard so you don't make the same mistakes I did. I know it doesn't seem like it, but I understand why you want to go to the city. When I was your age, it seemed like such a beautiful, mysterious place. Anything could happen there. But it isn't like that. The city will chew you up and spit you out."

"This is my only chance." I stood up and walked over to where she still sat on my patchwork quilt. "I can't just stay here making drawings in the kitchen and tailoring people's church clothing. I have to try to do it for real."

I rarely spoke to her so freely, and I searched her face for a hint of understanding, anything that showed she knew I wasn't trying to hurt her.

"I've spent my whole life trying to show you what is

23

important," she said. Her eyes darted around the room, and when she spoke it sounded like she wasn't even sure what she was saying. "And you haven't learned."

"You sound like Grandfather."

At the mention of my grandfather, her eyelids fluttered, her head bending forward at the neck. Her hair was pinned up into its normal workday bun, and the pearl-like outline of her spine jutted out against her skin just above her collar. I thought she might cry, but even in her darkest moments—like when the men had come to take her beloved piano away to sell at public auction over in Evert—she never did.

During his life, my grandfather was a deacon here in Shy. We lived with him until he died, and my mother bought the pub with her inheritance. He and my mother had always had the same conversation—or at least that's how it seemed to me.

She would say, *Emmy is your granddaughter. Why won't you even look at her?*

And he would reply, *She has the face of her father.*

"I am nothing like your grandfather," my mother said harshly. Her eyes darkened, and I held my breath, knowing I'd pushed too far, that I'd never reach her now. We both sat in silence. Then, slowly, she softened and held out a hand. I thought she was going to stroke my hair like she did every night, but she stopped, uncertain. "You don't have to do this." There was a hint of pleading in her voice and suddenly, I thought *I* might cry. "You can stay, and we can forget this happened. We can go downstairs and have some tea and scones like we always do. We can use the blue china." Her voice became a whisper, and she finished the gesture she'd begun, gently brushing my hair back from my face.

I wanted to stay still. I wanted to let her run her callused fingers through my hair and sink into her arms. But I couldn't, and anger rose from the pit of my stomach. It wasn't my fault. It was hers, forcing this choice on me, forcing me to hurt her.

"You know I need to go." I struggled to hold back tears and somehow managed to succeed.

My mother pulled back her hand and stared at me for a long moment. Then she said, "Very well."

She left me standing in my bedroom in my purple dress, the yellow feather falling halfway out of my hair. As I packed, I kept listening for her footsteps on the stairs, kept looking up to see if she would open my door, kept waiting for her to come and say she understood. It wasn't like us to shut each other out. Then again, it wasn't like us to be apart.

I thought for sure we would say goodbye to each other, but she went to bed early. The next morning when I went to her room, her door was ajar, and she'd left a note saying she'd gone out. I looked for her, but she wasn't in the vegetable garden or at the bluffs overlooking the pond. I waited until I would nearly miss my train and then, glancing over my shoulder every few moments in case she was there, left for the station outside Evert.

CHAPTER TWO

ON THE TRAIN, the views outside my window sped by, accompanied by the train's *click-clack*ing chorus. They changed from rolling farmlands to clustered factories and, finally, to elegant storefronts. Growing up, I'd heard the refrain "farmers, factories, Fashion House" constantly—it was taught to all the schoolchildren as an easy way to understand how the farmers provided wool and silk threads, the factories turned those into fabric, and the Fashion House designed the styles—but now, seeing each link of the refrain passing by my train window, it was clearer than ever before.

I arrived in Avon-upon-Kynt one day later. I had slept fitfully throughout the trip, my sleep filled with troubled dreams. After slumbering and waking repeatedly, it was hard to tell the time of day. When the train lurched to its final stop, everything felt odd and surreal. The unfamiliar steam-engine fumes hung rank in my nose and seeped into my clothes and hair. My head was heavy and sluggish. I'd spent the past day and a half sitting in a plush train seat and dozing in a comfy bed in the sleeper car, yet my body throbbed, and there were knots in my neck and shoulders. I told myself it was just worry about going someplace new—not homesickness, not so soon.

As I stepped off the train, I discovered I had been deposited inside a cavernous marble building, not outside, as I had initially thought. Dull sunlight filtered in through skylights high above my head, bleaching the marble walls stark white. Voices echoed in the station, rising above the hissing of steam and thuds of trunks being wrangled out of the luggage compartment. It was chilly. Fall came much quicker to the capital city.

I'd kept my carpetbag with me, and I clutched it as I slowly walked through the station. People streamed by me in a flood of colors and textures. They wore the latest fashions: elegant suede coats, headwraps, and black boots with pointed toes. Huge mirrors lined the walls, multiplying everything by two.

Mirrors were as much a part of Avon-upon-Kynt as fashion was. I'd heard the capital city had more mirrors per square foot than any other city in the world because the citizens needed to see their fashions. It was true. People glanced at their reflections as they walked, adjusting their coats and smoothing their hair. Normally I would've been enthralled, but I was more alarmed that no one seemed to be waiting for me. Nervously, I glanced from one side to the other and then—

"Ooof!" I ran right into a man. Or, more accurately, his midsection. As his shoes trampled my toes, my carpetbag slipped from my hands and I stumbled, nearly falling onto my backside. "Ouch!"

The man grabbed my shoulder, steadying me. He towered

over me, a striking figure in a black suit with a ruffled black necktie. I was about to apologize when he said, "Watch yourself, girl."

His annoyed tone seemed to imply it was my fault my toes were burning and bruised from his heavy shoes.

"You stepped on my feet," I said, unsure if I was more angry or more hurt.

Even though I knew he'd heard me, he continued on his way, disappearing into the crowd without another word. Moving quickly, I picked up my carpetbag and limped over to a wall. I fanned myself with my hand, trying to cool my hot face. This was the city. These people obviously cared more about beautiful clothes than saying "Excuse me."

The wall I was standing against was covered in canvas. I thought there would be a mirror underneath it, but as wind funneled through the station from the open doors, the canvas lifted and revealed a flash of blue and red. I had other things to focus on—my throbbing feet for one, getting to the Fashion House for another—but I caught the edge of the canvas and peered underneath it.

For a moment, it was hard to make sense of the image because I was so close to it but, as I stared, the shapes started to fit together in a mix of colors and lines.

A woman in eighteenth-century garb stood on a pedestal, cradling a cuttleworm in one hand and stroking the head of a sheep with the other. A banner reading *Britannia Secunda Forever: Our Fashion to the World* swirled over her figure. I recognized her from our currency: Queen Catherine. A century before I was born, just after Britannia Secunda had secured its independence from England, Queen Catherine had assumed the throne. According to our stories, Britannia Secunda had been too small to support itself and was on the verge of collapse. Queen Catherine used the remaining reserves to hire explorers to find resources or innovations that we could use to support ourselves. One returned with a cuttleworm—a strange creature that could be raised on the farmlands to spin silk threads. With her exquisite taste and aesthetics, Queen Catherine guided our country to its independence by not only manufacturing the best fabrics in the world, but also by turning them into stunning fashions.

"They are going to paint over it." I dropped the canvas. A young blond man was standing next to me, staring up at the same wall. "It's a shame."

Blue. The word popped into my head. His eyes were bright blue, like a Shy sky in spring. But it wasn't just his eyes. Tired circles were etched beneath them, forming blue half-moons below his lids. A bluish hue distorted his bottom lip, as if he'd recently been socked in the mouth with a large, clenched fist, and a herringbone-patterned blue scarf was tied tightly around his neck. Something drew me to him—maybe the bruises or his sleepy eyes. I'd always liked things—and people—who were different.

"They are?"

I caught a whiff of his aftershave. A deep, clear scent.

"Yes. It's an initiative from the Reformists Party."

The Reformists Parliament Party. That name was often splashed across the newspaper headlines. Every year, Parliament granted the Crown an arts budget. And, every year, the

Crown had given a large portion of it to the Fashion House . . . until now. The Reformists, who formed part of Parliament, had voted to cut the arts budget so they could invest in new factories that would create cheaper fashions to export.

"It's such a beautiful painting," I said.

The young man pulled the canvas aside again, so we could both see it. "It is," he said. "I've always liked it, especially how the artist put a hat on the cuttleworm and a dress on the sheep."

Another gust of wind rushed through the station, catching at the canvas and making it billow like a sail, ruffling the young man's hair. He laughed and let it go. The sound was cheery, and I couldn't help but laugh with him. The canvas settled back over the mural, obscuring it once again.

"Are they really going to paint over it?" I asked.

"Yes. And it's probably just the start. The Parliament appointments are happening this year, and it looks like the Reformists will get the majority over the Classicists for the first time," he said. "If that happens, they'll do more than just paint over murals." He stopped then, hesitating, as though worried he'd bored me.

"I've read about that," I said encouragingly. The same brightness that lit up his eyes spread to the rest of his face. "The Reformists aren't fans of couture, right? They want cheaper fashions."

"It's true," he said, and paused. "So, are you coming or going?"

"Coming," I said.

"Good. It'd be a shame if we'd just met and you were off to

somewhere far away." His smile was easy, relaxed. But those blue eyes of his studied me. Our shoulders were nearly brushing. Had he stepped closer to me at some point? Maybe this was how young men acted in the city. Or had I leaned in toward him without realizing it?

"I'm trying to get to the Fashion House." There. Safer ground.

"The Fashion House? Is that so? Are you the girl from the North? The one picked to be part of the Fashion House Interview?"

I tucked a strand of hair back behind one ear. "Yes."

"If that's the case, can I get a comment?" He procured a notepad from his coat pocket and quickly flipped through its worn pages.

"A comment?"

"I'm a reporter for the *Eagle*." A pencil appeared from the same pocket. "The Fashion House told the press you were going to arrive tomorrow—probably trying to throw us all. I've come to check the rail times, so I could come back then. But look. Here you are and here I am. This, my friend, is what you call an exclusive scoop. Now, what is your name?"

He waited, pencil poised over notepad.

"Emmaline, but everyone calls me Emmy." At my words, he started scribbling furiously in the notepad. "You write for the *Eagle*?"

"Well, yes." His shoulders slumped a little and he sighed. "For now. But don't hold that against me!"

"I'm not so sure I should be talking to you."

The *Eagle* was a tabloid notorious for running fascinating stories with dubious origins. Of course, every now and then the tabloids broke big stories. Unlike the more serious papers like the *Avon-upon-Kynt Times*, they operated independently from the government, so they could print whatever they wanted.

Usually, though, they took this freedom a little too far. In fact, even now I could see the front page of the *Eagle* displayed on a newspaper stand just behind the young man. Its headline read, "MYSTERIOUS MERMAID FOUND IN THE TYNE RIVER." He followed my line of sight to the paper and grimaced.

"I didn't write that one, promise. And now you see what I'm up against. Give me a good quote and you'll make my day."

His voice took on an unabashedly pleading note. I opened my mouth, ready to talk, drawn in by his easy charm.

Then, just before I started to recount meeting Madame Jolène back in Evert, I stopped. I might be from the country, but I wasn't stupid. My mother had taught me to be wary of handsome men.

"I'm sorry," I said. "I don't have anything to say on the matter."

The train exhaled more steam onto the platform and it whirled around us in a damp, white cloud. He was nothing like Johnny Wells. As pathetic as it was, Johnny was the only young man I could compare him to. My mother had always kept me away from the few boys in Shy until she started pushing Johnny on me.

"Nonsense!" He made a swirling motion in the air with his

pencil as though the gesture could command words from my tongue. "I'm sure you have something to say. Everyone does. You've left your home and traveled all this way with a carpetbag and a dream. Hoping to make something of yourself, possibly. Or perhaps hoping to prove someone wrong."

He spoke quickly, like his mind was jumping from point to point and he could barely keep up.

"Sounds like you're telling me my own story."

"Is it accurate?"

"No comment." I smiled back at him, and he sighed, shaking his head. "Though if you do describe me, can you add a few inches to my height?"

He laughed then, the sound ringing merrily through the station, the sole note of happiness amid the travelers sniping at each other to move or step aside.

"Very well. How does this headline sit with you? 'MADAME JOLÈNE'S NEW COUNTRY MOUSE ARRIVES TODAY, AND SHE IS QUITE TALL.'" He seemed inspired by his fake headline. He lowered his notebook, giving me a peek. Indeed, he had even written down "country mouse," with a poorly drawn slice of cheese beside the words. He cocked his head to the side as he stared at me. I tucked my hair behind my ear again. "You look different from what I was expecting."

"Different?"

"Yes. It's been the talk of the city. The Reformists Party has always tried to force Madame Jolène to do things this way or that. Normally, she ignores them, which was just fine because the Crown has always supported her. Until now, that is.

Everything is shifting, and the Reformists have more power."

I already knew Madame Jolène didn't want me at the Fashion House, but from the sound of it, neither did any soul in Avon-upon-Kynt, aside from the oft-mentioned Reformists Party. I glanced from the reporter to the other travelers. Suddenly, their passing gazes seemed cold and mocking, even though they couldn't possibly know who I was.

"What were you expecting?" I asked almost desperately.

"Oh, you know, a girl with a humble way of talking and lots of freckles," he laughed. "The Reformists Party wanted some-one who looked the part, but Madame Jolène didn't listen, it seems."

"Well, people in the country aren't all humble and freckled."

"That's the Reformists Party." He shrugged. "They tend to caricature the people they claim to help."

"Emmaline!" A bulky figure emerged from the steam and walked briskly toward me. I stepped back from the reporter. "Don't say anything to him!"

Francesco. He swept up to me, his dark mink coat extending all the way down to the train-station floor. A hint of a frilly purple tunic layered over fitted leather pants peeked out from beneath the fur.

The reporter turned to Francesco but not before winking at me. He cleared his throat, straightened his shoulders, and asked in a brisk, professional manner, "How does Madame Jolène feel about Parliament cutting the Crown's arts funding?"

"No. Comment." Francesco put his arm protectively around my shoulders.

Without missing a beat, the young man asked, "Will she ask the Crown to renegotiate the budget?"

"We must be going." Francesco guided me away. "Reporters!" he huffed, even though the young man was still within earshot. "Earth's scum, feeding on information." His hand was reassuringly warm and strong on my shoulder. "Welcome, my little scarecrow dresser. We must hurry. Orientation is starting soon, and we must get you . . ." He trailed off, glancing at my travel-worn, simple-cut overcoat before saying, "*Presentable.*"

I barely heard him. I twisted around, trying to see the reporter one last time and glimpse his blue, blue eyes, but he was already concealed by the train's thick, white steam.

We took a hansom cab to the Fashion House, the driver shouting at the crowd from his perch behind the passenger carriage. Francesco prattled on about how ridiculous it was that journalists who wore cotton trousers and boots without spats dared to critique the Fashion House—oh, and no, Francesco wasn't wearing spats either, but it was a "deliberate fashion choice," not a "casual attitude about booting." His monologue slipped into the background with the driver's cries. I realized I didn't even know the reporter's name.

Finally, the cab pulled to a stop and we stepped out into a cobbled courtyard, the cool city air stinging our faces. It was a stark change from Shy, where the summer heat lasted into September, sometimes even October.

"Hurry now. We must give you time to change"—Francesco paused to face me and wave a hand over my entire being—

"everything, before orientation."

I nodded, but I wasn't looking at him. I was staring up at the Fashion House. The stately brick building was covered in ivy and surrounded by a tall iron gate. Its white-trimmed gables stretched toward the sky, nearly covering the smokestacks emerging from its roof. Unlike the other businesses we'd passed, it wasn't joined to any other buildings. Instead, the Fashion House stood alone, a striking silhouette against the gray sky.

It appeared we were in the back. A man with a horse-drawn cart was delivering meats wrapped in brown paper, and a woman emerged from the door to dump out a bucket of water. Despite the mundane activities, the place exuded luxury. Through the open upstairs windows, I could see chandeliers, gilt-framed mirrors, and silk curtains, intimations of the beauty and glamour contained within the walls. Francesco called to me, "Come along, Emmaline."

"You can call me Emmy," I said, reluctantly dragging my eyes from the Fashion House to him. "No one calls me Emmaline."

Francesco wrinkled his nose and shook his head. "Emmy? You aren't a simple milkmaid any longer, dear child. Emmys, Suzys, and Beckys belong on farms, just like Franks belong in law offices or seminaries. No. Here, I am Francesco, and you are *Emmaline*." He whispered *Emmaline* and it sounded grand, like the kind of name a designer would have.

Still, it wasn't me. No one from home ever called me Emmaline. Suddenly, everything seemed to be moving too fast. I didn't have much—just a carpetbag, a few dresses, and me—and I wasn't ready to relinquish any bit of myself just yet.

Francesco gently rested a hand on my shoulder, as if he knew my thoughts. "We all make sacrifices, dear. It's the Fashion House way. Everything tells a story here, names included."

I nearly protested, but he had already whirled around on his heel to continue inside. I followed him. We entered a narrow lobby and, before my vision could adjust from the light, we started up a staircase lined with art. The first painting was small in comparison to the others, and it depicted a man in a tweed suit. I wondered if it was Lord Harold Spencer. I didn't know much about him, just that he'd been the previous owner of the Fashion House, years ago, before Madame Jolène had taken it over. Now he was merely a forgotten footnote in Fashion House history.

The rest of the paintings were of famous Fashion House designs, their enormity magnifying the details of the couture. I squinted at them. The first two showed the queen's watercolor coronation gown and the light, airy red dress with the twenty-foot chiffon train that the wife of the Moroccan ambassador had worn during the Parliament vote several years ago.

The third painting featured a woman in a sky-and-midnight-blue sparkly gown. I stared at it as we passed by, certain it was Princess Amelia in the gown she'd commissioned for the queen's Diamond Jubilee. It was one of Madame Jolène's most famous looks and had always been my favorite.

"This way, Emmaline."

On the landing above me, Francesco turned down a separate hallway. With one last glance at the blue dress, I stepped into the corridor. It was lined with cherrywood doors and paraffin-oil lamps with glass shades that threw squares of colorful light onto the carpet. Francesco opened one of the doors.

"Enter your new paradise. There is a dress lying out for you. As soon as you are ready, return to the foyer and line up with the other girls. Madame Jolène will direct the orientation."

My breath caught in my chest like a hiccup as I stepped over the threshold. I barely noticed the door closing behind me or the sound of Francesco's footsteps retreating down the stairs. A wash of muted colors overwhelmed me—ivories, champagnes, blushes, and soft blues—and I had to blink before I could see any one detail. It was all so still, as though there wasn't any air in the room and hadn't been for a long time. Everything was mirrored in the light-blue marble floor—the two vanities, the two canopied beds, and the two full-length mirrors.

Two.

A bottle of violet–witch hazel perfume and a closed sketch-book sat on one of the vanities. The wardrobe closest to it was open, revealing black and burgundy dresses hanging in a neat row. Someone was already living here.

My roommate? I stared at her etched perfume bottle and engraved leather sketchbook and set my raggedy carpetbag down on the marble. I'd never really had any friends in Shy. I'd always told myself it was because Shy was so small, but I knew most of the families didn't want their daughters hanging around at a pub . . . or with a girl born out of wedlock.

But this girl wouldn't know any of that. I could be whoever I wanted here. That was the power of the Fashion House, of the city. Whoever she was, I would smile at her and tell her she was pretty, and I liked her dress. Wasn't that what city girls did? And perhaps then, hopefully, we would be friends.

I let out a long, slow breath and briskly walked forward. My shoes made clicking sounds with every step, disturbing the chamber's pristine, static beauty. They seemed too loud and, without even knowing why, I tried to muffle them.

You're fine, I told myself. *You're fine.* I was tired. That was why, even though I was exactly where I wanted to be, I suddenly was overwhelmed.

I made my way over to one of the beds. The rococo-style headboard was elaborately carved with roses, scrolls, and cherubs, and covered in frosty white paint. A pink gown was laid out, its wide skirts nearly covering the whole duvet. The gown appeared to be two pieces, but it wasn't. The top reminded me of the precise, collared shirts I'd seen Shy's judge wear to our parish, only in a soft blush. Small buttons ran down the front, and quarter-length sleeves ended in pressed cuffs. Monogrammed inside the gown's back collar were the letters *FH*. Next to the dress were the necessary undergarments.

I undid the clasps of the dress I was wearing and slipped out of it, followed by my camisole, crinoline, and drawers.

Knock, knock.

I whirled around, almost tripping over my dress, which lay around my ankles with my undergarments. Only my stockings covered my legs to my thighs, and the realization sent my skin puckering into goose bumps.

"Just a minute," I called out, turning to awkwardly reach

up onto the bed for the gown and struggling to step free of my mound of clothes. "I'm not—"

The door opened, and a girl in a high-necked black dress accented with bobbin-lace appliques entered. I backed up against the bed, clutching the dress to cover myself. I recognized her outfit. The maid who had attended Madame Jolène back in Evert had been dressed in the same lacy, high-necked black dress. This girl was a servant.

"Francesco sent me," she announced. "Orientation is about to begin. I'm here to help you dress."

"Help me dress? Oh, I can manage." I faltered, desperately trying to shield myself with the gown. I could only imagine what Madame Jolène would say if she saw me using one of her dresses in such a manner. My cheeks burned bright pink, much brighter than the gown.

"You're the contestant from the North, aren't you?" the girl asked, walking toward me. I tried to back up more, but I was already trapped against the bed. "Well, here at the Fashion House, you don't dress yourself."

She whisked the gown out of my hands. I gave a squawk of embarrassment, holding my hands up to conceal myself. The hot flush in my cheeks suffused my entire body. I didn't know what was more embarrassing: being naked in front of a stranger or being lectured by one.

"Here." She reached for the new undergarments while I grabbed at the blanket on the bed, futilely trying to use its edge to cover my body. "Foundational garments first."

She handed me a pair of drawers. I slipped into them and

reached out for the camisole and crinoline, but instead of giving them to me, she held them up, sliding the camisole and then the crinoline over my head. Afterward, she wrapped the corset around my waist, fastening the clasps running down the front of it. I was grateful to be clothed again, even if it was only in underwear.

"Corsets have to be worn at all times at the Fashion House," the girl said as she turned me around to tighten the lacings in the back. I placed my hands flat against the corset. The fabric was thick beneath my fingers, and it extended down to my hips, encasing my entire torso. Satin and lace were molded together over the stiff pieces of whalebone.

"It's really beaut—" My word cut off as she gave the corset strings a jerk, pulling it tight up against my midriff and forcing the air out of my lungs. My ribs and hips submitted to its molding. I occasionally wore corsets at home, but never this tight. Half the time I only wore my bodice.

"You have a small waist," the girl said in an observational tone. I wanted to turn from her, but I was like a helpless puppet, the corset ties in her hands keeping me from pulling away. "It helps since you don't have much by way of hips."

"Are you a maid here?" I asked. Only a few people in Shy had maids. The ones I'd met were older women. None of them were like this girl.

"I am."

"What is your name?"

"You're sweet," the girl said, all fake saccharine. "Girls from the country are *so* sincere."

41

"Are we? And here I thought we were known for our scathing wit." I couldn't help being sarcastic. No one in Shy would be rude for no reason.

"Here, hold your arms up," she directed, lifting the gown over my head. She didn't respond to my comment, but she also didn't say anything else.

The dress smelled of fresh new silk. It was the nicest thing I'd ever had on my body. Even though I wasn't close enough to the mirror to see myself, I sensed its beauty and craftsmanship, from its fabric to its structured bodice. But staring down at the girlishly pink color, I felt something was . . . *off.* I cleared my throat.

"There aren't any other options, are there?"

"Options?" She made it sound as though I'd asked to attend the orientation in animal skins.

"To wear," I said, running my hands over my skirt, making sure my voice was even. "It's just that I'm not quite sure this is the best style for me."

The maid was silent a moment and then let out a harsh, singular, *"Ha!* If you want to choose how you dress, then the Fashion House is not the place for you." She pushed the last button through its corresponding hole. "Now, let's fix that hair."

She gathered my dark-blond hair, saying something about country hairstyles versus city ones, but I barely heard her. The Fashion House had always represented freedom to me—creative freedom. I stared down at the pink skirts puffing out around me. Their luster seemed to diminish, and I shifted uncertainly as the maid roughly twisted my hair up into a bun, pulling my head back as she did so. She procured hairpins from her apron pocket and stuck them into my hair, fastening the bun to the back of my head. By the time she was done, my scalp tingled with her pricks and stabs.

"There!" she announced. She took a few steps back and beheld me from head to toe. Despite her prior rudeness, she seemed pleased with her work.

I turned to the mirror over the vanity, finally able to see myself. For a moment, I stared, entranced. I thought I'd understood the gown from how it felt, but that was a mere glimpse into its beauty. It was a second skin, gliding over the contours of my body. It highlighted my waist and balanced out my hips. The sight drew me in and filled me with excitement. Soon, I would make beauty like this dress.

I wished I'd been wearing something this stunning when I'd met the reporter from the *Eagle*.

"You need to head downstairs to orientation and assessment," the maid said. "Be sure to hurry. They are waiting."

"They?"

"The Fashion House Interview contestants line up so Madame Jolène can review the rules of the competition. It's in the main lobby." She grinned and shook her head, as if deeply amused.

I knew exactly what she was thinking. That I was the only poor contestant, the only one from outside the city, the only "primitive" girl here.

All in a line? There would be no hiding it.

CHAPTER THREE

I LINGERED ON THE LAST stair, peeking into the lobby. The white marble floors were speckled with black, and the walls were covered in mirrored panels and eucalyptus-leaf print. I recognized the ornate coral-and-green Morris & Co. wallpaper from ads in the newspapers and the *Family Friend* magazine. The magistrate's wife, who was the richest woman in Shy, decorated her home with an older Morris & Co. wallpaper.

Five girls with coiffed hair, artful gowns, and perfect posture stood in a line. They had *it*: fearless confidence in one's own beauty. It exuded from them like a powerful perfume. Usually the Fashion House Interview had only five contestants. I was the odd one out, the one tacked on at the very last minute. I placed a hand over my chest. My heart pounded underneath the silk. With a deep breath, I slipped in to join the end of the line.

"Nervous?" the girl standing on my right chirped, tilting her head to the side to consider me. Her auburn hair pooled over her shoulder. "I'm Kitty. I heard Madame Jolène was taking on a girl from the country. Is it you?"

"Yes," I said. I didn't want to seem too desperate, but my

words came out in a grateful rush. One of the contestants was talking to me, and from what I could tell, she seemed genuinely sweet. "My mother owns a pub there."

Kitty gave a soft, lyrical laugh.

"That must have been fun. Lots of men, no?"

I didn't bother to tell her our pub was a sleepy place where customers came more for my mother's blackberry pie than anything else. Our patrons were men who ambled in after a long day of work, eager to get back to their families after a pint or two.

Just beyond Kitty, two girls whispered to each other, glancing at me. Even as my toes curled inside my shoes, I stared back at them to prove I wasn't unnerved. The first girl was on the shorter side, with thick black hair falling over her shoulders. Her lips were full and her eyes were dark. A few freckles sprinkled her nose, barely discernible in the dramatic chandelier light.

"That's Ky," Kitty said softly, following my line of sight. "Her father is our ambassador to Japan. Her mother is from one of the provinces there."

Ky's clothes were exaggerated and theatrical. She wore a gown covered in floral cutouts and a cuttleworm brooch. The hem rose above her ankles, showing white heeled boots and striped stockings.

"Who is her friend?" I asked.

"Alice. Her father passed away, but her mother is a well-known socialite."

Alice's skin was the color of skimmed milk, and her blond hair fell in ringlets. Her dress was layers of lace, each tier accented with a small purple bow. While both of their gowns had the full Fashion House skirt (Madame Jolène was known for using voluminous silhouettes and thick, structured fabrics), the girls didn't look anything like each other. Obviously, Madame Jolène had distinct visions for Ky and Alice.

The rest of the contestants also had clear styles. Kitty was all ladylike elegance in a navy-and-ivory dress, while another girl was outfitted in dramatic black. The last contestant at the end of the line was wearing . . . trousers? Yes. Wide-legged trousers topped with a fitted blazer. I ran my fingers over the satin of my own gown. Was this Madame Jolène's style for me? Certainly, the dress was classic. But it was made from such basic shapes—straightforward bodice sewn onto a full A-line skirt. In my chambers, I'd thought it was lovely, but in comparison to the other girls' outfits, it suddenly didn't seem like much of a style at all.

"They are so stunning," I said. I fidgeted in the pink dress, my hands antsy against its skirts. I wanted to change its color to a brilliant ochre silk with hints of red woven into the fibers. I wanted to transform its silhouette to an overly dramatic mermaid or drape my neck in too many jeweled necklaces. Anything to make it *something*.

"Yes," Kitty agreed, unaware of my thoughts. "Madame Jolène knows how to dress for both a woman's body and her type of beauty. She is, after all, the world's fashion maven."

Both Ky and Alice, I noticed, had gold amulets around their necks engraved with letters: *K & G, A & F.*

Gifts from suitors.

My skin prickled around my bare neck, and I resisted the urge to cover it with my hand. The reporter's image flashed in my mind.

Seeming to sense my uncertainty, Kitty touched my arm. A large stack of diamond bracelets encircled her wrist. They seemed cumbersome, but she wore them naturally, as though they were as much a part of her as her hair or eye color.

"Ladies, good afternoon!" The commanding voice of our employer and benefactress, Madame Jolène, rang out. The contestants immediately straightened into a perfect line as she glided into the room.

"Good afternoon," a few girls chorused back. I didn't say anything. This was only the second time I'd ever seen Madame Jolène.

She was wearing a sage evening gown styled in obvious reference to the Grecian goddesses. It had a long train that she draped casually over one arm like a wrap. A thick strand of black pearls wrapped around her hips and her hair was pinned with a peach brooch. The gown's drama and fluidity contrasted with the round spectacles perched on the bridge of her nose.

The society pages had recently featured several illustrations of Madame Jolène's glasses. The lenses were impossibly thin and set in intricate frames. Blue and red stones fanned out around the rims, cut to replicate the wings of a butterfly. When Madame Jolène had first started wearing them, everyone copied her, impaired vision or not. Ladies were said to be seen tripping up and down the streets of Avon-upon-Kynt, wearing glasses they didn't need. I'd read about how an oculist had started producing frames with just glass in them, as opposed to magnifying lenses.

Of course, Madame Jolène's eyeglasses had always been glass. She had kept that bit of information to herself. It was actually the *Eagle* that had broken the "news" by publishing an editorial calling Madame Jolène's eyewear "pointless."

Not only did Madame Jolène continue wearing the "pointless" eyewear, but she created even more elaborate designs. She was quoted as saying, "Beauty is never pointless." I loved the idea: beauty, pure and unadulterated, made just for the sake of itself. When I told my mother about the oculist and the eyeglasses, she had laughed loudly, cutting me off before I could finish the story.

"It would serve them right to go blind, Madame Jolène most of all," she'd said.

"I trust you are all well rested from your travels and ready for the Fashion House Interview to begin," Madame Jolène said as she moved down our ranks, peering at us through those useless, glimmering eyeglasses. "Some of you have been here for over a week, waiting for the remaining contestant positions to be filled. Your time here has been leisurely, but that will soon change. I will demand much from you, because our clientele demands much from us. Our house dresses the highest-ranking aristocrats and royals in Europe. What we dress them in, people the world over will copy. Francesco, brief them on how the Fashion House Interview will run."

By this time, she had made one trip down our line. She

abruptly stopped, one hand resting on her hip, the other intentionally, casually, touching her spectacles. Madame Jolène was posing for us, for me. And she took my breath away.

"Welcome, ladies." Francesco sashayed forward. He had changed since that morning. Instead of the purple tunic, leather pants, and fur coat, he was now wearing a crisp white jacket with matching white pants. The pants hems were cuffed, showcasing red shoes with huge black ribbons.

"All of you, of course, know me by now," he said. "I am the Fashion House's creative director. I make sure everything runs smoothly. However, I also design when I can, and Madame Jolène most graciously lets me create a line of handbags to go with the Fashion House's collections. Last year, Princess Amelia exclusively used my handbags at her events."

I wasn't sure how Francesco wanted us to react. He seemed tremendously proud, so I nodded and smiled. It wasn't hard. I was impressed. But it was more because of Francesco himself than his line of purses.

"Anyway, enough about me." He laughed with feigned modesty. "You should be getting to know each other. You can learn much from each other's strengths. And even more"—he lowered his voice melodramatically—"from each other's weaknesses. It is a competition, after all." He clasped his hands together, as though anticipating the drama to come. I swallowed hard. "Let's introduce everyone."

He ran through the name of each girl, starting with Kitty. I already knew Alice's and Ky's names, but I learned that the menswear girl was Cordelia, and the last girl, the one all in black, was Sophie.

"Now," Francesco drew out the word. "About the Fashion House Interview." At the mention of the competition, the girls quieted, their eyes sharpening. "There will be six challenges designed to determine your creativity, technical skills, and ability to manage clients. You won't know what the challenge is until it is announced. The results will be judged by Madame Jolène, myself, and the rest of the design board. There will be one winner for each challenge. To help you understand your performance in the competition, you will also receive a rank. As everyone knows, once this season concludes, one or two of you will be invited to join the Fashion House as design apprentices."

The girls broke into smiles as he mentioned the apprenticeships, and some of them glanced up and down our line, sizing each other up. Everyone's gaze seemed to pass right over me, but I didn't care. Resolve formed deep inside me. I would get one of those positions. Hadn't I managed to get this far, after all? I would work harder than everyone else, hone my design skills, and get the apprenticeship.

"When you aren't participating in the challenges, you will assist in the daily operations of the Fashion House," Francesco continued. "You will meet with titled women and show them the designs from the current collections. In addition to the gowns, you will have access to the private jewelry vaults for accessorizing during the fittings. If a customer selects a gown, you will measure her and tailor the pattern for her. Our sewing staff will create the piece. Most contestants seem to think this work is below them, but it is an important part of learning to work with clients and gaining intimate knowledge of the Fashion House designs. Any questions?"

"Will we receive feedback after each challenge?" Ky asked.

"Of course. Critiques will be given for every challenge, and a winner will be announced at the end of each. However, don't be too dismayed if you don't win the early challenges. I've seen girls come from behind many times."

"It's hard to believe that only two of us will be hired," Kitty whispered to me. "And the rest of us will be fired." She nervously shook her hair back from her face. She wanted this as much as I did. In fact, they all did. I looked up and down the row at the resolute faces and narrowed eyes. They were stylish girls, yes, but more than that—they were also determined. I needed to beat them, or I'd be back in Shy, washing dishes and waiting on tables and resisting my mother's campaign to wed me to Johnny Wells.

"You will, of course, enjoy the lifestyle the Fashion House provides during your time here," Francesco said. "We create luxury, so we live in it as well. You are as much a part of the Fashion House aesthetic as the wallpaper or the marble."

Everyone nodded. It was well known that the Fashion House was a unique place—even the servants wore couture.

"Madame Jolène!" It was Sophie. The girl in the black gown. I had to lean forward to see her face. For a moment, I thought she was looking down, but it was just her lashes, so thick and black that they shielded her eyes. Black hair, as shiny as her black silk gown, twisted into a knot at the very top of her head. Her porcelain-white features were beautiful, each one perfectly formed and placed. By all accounts, she was stunning—I couldn't find any flaws—but there was something grim about her, as though her beauty didn't extend below the surface.

Slowly, Madame Jolène, who had remained perfectly still during Francesco's speech, unwound from her pose to stare down at her. I wasn't sure how she did it since the girl was taller than Madame Jolène.

"Yes?" Madame Jolène asked.

Sophie didn't flinch or blush. She did hesitate, though, before saying, "What about her?" She pointed at me.

Me.

I stifled a gasp and took a step back, almost knocking into Kitty. Sophie's finger remained pointed. The girls watched, their eyes flitting from the black-haired girl to me, and then to Madame Jolène.

"What about her?" Madame Jolène asked.

"It seems you are including a different class of contestant this season," Sophie said. "Have the requirements changed? I'm just wondering because a reporter asked me yesterday if the Fashion House is becoming more . . . well, like a factory that mass-produces shirtwaists."

As she spoke, my breath grew short. My ribs tried to expand, but they couldn't. It was as if my new dress was suffocating me. I would faint, right here in front of everyone, and then they would really know I didn't belong.

"Well," Madame Jolène said. Her expression remained neutral even as something behind her face darkened. The single syllable hung in the air. Sophie shifted, and beside me Kitty softly exhaled. Then Madame Jolène spoke again. "Things are changing in Avon-upon-Kynt. But the Fashion House has never been and will never be a place that produces standard things, even when forced to include . . . some standard people."

Madame Jolène didn't glance at me even once. The other girls did, though. They openly stared at me and then turned to each other, their whispering punctuated by little snorts of laughter. Even Kitty took a small step away from me, as though trying to distance herself.

They thought I was a joke, just like Madame Jolène did. I kept my shoulders back and my chin raised, but my stomach twisted into unrelenting knots. I felt as small and ridiculous as they all thought I was.

CHAPTER FOUR

"ARE YOU ALL RIGHT, EMMALINE?" Kitty asked, noticing I was lagging as I followed her up the stairs. Our rooms were located on one of the highest floors, far above the sewing rooms and fitting areas. I wasn't sure I'd recall which one was mine, so I'd asked Kitty to help me. I was worried she might not want to be seen with me, but she had agreed.

No, I'm not all right. "Yes, I'm fine."

"Don't worry too much," Kitty said. She paused on a stair. "Sophie is a strange one. She's a Sterling, after all."

"A Sterling?"

"Yes. You know, the Sterling family."

For a second, I wavered between pretending to know who this family was—from Kitty's breezy tone, it seemed like I should—and just admitting my ignorance.

The delay was enough to tip Kitty off. "They are, or were, I should say, a well-known family. Sophie's parents died a few years ago, and it caused quite a stir. They weren't titled, but they were wealthy. Her parents were always getting attention for doing things like dancing in the city fountain at midnight or showing up together at the Gentlemen's Club. But try not to worry about Sophie. Such things will distract us from our work if we let them."

I nodded. Everything was happening so fast: the rude maid, Sophie's cutting comment, Madame Jolène's icy response. I arched my neck, trying to ease the throbbing at its base, and my eyes settled on the gilt-framed painting of Princess Amelia in her dazzling midnight gown, the one she'd worn to the queen's Diamond Jubilee. Without Francesco rushing me along, I could stare at it for as long as I wanted. Kitty stopped next to me.

She grinned. "It's beautiful, isn't it?"

"Yes," I breathed.

Even more than the gown, I loved the story behind it. I was ten when Avon-upon-Kynt celebrated the queen's Diamond Jubilee. Everyone said Princess Amelia wouldn't attend the festivities. Rumors had percolated for months that her husband, Prince Willis, had taken up with the nubile Duchess Cynthia Sandringham. And just two months before the jubilee, he had gone on a weeklong trip with the duchess in Italy, while Princess Amelia stayed with their children, Prince Andrew and Princess Astrid, back at the main palace.

According to the society pages, Princess Amelia had shown up, resplendent and with her head held high, wearing a sheath gown of raw silk dyed a rich blue. Now all the details were right in front of me. I hadn't known the fabric was a mixture of blues, both bright and dark. The gown had long sleeves and a high neck. In fact, it might have been considered prudish if it wasn't so tight that one could see the outline of Princess Amelia's entire body. Starting mid-thigh, crystals sparkled and glinted over the skirt, pooling around the hemline like shimmering raindrops. Layers of black and gray tulle fell from the back of the waist, creating the impression of a ball gown from behind.

"I was eleven when it happened, but I remember it all like it was yesterday," Kitty said. "It was quite past my bedtime, but my parents let me stay, and I was the only girl my age there." She smiled proudly. "Prince Willis and the duchess arrived before Princess Amelia did. Did the society pages mention that the duchess was formally introduced? It was awfully vulgar." Kitty shook her head. "The duchess was wearing a horrid gray silk A-line gown—and *pearls*, of all things. As if she were fifty! 'Dumpy' was the only word to describe her." A wry smile tugged at the corner of Kitty's mouth. "My mother told me Madame Jolène had canceled the duchess's appointment at the Fashion House because Madame Jolène is a personal friend of the princess's. The duchess has been blacklisted from the Fashion House ever since."

"So it's true."

I'd read about the blacklisted duchess in the society pages, but since I was so far away from the city, it was easy to forget the people in Avon-upon-Kynt existed beyond the confines of the articles. According to the papers, the prince and duchess had separated shortly after the jubilee, and the duchess had never been featured in any fashion spreads since.

"When Princess Amelia was announced, I'd never seen anything like it," Kitty continued. "There was so much noise—you know, people jostling, vendors yelling, that type of thing—and it stopped. The moment Princess Amelia stepped out onto the steps of the Parliament building, you could hear a pin drop. No one could look away. The gown was unlike anything I had ever seen, even here, where everyone lives for fashion. There was something about it . . . I don't know . . . it was glittering, glowing, even . . . it was like seeing something divine."

Kitty trailed off, and we both stood facing the painting, lingering, held by the blue gown's spell. For the first time, it made sense to me. The gown was exquisite, but more important, it told a story. It allowed a scorned princess to show her prince she didn't need him anymore.

"Come," Kitty said. "It's getting late, and we need our rest for tomorrow."

I followed her the rest of the way up the stairs, but the blue gown's image floated in front of me, filmy and ghostlike. Blue. It reminded me of something . . . but what?

The reporter's eyes.

They were as blue as Princess Amelia's gown. I shook my head vigorously, enough to make Kitty glance curiously at me.

No matter. There wasn't time for men. I needed to work hard and make sure that at the end of the season I was offered the apprenticeship. And then one day I could dress someone like Princess Amelia and tell her story, one stitch at a time.

I said goodnight to Kitty and opened the door to my chamber. Everything gleamed just as before. Now, though, night had fallen, casting the room in a golden light. The chandelier sparkled, and the room, warmed by its glow, seemed less clean and frigid. *It's like living inside a jewelry box*, I thought.

I wasn't alone. There was a girl sitting at one of the vanities. Her evening robe had fallen off her shoulders and it hung from the crooks of her elbows, revealing snowy skin and a black nightdress. With her long fingers, she pulled pins from her hair, sending cascades of dark waves down her back. She turned slightly so her reflection appeared in the vanity mirror.

Sophie.

Every single one of the emotions from the lobby came rushing back, as though I was standing there again, and she was pointing at me, making all those eyes fix on me. For the second time since I'd arrived, scorching heat rushed to my face, turning my cheeks pink.

Sophie's eyes flicked up to mine in the mirror. Then, just as quickly, she returned her gaze to the vanity's marble top.

"Sophie," I breathed. "I didn't know we'd be sharing chambers."

"It appears as such."

After her bold comments at orientation, I expected her to say something disdainful. This emotionless response was unnerving, much more so than a sarcastic comment or insult would have been.

"So, what did you think of the orientation?" Sophie asked, glancing at me once more in the mirror from under her black lashes. She picked up a pencil and began to draw long, harsh lines on the paper in front of her.

"I was quite impressed," I said finally, with a touch of derision. It seemed like the safest response. One that wasn't weak or threatened. "It was terribly exciting for me, especially since I'm a 'different type of contestant.'"

Sophie picked up her sketch and tucked it behind the vanity mirror. I was still standing in the doorway, as though I were a guest in my own chambers, waiting for permission to enter. Hastily, I crossed the room to my vanity and sat down on its cushioned stool.

How could this be happening? Of all the contestants, I was rooming with Sophie, a girl who already seemed to hate me, a girl who didn't think I should be in the Fashion House Interview just because I was poor and from the country.

I realized I was sitting motionless on the stool, staring at her. I needed to look busy, occupied, not intimidated. Quickly, I opened the top drawer of the vanity. Its shiny glass knob was odd beneath my fingers. It was so much smoother than the brass latches on my drawers at home, the ones that were so badly warped that I had to develop a complex strategy for opening each one.

"I saw you looking at Princess Amelia's gown with Kitty."

I twisted around on the stool so we faced each other. She had been watching me? I hadn't even seen her. The thought of those black eyes following me sent a chill through my bones.

"There hasn't been a 'big' dress since then," she said. "Or at least, not one that has shaped society and fashion in one swoop. I'm going to design the next one."

"You are?"

"That's why I'm here." Sophie spoke in such a deliberate tone, it sounded as if it had already happened. She had already created the next big gown. The public had already loved it. She already was a celebrated designer. There was no bravado in her manner, just frankness.

"How are you liking the city?" She picked up a chocolate-covered strawberry from a silver platter on a nearby end table and nibbled at it. "It must be quite a change from Shy."

I looked down at the contents of the vanity drawer, trying to think before I spoke. Corsets of pink and white, each one adorned with delicate lace and gems. Clearly everything was beautiful at the House, even the garments no one would see.

"You've heard of Shy?"

Shy was so small, it wasn't on most maps of Britannia Secunda. Since most of it was rural, travelers always had a hard time knowing where it began and ended. It simply rose out of the farmlands, built into a few simple buildings and forests, and then faded away into roads leading to other places.

"Of course not." She gave a smug little smile and licked a smear of chocolate off the back of her hand. "I researched the other contestants. Where they came from. What they want."

Her black eyes focused on me the way our cats stared at mice before devouring them. I turned away from her to re-examine the corsets in the drawer. I pulled one out to inspect the stitching.

"Why did you research everyone?"

I ran a finger over the corset, my body as stiff as the strips of whalebone lining its seams.

"Madame Jolène is only accepting two girls to apprentice as designers. And that's only if they're good. I am going to be one of them. I wanted to familiarize myself with the other contestants. I have to say—overall, I was impressed. Oftentimes, it seems like the contestants for the Fashion House Interview are only in it for the prestige. This time, though, it looks like it'll be a real competition."

"Really?" My voice faltered. What if the other contestants were already so much better than I was that I didn't stand a chance? Sophie seemed to think as much. "How so?"

"Well, Alice's mother hired a former Fashion House designer to tutor her, and Ky has spent years studying fashion in Japan. Cordelia's family petitioned for her spot before Madame Jolène even began making her list of girls to invite." Sophie rattled off each girl's background with ease. "I'm not too worried about Kitty. I'm sure she'll be strong with the technical skills, but she hardly seems to have any creativity, and I bet her parents bought her entry into the competition."

"Bought her entry?"

"Yes. She's from the Quincey family, and they lost their title some time ago after Kitty's grandfather led the Crown into an illegal investment. They've been trying to regain their social capital ever since. But their money can only get them so far—it certainly can't buy Kitty an imagination. So you aren't alone."

"Excuse me?"

"You and Kitty."

"What do you mean?"

"Well." Sophie's eyes flashed with something. Something I knew too well from the families who would give my mother and me bags of used clothes back in Shy. Pity. Sophie didn't continue, but she didn't have to. I knew what she was saying. Kitty and I weren't real competition. Not in her eyes.

That's fine. Let her underestimate me. Yet even as I told myself that, I faltered. Maybe I really was outmatched. Maybe I really was beaten before I even began.

"Oh, don't look so glum," Sophie said. "Perhaps you can get hired as a private seamstress to an aristocrat once the competition is over."

Her tone reminded me of the maid's from earlier. Too sweet. She was still watching me, her hand still over her sketch. I forced my face to relax, my eyes to soften. It made sense that she didn't consider me real competition . . . but it also made sense that she would want me to give up. I'd never considered that there might be another aspect to the Fashion House Interview. I'd never considered that the other contestants might just try to slip into my head and defeat me before I'd even sewn a stitch.

"Maybe." I mimicked her overly sweet tone. "I'm not too worried. I think training in the country gives me fresh perspective."

Training was a ridiculous stretch of the truth. My training, if one could even use such a word, was entirely self-directed and had occurred at the dining room table in our pub and over the threadbare quilt on my bed, where I'd spend hours sketching, studying the fashion pages, and sewing my own creations.

Sophie's eyes widened in a moment of surprise, and then she smiled. It was a small smile and the last thing I expected. I glanced down at the patterned paper lining the bottom of my vanity drawer, unable to hold her gaze.

"Well." That small, secretive smile still hung around her lips. "We shall see, Emmaline Watkins."

My name sounded strange in her low voice, as though I was hearing it for the first time. I didn't know how to respond to such a comment, so I pretended to be occupied with the corset I held. Yet while my eyes were fixed on it, my mind raced. I didn't want to be a private seamstress to an aristocrat, even if everyone assumed that was the highest I could climb. I wanted to *create*, to actualize the visions living in my head, even if my dreams were preposterous for a girl from the country with no family name or wealth to speak of.

"Oh, usually the maid unpacks for us, but I don't think she did for you." Sophie suddenly changed the subject, motioning to my carpetbag. It sat near my bed, a blight on the beautiful room, still full of my things.

I put the corset back into the drawer and walked over to the bag. Leaning over, I intended to shove it beneath the bed's dust ruffle and unpack it later, when I was alone. But as soon as my fingers touched the soft, familiar fabric, I couldn't shove it away. No, it wasn't very nice. But it was one of the few things I had, and it was part of me, as much as my work-callused hands.

I pulled my pencils and a ream of paper out of it and carried them to my vanity. I wanted the rhythmic comfort of my pencil tip against a blank page. Sophie observed, still turned in her chair.

"Can I see your designs?"

"Um . . ."

"What's wrong? I'm sure they're very good." She arched an eyebrow as she spoke, as though she'd already decided my sketches were terrible and was challenging me to prove otherwise.

"Fine." I pointed to my carpetbag, where several loose

sketches rested atop my other sketchbook. This girl wasn't my friend, that was for sure. But I didn't want everyone thinking I was a talentless pity hire. Sophie got up, her black silky robe sliding even farther down her elbows. As she brushed past me, the scent of violet–witch hazel perfume filled my nose.

She laid my sketches out evenly on the floor, one next to the other. My pencil stilled on the paper as she knelt to examine them.

"Detailed, aren't they?" she asked.

"I suppose so."

She held a sketch of a midday organza gown with a wide belt of round crystals accenting the waist. I'd titled it *My Mother Going to the City.* As I'd drawn it, I'd told myself a story about my mother deciding to return to the city and walking through Shy in the gown before leaving. Our neighbors, especially the ones who judged and pitied us, stared at her in awe. Out of all the sketches, Sophie had found the one that I thought about the most.

The sketch was a little silly—my mother would die before she'd wear a dress like that, yet I'd designed it to fit her bony form and sallow skin, deliberating over each decision until it was perfect.

The sight of it stung in the sharp, instantaneous way saltwater stings an open cut. I didn't want to think about my mother alone in the pub. I needed to write her. In fact, I would write her tonight and tell her I was sorry I didn't get to say goodbye.

Then she would write me back and I'd know everything was right between us.

PART I

"They aren't too bad."

"You sound surprised."

"I am," she said. "I have to admit—I thought you a token contestant and nothing more. But you are . . . capable."

She considered me, a new look in her eyes. It wasn't quite admiration, and it wasn't quite respect. But it was something close to those. I self-consciously ducked my head, quickly trying to change the subject.

"Can I see your sketches?"

"Not now," Sophie said. "Maybe later, once I've finished some new ones."

The pleasant feelings vanished. I'd just shown her mine and she wouldn't show me hers? I wanted to snatch my sketch away from her. I should have never let her see my work. Now she knew things about me, about what I could do, and I didn't know anything about her in return.

"As I said, you are capable, Emmaline." Sophie's tone was brisk, professional. "I'll give you a bit of advice. The other girls will try to trip you up. Be wary."

"Advice? Just earlier, you were embarrassing me in front of everyone."

"Oh, come now. I was feeling out Madame Jolène. That exchange had very little to do with you."

"Certainly didn't seem like it."

"However it may have appeared, that's what I was doing. I'll be frank. I don't need to worry about undermining you. I look forward to a fierce competition based on talent alone, not stupid mind games."

I didn't know if I should feel reassured or even more uncertain.

Sophie carried on. "As I said, you're in a difficult place. But I am too." Her eyes roved restlessly over my designs.

"What do you mean?" I turned back to the paper in front of me, feigning interest in it while waiting for her to respond.

But Sophie stayed silent.

"Sophie. What do you mean?" I repeated. It was awkward to ask the same question twice, but I persisted. Somehow, it seemed like Sophie knew more about my place at the Fashion House than I did.

Sophie sighed. She turned her head to the side, and her long black hair fell over her shoulder, blocking me from her vision. "Never mind," she said.

I stood up, part of me tempted to walk over to her and touch her shoulder and make her answer me. The other part of me, though, didn't know if that was too much, if it was better to just ignore her.

"Fine. I think I shall go to bed." Abruptly, I pushed back my vanity stool and stood up. I was done with her and our conversation—if it could even be called a conversation.

"Have you seen this?" Her words were sudden but her tone was nonchalant, as though we'd been conversing about something frivolous the whole time. She held out a piece of paper.

I walked over to her, tripping slightly on my overly long hem, and took the crisp page from her hand, thinking for a moment it was one of her sketches.

Instead, it was a letter, etched in black ink on thick Fashion House stationery.

"What is it?"

"My welcome letter."

A welcome letter? I glanced abruptly from the letter to Sophie and then back. Slowly, I sat back down on my vanity stool and read it.

Dear ladies:

Welcome.

As a Fashion House Interview contestant, you are in a position of esteem. As such, all behaviors must align with the dignity of the Fashion House and your benefactress, Madame Jolène.

RULES FOR THE FASHION HOUSE INTERVIEW:

Violations of these rules will result in immediate termination from the Fashion House Interview.

All designs must be conceived and created by the contestants without any references to pattern books.

Garments for the various challenges must be completed in the limited time frame set by Madame Jolène.

The Fashion House will provide each contestant with a sketchbook, pencils, a mannequin, fabric, supplies such as buttons, beads, etc., and a sewing kit. It is prohibited to use any other items during the challenges.

GENERAL:

Please be advised—contestants may be seen in public only if they are wearing House fashions. Contestants must present themselves to Monsieur Francesco for approval of all outfits prior to leaving for any engagements.

When working with Fashion House customers, contestants are strictly prohibited from sharing any private information about their customers to the press. Doing so shall result in immediate termination. Contestants are permitted to keep any tips, gifts, or benefits bestowed upon them by their customers, though all such items must be registered.

ADDENDUM:

This season, it is of particular importance that all interviews with the press be handled with discretion and delicacy. Interviews will be granted per Madame Jolène and only when necessary to advance the Fashion House's visibility. Be aware that any unsanctioned comments may be grounds for dismissal. Additionally, please be wary of conversations conducted outside the Fashion House. Press members have become particularly aggressive and sometimes do not identify themselves when collecting information.

SCHEDULING:

The first challenge will be held on September 5. Report to the sewing room for instructions.

—Mme. Jolène

"September fifth . . . But that's tomorrow!"

I knew the contest would start soon, but I thought I would have a day or two to at least settle in. I still didn't know my way around the Fashion House.

"Nervous?" Sophie asked.

"Are you?"

There. I turned the question back on her.

"No. It should be interesting. You'll soon notice everything is very . . . *interesting* here. You can keep the letter if you want. Otherwise, put it in the rubbish bin. I don't need it."

I held the letter in both hands. *Miss Sophie Sterling* was written across the top in an elaborate script that dipped and twisted across the page. I hadn't received a welcome letter. In fact, if Sophie hadn't shown it to me, I wouldn't have known that there was a challenge tomorrow.

Perhaps it had been an accident, an oversight. But that seemed like too easy an explanation. Especially since everyone, from Madame Jolène to the maid, seemed to think I was a joke.

"What's wrong?" Sophie asked, though there was no hint of sympathy or kindness in her voice.

"When did you get this letter?"

"It was on my bed when I got here a week ago."

I searched around my pillow. Nothing. Same with the foot, where an extra gold blanket was folded into a swan. Had someone taken my letter? Or had it never been here to start with? Maybe Sophie had taken it . . . but then, why would she show me hers? And, if she was being honest, she didn't have time for or interest in pettiness. I put my hand to my head, wishing I could wipe away the ache just underneath my forehead. I was being paranoid. All I needed was sleep and everything would be fine.

Still, my limbs were as rigid as the scarecrow Francesco always associated me with, and as I sat on the edge of the bed, I glanced at either side of it, hoping the letter had fallen off.

No such luck.

CHAPTER FIVE

KNOCK! KNOCK! KNOCK!

I lurched upright in bed. A ray of sunlight shone brightly on the floor, streaking the light-blue marble almost white. Holding up a hand to shield my gaze, I blinked. Sophie's bed was empty. In fact, it was neatly made, as though she'd never been there.

Groggily, I scanned the room. As I did, confusion roused my mind into wakefulness. Were my eyes playing tricks on me? Sleepiness gone, I looked around. No, things were different. Sophie's vanity had been moved to the far side of the room, along with her chaise longue. Her wardrobe had also been nudged over by a foot and its door stood open, revealing her black and burgundy dresses. And yet my furniture was in the same configuration as yesterday.

Last night, I'd thought I'd heard scraping and pushing and had even looked up once to see Sophie's shadowy figure moving around the room. I'd been so exhausted, though, I'd thought it was part of a bizarre dream.

"Emmaline?" A muffled voice came from the other side of the door. I kicked my feet, trying to free myself from the twisted mounds of satin blankets and tasseled pillows.

"I'm coming!"

How long had I slept? There were no clocks in the room, but the sunny quality of the light leaned dangerously toward midday. I fumbled my way across the room and opened the door.

"You aren't dressed?" Kitty stood in the doorway. Her hair was swept up into a low bun, her dark-blue gown accessorized with a gold necklace. Her eyes widened as she took in my night-gown and hair, which I could tell was forming a bird's nest of wisps and knots around my face.

"What time is it?"

"You aren't ready at all? It's time for the first challenge!"

"That's right now?"

"Yes! A maid didn't wake you?"

"No!" Panic, raw and sharp, shot through my chest. "What should I do?"

A maid—the snide one from the day before—was walking by, and Kitty stopped her.

"Help her dress, Tilda. She needs to be at the showcase in five minutes."

The maid smirked, as though pleased at my dilemma.

"Fine."

"I have to go, but come down as soon as you can." Kitty smiled at me. I figured she meant it to be comforting, but it was the sort of pitiful smile one gives a chicken before its head is chopped off.

Tilda followed me into my room, sighing. The soft sound

sent something else through me. Anger. I turned to her as she opened my wardrobe.

"Were you supposed to wake me up?"

She pulled out (yet another) pink dress with an asymmetric neckline and soft ivory overlay and pursed her lips.

"Did you put in a request?"

"A request?" I pulled my nightgown over my head, motioning for her to hurry. Just the day before, I'd been embarrassed to be naked in front of her. Now I only cared about the seconds tick-ticking away and, with them, my Fashion House future.

"You must register wake-up requests the night before." Her tone was excessively innocent and she smiled sweetly at me. "Isn't that how it works in the country, too?"

How was I supposed to know these things? These questions were like a corset, constricting tighter and tighter around me until every bit of air was forced out of my lungs.

With the dress over her arm, Tilda opened the top drawer of my vanity. She took out a simple daytime corset and brought it over to me, each step long and measured.

"Hurry," I urged, my fingers jumping around the corset, trying to help her fasten me into it.

"I am," she huffed, yet it seemed to take forever for her to lace up the corset strings, lift the dress over my head, and brush my hair into something resembling a decent hairstyle. "It's the first challenge today, isn't it?"

"Yes, so please go faster!" I implored.

"I'm going as fast as I can," she said, twisting my hair up. "The first challenge is always the most . . . amusing. To me, anyway.

Girls always try to go too big and do something impressive. They hardly ever succeed, and the results are simply hilarious."

"It won't matter if I'm not there to compete." I struggled to step into heels while she tried to push a few more pins into my locks. By then, I was sweating, and the gown stuck to my legs. "That's enough."

"No accessories?" Tilda asked, eyeing me as I stumbled toward the door, grabbing my brocade sketch.

"No time."

I dashed out into the hall and to the staircase. As I tried to run down the steps in heels, while also holding the brocade sketch and the banister, thoughts rose one after another in my mind. Maybe someone had told Tilda not to wake me, so I'd miss the showcase. Could it have been Sophie? Or one of the other girls?

That was the alarming thing. Not knowing if someone was intentionally trying to force me into missteps . . . or if I simply didn't know the ways of the city. Whatever the case, I needed to figure things out, and quick, before anything like this happened again.

I slowed my pace once I got to the sewing room, my mind a buzzing hornet's nest of thoughts. Perhaps I could slip in when no one was looking? Then Madame Jolène wouldn't even know I was late. The double-wide doors to the sewing room stood open, and I cautiously peeked inside.

The ceiling soared far above everyone's heads. A sea of iron sewing machines anchored to cutting tables stretched out in rows. Natural light spilled into the room from a series of windows running just beneath the ceiling. While it didn't have the glamour of the wallpapered, chandelier-lit lobby, the room was artful in its simplicity and balance.

Sophie, Alice, Ky, Kitty, and Cordelia stood at the tables. Madame Jolène faced them, flanked by Francesco and two women from her design board—I recognized one of them as the horsehair woman from my interview. They wore matching dresses with bateau necklines.

Standing against the far wall were a group of men in plaid shirts and denim trousers with overcoats and women in peplums and ruffled skirts. They held notepads and pens. Reporters, I assumed.

Reporters.

I ran my eyes over them, looking for a shock of blond hair and flash of blue eyes.

Almost immediately, I found them—found him. The reporter from yesterday. He was standing near the back, notebook and pencil poised and ready. My heart seesawed up and down, torn between a new form of excitement and nerves.

Focus. I tore my gaze away from him. The last thing I needed right now was to be distracted from the task at hand by a boy. Carefully, I took another quiet step forward.

Madame Jolène wore a voluminous burgundy gown embroidered with cuttleworms and a dark-blue head wrap that covered every wisp of her hair. She must have been speaking, because the thrill of the room was palpable, and every eye was fixed on her.

For once, her terrifyingly commanding presence worked in my favor. I took the opportunity to sidle into the room and slip up to the nearest cutting table, next to Sophie. I struggled to gather myself, so it would seem as though I'd been there all along. It was a silly hope, when there were only six of us. But I desperately clung to it as beads of sweat rolled down my back.

The silence in the room continued, and I cautiously glanced up. The first thing I saw was Madame Jolène's gray eyes, leveled straight at me. I cringed, ready for her to berate me or even tell me to leave. But when she spoke, it wasn't to me. It was to everyone else.

"As I was saying, you will have the rest of today and tomorrow morning for the challenge." It didn't matter that she hadn't outright scolded me. In fact, I might have preferred it to the dismissive derision that flitted across her face and then was gone. I stared down at my heels. I didn't dare look at the reporter now. Madame Jolène continued.

"You will sketch your designs in your chambers and then Francesco will escort you down to the Fabric Floor, where you will select your materials and bring them back here for the sewing portion. You will present your finished pieces at noon tomorrow. We will review your work and give feedback at that time." There was another dramatic pause, and I looked up just in time to see her extend a hand upward. "You may begin"—she paused, and everyone leaned forward in one collective surge of excitement—"now."

As though released from Madame Jolène's hold, the room burst into motion and sound. The reporters rushed forward.

75

Most of them hurried up to Madame Jolène, asking her questions. Her design staff formed a barrier around her, and they moved like one body toward the door. Madame Jolène's face was completely calm, as though she was alone in the room and not surrounded by a throng of reporters shouting questions at her. One or two approached Sophie and Ky.

The rest came up to me.

"Are you the contestant from the North?" a reporter demanded.

"What is your design aesthetic? Is it"—another one, this one in black-and-gray striped trousers, looked me up and down—"pink?"

"What do you think about the Reformists Party demanding your inclusion in the Fashion House Interview?" a particularly loud-voiced reporter shouted over the others.

"I . . ." Everywhere I turned, their bodies pressed up against me, their eyes hungry for my words. "I need to get by—"

I struggled to break through their circle, but they seemed to grow in strength, jostling me this way and that. Suddenly, a familiar face joined them. One with blue eyes, blond hair, and a bruised lip.

"Is it true that Madame Jolène will only be using yellow in the upcoming fall collection?" he yelled, his voice carrying over the din.

"Yellow?" the loud-voiced reporter shouted. "*For fall?*"

He darted away, yelling, "Madame Jolène! Wait! Just one comment."

The other reporters followed him like bloodhounds on a

scent. All of them except the blond reporter. He stood in front of me, arms folded across his chest, a lopsided smile on his bruised lips.

"Thank you," I said self-consciously, tucking a strand of hair behind my ear.

"Anytime," he replied. "But you'd better get going. The challenge has already begun!"

"You're right!" I was the only contestant still in the room. Frazzled, I gathered up my skirts. "I need to hurry."

"Good luck," he said. Skirts still gathered, I paused for one second longer. Light from the high windows fell across his face, turning his hair into an even lighter blond and softening the blue from his eyes so that they were as clear as water.

"I still don't know your name," I said.

The lopsided grin on his lips grew and evened out so it was one full smile. But just as he opened his mouth to reply, Francesco called to me from across the room.

"Emmaline! No time to chat, darling. This is a competition, not an ice cream social." He motioned for me to go, and I obeyed.

Ky, Alice, Kitty, and Cordelia were already on the staircase by the time I crossed the lobby floor. They hurried, their steps somehow loud, even though the stairs were covered in plush carpet. I rushed after them and managed to catch up to Ky.

"Ky," I said. "What are we supposed to design for the challenge?"

For a second, she paused. Like last night, her style was all clash and contrast yet somehow worked. Her green gown had a fleur-de-lis print, and her gold heels had actual nails driven through the leather.

"It's a—" She suddenly cut herself off, a shrewd sharpness coming to her face. "Maybe you should go ask Madame Jolène."

"What? Just tell me what it is."

"You really should ask Madame Jolène. I wouldn't want to tell you the wrong thing." She gave me a fake, apologetic smile, as though there really was nothing she could do.

She moved past me, leaving me alone on the stair. I took a breath, trying to steady myself and calm down. This was a competition. No one was going to help me. Still, my face burned hot with frustration.

"It's a coat," someone said behind me. I turned, the scent of violet and witch hazel filling my nose. Sophie, her hair wrapped up into a knot at the top of her head, stood at the bottom of the stairs. "We have to design a fall coat. The only requirement is that we incorporate feathers."

"Really?" I blinked in surprise. Cool and aloof Sophie was the last person I expected help from. "Thank you. I really appreciate it. I asked Ky, and she wouldn't tell me."

Sophie proceeded up the steps, coming to stand next to me on the same narrow step, her black skirts brushing against mine in a swish of cool silk. I leaned back, unnerved by her closeness. Everything about her seemed *more* up close. Her hair seemed blacker and her skin seemed whiter. Even her perfume suddenly seemed stronger.

"I suppose she was trying to gain some sort of competitive edge," she said. "It's quite funny. Some girls are so easily threatened."

She stared evenly at me, as though waiting for a response, but I didn't know what to say. A soft half smile crossed her mouth and then was gone. My face blazed hot again. She found me amusing. Pitiable.

With that, she continued up the stairs, leaving me behind.

When we got to our chambers, Sophie picked up her leather sketchbook and took the chaise longue. Her skirts spread around her like a pool of black water. An identical leather sketchbook sat on my vanity. Three graphite pencils, their wood encased in gold leaf, were next to it.

I picked up the sketchbook and one of the pencils, and glanced around. At home, I sketched at our dining room table. Our table was old and its rigid edges sometimes distorted my lines. I wouldn't have that problem here, where every surface was smooth and glossy.

I sat down at the vanity and flipped back the cover of the sketchbook.

A coat. A fall coat with feathers.

I closed my eyes, like I always did right before I sketched. Usually a dreamlike fog filled my mind, one full of colors and forms. But this time, my mind was a scattered mess. I opened my eyes. Sophie sketched quickly, her hand moving assuredly across the page. She looked like a real designer, like someone who knew exactly what she was doing. The sight of her confidence made my nerves grow even more.

Focus.

Coat. Feathers.

I took a breath, a deep one that filled my lungs with air and made my chest expand. I let it out slowly and pressed my pencil tip to the page.

A slim coat.

There. That was a starting point. That was a silhouette.

Slowly, I outlined a fitted coat, one that would follow the lines of the body.

Should it be navy? Black?

Usually, I never had to ask myself these questions, because the answers always seemed to be there inside me, simply waiting to be discovered. Now I felt like I was designing outside of myself, that I was forcing myself through each step.

Nude.

I didn't think the word so much as feel it. *Yes.* The coat would be nude wool and I'd cut out black leather pieces. I would sew the pieces onto the body of the coat so that, at first, it would seem like it was entirely black leather. Then, as the wearer moved, bits of the nude would show through.

I couldn't help but smile. The mix of shiny leather with soft wool was completely me: functional yet fantastical, and articulated in the slimmest of silhouettes. I'd sew red feathers around the collar. They would stand straight up, creating a high neck. The wool would be in homage to Shy, along with red robins' feathers.

I worked quickly, labeling which colors went where and the types of fabrics I'd use.

Our chamber door opened, and Tilda entered, holding a feather duster. She flitted about, dusting here and there. She gave Sophie a wide berth, but when she came near my vanity, she peered over my shoulder at my sketch.

"My," she said. "That's quite the look."

Quite the look?

My fingers tightened involuntarily on my pencil, and I stared down at the sketch. Just moments ago, I'd thought it was strong. Creative. Me.

"You do realize you are designing for the Fashion House, don't you?"

"What do you mean?"

"The Fashion House silhouette is full. Traditional. Not all skimpy like this." She jabbed her feather duster at my sketch. The duster emitted a gentle cloud of dust and I almost sneezed. "And nude? For the fall season?"

"Shouldn't you be cleaning?" Sophie asked from her spot on the chaise longue. Her head was still bent over her drawing and she didn't stop sketching. She spoke in the same commanding and impersonal tone that Madame Jolène used when addressing the maids. Tilda immediately stepped back, lowering her head.

"Yes, miss."

She went back to dusting, and I slowly started drawing again, filling in the details on the coat. But as I did, doubts plagued me. The design was different. Too different. Tilda was right. I was designing for the Fashion House now, and my coat didn't fit the Fashion House style at all. Tilda's words replayed in my head. Not the ones from now but the ones from earlier.

The first challenge is always the most amusing. To me, anyway. Girls always try to go too big and do something impressive. They hardly ever succeed, and the results are simply hilarious.

Everyone already thought I was ridiculous. The last thing I needed to do was prove them right by designing something completely outside the Fashion House canon.

"Ready?" Sophie flipped her sketchbook closed.

"Ready?"

"Our sketching time is up. We need to meet Francesco on the Fabric Floor to get our materials."

She got up, tucking her sketchbook under her arm. I picked up my sketchbook, too, and followed her out of our chamber. There wasn't time to draw a new sketch, but I couldn't use the nude-and-black one. Somehow, I'd have to come up with another one in my head by the time we got to the Fabric Floor. I tried to think, but my thoughts were as scattered as a child's blocks across the floor. A plethora of silhouettes ran through my mind. Instead of flowing over me in a warm fog, they came with sharp flashes and blinking lights. Desperately, I willed them to turn into one look I could use but, as hard as I tried, I couldn't pull one out of the chaos.

Luckily, the Fabric Floor was down in the basement of the Fashion House—it gave me more time to think. To plan.

"Are you all right, Emmaline?" Kitty asked as we gathered outside the Fabric Floor doors. "You look stressed."

"I am." I forced myself to smile at her. "Just trying to figure out my design."

"Don't worry. Trust yourself."

I smiled a real smile. Everyone treated me coolly or with disdain. Everyone except Kitty, whose sweetness reached me through my distress.

"You're so kind, Kitty. Everyone else is so"—I lowered my voice so only she could hear me—"intense."

Especially now. No one chatted or even smiled. The other girls looked like soldiers readying for attack, their sketchbooks and pencils reminding me of shields and swords. Ky had wrestled her way to the spot closest to the Fabric Floor door, the epaulets on her wide-shouldered gown flashing. Cordelia came next to her, but Ky refused to give up any space.

Kitty watched them elbowing each other and quietly replied, "My family was titled, long before I was born, but we lost the title. I grew up seeing my parents look down on everyone else, even though we aren't any different. They were always nice but in a horribly fake way. I promised myself I wouldn't be like them. I promised myself I'd follow the rules." She sighed. "All they want is for me to win the Fashion House Interview—they'll do anything to move up in society."

I'd thought everyone else in the Fashion House Interview had charmed lives. They were wealthy, after all, and established enough to be invited to the competition. But Kitty's story about her disgraced and desperate family didn't fit my assumptions.

"Ladies, welcome." Francesco stood in front of the double doors leading to the Fabric Floor. "You will have twenty minutes to get any fabric, buttons, appliques, or trims. No need to worry about thread—we will provide you with the appropriate colors for your designs in the sewing room. Since this challenge includes feathers, we've brought in several options. You'll find them at the back of the Fabric Floor. There are carts that you can use to collect your items."

He turned to grasp the two knobs, pausing for dramatic

emphasis. After a few beats, he flung the doors open wide and stepped aside.

For a moment, I was nearly swept away by the room. It seemed to go on forever in every direction. Rows and rows of towering shelves displayed bolts of fabric. Signs were affixed to the shelves, denoting the types of textiles. I grasped the handles of a cart and walked forward, taking in the hundreds of colors, patterns, and prints, my imagination set afire by the countless options.

The other contestants rushed past me, pushing their carts, jolting me into action. Fabric. I needed to get fabric, even if I wasn't sure what my design was. And trim and buttons. And, oh God, feathers, too.

I spotted the sign for wool and headed there first. My eyes landed on a sumptuous navy wool with a slight herringbone pattern running through it. But, just as I reached for it, someone slipped between me and it and snatched the entire bolt off the shelf. Cordelia. She stuck it into her cart.

"I was going to use that!" I protested.

"So sorry," she smirked. "Maybe go to the burlap aisle? I think that would be a better fit for you."

The urge to snatch the bolt out of Cordelia's cart rushed over me, but there wasn't time to get into a fight with another contestant. I turned away from her, so angry that I could barely see straight. Almost blindly, I yanked a bolt of navy off the shelf. It didn't have any print, but its texture was soft and the Fashion House always used clean, classic fabrics.

Feathers. I needed to get those next.

As Francesco said, they were at the back of the Fabric Floor. Bins displayed everything from luxurious peacock plumes to tiny swallow feathers. Ky and Alice were already elbow-deep in the bins. Their quick motions sent feathers tumbling up into the air, where they spun and drifted back down to the floor.

"Get the black crow feathers," Ky snapped to Alice. "I'm sure Sophie will want to use those."

Apparently, I wasn't the only one they were trying to trip up.

"Ten minutes, ladies," Francesco's voice echoed through the basement. Normally, I would've politely waited to start digging in the bin of gray feathers that Alice was pawing through. But, in my short time in the Fashion House Interview, I'd learned. I elbowed my way next to her and grabbed some of the feathers.

"Ouch!" Alice cried out as I knocked into her. I didn't stop. I held the feathers up to the fabric in my cart. It matched well. Maybe a little *too* well, but I didn't have time to question myself. There were small sacks hanging next to the bins, and I took one, stuffing four handfuls of the feathers inside.

Now I just needed buttons and maybe some trim and I would have everything required to make a coat. My hands were slick with sweat. I didn't know if it was from the time limit or the fact that I wasn't even sure what I was going to design. The wheels of my cart screeched as I hurried to the side wall, where tins of buttons, trims, and appliques sat in stalls, displayed almost like fruit at the open-air market that came through Shy every spring.

Sophie stood by one of the stalls, holding up a black jet button. She turned it this way and that, as though she had all the time in the world. With a slight shake of her head, she set the button down and then picked up a black enamel one. I paused for a moment, pulled into her calmness. Her cart sat next to her, several bolts of fabric arranged neatly inside it. I glanced at my cart. My single bolt of navy wool stuck up out of it, and one of my sacks of feathers had tipped over. It was as messy and disorganized as I felt inside.

"Only five minutes left, ladies!"

Five minutes? Where on earth had the time gone? With fumbling fingers, I grabbed some brass buttons. Their sharp edges dug into my skin, but I didn't have time to be careful. I wasn't sure how many I needed, so I took several, dumping them into one of my feather bags. Breathing hard, I glanced around, at a loss. I needed more than buttons to adorn my coat.

Desperately, I grabbed some braided cord, a length of gunmetal-colored chain, and a spool of black fringe. Did I need more?

This is all wrong.

The thought hit me hard, and even though I shouldn't have wasted any time, I leaned against one of the stalls. I was grabbing elements for a design that didn't even exist. That wasn't what designers did. It wasn't what *I* did. How had I ended up like this? How had I gotten so lost?

"Two minutes, ladies! I suggest you head back to the front to avoid disqualification." Francesco's bellow reached through the basement. For better or for worse, everything I would use for my first Fashion House Interview challenge was in my cart, and I couldn't change it now. As I reached the front, my heart was as heavy as an iron weight.

I didn't want to admit it, but I couldn't shake the feeling that I'd already lost.

The maids took our carts up to the sewing room, so when we got there, our items and sewing kits were laid out on individual cutting tables. Mannequins stood next to each table. I recognized my table instantly from my bolt of plain navy wool and mismatched assortment of buttons, cord, chain, and fringe.

The other girls streamed past me to their tables. Within moments, the room filled with the sounds of heavy sewing scissors slicing through cloth, the rustle of fabrics being unfurled, and the rattle of buttons and beads scattering across tabletops. I touched the navy wool.

Get yourself together.

Navy coat. Full skirt, voluminous collar, detachable cape trimmed with cord.

With a deliberation I didn't feel, I picked up the heavy paper inside my sewing kit and the measuring tape and began to measure out my pattern.

Sophie's table was nearest mine, and when I saw her unpack her materials, I stopped mid-snip, startled. Instead of the black silk, feathers, and buttons from earlier, she carefully sorted through fabrics of dusty rose, dark gold, and light brown.

"You switched your colors," I said, unable to stop myself.

"Hardly," she replied, picking up the pattern paper. "I had them the whole time, hidden underneath the black fabric. I didn't want anyone to copy me."

"Those colors are so . . ." I faltered, staring at the cornucopia of hues spread across her table. The pinks had undertones of tan and sable, while the browns were the exact shade of milky tea.

"Like fall," Sophie finished for me. "Everyone uses dying leaves as the color inspiration for fall. They use red, orange, and black . . . but these are the true hues of fall."

Her color scheme was warm, whispery, winsome. It made me think of a wheat field just at sunrise, when the sky is punctuated with soft pink clouds rimmed in yellow and the wheat stalks gleam like gold. Ky, though she might have tried to sabotage Sophie, hadn't anticipated this. And neither had I. I glanced at my plain navy and my stomach twisted.

"I thought you would use black," I said.

"If I was designing for myself, I would. And it would've been fantastic. But this is for the Fashion House Interview," Sophie said, her tone turning hard and bitter. "One must go for the unexpected, obviously."

She'd pushed her decoy black fabric to the edge of her cutting table, but now she stared at it longingly. Then, without saying another word, she began setting out her buttons.

Slowly, I turned back to my table. The image of my first coat—the nude-and-black one—rose in my mind. I forced it away, even as it called to me. With a motion more decisive than I felt, I cut into the pattern paper.

I thought a full day devoted to designing would be more than enough to create a coat. Back in Shy, I'd never had such a block of time to design anything. Even on Sunday, when our pub was closed, we were scrubbing the dining room and kitchen clean and getting things ready for the coming work week. My creativity happened in stolen moments, often interrupted by the need to check the taps and wash the pint glasses. But even though we had the entire day and the following morning until noon, the minutes flew by.

As the day ended, I stepped back to survey my coat, my neck and feet aching from the work. My fingertips were raw from hours of manipulating the heavy wool and holding the sharp edges of the brass buttons in place as I sewed them on. I didn't dare think about my appearance, but I could tell that my hair was a mess of wisps, and my dress clung to my sweaty body. I'd long since kicked off my heels, and my feet were grubby from walking around barefoot.

At least I wasn't the only one who was worse for wear. Cordelia impatiently blew errant strands of hair out of her face, and Alice wiped her brow with some extra strips of her lace. All the other girls had also taken off their heels, including Kitty, who'd fretted that we weren't supposed to. All of them except Sophie.

I looked at the different coats. Alice's was covered in Chantilly lace and white swan feathers. Kitty's coat was traditional blue toile, and Cordelia's menswear coat was in that navy fabric she'd snagged from me.

Sophie's stood out, as did Ky's. Ky's coat was a dark plum with a jagged hem and crane feathers accenting the waist. She'd stitched the word *Happiness* across the back of the coat and embroidered a crane just beneath it.

"Why 'happiness'?" Alice asked. Her voice was so girlish, she sounded much younger than she was, and, with her ringlets and bows, she looked much younger too.

"It ties in with the crane feathers," Ky replied. For once, her competitive manner eased, and she touched the swirling *H*. "In Japan, cranes are the birds of happiness."

"Oh, how sweet!" Alice said. "I've always wanted a crane. I'd tie a ribbon around its neck and walk it around the city."

I stared at Alice, wondering if she was serious or not. It was hard to believe her bubbly, vapid personality could be real, yet I'd never seen her act any other way.

"This is a red-crowned crane," Ky said sharply. "It's not the sort of creature you'd treat in such a way."

"Touchy, touchy," Alice purred. She spun around and flitted back to her coat.

Ky rolled her eyes and carefully tied off her thread. She ran a finger around the outline of the crane, a wistful look coming over her face. Perhaps she missed Japan. I could only imagine how strange it would be to be raised in two different countries. How would one know where one belonged?

Even though I'd never set foot outside the country (before now, the farthest I'd ever been was Talley, the small town just past Evert), I felt a strange kinship with Ky. I never belonged in Shy, and I wasn't so sure I belonged in Avon-upon-Kynt, either. Though Ky never said as much, I understood that wistful expression. It was longing—for her old home, most likely, but maybe also for something else. A place that didn't exist for her . . . or me.

I turned back to my coat, forcing myself to focus. I'd made sure every stitch was precise and the fit was perfect. I'd created a strong piece, one with masterful tailoring. Even so, I couldn't shake the feeling that the coat wasn't quite right.

The next day came quickly. Like the morning before, Sophie was gone when I woke up. Unlike the morning before, I managed to rise before Tilda came in, and picked out my own clothes. I'd been at Tilda's mercy twice before and I was quite done with it. By the time she arrived, I'd decided on a simple peachy-pink-colored dress. It still wasn't a hue I liked—the soft orangey-pink tones reminded me of a grandmother—but the design was elegant enough.

I was so nervous that I skipped breakfast and went straight to the sewing room. A lone girl was in it: Sophie. The room was quiet aside from the soft squeak of her mannequin as she adjusted its height. The coats stood like headless (quite fashionable) ghosts.

I walked over to mine. At least it wasn't pink. But then, it wasn't much more "me" than the ridiculously peachy-pink dress I stood in.

The other girls soon came in, each one heading to her station. Nervous, tense silence filled the room as we made our final alterations.

I thought there would be some sort of official announcement before our work time concluded and the evaluations began, but as I was tacking down the last bit of fringe on my coat, the doors to the sewing room were suddenly flung open. I jumped back, startled.

Madame Jolène entered like a monarch at the head of a royal procession. She wore a sky-blue gown painted with red leaves and gold birds. A sheer piece of shimmering fabric draped from her shoulders, flouncing behind her with each step she took. Her presence sent my heart into my throat, and I barely managed to tie off my thread.

Her sewing staff, in identical frilled dresses, and Francesco, who sported a hat adorned in red feathers, hurried along behind her, all jockeying for position near her. One of her designers got too close, though, and brushed her skirt. Madame Jolène didn't turn around, but she arched one eyebrow and the entire entourage froze. She kept moving, and they immediately redoubled their efforts to get close.

They came to the front of the room and faced us. Madame Jolène stepped forward.

"Ladies!" Her commanding voice resonated through the sewing room. "We will evaluate your fall coats one at a time. Starting with . . ." I expected her to proceed to Ky, who was closest to her, but instead she scanned the room. "Emmaline."

Me? I was going first? She stepped around the rows of desks, moving lithely until she was right in front of me.

"I—" Frantically, stupidly, I felt like I needed to say something. She held up her hand for silence and stared at my coat for a long moment. I didn't know where to look or where to even put my hands. The quiet stretched on, everyone waiting and watching. I stood there, feeling the excruciating length of each second, desperately wanting to point out that my coat was well made and that it truly embodied the Fashion House look.

At least I could be certain of that. The coat was thick and voluminous with gray feathers sewn around the neckline and a detachable cape. Fringe trimmed the cuffs, tacked in place with the braided cord.

"Very . . ." Madame Jolène drew out the word. I held my breath, hoping against hope that she would love it. "Classic with subtle details."

My heart leaped, suspended between hope and terror.

"Write that down," one of her designers hissed to the other.

"No need to write it down," Madame Jolène said. "Ladies!" she swiveled away from me to address the other girls. "This coat is well made and has some distinctive elements, like this fringe." She brushed the fringe with one finger, making it dance. "But this is the Fashion House Interview. Overall, there is nothing memorable about the coat, and it is quite substandard. In addition, the feathers were used in an expected way, when we wanted to see them given new life."

Madame Jolène's designers nodded sternly, as though they'd been thinking the same thing the whole time.

Nothing memorable. Quite substandard. Expected.

I wanted to explain. I wanted to tell her that I was just trying to give her what she wanted and that I could do so much better. Staring at the coat, seeing it through her eyes, I hated it more than I'd hated anything before. I wanted to will it away and replace it with the nude-and-black coat I'd originally drawn.

"I . . . I was trying to go for an iconic look." My voice was as wispy as the feathers adorning my coat. Across the way, Ky smirked, while Kitty looked at me with sympathy. Alice blinked several times, as though she wasn't quite following what was happening. "And, personally, I think that the feathers—"

"I am not interested in your explanations, Emmaline," Madame Jolène said. "I am only interested in your designs, and this one has spoken for itself." Invigorated by our exchange, she turned on her heel. "Moving on!"

She headed toward Sophie's mannequin. I sank back against my cutting table, dully feeling its edge dig into my back. I'd wanted to come out strong for the first challenge. Win it, even. Instead, I'd turned out a mediocre coat that I wouldn't even want to wear. And why? Because I'd listened to Tilda. She'd made me doubt myself, much more so than any of the other competitors.

But even as I tried to blame Tilda, I couldn't quite believe my own excuse. In the end, I was the one who'd picked out that basic navy wool, and I was the one who'd turned it into a boring coat that could hardly qualify as couture.

"This is beautiful, Sophie." Madame Jolène's cool voice cut through my thoughts. Numbly, I lifted my head. Sophie's coat was a mix of knits and lace in the buttery hues I'd seen earlier. "Exceptional color choices."

"Thank you," Sophie said.

"This could work for Duchess Kent," Madame Jolène mused, addressing one of her designers.

"Most definitely. It would be perfect," the woman said. Instead of looking at the coat, she watched Madame Jolène's face, searching for approval.

"Take the pattern and notes," Madame Jolène said, and the designers scurried to gather up Sophie's papers. I stared, feeling the bitter bite of jealousy.

A soft red settled across Sophie's fair cheeks. At first, I thought she was blushing with pride. But then her fingers twitched agitatedly, and a furrow puckered her brow. She didn't look happy. Or proud.

"I wasn't quite finished with the pattern," she said.

Madame Jolène turned to face Sophie. A smile pulled at her lips, but her gray eyes remained as cold as ever. The reds and gold of her attire suddenly seemed more vivid, as though flaring with her displeasure.

"Sophie," she said, "your work is now Fashion House property. That is a critical component of being here."

"Of course," Sophie murmured. She didn't meet Madame Jolène's gaze. Instead, she stared at her pattern.

"And on a different note, you wear too much black." Madame Jolène was stern. "You have white skin, black eyes, and black hair. Your appearance is much too dark for the Fashion House. I've included several burgundy dresses in your wardrobe. Wear them as well and accessorize with other colors."

The pink in Sophie's cheeks turned a deeper shade of red. But Madame Jolène didn't seem to notice. Or if she did, she didn't care. She simply swept on to Cordelia.

Everyone watched her, but I was transfixed by Sophie. With sharp, intentional motions—the assured kind that reminded me of my mother butchering a duck—she collected her few remaining notes into a neat stack and sheltered them against her chest. Then, seemingly out of nowhere and for no reason, she looked directly at me, those enigmatic black eyes latching on to mine. I nearly ducked my head, flustered, but she simply smiled a bit and gave a half shrug.

I was the first one to look away.

CHAPTER SIX

THROUGHOUT THE NEXT WEEK, we had standard Fashion House duties. There wouldn't be another challenge until the following Monday, and I looked forward to the change. I needed something to distract myself from the embarrassment of my boring navy coat. It was an unpleasant ache that followed me through the halls of the Fashion House.

Kitty kept reassuring me that the coat really wasn't that bad and, to a certain degree, she was right. The coat wasn't bad. But it wasn't good, either.

I tried to reassure her as well. After the first challenge, the rankings had been posted outside the sewing room, and they showed that she also hadn't done very well. We were judged in three categories: workmanship, creativity, and how well we'd followed the theme of the challenge. Our scores, which were out of ten, totaled to create our rank. Sophie was at the top, with Ky close behind her. The other girls filled out the middle, and then Kitty and I were squarely at the bottom.

As the first day of Fashion House duties began, I took solace in the fact that I'd registered a wakeup call—at least I'd figured that out. I would report to the fitting rooms with time to spare.

I stepped down onto the landing just as Ky and Alice breezed by, coming down from their rooms on the floor above. They chatted, and I strained to hear. The biggest key to succeeding at the Fashion House Interview was to design beautiful couture. But I sensed there was more to it than just that. I needed to figure out how to fit in. How to belong, how to act like someone from the city. Ky and Alice were the epitome of city girls, and I could learn from them.

"By the way," Ky said. "Sophie and I are having lunch together today. You should join."

"Definitely," Alice chirped. She linked her arm through Ky's so they were walking side by side. "Also, I've been meaning to ask—do you have some sheepskin?"

Sheepskin? I inched closer.

"I have some in my room. Are your heels hurting?"

"Yes. They're just the prettiest things ever, but they feel like they're made of nails." She paused midstep to lift her skirt and extend her ankle, showcasing the heeled boot on her foot.

"Well, we can go to my chamber after your first appointment. I have loads of sheepskin because Sophie gave me hers."

At the mention of my roommate's name, I craned my neck. I'd hardly seen her since our first night—she didn't seem to come into our chambers until the sky was turning from black to inky blue. It was perplexing, but with everything else on my mind, I hardly had time to figure it out.

"How does she do it?" Alice asked. "She wears the highest heels all day long and she never seems to feel them."

"It's because she likes to be tall," Ky said. "Even though

heaven knows she's already the tallest girl here. And she never wears sheepskin. Says she can't handle the thought that it might peek up out of her shoes."

Ky suddenly stopped, dragging Alice to a standstill with her. She looked over her shoulder at me. I hadn't realized it, but I'd gotten much too close, and she'd sensed my presence. I took a few steps back, but it was too late. "Can I help you?" she demanded.

"Oh, sorry." I blushed. They glared at me with twin looks of disdain before sweeping by. As they did, they leaned into each other to whisper. They didn't bother to make sure I couldn't hear.

"She's so uncouth," Ky said.

"I know. It's embarrassing, really. She's better suited to be a maid."

I knew they didn't think much of me, but hearing it out loud made my insides shrivel. I watched them go, their arms still intertwined.

Down in the fitting room hallway, a large schedule was posted on the wall. It listed our names and individualized schedules for the day: which customers we would see and at what times. Beneath the list were the white cards for each client tucked into a corresponding pocket, specifying her measurements and wardrobe needs.

My name was near the bottom of the alphabetized list.

EMMALINE WATKINS, FITTING ROOM 7—

LADY ELLEN PAIGE RAYMOND—FINAL WEDDING GOWN FITTING

LADY MATILDA DAWSON—FINAL EVENING WEAR FITTING

LADY ELEANOR WESTON—FINAL EVENING WEAR FITTING

I skimmed over the other contestants' schedules, coming to Sophie's.

SOPHIE STERLING, FITTING ROOM 1—

DUCHESS EMERY CROSS—CUSTOM GOWN CONSULTATION

All the other girls had custom gown consultations as well or, at the very least, first fittings or accessorizing appointments. I'd been given the leftovers, the nearly completed clients. My heart sank—Madame Jolène didn't trust me with the more complex appointments. That much was clear.

I grabbed my clients' measurement cards (not that I needed them) and headed down the hallway to fitting room seven. It was at the very end, and I passed the other girls to get there. They didn't say anything, but their eyes followed me.

They knew.

They knew I'd failed at the first challenge and that I really was there just to improve the Fashion House image. I wanted to close the curtain of my fitting room and curl up on the uphol-stered bench inside. But I couldn't. I had to keep going.

I hoped that I would get more advanced appointments the fol-lowing day. Or the next. But each morning, the schedule was the same. Last fittings for me, gown consultations for everyone else. It went on this way throughout the next week. Even on the morning of the second challenge, I stood in my fitting room with yet another final fitting. My client, Lady Ellen Paige Raymond, exclaimed, "I can't breathe! I can't breathe!"

Her eyes bulged and sweat plastered her curls to her face. I was gasping for breath too. A tingling sensation shot to my wrists as I forced my fingers to loosen their grip on her corset strings.

"No! No! Tighter!" Lady Ellen and her mother, Lady Vienna, cried in unison.

"Are you sure?" I didn't want to be responsible for cracking Lady Ellen's rib cage. Not when her wedding was only four weeks away. Still, I needed to make sure the ivory silk satin bridal gown hanging on the dressing room hook would fit over Lady Ellen's girth. According to the notes pinned to the garment bag, the dress had been sized down in hopes of Lady Ellen's weight loss. Whoever decided on this may have been a tad too optimistic.

"Of course she is sure!"

Suddenly Madame Jolène was striding toward me, resplendent in a mint-and-brown Persian-inspired brocade gown. Startled, I dropped the corset strings.

Madame Jolène slipped her spectacles into her bodice and placed her hands on either side of Lady Ellen's waist, her rings sparkling in the dressing-room light.

"The dress is designed to pull your waist in three inches." She unwound the measuring tape circling her neck like a yellow snake and wrapped it around Lady Ellen's circumference. "Two more inches," she declared. "Is that a problem, Emmaline?"

"Oh, no, of course not!" I exclaimed, my numb fingers fumbling for the corset strings.

"You can't be tired from doing one little corset. After all, that is a basic element of your job. Is this fundamental skill too strenuous for you?"

"I'm not tired at all." My already flushed face grew even hotter, until my skin was burning. The corset creaked around Lady Ellen's width, and even though the fitting rooms were humming with the Fashion House sounds—snipping, ripping, rustling—an angry buzzing in my ears drowned it out.

"Well, please try to make more of an effort," Madame Jolène said. She stepped back. "Are those *flats* you are wearing? Where are your heels?"

"I'm sorry," I murmured, subtly trying to pull my skirts down to hide my satin flats.

"Madame Jolène," Lady Vienna broke in, "why is this dress too tight? This is the most important day in Ellen's life. Everyone will be looking at her! *Everyone!* I can't have her looking like a—"

"What she is trying to say—" Lady Ellen interrupted. She had to stop to catch her breath midway through her sentence, one hand pressed to her confined midriff. "Is that I cannot . . . look like . . . a . . . fat pig in a white . . . dress. This is my day, and I will not look like a pig!" Drops of sweat flung off her face, spraying my cheeks. I didn't dare wipe the moisture away, certain any motion would draw Madame Jolène's attention and disapproval.

"If you did not look good in one of my gowns," Madame

Jolène said, "I would not let you wear one." I expected her to leave on that cutting comment, but instead she said to me, "When you are finished with Lady Ellen, report to the lobby."

"The lobby?" I asked. Madame Jolène had already scolded me—what else could she want?

"Yes. Alice has been instructed to finish your appointments."

Without another word, she turned and continued down the hallway, swooping into the other fitting rooms to the delight of the customers and stress of the other contestants. It was her modus operandi. She came down to the fitting rooms several times a day, even though she had her own more prestigious customers. She reminded me of my mother, fully invested in her business and involved in every aspect. But while my mother lived by routine, Madame Jolène did her rounds at random times, so I never knew when she would appear to drop a scathing comment.

As soon as I finished the appointment, I practically ran to the lobby. Nothing, not even Alice's pouty expression at having to take over my final fittings, could distract me from wondering what awaited me.

The lobby was empty except for Francesco. He faced one of the mirrored panels, carefully redoing the knot on his crushed-velvet bow tie.

"Aren't you a sweaty mess?" he said, seeing my reflection in the mirror behind him. I almost smiled. Only Francesco could say something insulting and make it sound affectionate.

"Is Madame Jolène here?" I came to stand next to him. "She pulled me out of my fittings."

"Yes, she did," he said, concentrating on the bow tie. "You need to change."

"Change?" I blinked at him and glanced down at my simple pink consulting dress. "But I still have other appointments."

"Those have been reassigned. Today you begin your other Fashion House duties."

"What?" Aside from the Fashion House Interview and working with clients, there weren't any other duties. And I didn't want there to be. As hard as my time at the Fashion House had been so far—I'd fretted I'd fallen irrevocably behind in the competition—I could feel myself sinking into its rhythm of creativity and beauty.

"Yes. You didn't have any yet because we were finalizing your press wardrobe."

"Don't I already have a Fashion House wardrobe?" I thought about those dresses hanging upstairs in my chamber in their nauseating row of pink.

"Oh, those dull things? Those are just your basic outfits," Francesco said. "Every contestant receives at least five styles upon arriving here. But you get more. You will need a new dress and accessories every time you appear publicly. We aren't outfit repeaters, darling, and every appearance is a fashion opportunity!"

"Appear publicly?" Instantly, the knots of tension doubled in my neck. I frowned, and Francesco, seeing my expression in the mirror, stopped fussing with his bow tie to turn around.

"Why, yes. You are here for a reason, Emmaline. The Reformists Party wants to see the Fashion House making changes, and you are one of those changes. Starting today, you'll be attending a variety of political and social events. You won't have to say anything, just look pretty and a little . . . provincial, if you can. And, later this week, you'll have some interviews—we'll give you instructions on those."

Cold fingers of dread wrapped around my heart. Events. Looking pretty. *Not designing*. How on earth would I have time to focus on the competition if I was away?

"You should be excited. Madame Jolène herself oversaw your new looks. They are fabulous. You'll adore the handmade rosette accents. The dresses are pink, of course, but each one is stunning." He said the word *pink* quickly, as though he knew I hated it.

"Francesco," I said, trying to sound calm, "will I still meet with my customers?"

"What customers?" Francesco blinked at me. "You've had nothing but final fittings. But don't worry, I'll still schedule you as many as possible."

"Will I have enough time for the next challenges?"

A long pause stretched out between us, and I waited, a metallic taste in my mouth.

"I'm not sure," he said, the showy drama gone from his voice. He spoke simply, gently.

"Is there a problem here?" Madame Jolène entered from the fitting-room hallway. Her spectacles sat high on her head like a delicate headpiece, and her measuring tape still hung around her neck. She kept moving toward her private staircase, as though she had no intention of stopping to hear our responses.

"No, of course not—" Francesco quickly started to say.

But I said, "Madame Jolène, may I have a word?"

She stopped but didn't turn toward me, as though she might continue walking away at any moment. One of her little dogs (Apollo, as distinguished by his leather neck ruffle) came padding into the room and, upon seeing her, hurried over to sit at her feet.

"Yes?"

"Francesco just told me I have additional Fashion House duties." I spoke slowly so my voice wouldn't waver. "I just wanted to make sure I will still have ample time for the competition—"

"Emmaline," Madame Jolène said, finally turning around to face me with serpentine grace. "You were brought here for a specific reason. Your first and foremost obligations are appearances and interviews."

I took a quick breath. I knew I'd been brought to the competition to improve the Fashion House's image. But I hadn't anticipated that I'd be sent out and about, or that I wouldn't have the same time to compete as everyone else.

"I just want to make sure it doesn't compromise my place in the Fashion House Interview. I know my first coat was basic, but I promise I can design so much better—"

At the word *design*, Madame Jolène let out one of her short, imperious laughs.

"Dear Emmaline," she said, "you forget your place here. Being a designer requires many skills beyond talent with a needle or sketchpad. Skills you neither understand nor possess—and certainly cannot attain in one season. Do good work, and when you are back home, you will be the better for it."

Back home?

When I was little, I loved knitting together a few stitches of yarn and then pulling them so the fibrous strands came apart in a single instance. I marveled at how, with just one tug, something that was the start of a scarf or sock could be just a string of yarn once again.

With those two words, *back home*, I was back in Shy. Only, things were different, warped. I wasn't the little girl pulling apart the scarf. I was the yarn, suddenly becoming nothing in one second.

Had she decided I wouldn't get one of the designer positions? Already? No, my navy coat hadn't been very good. But I'd been confused. Lost. I knew I could do so much better, if she just gave me the chance.

"Why?"

The word came out louder than I expected. Beside me, Francesco gave a wordless murmur, and Apollo cocked his head, looking from me to Madame Jolène. The question didn't quite make sense in the context of our conversation, but she understood. The perpetually tense muscles in her face eased slightly and she tilted her head to the side, as though I were an exotic creature she had never seen before.

"'Why?' is a good question. I ask it quite a bit myself. For example, why can't I run my Fashion House the way I desire, without the interference from some young, upstart members of Parliament? I've worked to create an empire, and yet I'm not the ruler of it. So why, Emmaline, is a very good question. The problem is that there are few answers to the whys."

There was nothing harsh in her tone, but her calm voice and the sweet expression didn't fool me. She loathed me. The realization hit me as clear as lightning across a blue sky in Shy. Maybe not me personally. But what I represented: her limitations. We stood there, staring at each other for a long moment, my blood throbbing in my ears.

I took another quick breath and then a slower one.

"Please," I said. "Give me a chance to prove I belong here."

Slowly, she reached up one hand to touch the measuring tape around her neck. She didn't play or fidget with it like a normal person might. She simply placed her fingers over it, her gray eyes keen and sharp. Then she said, "Of course. When it comes to picking the design positions, I choose on talent alone, as shown throughout the competition. If you are the best choice, you will be selected."

She turned away with such force that her skirts swept out over my shoes, and she glided toward the staircase. Apollo followed her. She paused right before the steps to gracefully collect him into her arms, her posture still somehow perfect. Then the two of them disappeared up the stairs.

I looked at Francesco.

"She doesn't think I'll be one of them, does she?" I asked. "She thinks I'll be so busy with these events that I won't learn enough or even have time to showcase my skills."

Francesco opened his mouth and then shut it. Finally, he said, "Madame Jolène will always do what is best for the Fashion House. Don't give up." He gave my arm a little pat, but even though he was trying to be reassuring, I saw his eyes. There wasn't any hope in them. Only sympathy.

He didn't think I had a chance, and neither did Madame Jolène.

Two hours later, I sat in the front row of a small audience, practically drowning in pink ruffles and semiprecious gemstone necklaces. The dress had a flowery print and high neck. I imagined it was Madame Jolène's take on what a country girl might wear to a party. It was effective. Nearly everyone who saw me glanced from my face to my dress and then turned to whisper to each other about the "new country contestant." Madame Jolène had wanted me to stand out, and she'd done a good job.

But while the dress was an elaborate concoction of frills and lace, she hadn't bothered to make sure it was wearable. The whole thing itched, and the sensation, combined with the dread in my stomach and knots in my neck, nearly drove me mad.

"This library signifies the commitment of the Reformists and Classicists to work together," a man droned on from his spot behind a podium. No one had told me what exactly the event was, but it seemed to be a dedication for a new library wing. I'd been sent alone. Francesco had hired a hack that had picked me up behind the Fashion House, the same place I'd first entered it, and whisked me the short distance from the Fashion House to this library.

If I hadn't been so frustrated, the trip would have been exciting. After being inside for so long, I was finally out and about in the Quarter District, the wealthiest commerce borough of

Avon-upon-Kynt. We'd driven along the River Tyne, which threaded its way down the center of the city. As we'd passed auction houses, restaurants, and galleries, my eyes searched the different windows—not to look at the wares, as gleaming and glistening as those were—but to see which Fashion House Interview contestants were favored. I saw most of our names displayed on signs, but Sophie's showed up the most, often encircled in black roses.

I wasn't sure whether I would see mine, but, as we'd turned past a small teashop, there it was. A sign just for me. It read: *Wentworth & Co. Tea Salon Supports Emmaline Watkins, the Fashion House Interview.*

"And now, Parliament Member Richard Davies will share some thoughts," the man up front announced, and everyone applauded as the next speaker came up.

I couldn't muster the will or care to clap. As I sat here, the contestants back at the Fashion House would be starting their fourth appointments of the day. They would be taking measurements, making quick sketches, cajoling customers to try a new color or new style. More importantly, they would be showing Madame Jolène that they could adapt to the Fashion House ways, that they would be a good fit for the apprenticeships. And while they were making progress in the challenge, I was here, sitting in a chair.

Parliament Member Richard Davies, a rotund man with a receding hairline, took his place at the podium. Everything he said sounded the same as the man before. He referenced *progress* at least ten times and *the vision of the Reformists Party* approximately eight times. He cleared his throat in a most obnoxious way twice, and then finally concluded, saying, "The Parliament Wives' Association has thoughtfully provided us with some refreshments. Let us enjoy."

I jumped to my feet, trying to adjust my dress so it didn't rub against my neck and underarms quite so much. When my movements didn't help, I sighed and surrendered to the gown's itchy embrace and joined the line of people at the food table.

Morosely, I picked up a small plate with an even smaller scone on it. A server offered me two different options for wine and, uncertain, I pointed to one of the bottles. I moved to the side as the people behind me pressed in, reaching for refreshments before falling into small, conversational groups. I pretended to concentrate on eating the scone and sipping at the bitter wine.

"My dear!" I turned to see a portly, smiling woman addressing me. She'd been introduced at the very beginning as the head of the Parliament Wives' Association and the sponsor for the event. Lady Weber, I believed her name was. "It's a pleasure to have a Fashion House Interview candidate here. We've been so curious to see Madame Jolène's new contestant—and aren't you darling!"

I smiled, awkwardly brushing scone crumbs from my mouth.

"Someone requested to meet you. Come, come." She gestured for me to follow her. I did, leaving behind my plate but taking the wine. Lady Weber led me across the library and over to a tall gentleman who stood staring up at a landscape painting, his back to us. "Mr. Taylor, this is Madame Jolène's new country contestant." At her introduction, the man turned around. "This, my dear, is Mr. Alexander Taylor. He's quite a prominent fixture here in the city and a wonderful proponent of the arts. He is also a member of Parliament and the head of the Reformists Party."

The man held out his hand. I shifted my glass from my right to my left and took his hand, uncertain if he was going to shake it or not. Stepping closer to me, he bent at the waist and kissed it. His skin was bizarrely soft, and when he withdrew his hand, there was an oily residue on my fingers. It was some sort of fragrant, musky lotion.

"Oh, Mrs. Clark is leaving—I must say goodbye." Lady Weber bustled away. The man considered me with an expression that was somehow both uninterested and arrogant. He stood centered against the painting, making it seem like the gilded frame existed to showcase him, not the landscape.

"It's nice to meet you," I said, clutching the stem of my glass with both hands, the sharpness of the wine suddenly more prominent on my tongue.

Mr. Taylor seemed to be about forty. He ran his hand through his hair, as though making sure each strand was in place—which they were. He wore a double-breasted suit that was completely black, from the buttons to the cufflinks. The only touch of color came from a burgundy neckerchief tied in an elaborate knot.

"So, you are the country girl."

"Um . . . yes."

"It was my idea to bring you here, you know. I proposed the idea to Madame Jolène as a way to advance the Reformists

Party's agenda," he said. His eyes fixated on my ruffled dress, and he nodded, as though pleased. "You certainly look the part."

I should have said thank you. If it wasn't for Mr. Taylor, I'd be back in Shy. But there was something about the way he looked at me, as though I was an object, not a person.

"I suppose so," I said.

"Anyway, you've been at the Fashion House. Have you had much interaction with Miss Sophie Sterling? She is . . ." He paused, and the indifference and arrogance vanished. When he spoke again, his tone was reverent, liturgical even. "She has black hair and eyes. *True* black—like obsidian or onyx."

I clutched my glass even harder, my hands slippery from sweat and the lotion residue. He obviously meant my roommate. Normally, if someone asked if we had a mutual acquaintance, I would answer without hesitation. But there was something disturbing about this man, something that went far beyond the rudeness of ignoring pleasantries.

"I've met her," I said, trying to sound nonchalant. Sophie was hardly anyone to me, and I didn't know anything about this man, other than he was the head of the Reformists Party. But I couldn't ignore the fact that something about him made the fine hairs on my arms stand up. "I haven't spoken much to her, though. If I do, should I tell her that one of her suitors is inquiring after her?" At the word *suitors*, his lips twitched.

"No," he said. "I am not just 'one of her suitors.'"

He took a step toward me and I flinched, unable to stop myself. He was tall, much taller than I'd first realized, and his lean frame couldn't mask the muscles rippling along his arms and shoulders beneath his jacket.

"When you speak to her," he said, "you tell her this: Alexander Taylor sends his regards."

I nodded, certain that if I spoke, my voice would squeak. Whoever this man was and whoever he was to Sophie, I didn't want any part of it. I broke his gaze to glance around, relief coursing through me when I saw Lady Weber motioning to me. She pointed out the open library doors to a waiting hack. It was there to take me back to the Fashion House.

"I have to go," I said.

"Remember to tell her," he said. "Do not forget."

I didn't respond. I just hurried away, only pausing to set down the glass of wine. As the hack pulled away, I wiped my fingers on my skirts, ridding them of Mr. Taylor's lotion. But even though I rubbed them dry, I couldn't get rid of the musky scent. It hung in my nose all the way back to the Fashion House.

"Where were you all day?" Sophie asked as I entered our chamber that evening. It was a strange question coming from her, considering she was the one always gone from our room. In fact, I was surprised she was there. Earlier this week, I'd asked her why she was always moving her furniture around ("I hate things that stay the same," she'd said) and why she was never in the room ("I need time on my own").

"I was at a library dedication." I stopped just inside the doorway, kicking my heels off, and pulling my necklaces over my head so I could drop them atop the vanity. I yanked at the closures on my gown and heaved it over my head. I left it where it fell, shedding my Fashion House self like a snakeskin. I was happy to be free of the dress, as though taking it off could wipe away the icky feeling I'd had since leaving Mr. Taylor at the dedication. "Sophie, I met someone at the event. Someone who asked about you."

"Oh? Who?" Her voice was a little higher than normal, and I walked over to where she lounged on her bed. As usual, she was attired in black and, even though we were in our chamber, she was wearing silver heels that glittered around her bony feet.

"Mr. Taylor." Saying his name made the musky lotion scent rise in my nose again, as though the smell and the man were indelibly linked. "He asked if I knew you."

Sophie, who had been leaning against a mountain of tasseled pillows, half propped herself up on her forearms. She lifted one hand to her dark hair and her fingers started twisting through it. Even though her gaze was fixed on me, her eyes dimmed in a distant way, as though the thoughts in her head were much more forceful and consuming than I was.

"Don't worry." I moved closer to her and sat on the edge of her bed. "I didn't tell him anything about you."

Wherever she'd gone in her head, my words reached her and she came back to herself, blinking and focusing once again.

"You didn't?"

"No."

"You—what did you say instead?"

"That I'd met you but hadn't spoken much with you."

My response seemed to startle her and for once she seemed unsure.

"You lied for me?"

"Well, yes. He seemed . . . a bit intense. I wasn't sure of the best thing to say."

Her brows drew together, and her fingers swirled through her hair. She seemed to be puzzling something out, something she couldn't quite grasp. Finally, she said, "That—that was very kind of you."

Now it was my turn to be startled. "Oh, of course."

Her frown deepened, and her lips opened a few seconds before she said, "Thank you." The pleasantry sounded odd coming from her, as though it was a phrase in a different language, something she could repeat but didn't quite understand. "I wouldn't have expected any of the other contestants to do such a thing."

She sat completely up on the bed, crossing her legs and straightening her back. She stopped fidgeting with her hair, and a pink hue warmed her cheeks, as though she was embarrassed by her frankness.

"That's a shame," I said.

"Well." She flicked her hair over her shoulder and her usual coolness descended on her in the same way that cold, gray clouds descend on the sun during Shy's bitter winters, obscuring any brightness. "I don't mind. They're threatened by me."

She spoke without any hint of boastfulness. I nodded. It was true. She was impressive—both beautiful and talented. I couldn't speak for anyone else, but I knew I was intimidated by her.

"Who is Mr. Taylor? Is he one of your suitors?" I realized she hadn't told me anything else about him.

"Yes, just another suitor." She spoke quickly and so assuredly

I found myself nodding even though I didn't quite believe her. "He's a supporter of the Reformists Party, so Madame Jolène doesn't let him visit. But he tries to send me messages any way he can."

"How did you meet him?"

She gave an impatient sigh and only shrugged in response. Whoever he was and whatever he was to her, she wasn't going to tell me. And maybe that was better. I shouldn't get involved with her and her volatile lovers, especially one like Mr. Taylor.

"By the way, while you were gone, Madame Jolène announced the next challenge." Sophie spoke a bit too eagerly, as though anxious to put our previous conversation aside.

"*She did?* She didn't even wait for me to get back?" I couldn't keep the note of frustrated panic out of my voice. The Fashion House Interview was happening without me—and no one noticed.

"Calm down. I told her I would tell you what it was."

"Did Madame Jolène care that I wasn't there?"

"Well"—Sophie smirked—"I wouldn't go so far as to say that. But she did mention that you were away on press duties. Anyway, the new challenge is quite interesting. It begins tomorrow morning and concludes tomorrow evening. It's a bit of a scavenger hunt. We need to find three fashion elements around the Fashion House—like a gown or a hat or a handbag—and sketch out how we would change them."

"How we would change them?"

"Yes. Make them better. Make them our own while still honoring their past."

Make them our own. I certainly hadn't done that with the last challenge. Anxiety rose from the pit of my stomach. So much rode on this new challenge. I needed to redeem myself since I'd failed so colossally before, and prove to Madame Jolène that I was more than her press puppet. For a moment, I teetered on the brink of falling apart.

Stop. Stay calm.

Last time, I'd panicked. I'd panicked so badly that I'd drowned out the sound of my own voice and made something I wasn't proud of. I wouldn't do that again. I pushed myself up off Sophie's bed, letting the decisive action drive me, and I walked around to my side of the chamber.

I'd been so preoccupied with Sophie and Mr. Taylor and the new challenge that I hadn't noticed my part of the room had been transformed. A new wardrobe had been brought up and its doors stood open, a profusion of pink exploding from it. Several white boxes sat neatly next to it, their lids removed to reveal hats, handbags, and gloves nestled on delicate tissue paper. "What's all this?"

"I think it's for you." Sophie surveyed the items. "Francesco said it's your press attire. He left a letter for you on your bed."

The dresses and accessories were in the softest shades of pink, but it didn't matter. If they'd been vomit-green, I'd have been less repulsed.

"I should redesign one of these for the challenge," I muttered. "Honestly, the only time this shade of pink should be used is for baby bonnets."

Sophie laughed appreciatively as I walked over to my bed, where a large envelope was propped against my pillow.

The sight of the envelope made my stomach twist. I'd written my mother at least four times since arriving, and she should have gotten at least one of the letters by now. A letter could still be on the way—but I hadn't heard anything from her.

I thrust my thumb under the flap and yanked the letter out, reading it quickly.

Emmaline:

You are scheduled for three interviews tomorrow starting at 12:00 p.m. in the Grand Salon:

Mr. Tristan Grafton for the Eagle at 12:00 p.m.

Mr. Harold Winston for the Avon-upon-Kynt Times at 1:00 p.m.

Ms. Eugenie Walker for the Ladies' Journal at 2:30 p.m.

Be ready by 11:00 a.m. I will come and approve your appearance. Your press wardrobe has been sent up, and you will notice that the outfits have been labeled for your various events and interviews.

More notes will be sent up, but your points during the interviews will be:

—The Fashion House's generous decision to admit you as a contestant in the Fashion House Interview

—Your excitement for Madame Jolène's fall collection

—The tangible ways in which the Fashion House has worked to become more accessible to the middle-class customer

The following day, you have three social functions. More information on those will be sent up later.

Regards & Kisses,

Francesco

Three interviews, lasting from noon to three thirty, and I'd have to start getting ready at ten. Before then, I'd need to study the interview questions. I wouldn't have any time to look around the Fashion House for items to improve.

"These will take forever," I said, more to myself than to Sophie.

"What will take forever?"

"I have three interviews tomorrow."

"Who are they with?"

"The interviews? The *Eagle*, the *Avon-upon-Kynt Times*, the *Ladies' Journal*." I crawled onto my bed, holding the letter. I lay down, letting the mattress cradle me and the letter drop from my grasp.

"No, who are the different reporters *conducting* the interviews?" Sophie asked. I groped for the piece of stationery and found it lying next to me. I held it up in front of my face and squinted at the cursive.

"Mr. Tristan Grafton, Mr. William Harding, and Ms. Eugenie Walker."

There was a long pause and then Sophie said, "I see."

I swallowed my angst long enough to ask, "Do you know any of them?"

"Only Tristan Grafton."

I reread the name. I wondered if Mr. Tristan Grafton might be the reporter from the station. He worked at the *Eagle*. Tristan. Tristan Grafton. It had a pleasing sound to it, the sort that would fit a blue-eyed, blond-haired young man.

"Is he nice?" I asked. I wanted to ask what he looked like, but that seemed too bold.

"He is."

Her usually distant tone had an awkward hitch, enough to catch my attention, but she fell silent.

Giving up on a further response from Sophie, I sat up and slid off the bed, my skirts catching in the blankets. I noticed another Fashion House envelope on my dresser.

What would this one say? That my entire week would be interviews and press events and not to even bother thinking about being a serious contestant?

I opened it. Inside was a slip of paper and four bills. The slip read:

FASHION HOUSE INTERVIEW
CONTESTANT: EMMALINE WATKINS
COMPENSATION FOR TWO WEEKS OF WORK
DEDUCTIONS: BOARD, ATTIRE

I pulled out the crisp bills and, for the first time that day, I felt something other than frustration. I counted them, hardly believing how much was there. Even with the deductions for board and attire, there was enough to cover a third of the Moon on the Square's mortgage payment. I clutched them tightly—I'd known contestants were paid, but I hadn't antici-pated it would be this much. Money like this changed things. Money like this could justify me leaving my mother behind and coming here. I would send all of it home, aside from a small bit to keep to send her a gift later on since her birthday was in a few months.

There was a sketch page and a pencil sitting on my vanity. Eagerly, I sat down on the stool. I slipped the bills into my pocket, picked up the pencil, and wrote,

> *Dear Mother,*
> *Please use this toward the mortgage.*

I started to write about the press events and how Madame Jolène made me wear pink and how I'd created the most basic navy coat in all of Avon-upon-Kynt. Then I scribbled out those lines, my motions so violent they tore the paper and left a faint scrawling mark on the vanity top. Across the way, Sophie softly cleared her throat but didn't say anything.

Slowly, I sat back on the stool, my reflection staring back at me from the mirror. My face was white beneath my suntanned skin, the color drained away. Nothing, not even the thrill of making money, could make me feel secure here.

I picked up the pencil again, but instead of writing a letter, I started sketching a design. As I did, it came alive in my mind: an exquisite purple-gray gown with thin lines of beading and crystals running down the skirt. I lost myself in it until all I saw was the dress and all I thought was, *Even if Madame Jolène discounts me, I will find a way to succeed in the next challenge.*

CHAPTER SEVEN

THE NEXT MORNING, I pulled out the dress and accessories specified for the interviews. It was, of course, a blush gown. Francesco sent up styling directions, dictating everything from which wrists I was supposed to wear the bracelets on to how to carry the handkerchief. There was even a small vial of perfume for me to wear.

Kitty helped me lay out the look on my bed. I surveyed the dress, jewelry, shoes, and perfume, morosely eating macarons from a hamper Kitty's parents had sent.

"Even this macaron is pink," I sighed. I popped the last bit of the meringue in my mouth. "That's the last one I'll eat. I don't want to take your entire box."

"Oh, please do," Kitty said. Her tone sounded earnest, as though she wasn't just being polite. "Eat them all, if you wish."

"Kitty, have you finally set aside your rule-following? Are you trying to sabotage me with a stomachache?"

"Certainly not." Despite my teasing, she frowned at the hamper. "It's just that my parents send these each week."

"Sounds delightful."

"Perhaps. But you don't know them. All they care about are appearances. They want it to seem like they have lots of money and that they love me."

The macaron suddenly seemed too sweet. I swallowed down the last sugary bits. I'd already told Kitty about my schedule and how I wouldn't have enough time to dedicate to the Fashion House Interview.

She'd listened, her brow furrowing with concern, and had said, "That is a tight spot. But do your best and show Madame Jolène that you can offer the Fashion House a lot more than press attention."

"I doubt she'll ever believe that," I'd replied, nearly shuddering as I'd remembered the way she'd stared at me and how her gray eyes had filled with spite. "She's already decided I won't win."

Now I wanted to comfort Kitty in the ways she comforted me. But what did I know of cold, uncaring parents? My mother, despite her firm ways, loved me and did everything she could to give me a better life, while Kitty's parents demanded that *she* elevate their status.

"Don't worry about me," Kitty said, seeming to see my concern. "I find satisfaction in doing things the right way. It's my form of rebellion. And as for my parents"—she shrugged—"they are who they are. But never mind that. Let me help you into the dress. You're running short on time."

She helped me lower the gown over my undergarments. Tilda was scheduled to come and help me and, as usual whenever I needed her, she was nowhere to be seen.

Yesterday, I'd been dressed so quickly and sent off to the library wing dedication that I'd hardly had time to look at myself. Today, I could fully see Madame Jolène's vision for me. The pink dress had an angular row of ruffles running from the waist to the hem. Thankfully, the ruffles on this gown were stiff, sharp, and modern, even if they featured a faint vine pattern.

Kitty turned me toward the mirror. "Ooooh, Emmaline, you look beautiful!"

I stared at my reflection. Kitty was right. Madame Jolène was right. The gown had a huge skirt, which accentuated my slender waist. The Queen Anne neckline enhanced my lacking bust. The manipulation of the fabric and the sharp crease of ruffles running down the front inspired drama. Somehow everything fit . . . yet too well. I shifted, staring hard at my image. It was too perfect.

"It's so expected," I said to Kitty.

"It's classic. You look like a country princess."

"I suppose so."

The door jostled open and we both looked up to see Tilda enter, her expression as dour as ever.

"You're late," Kitty said. She didn't adopt the harsh tone that Madame Jolène and Sophie used when speaking to the maids, but she was stern. "You should've been here an hour ago."

"So sorry," Tilda said, but she didn't bother to offer an excuse. She came up to me and motioned for me to sit down so she could do my hair.

"Well, I have to go," Kitty said. She didn't say it, but I knew she needed to search for Fashion House items to redo for the challenge. The other girls were combing the different floors for gowns and accessories to improve as we spoke. "Good luck with your interviews."

"Thank you for taking the time to help me," I replied. I watched her leave, wishing I too could go and rifle through sketches at the Fashion Library and stare at the gowns displayed on mannequins in the Presentation Lounge. There were thirty minutes between my second and third interviews. That would be my time to strike. I'd have to rush, undoubtedly. But it was my only true chance to find three items to redesign.

"Floral headband . . ." Tilda read the instructions for my look. The headband sat on my vanity and she picked it up, smiling amusedly at its overly girly print. "Well, isn't this sweet?"

I bit the inside of my lip, hard. Tilda would never dare to be so familiar with the other contestants. Then again, they wouldn't allow it. They—and anyone else of note at the Fashion House—treated Tilda and the rest of the staff with impersonal coolness. I couldn't bring myself to do the same. I knew what it was like to do thankless work, the kind that ended in dishes that would just need to be scrubbed again the very next day.

But there was something about the way Tilda treated me. She wasn't just familiar with me—she was rude. And, though I assumed she hadn't meant to, it had been her words that made me doubt myself for the first challenge.

"The next time I need you, please be here." I didn't speak harshly, but I channeled the voice my mother used when speaking to vendors who were late on deliveries. Not mean, but firm.

"Of course," Tilda said, yet she sounded flippant. She gathered my hair up in her hands. "I saw your coat."

"You did?"

"Yes. Madame Jolène had me pack up the . . . well, the *less successful* coats. They were donated to charity."

Donated to charity. With just those three words, I was wavering on the brink of despair again. Had I really done *that* poorly in the first challenge? I swallowed hard, struggling to contain myself. I couldn't give in to doubt. I wouldn't let myself.

"Is that so?" I evenly met Tilda's gaze in the vanity mirror. "That's kind of her."

Tilda stopped running the brush through my hair for a moment, sulky disappointment crossing her features.

She pursed her lips and said, "Have you started on the next challenge? Last I heard, Ky and Sophie had already found all three of their items."

"Oh, have they?" I still sounded calm, but my stomach clenched. All three? I'd yet to find even one. I couldn't help it—the stressed, scrambled feelings I'd experienced during the first challenge came over me, stronger than before. I shouldn't be sitting here, getting my hair done. Desperately, I glanced around the chamber, as though I could find gowns and accessories from the Fashion House collection lying about the room.

"Yes," Tilda said, twisting my hair into a low bun. "And Alice has at least two."

She held my hair in place with one hand and pulled hairpins out of her pocket with the other. The morning light rippled off her black taffeta skirts, gleaming across the fabric like moonbeams across a nighttime sky. I stared at the effect in the vanity mirror, tilting my head to the side. A thought slowly developed in my mind.

"Your uniform," I said. "When was it designed?"

"This?" Tilda glanced down at her black dress with its bobbin lace trim. "I don't know. Madame Jolène probably designed it years ago, when she first took over the Fashion House."

Abruptly, I stood up, wrenching my hair out of her hand. It hurt but I barely noticed. I stepped back, looking Tilda over. Or, more precisely, looking her dress over.

"You ruined your hair," she complained. I ignored her and opened my vanity drawer, where I kept my Fashion House Interview sketchbook and pencils. I flipped open the book and quickly sketched the general outline of her dress: floor-length A-line gown with bobbin lace edging the cuffs, neckline, and hem. It wasn't very functional, not with its thick fabric and wide skirts. I couldn't imagine doing a full day's worth of work at the pub in such a garment. And while it was pretty, it didn't feel modern or fresh, even though most of the Fashion House maids were around my age.

Drawing over the original dress, I drew a new one. Slimmer. Shorter. It didn't have any lace, but it had deep pockets. When I was finished, the new gown sat within the outline of the old one.

"There." I would need to sketch it out again in greater detail, but it was a start—and a plan.

"Are you redoing our uniforms?" Even though Tilda tried to sound unengaged, she leaned forward to peek at the sketch.

"Yes. The current ones are dated and hardly functional." I held out the drawing so she could see it. "Wouldn't it be easier to work in a slimmer dress with a shorter hem? And wouldn't you like it if it was a little more stylish and fresh?"

"I don't think that's the point of the challenge," Tilda protested. She reached for my hair again, and I sat down so she could finish it. "You're supposed to improve on a Fashion House design. Like one of the dresses or accessories made for clients."

"But Madame Jolène did design the uniforms," I pointed out, wincing as Tilda twisted my hair sharply into a bun and slipped the headband over my head. "So technically, it qualifies."

"Seems a little desperate, no?" Tilda's snide tone came back, even as she kept staring at the redone uniform. "Perhaps you're just worried that you don't have time to do anything else?"

I played with the ruffle on my interview dress. She was right, to a certain degree. But redesigning the maids' outfit—as unorthodox as it might be—made sense for me. I knew about work and I knew about fashion. Even if I had all the time in the world to find a subject, this project would intrigue me.

"Emmaline!" Francesco opened the chamber door and poked his head inside. "What on earth is taking you so long? Mr. Grafton is waiting for you."

Tilda sprayed the perfume that corresponded to the dress—an airy scent of lilacs, apples, and vanilla—from my head to my feet. It settled on my skin in a misty, aromatic cloud.

I followed Francesco out of my chambers, carrying my sketchbook and pencil. I would need them for that thirty-minute break when I would search for my other two items. I thought Francesco might tell me to leave the sketchbook, but his head was buried in the large leather book that contained the Fashion House agenda. He didn't say anything until we reached the stairs. "Pretend you are a rich society lady, Emmaline, and you are attending a gala. Would you want a clutch made from an edgy leather with metal trim? Or a white linen one with a gold clasp?"

"I'm not sure I'm the best person to ask," I said, my mind still on my redesign of the maids' outfits. "I've never been to a gala."

"The leather is navy while the linen has an embossed pattern on it," Francesco said, ignoring my initial response.

"Um, I suppose—"

"The leather, right? I knew it. I just knew that was best. No boring linen." He scribbled a note in the agenda, next to the daily schedule. I wondered if Madame Jolène knew he was using the agenda for his personal notes.

"Yes," I said, smiling.

"You studied the guide of possible questions and appropriate answers, I assume?" His head remained buried in the agenda.

"I did." Those had been sent up that morning with directions to have them memorized in time for the interviews.

"And what are they?"

I blinked, my mind as hazy as the cloud of perfume Tilda had sprayed over me. I collected myself, pulling my thoughts from the day's challenge. "The upcoming collections, how excited I am to be here, how generous Madame Jolène is to include me this season." It was hard to say the last one in a measured tone.

"Yes, be sure to stress that last point." Francesco raised his head, his face mournful. "The Reformists have gotten even more impertinent. Recently, they brought a proposal to Parliament stating that the Fashion House itself should create designs for factory-produced styles."

"I didn't know." I'd never given much thought to the political aspects of the Fashion House, but the idea instantly bothered me. I couldn't imagine the Fashion House creating cheap designs. It seemed wrong, like asking a prize racehorse to pull a plow.

"This is an important interview, Emmaline. Fashion House Interview contestants rarely get to speak officially to the press," Francesco said. As he spoke, his usually theatrical expression was replaced by a quiet intensity. "I'll join you for your other two interviews, but I'll be attending the queen at her fitting with Madame Jolène during the first one. Be sure to stress that the Fashion House has always been and will always be the future for Avon-upon-Kynt."

"I will."

"Now, wait here for a few moments. Mr. Grafton is in the main parlor." He motioned me to the side of the hallway. "I'll be right back. Oh, and did I mention the leather clutch would have a knuckle-duster holder?"

He didn't give me a chance to respond, continuing with his head buried in the daily agenda. I glanced up and down the narrow hallway and stifled a half-frustrated, half-panicked huff. I needed to be working on my redesign, not standing here. I opened my sketchbook, balanced it against one knee, and awkwardly added gold epaulets to the shoulders and a separate choker to the neck.

The soft mumble of conversation came from behind a thick door with a large glass doorknob. Normally, it would have been impossible to hear through it, but whoever was inside had left the door slightly ajar, and a hushed voice slipped out. It sounded strangely familiar, though I couldn't quite place it. I lowered the sketchbook, stepped closer, and stretched my neck forward so I could see through the narrow slit of space between the door and its frame.

There was a dark-haired girl inside. She was turned away from me. All I could see was her overly straight posture, black gown, and the snow-white expanse of her neck, visible beneath a chignon of waves.

She was facing a young man. It seemed like they knew each other well. He was tall, but the girl, in her heels, was his height. Dark blond hair fell over his forehead and he said something quietly to her, his eyes fixed on hers. His blue, blue eyes.

I clamped my hand over my mouth to keep from gasping.

The reporter I'd met at the train station and had seen in the sewing room.

A shiver ran through me, just beneath my skin, and I leaned forward even farther, trying to see his face better. His lip was healing. Only a hint of discoloration remained.

The girl asked, "Does it hurt?"

My heart plummeted down to my feet. I recognized this voice as well. There was only one girl with that low, cold cadence. Sophie. Was the reporter—*my* reporter—courting Sophie?

"You know me," he said. The smile I'd seen at the train station was gone, replaced by a questioning, grave expression. "A reporter's job is dangerous. It's not the first time a subject has punched me for asking impertinent questions."

"And it's not the first time you've punched someone back." Sophie moved closer to the reporter, closing the distance between them. Their bodies formed a single, strange silhouette in the middle of the room.

"Sophie," he said as she leaned in even closer. I held my breath and leaned in, too, as if I were Sophie. Slowly, she tilted her head forward, but just at the last moment, he stepped back, and her long fingers drifted through the air between them.

Numbly, I returned to my former spot in the hallway. I leaned back against the wall and let out a long, slow breath just as Francesco came rushing up the stairs.

"I had a tea tray set up," he said, pointing to the parlor doors. "A maid will come serve it."

I blinked and nodded dully. I remembered how Sophie had asked me about him the night before. She'd said he was "nice." Apparently, he was very nice to her. And what man wouldn't be? She was as breathtaking as a crescent moon in a pitch-black sky.

Then again, he'd stepped back. She might fancy him, but perhaps the feeling wasn't mutual.

"Now, where is Mr. Grafton?" Francesco put his hands on his hips and glanced around, as though he—the reporter—might be hiding behind a vase or side table.

"I think he's in the other room," I said. My face flushed, and I didn't dare look Francesco in the eye.

"Is he with Sophie?" Francesco shook his head, his face

pinched with impatience. "How unprofessional. Go in and get ready. I'll send him in."

I pulled the heavy doors open and slipped into the bright, airy parlor. I walked over to the grouping of tufted Chesterfield furniture—two armchairs and a fainting couch—and settled onto the fainting couch, arranging myself so my ruffles lay neatly against my skirt. I stored my sketchbook and pencil underneath it.

There was a window behind me, and I twisted around on the fainting couch to glance out of it, seeking the soothing familiarity of the sky. The parlor was on the second story, so it was all I could see—one square of blue, dotted with a few gray clouds. But it wasn't enough. I wanted to be out there, to smell the air and feel the fingers of the wind in my hair.

Then I could let nature overwhelm my senses and forget the reporter and Sophie.

Impulsively, I went over to the window and placed my palm flat against the glass. If I stared straight at the sky and the perfumery's gables across the way, I could feel like I was out there, hovering between the roofs and the sky. *Almost.* No matter my imagination, I was indoors and had been—aside from the short walks from hacks to buildings—since I'd arrived. And yet, I still sensed the seasons changing, how summer was slipping into fall.

Though I tried to deny it, I was a country girl. For the first time since arriving, my hands itched for dirt in the same way they itched for pencils and sketch paper. I wanted to bury my fingers in the soil of my mother's vegetable garden. Just last fall, she harvested a bounty of carrots, yanking them from the earth with firm hands. After a while, she sat back on her heels, a bright orange carrot in her hands, and held it up close to her face, examining it. Dirt stains ran all the way up her forearms. She stayed that way for a long time, until I asked her what she was doing. She lifted her eyes to mine, and I had never seen them so . . . full.

"It's the most beautiful thing I've ever seen, Emmaline," she whispered, her voice reverent, like she was praying in church. "It's the most beautiful thing in this whole entire world."

"Emmaline?" I hadn't heard the doors open, and I jumped at the sound of my name, the image of the carrot in my mother's dirty hands dissipating as I turned to see the reporter enter.

I walked back to the fainting couch and settled down onto it. Instantly, I wished I'd chosen a different seat. The couch was lower than the other furniture, and its pink-and-orange rose pattern clashed with my gown's shade of pink.

He sat down across from me, reeking of violets.

The door opened again, and Tilda came in. She approached, her eyes lingering longer than necessary on Tristan's face.

"Would you care for some tea?" she asked him as she bent over the small table and set down the silver tea tray and a small plate of petits fours.

"Yes, please," he said.

She served it deftly, her hands moving quickly over the teapot. "Cream or sugar?"

"I prefer it black."

She handed him the teacup, her fingers overlapping his, and she glanced at me.

"Tea?" Her usual snide tone underscored the question. Normally, I would try to ignore it but now, in front of Tristan, the heat of embarrassment chased away the phantom sense of cold glass against my palm.

"No, thank you."

"They don't drink tea in Shy?" She glanced at Tristan in a knowing way, as though to say, *This country girl is ridiculous.* He frowned, and the sight made her jubilant expression dim.

"I just don't want any," I said. "But thank you."

I stared directly at her, daring her to say or do anything else. She hesitated, seeming to consider it. Then, she set the teapot down hard on the tray and flounced out of the room, as though she was Madame Jolène herself.

Once she was gone, Tristan took a sip of tea. I couldn't look at him, instead staring at the way his fingers dwarfed the porcelain teacup. His knuckles were malformed, as though he'd punched something hard at some point and broken them, and there was a bit of dirt under his nails.

"I'm Tristan Grafton," he said, and I barely stopped myself from saying *I know.* For a moment, I wondered if he'd somehow forgotten all about me. "They started painting over the mural. I thought you might like to know," he continued. "White. All white. They've gotten all the way up Queen Catherine's body, so she's a disembodied head now, Emmy." He paused. "Or is it Emmaline? The Fashion House contacted my editor and told us we had to print your name as 'Emmaline.'"

So, he remembered. The canvas, the mural. My name. An inane desire to smile built up inside me, even as Sophie's scent drifted toward my nose.

"The name 'Emmy' didn't exactly fit with the Fashion House aesthetic," I said. "You can call me Emmy, just . . . don't print it."

My back was to the window, but Tristan's eyes reflected the daylight back to me. The last time I'd seen him, in the sewing room, the white morning light had washed the color right out of them. But now, the day was bright, and his eyes were bluer than ever before.

"Very well." He wrote *EMMY* across the top of his notebook and underlined it. "Just a personal note for myself," he explained. "So, how are you today?"

"Good," I said, wondering if this was part of the interview or just pleasantries. "Busy. I have two other interviews, so I'm worried I won't have time for today's competition."

"A Fashion House Interview contestant who doesn't have time to compete," he said. "That's a sad thing indeed."

"Yes. And I need to do better than last time."

"Ah. The navy coat?"

I winced. It made sense that he knew about the coat—the papers printed sketches of our work. I wondered if he knew that mine was so disastrous that it'd been donated to charity.

"That was a misstep," I sighed.

"It's all right. It was just one challenge. There are more to come." The sincerity in his voice warmed me, but it couldn't dispel my worry.

"I suppose so."

"Don't let it discourage you. I've seen contestants get mired down by bad evaluations—the key is to shake it off."

"Easier said than done."

"That's true. But Sophie said she's seen your other designs and that you have talent."

"She did?" *They talked about me.* The thought zinged through me. Had he asked about me? I saw them in my mind, standing near each other yet apart, as though forces drew them together while separating them at the same time. I blurted, "Are you seeing her?"

Instantly, warmth rushed over my cheeks. I wished, with everything inside me, that I could snatch the words back.

"No. No, I'm not." If he was startled by my impetuous question, he hid it well. "I did. Before. But that was some time ago, and while I wish her well, I don't feel for her."

Giddy relief rushed through me, surprising me with its strength. I could feel my cheeks turning from pink to red.

"I see," I said, trying to regain control of my senses, which came alive with the flush of my face. "That question was irrelevant to the interview. I apologize."

"Don't." The single word was underscored by the intensity of his tone. I dared to glance up at him. "Don't apologize."

We stared at each other, caught between the things we'd just said and the things that we weren't saying. The cheerful look in his eyes was replaced by something new. Something strong, undefinable.

Does he fancy me?

For a moment, I couldn't catch my breath. I tried to hide it by inexplicably reaching for an empty teacup and grabbing the hot handle of the teapot. I'd never felt such feelings for a boy before—my only experience was with Johnny Wells.

Johnny once asked to kiss me. Our mothers had gone into the main dining room of our pub to give us some time in the kitchen. My mother beamed at me, her face practically aglow with happiness. Johnny and I made conversation—or, in reality, I talked about the latest trends in hats until he asked, "May I kiss you?"

I was startled. I'd always imagined kisses as impulsive things between lovers. My mother had certainly given me that impression. She had always said men were given to passion and that we women had to always fend them off. This polite question from Johnny, asked in the same way one might ask to have the sugar bowl passed at teatime, startled me.

My first instinct, after years of my mother lecturing me on the impropriety of the male sex, was to say no. But then I shrugged and said, "All right."

He leaned forward, eyes squeezed closed, lips puckered, and placed a neat, clean kiss right on my mouth. Afterward, he straightened up in his chair and took a long drink from a beer I'd poured for him.

Now I was the one grabbing for a drink at the thought that Tristan might desire me. With uncertain hands, I poured myself a cup of tea and took a sip. Hot liquid scorched my tongue and I jerked the cup away from my lips, trying to act natural while the burning tea seared the inside of my mouth.

"Are you all right?" Tristan asked.

"Yes." I gasped, struggling to remain emotionless, my face contorting against my will. "Just fine, thank you."

"Let me help." He took the teacup from my hand, where it

dangled precariously, about to spill onto my skirts and, no doubt, give me another burn. "By the way, who else is interviewing you today?"

He spoke nonchalantly, returning us to familiar ground. I was relieved, but part of me wanted to reset, to see that burning in his eyes and to go forward instead of backing away. But perhaps that was something to be saved and returned to, later on.

I hoped so.

"Two other papers," I said. "The *Avon-upon-Kynt Times* and the *Ladies' Journal*."

"The *Times*, eh?" A wistful glimmer lit his face. "I had a job interview with them earlier this week. Didn't go so well."

"Sorry to hear that," I said.

He gave a blustery shrug.

"It doesn't matter. I'll get hired there someday. I just have to keep working hard."

I nodded, sobered. Working hard. Our goals might have been different but, to a certain degree, we had the same plan to achieve them.

"Anyway, the *Eagle* wants to know everything about you. How would you describe your style?"

"My style?"

"Your designs," he prompted. "Your coat was characterized as 'classic' but I have a feeling that isn't really you."

"No," I said, cringing. The last thing I wanted was for everyone to think that I had no imagination. "I like to mix things."

"How so?"

"I—that's a good question."

Whenever I thought about my style, my thoughts filled with colors, shapes, and lines in grays and blues and purples. They drifted in my mind like water, sometimes smooth and placid, other times as tumultuous as a raging ocean storm. How did one funnel such a thing, such a feeling, into words?

I had to begin somewhere.

"I love to pair hardware elements—like brass buttons, metal hooks and eyes—with softer fabrics, like chiffon and organza." Once I started talking, the words came effortlessly to my lips. Talking about my designs was easy, almost as though I was standing next to him at the train station again, looking at the mural.

"Why?" His pencil stilled on the paper as he glanced up.

"Because it's all around me at home," I said. "It's what I know: hard work and functional items mixed with beauty. It's me."

"That's a good quote," he said, offering me that lopsided smile. He lowered the notebook and sat back. The smile still played at his lips, but his eyes stared at me, open, thoughtful. "You're an interesting girl, Emmaline Watkins."

"Is that so?" I stared hard at him, trying to determine if he turned on this charm for all women, or if he really did think there was something different about me.

"Girls in the city are *taught* to be stylish, but you . . . you figured it out by yourself." He spoke slowly, as if he was thinking hard about what he was saying. The spaces between his words were a change from his typical quick way of speaking. "And Madame Jolène picked you over the other candidates. That's pretty impressive."

I sighed, tempted to let him think I alone had caught Madame Jolène's eye, that she had specifically wanted me, Emmy Watkins, at the Fashion House. I wanted to sell him this piece of fiction in the way that Madame Jolène sold her designs to her patrons, as a mesmerizing story. He already knew I was the political hire, but I wanted him to think more of me. However, even though the story gathered on my tongue, I couldn't utter it.

"That's not exactly what happened. Madame Jolène didn't pick me so much as I forced myself on her." The truth—the fact that Madame Jolène would probably send me home after the Fashion House Interview ended—wanted to pour out of me, but I stopped. Tristan was a member of the press who no doubt wanted good stories more than most men wanted a pile of gold. And even if I was drawn to him, I needed to be wise. "I'm happy to be here; don't mistake me. But things are a little . . . limiting here for someone like me . . ."

I shrugged, leaving the thought hanging in the air between us.

"I'm sure it hasn't been easy for you." He leaned forward, his cunning smile gone for the moment. His eyes weren't just blue, I noticed. Small flecks of green dotted his irises. "I've seen the pressure on the Fashion House lately, and I'm afraid you're a pawn in all of it." That sly smile pulled at the corners of his mouth again. "Albeit a very lovely pawn. But it must be a hard spot, no?"

Yes, I wanted to say, but I couldn't discuss that.

"It can't be much worse than writing about mermaids."

He laughed then, brightly, unapologetically. It made me relax, the tension from the past days melting away in the warmth of the sounds. For once, I wasn't worrying about fitting in or covering up my lack of knowledge about this thing or that.

"At least I have interviews with actual people this week. You today, and then in a few weeks, Duchess Cynthia Sandringham."

"Who?"

"She's Prince Willis's former lover. It's an old story, but it still sells well," he said. "Everyone loves reading about a woman in disgrace."

Prince Willis's former lover. The painting of the blue dress hanging in the staircase. Every time I'd passed it, I imagined it lifting right off the canvas to hang in the air, invoking the scorned princess who wore it. I'd never given Cynthia, the prince's paramour who'd been blacklisted from the Fashion House, a second thought. Her part in that narrative was only to contrast the beauty of Princess Amelia and her blue gown.

"She's a sad figure," Tristan said. When he brought the teacup to his lips, it looked like he was gulping beer, not the Fashion House's finest Darjeeling. He returned the cup to its saucer with a sharp clink. "Always asking me to try to put in a good word for her to Madame Jolène. She doesn't understand I never actually interview Madame Jolène—and that Madame Jolène is many things, but sympathetic is not one of them."

"Then where does she get her fashion from?"

"Personal seamstresses, I think. All previous Fashion House Interview contestants, but their styles aren't anything in comparison to the gowns from the Fashion House. She hasn't been in the fashion pages since the jubilee—for a duchess, that's devastating. Lately, she's been in a pretty bad state."

"Bad state?"

He pantomimed someone drinking from a bottle.

"I think she might be desperate enough to show up at the gala for Madame Jolène's new designs."

Every season, Madame Jolène held a gala to introduce the theme of the upcoming collection. Anyone who was anyone in Avon-upon-Kynt's elite attended, and the *Times* always devoted several pages to covering it.

"She's not invited," he continued. "But she says she's going this year."

I nodded, unsurprised. Before, I would've said that behavior was ridiculous, but now I knew the truth. The Fashion House was enough to make anyone crazy. Or drunk.

"She's convinced herself that if she just talks to Madame Jolène, she'll be able to persuade her to take her back. She really shouldn't worry. Things are changing, and the Fashion House will probably have less influence very soon."

"Because of the Reformists Party?" I thought about the mural in the train station, now nearly covered in white paint.

"The queen is a Fashion House devotee, but the monarchy's power is dwindling. Have you heard about the Parliament Exhibition that's happening next month? The Reformists Party has been billing it as a fun event with food and entertainers— but everyone knows it's an excuse for them to give speeches and round up support for their causes."

"In Shy, the papers always make it seem like the monarchy is so strong," I said. "I guess that's not true."

"Not particularly," Tristan said. "The Reformists Party wants Britannia Secunda to be known for more than just our fashion."

"Oh yes, they want factories, right?" I recalled what Francesco had just told me. "I suppose the factories do create opportunities for people. . . . When my mother was young, she actually came to the city to work in one. Of course, there were only a few back then."

"Did she? A lot of country girls come here before going back home and getting married to good old country boys."

"I've always wondered about her time here," I said, ignoring his comment about country girls getting married. "Maybe I can figure out where she worked or what her time was like here . . . but it was a long time ago. Nineteen years, about."

"Nineteen years?" Tristan thoughtfully bit his lip. "You know, the textile factories keep records of their employees. It isn't hard for me to access them." He paused and then said, "I can check for you. I mean, if you like."

"Really?" I was edging toward a place with no handholds or stops, the sort of place where one lost herself to a young man with an eager manner and blue eyes.

"It's no trouble," he said, and he sounded excited. He was smiling, again, as though pleased he'd made me happy. "What's her name?"

"Edith. Edith Watkins."

He wrote her name on his notepad so close to mine that it looked like one word: *EMMYEDITHWATKINS*. Forward or backward, it was us, mother and daughter.

She still hadn't written me.

"I'll find her. Or the past her, I should say," Tristan said. "Everyone leaves something behind, whether it's a name in a record book, a bill, a payment stub."

"Thank you so much," I said. "I really appreciate it."

"Consider it done," Tristan said. "Now, I need just a few more comments for my article. Why don't you tell me why you love designing so much?"

"Well . . ." I leaned back on my hands, pushing away thoughts of my mother. "I almost don't know why," I said. "All I know is that I'm compelled to design. When I'm sketching, or sewing, I feel most like myself, like I was made for it." The last sentence poured out of me, and I stopped. "It . . ." I tried again, starting slow. "Designing lets me explore and create stories. . . . I'm just prattling."

"Don't worry." He was staring at me, his face completely serious. "I think I feel the same way about writing. Half the time I feel completely ridiculous running around town harassing people for comments or leads. But I know I could never quit. I must try to be the best at it. It's all part of it."

"Part of what?"

"Being seen," he said. He arched his back slightly and fidgeted, as though he didn't quite belong in the silk, pillowed armchair.

"Being seen?"

"There's something communicative about art. If no one sees it, there isn't much of a point." He reached forward to finally return the teacup to the saucer. He set it down gently, noiselessly.

"So, for me, it would be breaking life-changing news on the front page of the *Avon-upon-Kynt Times*."

"And for me, it would be designing a dress that shaped an entire fashion season," I said, nodding. Even though it was a maid's job and not mine, I picked up the pot to pour him more tea, this time barely registering the hot handle scorching my palm. He was right. Part of art was having it seen.

Madame Jolène wanted me to be seen, that much was certain. But not as a designer. I was her cheap token of progress and nothing more.

I couldn't let that be my story. No matter what, I would figure out a way around Madame Jolène's plans for me and make some plans of my own.

CHAPTER EIGHT

FRANCESCO JOINED ME FOR THE next interview. He practically took over, answering the questions with flair. Not that it bothered me. My mind was racing—my small window of time between the current interview and the next was approaching, and I felt like a horse at the start line of a race.

As soon as the reporter left, I pulled my sketchbook out from under my chair. I flipped open to a clean page and sketched out the maids' uniform, struggling to draw quickly yet neatly and keep an eye on the clock. Francesco sat back in his chair, drinking tea and watching. It took me seven minutes to draw out the uniform. It wasn't my best work—I sacrificed some of the more nuanced shading to save time. Once it was finished, I jumped to my feet.

"You have twenty-three minutes until the next interview," Francesco reminded me as I headed toward the door. He set his teacup down and picked up a petit four. He plucked the fondant flower off the top and popped it into his mouth.

"I know," I replied. "But I have to find two other items for the challenge."

"Well, I suppose I can stall a bit. Take thirty-five."

"Really? Thank you, Francesco!"

"Yes, yes. Now hurry!"

I burst out into the hallway but then stopped, realizing I didn't have a plan. I looked left and then right, the urgency of passing time bearing down on me. Where should I look, when I only had thirty-five minutes? I walked over to the staircase. Even if I wasn't sure where I was going, I needed to *move*. I hurried down the stairs, the Fashion House paintings staring down at me as I scurried by.

At the second landing, I stopped to lean against the banister. The paintings of the famous Fashion House designs stretched along the wall, rectangles of color and beauty, each detail so vivid that I felt like I could touch them and feel the smoothness of silk, taffeta, and chiffon underneath my fingertips.

Slowly, I continued down the stairs, staring hard at each painting. At the second-to-last step, I came to a stop. The painting staring back at me featured the Moroccan ambassador's wife in her red chiffon dress with the long train. The artist had caught her in motion, captured midstep. The chiffon floated ethereally around her, but her skirts were still huge, supported by an underskirt of thick red satin. Behind her, her twenty-foot train trailed through the air, following after her in a red streak. The dress was spectacular. I'd never questioned it or ever thought it should be changed, but now as I stared at it, revisions burst into my mind almost faster than I could process them.

I opened my sketchbook and lifted my pencil. Then I froze,

pencil pressed to page. What was I doing? Revising a beloved Fashion House design? Could I make it better? *Should* I? The dress was iconic, a piece of Fashion House history. But . . . I was running out of time. And the changes that I wanted to make came naturally to my mind—I didn't have to force them at all. I wasn't trying to conform to the invisible Fashion House rules. I was listening to myself.

And at least I'll be proud of this. Unlike the navy coat.

I drew in a long, steadying breath and started sketching. As I did, I lost myself to the beauty of the dress. In my mind, sights and feelings mixed. Bursts of red combined with the silky sensation of chiffon.

Carefully, I streamlined the silhouette, ridding it of the heavy satin skirt so that the chiffon fell against the body. I embellished it with gunmetal beading reminiscent of tarnished silverware. Nothing at the Fashion House was tarnished, but I always loved objects that showed a patina of age.

"Emmaline!"

Startled, I nearly dropped my pencil. Francesco stood above me on the stairs. "It's been forty minutes. Ms. Walker is waiting."

"Waiting?" I looked around, as though I could find a clock nearby. "I completely lost track of time."

"I should say so. You aren't successful enough yet to be demanding and have people wait for you. Though, to be fair, only Madame Jolène is on that tier. Someday, I hope to be as well. Now, come along, my dear."

I shut my sketchbook and climbed the stairs toward

Francesco, trying to stay calm. I was out of time, and I only had two sketches: the maids' uniform and the red chiffon gown. The now all-too-familiar feeling of panic rushed over me. What could I do? Sketch something out fast as I headed to the judging after the interview? Maybe I could do that. I could sketch and walk at the same time. Guiding myself with one hand on the banister as I moved upward, I looked over my shoulder into the lobby, desperately searching for anyone in a Fashion House gown. No one was down there. There was nothing to inspire another sketch.

I clenched my sketchbook and tried to ignore the sinking feeling in my belly. It was happening again. I was failing at the Fashion House Interview for the second time.

I was numb through the interview, my mind running rampant as I thought through my options. Vaguely, I heard the reporter ask me something.

"Yes," I said automatically. Francesco cleared his throat loudly, and I blinked.

"Ms. Walker was asking you how you felt about the first challenge."

"Oh! I'm sorry." I focused on the bespectacled woman in the blue serge office dress. I hadn't answered the question, but she wrote something down in her notebook. She was probably taking notes on how odd I was. "The first challenge . . . well, it was . . . I learned a lot."

"I'm sure it was overwhelming for someone from the country," Ms. Walker said. "When I heard you were included in the

Fashion House Interview, I wrote an op-ed about how it really isn't fair. To you."

"To me?"

"Indeed. You don't have the background of the other girls." Ms. Walker stared owlishly at me, her eyes magnified by her thick-framed glasses. They were terribly dated, the style popular a couple years ago. On top of that, they didn't flatter her face shape. Even as I focused on her words, my mind fixed them for her. "It isn't your fault, but you were set up for failure just to appease the Reformists Party. These artificial changes to the system don't benefit anyone."

"That certainly isn't the case—" Francesco started to say.

"It's true." I interrupted Francesco. He tried to kick me discreetly with his cheetah-print slippers, but his motion was overly dramatic, and Ms. Walker rolled her eyes. "I don't have the same background as the other girls, and because of my press duties, I don't have the same time for the challenges or Fashion House fittings. I must admit, it has been difficult."

"Keep going," Ms. Walker said at the exact same time that Francesco said, "Goodness, Emmaline, stop."

Just moments ago, my mind had been frazzled. Now, I was fully present, aware. Aware of Ms. Walker's hungry eyes, waiting for a juicy comment. Aware of Francesco's desperate attempts to shush me. And aware of my own heart, beating hard underneath my ridiculous dress.

"I may have been set up to fail, and I'm not like the other girls," I said. "I don't come from much. But I wouldn't trade who I am or where I came from for all the wealth and status in the world." My mother's face flashed before me. Yes, there were lines around her eyes and across her forehead. But there was something else. Not fire. Smoldering. A long-simmering power forged by a lifetime of hardship.

Everyone judged her by her mistakes and told her she couldn't run a pub on her own. Despite them, she'd done it. Was doing it. "My whole life, nothing has been handed to me. I get it on my own. You say that I'm set up to fail—and maybe I am. But I will design, and if Madame Jolène doesn't like it, I won't stop. I'll design another gown and then another. And another one after that."

I stopped abruptly and the three of us sat in silence. Ms. Walker nodded, slowly at first, and then faster. I thought Francesco might scold me, but when I looked at him, he smiled back.

"Emmaline is strong," he said softly. "I knew it from the moment I saw her outside that tent in Evert." He straightened his fitted suit jacket. "Now, then. I think you have enough quotes, Ms. Walker. Emmaline needs to get to the judging."

"I still have five minutes!" Ms. Walker protested.

"So sorry." Francesco stood up, motioning for me to do so as well. "But this contestant is needed elsewhere."

Outside the salon, I grabbed my sketchbook from a side table. Francesco had told me to leave it there during the interview, but now I clutched it to my chest.

"Thank you, Francesco," I said.

"For what?"

"Just . . . thank you."

"Oh, never mind! Now, get going to the judging. I'll see you there. I just need to freshen up and change."

I nodded, still smiling. I'd learned that people in the city changed at least three times a day because they were always looking for ways to show off their new styles. Francesco, though, sometimes changed four or five times.

A sudden sound of heeled footsteps and voices came from the stairway. It was the other girls—Kitty, Cordelia, Ky, and Alice were walking down to the challenge critique. Sophie was nowhere to be seen. I quickly joined them on the landing, sketchbook still held tight.

"How were your interviews?" Kitty asked.

"Good. Though they didn't afford me much time to work on the challenge. I only have two sketches right now."

"Just two?" Cordelia asked, glancing over her shoulder at me. Her sketches faced outward, and I could see detailed designs, complete with dashes of watercolor.

She wore a skirt held up with men's suspenders. A few days ago, I'd asked her about her style. I was familiar with Kitty's classic looks, Alice's girly fashion, and Sophie's dramatic aesthetic. Even Ky made sense to me—she'd cross-pollinated her style with looks from both Britannia Secunda and Japan. But I'd never met a girl who wore men's pants, blazers, and work boots.

"Menswear is interesting to me," she'd said. "In a way it's more limiting, but I love how strong the lines are. Growing up, I always dismantled my father's clothes to look at their patterns and shapes."

After I'd asked her about her style, she seemed a bit friendlier.

Before, she'd never have bothered to ask about the status of my sketches.

"Yes. For now." I flipped open to the middle of my sketchbook.

"Wait, are you sketching another one *right now?*" Ky demanded.

"I don't have much of a choice." I tried to sound calm, but Kitty's alarmed expression and Ky's triumphant face said it all: I was doomed.

Don't get distracted.

Anchoring the sketchbook against my stomach, I lifted the pencil.

"Don't trip!" Kitty exclaimed.

Each step made the sketchbook's hard cover jam into my middle. My first line jiggled across the page. Shaking my head, I flipped to a fresh sheet. But I didn't know what I was sketching. Just like the first time, no warm fog came to envelop me. My mind was empty, as white and blank as the page in my sketchbook. I couldn't wrestle anything out of it except basic images and silhouettes. They were jagged and rough, and none of them spoke of beauty or elegance.

And even if they had, any sketch I did right now would be rushed, without any detailing. It would be lines without life. Without *me.*

Slowly, I flipped the cover of the sketchbook back and closed it. During the first challenge, I'd submitted something I didn't love. I couldn't do that again. If I received an unfavorable judging (which I inevitably would) for only having two sketches instead of three, I'd prefer that to showcasing a sketch I wasn't proud of.

"Giving up?" Ky asked.

"Yes." I paused. "No. I have two strong sketches and I don't have enough time to do another one. Or at least one that represents my style and my skills. I'll submit only two."

For a moment, silence fell over the girls and they glanced at each other. Only Ky looked pleased.

"It really isn't fair that you didn't have the same time as the rest of us," Kitty said. The other girls didn't agree, but they didn't disagree either.

"Thank you, Kitty," I said softly. She was close to me, close enough to squeeze my arm. I focused on the warmth of the gesture, trying to ignore the fact that I was walking into the challenge with an incomplete entry.

We had only a few minutes to set out our sketches in the sewing room before the double doors swung open and Madame Jolène entered with her design board. She was coming from a fitting— her tape measure hung around her neck and a pincushion was affixed to her wrist with a huge gray ribbon. Her dress was a bit less extravagant than her usual looks—a duchess satin gown with architectural folds running across the neckline and hem. The skirt was a full A-line, no doubt to allow her the ease to stand and bend as necessary. Even though she'd probably spent the entire day attending the queen, her hair was still a perfect chignon of loops and spirals.

She came to the front of the room and scanned us with one swift, unblinking glance. I nearly cringed when her eyes passed over me. As if in anticipation of her scorn, every muscle in my body locked and tensed.

"Good evening." Madame Jolène didn't pause to let us respond. "This challenge is based on fashion updates and revisions. This is to measure your skills at breathing new life into a style while maintaining its original integrity. Since this challenge is based on sketches, you will also explain your work, so we may understand your mindset."

Explain your work. I didn't know we'd have to talk. My already tense body tightened even more. I tried to think about what to say and how, attempting to conjure up some sort of script. I let out a tiny sigh of relief when Madame Jolène approached Cordelia first.

"Sketches," she said commandingly, holding out her hand. Cordelia gathered them up and gave them to her. I was surprised to see her fumble. In my mind, the other girls were so confident. Superior, even. Yet Cordelia's movements were quick, antsy.

"As you know, I like to feminize menswear and turn it into something altogether different," Cordelia said. Her voice was devoid of natural inflection, as though she was reciting lines from memory. "I took a gown, a cape, and a blouse from last season's collection and redid them to reflect my style. I used the original fabrics for all of them. For the gown, I was inspired by a man's smoking robe and changed the silhouette to reflect that, complete with a loose fit and waist sash. I approached the cape and the blouse in a similar manner, turning them into pieces that a man might wear in the evening."

"So I see." Madame Jolène's attention was on the three sketches. She flipped through them once and then again. "The concept is strong. Your aesthetic is unique, so your pieces always feel distinct." Cordelia beamed, and the design board murmured in approval. "However! You've completely obliterated the previous history of the pieces. You've used the same fabric, but other than that, one would never know what the previous items looked like. It entirely defeats the purpose of revising an existing garment—one would never know this was a redesign because you've annihilated the original."

Cordelia nodded. She tried to look unbothered, but she wilted behind her smile, her shoulders drooping like a flower in the hot sun. Madame Jolène handed her sketches back, and she took them with a limp hand. The design board shook their heads, as though they'd known all along that Cordelia would fail at the challenge.

"Now let us see what"—her gaze swept the room once again—"Emmaline has done!"

Every step Madame Jolène took toward me seemed to make her grow taller. With her design board following her, I felt like I was in the pathway of a stampeding pack of stylish gazelles. I took my sketchbook and held it out before Madame Jolène asked for it.

"They are the first two sketches," I said.

"Two?" She took the sketchbook from me but didn't open it. "Where is your third sketch?"

"I . . ." Excuses leaped to my tongue. *I didn't have time*, I wanted to say. *You didn't give me any*. Frustration came with the excuses. It wasn't my fault I had two sketches, and she already knew that, yet she stood there, asking me why that was the case.

"Well, you see—" My voice was hard. Madame Jolène didn't say anything, but her chin lifted, and my words died on my lips. I cleared my throat, remembering what she'd said to me before. Excuses couldn't save me. Only my work could save me. "I did two."

"Well then. Let us see these two sketches." She flipped the cover of my sketchbook back and stared down at the page. One of her design assistants let out a gasp. Madame Jolène turned the sketchbook toward me.

Angry dark slashes covered the sketch of the red dress, mutilating the design. I nearly gasped like the design assistant, but I couldn't. All the air in my lungs was gone.

"What is this?" Madame Jolène's voice was measured, but there was iron in it. She turned away from me to hold the sketchbook up so the rest of the room could see. A twitter of surprise ran around it as everyone saw the destroyed sketch. "I assume this is some manner of sabotage. I will say it now—I have no time for this and neither do any of you. This had best be the last time that anything of this nature occurs. Is that understood?"

Scared silence filled the sewing room.

"Is that understood?"

"Yes, Madame Jolène," the other girls quickly chorused.

"I can still see the sketch underneath the lines," Madame Jolène said evenly. "I will judge your work based on that."

She held the sketchbook up, squinting hard at the design. I tried to catch my breath. In. Out. In. Out. It didn't help. The air caught in my chest. It was one thing for everyone here to dismiss me and look down on me. But to destroy my work? When I already was barely making it?

I turned to my left and right, searching the faces around me. Everyone was staring at me, but the minute I looked around, they averted their eyes. Everyone except for Sophie. She met my gaze. If she pitied me or was surprised, it didn't show.

Was it her? She was always at the top of the challenges—but that didn't mean she wouldn't try to stop me. Or maybe Ky? I cut my gaze to her. Everyone knew she was cutthroat. My eyes went from girl to girl, even Kitty, trying to read guilt in their expressions, their body language.

"Tell us about these," Madame Jolène said. Her voice was back to its usual tone—firm and commanding—as though there was nothing amiss. She turned the page of the sketchbook to look at the maids' redesign. Just like the red dress, it was slashed over with pencil.

"I—" My voice cracked and I struggled to collect myself. "I redid the maids' uniforms and the red gown that the Moroccan ambassador's wife wore." I was numb, barely hearing my own voice. "I thought they both needed some updating, but I still wanted to maintain the overall existing lines."

"Ah. The Parliament-vote dress. How did you see it? It isn't on display." Madame Jolène's voice was like cold water on my face, shaking me free of the red wash of anger that enveloped me. I forced my hands to relax and lifted my head. Whoever had done this to me wouldn't get the satisfaction of seeing me fall apart.

"The painting in the stairwell," I said, putting my breath behind my words. "That's where I saw it."

"How very . . ." She seemed to search for the right word. "Unusual."

"She took her inspiration from a painting and the maids' uniforms?" One of the designers murmured. "That wasn't what she was supposed to do."

"No," Madame Jolène said. "It wasn't."

I steadied myself against the sewing table. I'd failed. Again. I felt like my sketch—slashed over, torn apart.

"But the rules were to recreate a Fashion House design, and both are Fashion House designs," Madame Jolène said. "It shows ingenuity and creativity, and you can clearly see the existing garments in these new versions."

For a moment, I didn't feel anything at all. Not happiness or joy or even the mix of despair and anger from before.

She liked my work.

The thought centered itself in my mind, dispelling my tumultuous emotions. I'd succeeded. I'd succeeded at a Fashion House Interview challenge for the first time.

"Well done," Madame Jolène said. "Your take on this challenge was refreshing."

Even though my sketches were still crisscrossed with pencil scars, I couldn't help myself. I grinned at Madame Jolène. She stared impassively at me, but there was a twitch of a smile at the corner of her mouth. She abruptly turned away, declaring, "Ky is next."

She moved on, but I couldn't focus on Ky's critique. I'd done something right. Possibly even found my footing in the competition. I grasped my sketchbook tightly with both hands. The cover was still flipped back, revealing the maids' uniform.

I stared at it, wanting to enjoy the image, but the pencil lines gouging through the page demanded my attention. My breath was tight in my throat again. Whoever had done this had failed—this time.

Once again, I looked around the room. I knew most of the girls and certainly Madame Jolène didn't want me here. But I'd never imagined any of them would try to stop me. At least not this way. Another thought occurred to me. When I'd first arrived, I didn't have a welcome letter. Had someone been trying to sabotage me from the very beginning?

Abruptly, I closed the cover of my sketchbook, banishing the sight of my destroyed sketches. I clutched the sketchbook to my chest, as though it could protect me. But deep down, I knew nothing could protect me here.

CHAPTER NINE

THE NEXT MORNING, we assembled for the announcement of the challenge. I went to the meeting with a bitter taste in my mouth, the remnants from yesterday. Not only would I need to succeed at the challenge, but I now had to guard myself and my work.

Before walking into the sewing room, I glanced at the rankings. Sophie was at the top, but Ky and I were tied just behind, separated from her by one point. Cordelia was next. Kitty wasn't at the bottom—Alice was—but she wasn't far from it. It was exciting to see my name so close to the top, but I couldn't shake the unease that hung about me.

In the sewing room, Alice, Ky, and Cordelia stood in a companionable cluster. Kitty was with them, but when I entered, she came to stand next to me. Sophie was near the other girls and chatted with them, yet, as always, she somehow distinguished herself.

"How are you doing?" Kitty asked.

"Fine," I muttered. "Just a bit shaken."

"You should have heard Madame Jolène talking to Francesco

last night," Ky suddenly said, leaning forward to look at me.

"What did she say?"

"She was furious about your sketches. She said you've made this year's competition a joke."

"*I've* made it a joke?"

Kitty murmured something sympathetic in my ear, but I brushed her off.

"Yes." Ky smirked. I knew she was pleased by my response, and I tried to appear calm. "She said you're a distraction and you undermine the credibility of the competition."

"That's enough, Ky," Kitty interjected. She placed a protective hand on my arm. "I'm sure that isn't the case."

"Of course it is," Cordelia cut in. "Our futures rely on this competition, but all anyone focuses on is Emmaline. You didn't earn your spot here, but you get paraded around the city in new clothes."

"Do you think I want this?" My voice bounced off the high ceilings of the sewing room. "To be treated like a press puppet when all I want is to be a designer?"

"Ladies, ladies!" Francesco swept into the room wearing a gray-and-white suit with pointed shoes embroidered with peacocks. "What on earth is going on?" He tried to look stern, but his eyes flashed with interest. He clasped his hands together, as though he was about to devour a sumptuous meal.

"It does not matter." Madame Jolène entered from the opposite door with her designers. She held one of her little dogs, Calliope, and another, Clio, trotted along next to her. "There is no time for petty nonsense."

She was dressed in a champagne gown covered in a variety of ivory lace that formed an intricate patchwork across her skirt. Though her gown was made entirely of neutrals, a huge necklace in bright pinks, teals, and corals sparkled at her throat.

The mood of the room changed to nervous excitement, as it always did when she arrived. But as everyone quieted in anticipation, I felt like I was watching from outside Madame Jolène's powers of enchantment.

"The next challenge is one of the biggest," Madame Jolène said. "It will test all your skills: design creativity, workmanship, and client management."

Despite myself, I was intrigued. A big challenge. My fingers twitched in anticipation of cutting, threading, and sewing.

"We have a titled client who is engaged to be married, and she has agreed to let her wedding gown be the subject of the challenge," Madame Jolène continued. "You will have a bit of time to ask her about her preferences and vision. You will each have three weeks to make your gown, and she will wear the winning dress at her wedding. Of course, the final version of the dress will be revised and edited by me and my design board."

A wedding gown! Those two words sent tingles down my spine. Back in Shy, brides wore simple white dresses to their nuptials, but in the city, weddings were exhibitions of extravagance and style. Whenever there was a big wedding, it was reported in the fashion pages with elaborate spreads detailing the bride's attire.

"Contestants," Francesco said, stepping forward, "meet Lady Angelica Harrison."

He opened the sewing room door, and a young brunette woman stepped inside. She was dressed in one of the latest Fashion House gowns: an iridescent taffeta dress with a huge skirt. A dramatic hat with three giant plumes protruding from the brim sat atop her head.

"Hello, ladies," she said, smiling. "I cannot wait to see what you create for me."

"You may now ask Lady Harrison questions," Francesco said.

Ky's hand shot up.

"What is your vision for your wedding gown?"

"Oh, I definitely want something unique," Lady Harrison said. Her eyes ran over Ky's emerald-green dress with its coral lace trim. "But not *too* unique. Timeless yet creative."

"Timeless yet creative," Ky repeated slowly. I understood her hesitation. That didn't tell us much.

"Is there any area of your figure that you are a bit self-conscious about?" Alice chimed in. Her usually airy voice was a bit more serious. I'd read a few days ago that one of her sisters had gotten engaged to a lord. A very *old* lord. I'd asked Kitty about it, and she'd told me that Alice was one of five girls, and that their socialite mother was trying to marry them all off—that she'd trained them to have a doll-like manner to attract older, wealthy, and hopefully titled gentlemen.

Alice, though, didn't sound so breathy today. I understood. If she won a spot at the Fashion House, she wouldn't have to marry a man the age of a grandfather.

"My hips," Lady Harrison replied. "I almost always wear A-lines."

"Any favorite fabrics?" I asked.

"I like light ones."

"Like chiffon or organza?" I followed up, for clarification.

"Yes. And also heavy ones."

Across from me, Sophie let out a small exasperated sigh, but I suppressed a smile. I'd come to realize that clients could be confusing. The other girls continued asking questions, but I stared hard at what Lady Harrison was wearing. That would provide more clues to her style than would Lady Harrison herself. Quickly, I jotted down a few notes.

Iridescent taffeta. Statement hat. A-line bordering on ball gown.

"All right, question time is over," Francesco announced. "Lady Harrison will be back here in three weeks to see the designs and pick her favorite one."

He held his arm out to Lady Harrison and she took it, waving to us as he escorted her out. Once the door closed behind her, he smiled sympathetically at us.

"This is an example of how challenging it can be to work with a client," he said. "Half the time, they ask for contradicting things or say one thing and mean quite another."

"Which is where your skills as designers come in," Madame Jolène cut in. Unlike Francesco, there was no understanding or sympathy in her eyes. From her position in Madame Jolène's arms, Calliope yipped, as though to underscore the point. "It is up to you to figure out what is best for her. You will spend the rest of the day sketching, and tomorrow you will go to the Fabric Floor. I suggest you plan your time carefully. Three weeks is more than enough time to make a wedding gown, but with our upcoming events and your Fashion House duties, you will only have four full days to devote to it. Other than that, you will have to find work time around your schedules. You may begin now."

With that, she swept out of the room, Calliope still tucked under her arm. Francesco and her designers hurried after her.

"Well, that was confusing," Alice said. Her bottom lip extended in a pout. "What on earth does Lady Harrison want?"

"It's hardly fair," Cordelia complained. "How can I translate my menswear-inspired look to a wedding gown? Even if I do, she won't pick it."

"I have the same problem," Ky said. "I hardly doubt she wants something I'd come up with. She wants a traditional Fashion House design."

"Are you surprised?" Sophie spoke from where she sat on the edge of a sewing table. "We are supposed to be aesthetically distinct but, at the end of the day, we are supposed to fit the Fashion House mold. Our unique styles will only be trotted out during the Fashion House Interview."

The whole time I'd been here, I'd thought I was the only limited one. But perhaps that was the thing about the Fashion House. The only one who was truly free was Madame Jolène.

I returned to my chamber to sketch—I didn't dare sketch around the other girls. The last thing I needed was for my sketchbook to get stolen or my designs destroyed again.

I started out sitting in the middle of my bed but then moved to an armchair, turning it to face the window. I stared out, tracing the wispy waves of the clouds with my eyes. Their dreamy shapes floated across the sky and stirred up images in my mind, thickening to become the comforting fog that always descended on me when I designed. I tried to focus on that and not the worries that darkened my thoughts.

For the first challenge, I'd done something much too safe. For the second, I'd been myself. For this one—which, so far was the most important one—I'd have to figure out a way to blend my style with the Fashion House look.

I knew Lady Harrison wanted an A-line to balance out her figure. But that wasn't quite right. Her proportions already were balanced. There was no need to cover her up in a huge skirt. In fact, putting her in an overly big skirt would only make her seem fuller. No. The way to go was a slim dress with dramatic folds in the fabric. It would give the impression of a big silhouette without being one.

I drew quickly, the sketch spilling across the page. It sprang from my heart, easily, effortlessly. I was lost to it until the door opened and Tilda came in, wielding her feather duster. Immediately, I flipped my sketchbook closed. The last thing I needed was for her to weigh in.

"I heard your sketches were destroyed," she said, waving the duster around my vanity.

"Yes. But Madame Jolène was still able to judge them."

"Oh, was she?" Tilda's voice was airy and light, but I frowned. There was something about the way her lips tightened. She seemed . . . disappointed.

"She quite liked them." I watched Tilda carefully. She might not have had any real power at the Fashion House, but she was a maid, and that meant that people would talk freely around her—she was practically invisible. In fact, she might even know who destroyed my work. "You wouldn't happen to know who did it, would you?"

"Of course not," she answered quickly. A little too quickly. I set my sketchbook down and stood up. She noticed my movements and lowered her feather duster, watching me warily as I approached her.

"Are you sure?" I tried to look her in the eye, but she avoided my gaze. "Please, I could use your help. I'm—" *I'm barely surviving here.* The thought struck me hard. Unexpectedly so. "Please, Tilda."

"Don't bother asking. I can't help you." For once, her voice wasn't tinged with that fake sweet tone she always used with me. "If you can't handle this competition, you shouldn't be in it."

"I don't understand," I said slowly. "We're similar. I'm not from *this*, Tilda." I gestured to the opulence around us.

"I know that." Her words were short and snippy, all artifice of sweetness gone. "That's what makes it worse."

"Makes it worse?" I knew everyone else here would never deign to have such a discussion with a maid, but I was tired of doing things the Fashion House way. So far, going along with things had only gotten me limited competing time and a wardrobe of repulsively pink dresses.

"You're no one. If the Fashion House didn't need you to posture for the press and you'd come to the city for a job, you'd be a maid, just like me. I have to put up with everyone else here, but I shouldn't have to put up with you."

"You don't understand." I wanted to tell her everything, that coming here had been my lifelong dream but how, since arriving, I'd realized that the dream didn't exist—that I was blocked at every turn, dismissed, sent this place and that to look like a "country" girl—and that most of the time, I felt like I was falling down a bottomless hole. But even though Tilda resented everyone at the Fashion House, she was more like them than I ever would be, and like them, she wouldn't care.

"I don't understand what?" She challenged me with her gaze. Abruptly, I turned away and went back to my chair by the window.

"Nothing," I said. "Never mind."

She pressed her lips together in a thin line and raised her feather duster. She started dusting, and I started drawing, and there was complete silence again, a silence full of strain. My hand moved about my page, automatically filling in parts of the sketch, but all I could feel was the lump in my throat and the tears that stung the backs of my eyes.

We were supposed to go to the Fabric Floor the next morning, but I was scheduled to attend a reading by the new poet laureate. Even though it would limit her time, Kitty agreed to pick out my fabric. I gave her a list:

Warm ivory duchess satin

Silk-covered buttons

The list was sparse compared with Kitty's, which was full of different types of laces, silks, and embroidered appliques. Ky brushed by with hers, and it was covered with words like *embossed taffeta* and *ruffled tulle*.

"Are you sure you don't want me to get you anything else?" Kitty asked, frowning at my two-item list. "I can throw in some extra beads or lace."

"I'm sure." And I was. It was all I needed to make the gown in my head, and that was the secret of it: it would let Lady Harrison shine and enhance her figure without the distraction of frills and laces. "But can you please make sure it's the right shade of ivory? I want that hue that's just between candlelight and champagne."

"Between candlelight and champagne," Kitty repeated. Her brow crinkled. "I'll do my best."

I nearly launched into a description of the color that I could see so clearly in my mind. But that was the thing with colors—one had to see it in person to know it. I smiled reassuringly at Kitty, but the minute she looked back down at the list, I gritted my teeth, praying desperately that somehow she would get the right materials.

After the reading, I hurried to my chamber to see the silk that Kitty had selected for me. It waited on my bed, an ivory cutout against the blush duvet. I frowned, running my fingertips over it. It wasn't the right shade of ivory—there was way too much yellow in it. A package of buttons sat next to it. I spilled them out across the bed, my frown deepening. The buttons matched the silk, but they were much too small. They wouldn't look right at all. Defeated, I sat down on the edge of my bed, staring at the too-yellow silk and too-small buttons.

CHAPTER TEN

THE NEXT DAY, I wanted to start the pattern for my wedding gown, but we were scheduled for Fashion House duties because of the gala. The number of customers had doubled, and everyone was needed—including me, for once.

I headed down to my fitting room, stepping around the handymen bringing down extra mirrors and the maids clearing out the spare dressing rooms that stored extra mannequins.

When I got to my fitting room, I took a deep breath, inhaling the scent of the fresh flowers the Fashion House received every day to perfume the hallways. I pulled back the curtain to my room and stepped inside, shaking off my despondency at the silk and buttons. Every fitting room was the same—furnished with a trifold, full-length mirror, a circular pedestal, an upholstered bench pushed against the wall, and a garment hook on the wall.

Despite the uniformity of the rooms, I'd learned the nuances of mine, how my pedestal listed just slightly to the side when anyone stepped on it and how the mirror needed to be adjusted for the best light.

I took another breath, this one quick and short, trying to energize myself and push away my frustration. For now, I would focus on the customers, design in my head, and try to keep moving forward.

Three appointments later, I was gritty and sweaty . . . and bleeding.

"You've stabbed yourself," said my customer, Madame Solange, staring down at me as I knelt by her hem, taking out the basting stitches.

"Indeed," I said, standing. A drop of red blood welled up on my fingertip. I'd impaled myself on a straight pin. I sighed. It was common to stab oneself with a needle at the Fashion House. Straight pins and sewing needles were used every day and frequently lay scattered across the tabletops and floors. But the puncture was on my sewing finger, the one I used to push needles through cloth. It would be bothersome, especially for the detail work I'd have to do on my wedding gown. I needed to start wearing thimbles, even though I hated how they felt.

"Be careful not to get any of that on my gown." Madame Solange sniffed.

"I will," I said, holding my finger away from the dupioni silk. She was right to be wary. A bloodstain on silk was impossible to get out.

I glanced around my fitting room for some spare cloth, but I hadn't cleared my room between appointments. I picked my way across the fitting room, stepping over the mountain of wire crinolines and spools of thread littering the floor. I'd even left a few gowns wrapped in their muslin bags hanging on a hook. I held my bleeding finger aloft, terrified it would drip.

"Tell the maid to bring me another glass of champagne while you're out there," Madame Solange said. I nodded and walked out into the hallway, heading for the washroom. Sometimes Madame Jolène occupied the dressing room adjacent to the washroom. The spacious, private chamber was reserved for customers who were titled or wealthy enough to warrant Madame Jolène's attention, but not important enough to be invited to her private fitting rooms.

The curtain to the dressing room was closed, but I heard Madame Jolène's cool voice coming from inside.

"Yes, we will just raise the hem a quarter of an inch. It will be perfect. The tip of your shoes will show as you walk, but when you're standing still, the hem will extend to the floor."

I slowed, wondering if I should go to the washroom on the second floor. I didn't want Madame Jolène to see me with my bleeding finger. I was trying to change the way she saw me, and bloodstains on her gowns would not curry her favor. I listened hard. Madame Jolène's customer responded. They were obviously in conversation. If I was quiet, I could slip by without being noticed. I stepped forward, trying to be quick but noiseless. One step, two, and then—WHOOSH!

The curtain swung back on its rings.

I wheeled around to see Madame Jolène sweeping it aside. I stilled, finger held aloft.

"Emmaline? What on earth are you doing here?"

"I—" I started to explain, but then stopped. I had seen something just beyond Madame Jolène, something that bewildered me. Standing behind her was a woman I didn't recognize. I had the blurry impression of dark hair and olive skin. But beyond that she was inconsequential fuzziness; I only saw her gown.

The woman stood there, staring at me, enfolded in a jade jacquard dress. The pattern—*my* pattern, the one that had bold dramatic swoops accented by smaller straighter lines—was woven into the fabric with gold thread. Soft tendrils of chiffon pulled delicately across the neckline, almost like gentle curls. I stared at my brocade gown that was somehow *here*, in the world, a composition in thread and fabric.

"Is that my gown?" I turned from the dress to Madame Jolène, still confused.

"Your design was used for it, yes," Madame Jolène said. Those needle eyes of hers met mine, and there was nothing in them. No understanding, no guilt, no indignation. Nothing but empty grayness—and that was the deepest insult of all. She stepped aside, gesturing down the hallway, motioning for me to continue, dismissing me as she always did.

But I was done being dismissed. I planted my feet, distantly feeling the blood from my finger running down my wrist and soaking into my sleeve. My thoughts clarified, the confusion replaced with anger. She'd made my dress without telling me— even as she minimized my role in the competition, even as she used me to make the Fashion House look better.

"You didn't tell me you were having my gown made," I said.

"*Excuse* me?" The woman let out a haughty snort. "This gown was specially designed for me by Madame Jolène." She turned to Madame Jolène. "This is highly unusual, is it not? Whatever is she talking about?"

"Don't mind her," Madame Jolène said evenly. There was an

almost imperceptible change in her face. Slowly, the blankness tightened into coldness. I thought she would say something—anything—to explain or defend herself, but instead she asked, "Aren't you on your way to the washroom?"

"Yes, but—"

"This is neither the time nor place to discuss this." Madame Jolène's eyes narrowed at me.

"I don't understand." I wasn't really thinking now. I was just speaking, my words carried forth on my pent-up frustration. "I'm not an actual contestant in the competition, but you made my gown. You want to send me home at the end of this. But I'm talented. You know I am—"

"Home." A bit of a smile winged its way across her lips, and then it was gone. "If you wish to question me and my actions, Emmaline, you will be going there much sooner than I'd originally planned."

The threat hung in the air, and suddenly I hated her. I hated that she had the power, and that all I could do was stand there with my gown only a few feet away, and that no matter what I did, I could never possess it again in the same way. It was made; it had gone from sketch to dress, and I hadn't even known until a moment ago.

"Do you wish to go home now, Emmaline?" Madame Jolène asked smoothly.

For a few seconds, I didn't know what I would do. My rage swarmed and gathered inside me, my thoughts like bees readying for an attack. But, somehow, I suppressed those black points of fury.

Instead of continuing past the consulting room to the wash-room as Madame Jolène had instructed, I turned on my heel and made for the fitting rooms. I'd been holding my hand up, but now I dropped it to my side.

My finger pulsed with my heartbeat as I moved down the hallway. I fought to keep facing forward. Everything inside me wanted to turn back and behold my gown—*my* gown—one last time. Even though I'd barely had time to see it, I knew it intimately, from the godets sewn into the skirt to the fifteen jet-black buttons running down the back seam.

Behind me I heard Madame Jolène say, "Try walking in the gown. I'll make sure the hem length is correct." Her tone was the same as always: taut, professional, brisk.

I picked up my pace, rushing down the hallway, away from her and my gown. If I didn't make myself leave, I knew I would march back up to Madame Jolène and say things that would get me thrown out immediately.

My heels were slowing my pace, so I took them off and dis-carded them in the middle of the carpet. It was a tremendous Fashion House violation to be barefoot, but I didn't care. By the time I reached my fitting room, I was almost running, weaving in between customers mingling in the hall. I wasn't sure where I was going—just that I needed to get away.

"Excuse me!" Madame Solange called out as I brushed by. I kept going up the hallway, moving faster and faster.

"Emmaline? Emmaline!" It was Kitty. I came to an abrupt stop, which was just as well, because I wasn't even certain where I was heading. She was standing in her fitting room, refolding silk around a bolt.

"What on earth is the matter?" she asked. "Gracious! Where are your shoes? Your finger! Are you all right?" She motioned me into her fitting room and picked up a strip of cotton from her sewing case. "Here. Oh dear, you got blood on your sleeve." Wrapping the cotton around my finger, she applied pressure to the puncture. "What's wrong?"

"Madame Jolène—" I struggled to form a coherent thought. *"She made my gown."*

"What do you mean?" Kitty asked, frowning.

"My sketch, the one she took at the audition in Evert. She had it made for a customer, and she didn't even tell me!"

The creases in Kitty's forehead eased, and she let out a hesitant laugh.

"You should be proud. It's an honor to have your gown made by Madame Jolène. It happens all the time. The Fashion House is founded on the principles of collaborative design. But . . . maybe you just need a moment?" Kitty asked, patting my shoulder uncertainly.

I nearly retorted, *No, I don't need a moment, I need my gown back*, but I caught myself and nodded, attempting to smile. It wouldn't help anything to get mad at her.

"Let me get you a glass of water." She left the fitting room.

I took a few gulps of air. Something wet and sticky oozed down my finger. It was bleeding again, Kitty's impromptu bandage failing to stop it. I reached over to her sewing cabinet and opened the top drawer, searching for another strip of cloth.

A letter sat on top. I was about to move it away, but then I saw something that made my heart stop.

Slowly, I picked up the letter.

Kitten—

Your father and I have been following the Fashion House Interview rankings and it seems that you are consistently near the bottom. You know what we have sacrificed to put you in the competition. Please do not waste this opportunity to better our family, and do anything necessary—sabotage, even—to secure a better rank.

Regards,

Your Mother

Instantly, every interaction I'd had with Kitty rose in my mind, reframed in cruel clarity. Kitty helping me get ready for the interview. Kitty getting fabric and buttons for me. Kitty encouraging me when I was down. Before, the scenes had warmed me. Now they were cold sequences of manipulation.

She was kind, and I was so desperate for a friend that I had let her in, played right into her hands. I'd invited her into my chamber, confided in her, given her plenty of opportunities to sabotage me. I should've known. She was sweet. Too sweet. No one was that nice.

Not here, not in the city.

"Emmaline?" Kitty stood in the fitting-room doorway. Her eyes went straight to the letter in my hand.

"It was you. You told the maid not to wake me, and you destroyed my sketches. And the materials for the wedding gown. You intentionally got the wrong shade of silk and size of buttons."

Quickly, Kitty pulled the curtain to her fitting room closed.

She set down the glass of water, slowly, carefully.

"I know how this looks." Her voice was matter-of-fact, its usual gentleness gone. "And yes, I haven't been . . . completely honest with you."

I stared down at the letter. My finger left a bloody imprint on its grainy surface. I fixated on its rigid outline, desperately trying to make sense of everything.

"I'm not here to win the Fashion House Interview apprenticeship. I would like to, but I'm a realist. I'm here for the connections."

"What?"

"After the competition concludes, I'm going to apply to the royal family as their in-palace seamstress. You don't have to be a great designer—you just have to be good at mending, and I'm one of the strongest technical sewers here."

"The in-palace seamstress . . ." I tried to clear my thoughts.

"Nothing would make my family more furious than if I was in the graces of the royal family and they weren't. I'm sick of being controlled by them, but they won't be able to reach me if I'm there."

"This letter instructs you to sabotage the contestants."

"I haven't, though. Think about it, Emmaline. Even if I did sabotage someone, what would the point be? It wouldn't make me win the challenges. No, my goal is to establish myself as a strong sewer and use that to gain a new life."

She spoke with practiced ease. There was no sweetness in her tone or eyes—just calculating thoughtfulness. I watched her, feeling like she was transforming right in front of me and that I was seeing the real Kitty for the first time.

Now that I thought about it, Kitty always turned in well-made clothes. And when she explained her work, she always emphasized its tailoring and fit. Since the royal family only wore Fashion House clothing, she'd be an ideal applicant for a palace seamstress because she'd participated in the Fashion House Interview.

All the pieces seemed to add up. The question was whether to believe the story they created.

"My family uses everyone." Kitty pressed on. "Even me. At first, I thought I'd been accepted into the Fashion House Interview because of my skill. But my parents purchased my spot to elevate their status. I told them I was done with them, but they don't care. They still try to use me, still send me those ridiculous hampers, still go around telling everyone how I'm going to win the whole thing. Little do they know that I'm going to .elude their grasp entirely—using the scenario they put me in."

"But—you are like them. You pretend to be sweet, and it's an act."

"I suppose you're right. They want me to be competitive, so I've been overly nice and helpful to everyone, hoping they'll hear about it and go mad with frustration."

Slowly, deliberately, I folded the letter in half and put it in my pocket. For all I knew, this was a performance, too.

"I'm going to keep this, and if I get even the hint that you're sabotaging anyone, I'm going to take it to Madame Jolène." I could've turned it in right then and there, but maybe Kitty was telling the truth. If there was the slimmest possibility she was,

I wanted to give her the chance to break free from her family. But I needed to be careful. "And from now on, I think it's best if you stay away from me."

I wasn't prepared for the hurt that filled her eyes. It was swift and deep, a duplicate of my mother's eyes when I told her I was leaving for the city. I steeled myself against it—I couldn't trust her.

I left her there and went back up the hallway to where my shoes were sitting on the carpet, one upright and the other a few paces away on its side. I slipped them on and headed back toward the lobby and the stairs. I walked several yards before my feet started tingling, the pain from the heels renewed after being dulled all day long.

"You look . . . tired," Sophie said as I entered our chamber. She watched me from her perch on the wide windowsill. I stopped in the doorway, kicking off my heels. I jerked myself out of my gown. I wanted to divest myself of everything that was the Fashion House and Madame Jolène. Luckily, it was my consulting gown, so I could get out of it without assistance.

"I am," I said shortly, undoing the clasps running down the front of my corset and letting it fall to the ground so I was wearing only a slip. I was aimless for a few moments, my mind still half in the fitting room with Kitty and half in the hallway with Madame Jolène and my gown.

It was all so much.

Too much.

I forced myself into action. I unfolded the wedding gown silk and retrieved a measuring tape from my sewing case. As I did, I noticed Sophie's vanity had been moved yet again. "Will you stop moving things around? And what are you even doing here?"

My snappish tone got her attention, and she set down the recent issue of *La Mode Illustrée* she held. She was immaculate in her slim, French-bustled skirt and high-necked blouse. The two pieces were made of a shiny black satin. The only sign she'd come from consultations was a pincushion tied around her wrist.

"I have to change things," she said, giving a careless shrug. "Things that stay the same bore me. And Madame Jolène lets me take my breaks when I wish."

I didn't bother to reply. My hands held the silk and tape, but my mind was loose again. I wondered, for the first time, about the woman who had purchased my dress. How had she felt when she saw it and slipped it on? Occasionally we tried on Fashion House pieces to get a sense for their fit. I always loved the moment when a new gown was in place on my body—how it was completely separate from me yet encased me. There was always a bit of surprise.

Dresses were different once they were on a figure. Garments needed bodies to complete them, to incarnate them, and I always marveled at how they appeared one way on a hook and another on a woman. Did the owner of my dress feel transformed? Did she feel more or less like herself? I hated that I would never know.

"I need—" I started and stopped, cutting myself off because I didn't really know how to finish the statement.

"What?"

"I don't know. I've had an eventful day." *To say the least.* I couldn't tell her about Kitty. If she was trying to escape her parents, I wanted to protect her. But I could tell Sophie about my gown. "Madame Jolène took my design and had it made for a client. I know I shouldn't be surprised. The Fashion House owns our designs. But I never anticipated how it'd feel to see it made."

Sophie didn't seem startled. Instead, she slowly set the magazine down on the window ledge and swung her legs over the windowsill so she was facing me, her black skirts spilling down onto the floor like silken ink. Her full attention took me aback. I expected a sardonic comment or an empty platitude. After all, that was Sophie: always fluctuating between sarcasm and vague detachment.

"What happened?"

"Madame Jolène had my gown commissioned for a client." I played with the edge of my measuring tape. "I didn't even know until I saw it just now."

"How did it look?"

"It looked . . ." I thought for a moment. It was beautiful. But there were things—subtle things—that had been changed. The skirt was fuller, as was Madame Jolène's signature. The bust-line was higher to provide more coverage, and the gold pattern in the jacquard was softened, the drama mediated by smaller swirls. Even though the dress was mine, Madame Jolène had commercialized it.

"It looked different. Too different. I've been dreaming about creating that sketch, and now it's done."

Sophie listened, running her hands through her black hair and wrapping the ends around her fingers.

"I see," she said. A glint, like a white flame, lit up her eyes. "We are similar, you and I. We have to do things our way."

My hands, which had been fussing with my silk and measuring tape, stilled. Similar? Sophie and I? Hardly. Aside from her also being a contestant, I didn't think we could be more opposite.

"Not really," I said. "You're at the top of the competition. Everyone already knows it. I'll be fortunate if I get to do a few designs before I get sent home."

"That's hardly the future I want," Sophie said. "I don't like designing for someone else."

"What do you mean?" I stared at her, perplexed. "You'd give up designing if you have to do it under Madame Jolène's label?"

"I'd never give up designing. I might as well try not to breathe," Sophie said. She pulled her legs back up onto the windowsill, wrapped her hands around them, and then rested her chin on the tops of her kneecaps so she seemed to only be face, arms, and legs.

"Then what else would you do?"

"I don't know." She gave a small sigh, stretched out her legs, and picked up her magazine once again. I sat back on my heels, staring at her. I'd always thought that I was the only one who felt held back at the Fashion House. I'd never thought anyone else—especially Sophie—might feel the same way.

I picked up a straight pin, but instead of slipping it into my silk, I played with it, pressing my finger lightly against its sharp tip. Enough for its sting to register, but not enough to break the skin. The calluses from home—from scrubbing floors, weeding, lugging casks of beer—were disappearing, leaving my fingers sensitive and soft.

For a moment, I let myself think about home. My mother still hadn't written me, even after I'd sent the money home. It could only mean one thing: she was mad at me. The thought followed me everywhere I went. It was a shadow I couldn't shake, darkening everything with its presence.

I wondered what she was doing now. She probably was sitting at the kitchen table, poring over the ledger. She recorded everything in there: the sales, whether they were for a dinner for five or a single pint; the payments due to the beer vendors and the bank; the dates our keg shipments would arrive. Everything went into that book, and she spent hours analyzing the numbers, seeing where she could cut, where she could spend, when she could schedule things. Above all, she was a shrewd businesswoman.

I stopped still. A businesswoman. No one had ever shown her how, just like no one had ever shown me how to design. She had figured it out, bit by bit, and with no money or support from anyone else.

A realization flashed in my mind like a zigzag of lighting, nearly making me drive the pin into my skin. I let it drop to the floor.

My mother, against the odds, had opened the Moon on the Square—and even though it was hard work, she ran it the way she pleased.

Perhaps, just perhaps, I could do the same thing. Only not with a pub.

With a fashion house.

I saw it: a beautiful showroom lined with gowns in shades of purple, green, and gray. It would be my domain, where I could design whatever I desired and be judged on my work alone, not on where I came from. I wouldn't have to fight for respect in a place that didn't want me or even saw me as a future designer. I wouldn't have to worry about limited competition time or sabotage or having to make a wedding gown from a silk I would never have picked.

Yet . . . why hadn't anyone done it before? The vision couldn't appeal to me and me alone. In Britannia Secunda, where good fashion sense was akin to nationality, there had to be droves of other girls who wanted the same thing. But, as far as I knew, there had never been two fashion houses at one time.

"It's too bad there is only one Fashion House," I said, trying to sound glib. "Have people tried to start others?"

"Yes." Sophie didn't look up from her magazine, but I waited, hoping she wouldn't fall into one of her strange silences again. "But Madame Jolène has the Crown's favor. And while the Crown isn't as powerful as it was before, it still wields lots of influence. A few fashion houses tried to spring up in the past several years, but they can never get financing from any of the banks, and the *Avon-upon-Kynt Times* never reports on any of their designs."

"So, Madame Jolène will always control fashion in Avon-upon-Kynt?"

"Probably." Sophie was still focused on her magazine, but she hadn't flipped a page for a while, and her gaze didn't move. She'd stopped reading some time ago. "Though I must say, I don't think she's as untouchable as it seems. If someone wore something new, or if a collection started without funding from the bank, it could gain enough traction to evade Madame Jolène's reach."

"You really think it would be that easy?" I asked, my mind whirling faster than ever before with thoughts, dangerous thoughts.

"A lot of Madame Jolène's power comes from the impression that she has it," Sophie said, unaware of my internal frenzy. "As it is now, though, the Fashion House is the only way to design." She shut the magazine cover, but she didn't pick up another one. She remained languidly lounging in the window seat. Though her body was loose and relaxed, she frowned, a line of focused attention rising between her brows. Abruptly, she looked at me. "Why?"

"No reason," I said quickly. What on earth was I thinking? I rubbed my aching forehead, the weight of the day descending on me. I was tired. Too tired. My anger made the idea of starting my own fashion house seem viable. But that's all it was. An angry, exhausted fantasy. Even if it was possible, I didn't have the means or knowledge necessary. I was new to the city, new to fashion.

I picked up the straight pin from the floor and used it to secure my measuring tape in place on the silk. There was no time for daydreams.

CHAPTER ELEVEN

THE NEXT DAY, I had another press event—a knighting this time. I didn't want to leave my silk or buttons in my chamber where someone could ruin them, so I tucked them into the rose-colored handbag assigned to my outfit and brought it with me. A few people eyed my bulging bag, but I ignored them. I'd been sabotaged once. It wasn't going to happen again.

The knighting included a formal dinner, so it was nighttime when I finally got into the coach to head back to the Fashion House. I struggled to work on my wedding gown in the coach, despite the way it jostled back and forth over the cobbled streets. I'd lost almost a whole day at the event.

When I arrived at the Fashion House, I hurried up to my chamber, arms full of my silk wedding gown. There was still a bit of night left. Sophie, of course, wasn't there, but sitting on my vanity were two white envelopes. I set the wedding gown down on the chaise longue. One envelope made sense. It would be my Fashion House pay. But the other one had a postage stamp in the corner.

My mother.

She had finally written me. A rush of tears sprang to my eyes, and I ran over to the vanity, snatching up the envelope so fast that I knocked over a small container of straight pins onto the floor.

Only . . . the writing addressing it to me was a scratchy scrawl, nothing like my mother's clear, even print. The ache flared up again, as strong as before. I lowered the envelope and the relieved tears in my eyes turned hot. For the first time since coming to the Fashion House, I couldn't stop them, and they ran down my cheeks. I wiped them away, but they continued to spill down my face.

I opened the envelope. There wasn't a letter inside. Instead, there was a tourist card, the sort people buy as a souvenir on a trip. It was a glossy print of the train station, featuring the mural of Queen Catherine. Two stick figures—one a boy and the other a girl—were drawn crudely onto the image in graphite.

I flipped it over, and the other side read,

Emmy,
  I thought you might like to remember the mural. Also, I added us for posterity's sake.
—Tristan

I wiped my face with the back of my hand and sat down on the vanity chair. I turned the card back over and stared at the two figures Tristan had sketched onto the picture. Slowly, a smile came over my face.

He was a terrible artist. I didn't know if it was an accident

191

or not, but the stick people's hands overlapped. My smile grew wider. I pictured him passing by one of those stands selling newspapers, maps, and postcards, his bright blue eyes landing on the mural card. It had made him think of me.

I tucked the card into the vanity mirror so I could see it from anywhere in the chamber. With my eyes still fixed on it, I picked up the other envelope, the one with my pay, and slid the flap open. I was so preoccupied by thoughts of Tristan that I didn't realize something was wrong for a few moments—that there wasn't any money in it, just the usual white slip. I pulled the paper out, tearing the envelope in the process. Not a single bill was inside it. I read the slip.

FASHION HOUSE INTERVIEW
CONTESTANT: EMMALINE WATKINS
COMPENSATION FOR ONE WEEK OF WORK
DEDUCTIONS: BOARD, PRESS ATTIRE

No pay at all? There had to be some mistake. I glanced at the clock. I knew Francesco and Madame Jolène dined together in her private apartments at the top of the Fashion House and that after the maids brought down their trays, they would have a glass of wine. If I went now, I could catch Francesco as he left Madame Jolène's rooms, and he could make sure I was paid first thing in the morning.

Then I could post the money to my mother right away.

Quickly, I jumped to my feet. I clutched the envelope and slip in my hand, not bothering to use the banister as I rushed up the staircase. It led to the fifth floor, where Francesco's rooms were located, but it didn't go all the way up to Madame Jolène's apartments. Only her private staircase went to the very top, and that was on the opposite side of the Fashion House.

There was a small landing outside the double doors leading to Francesco's chambers. A gas lamp gave off a weak yellow glow into the night, illuminating a zebra-hide rug, reminding me of his zebra pocket watch. The walls were covered in a bamboo print wallpaper. It gave the impression that an elephant or rhinoceros might emerge from between the stalks at any moment. I stood in the lamp's small circle of light, my body tense and aching.

I didn't have to wait long. Francesco appeared on the landing, attired in a loose caftan with fur slippers. His cheeks were ruddy in the dim light and, upon seeing me, he held his arms out to me.

"Emmaline," he said, the thick smell of wine billowing with his breath. "What on earth are you doing here?"

"I'm sorry to bother you." I raised the torn envelope and slip. "But I just got this and there wasn't any money in it. I think there must have been a mistake."

The loose smile around his lips immediately disappeared and his chest rose and fell with a deep sigh.

"There wasn't a mistake. After the fashion deductions, there wasn't any money left."

"Deductions?" My tenuous hold on my panic slipped even further. "But my contestant wardrobe was already taken out of the first payment."

"Yes. But we hadn't tallied up your press attire yet, not to mention all the accessories. In fact, when we did, you actually owed us—quite a lot—but the Fashion House covered the rest."

"*I* owed the *Fashion House?*" I sputtered.

"Well, yes," Francesco said. "Couture is very expensive, and you need a new dress for every appearance. And we had to use outside vendors for most of the hats and jewelry."

"This can't be happening," I said, more to myself than to him. Money was the last bridge between my mother and me. No, I hadn't come to the Fashion House for the pay. But when I had it, I knew it would keep the bank at bay and ease those deep lines in my mother's forehead. When I had it, I could justify leaving her all alone because I could still help her, still show her I loved her. "That was for the past week. Will I get paid again?"

Francesco glanced down at the zebra hide at his feet, as though it might tell him the answer. "Things should calm down after the Parliament elections. Once they do, I'll talk to Madame Jolène about reinstating your pay."

"And, until then, I work for free?"

A long time ago, a neighbor woman had brought my mother her old china. She'd unpacked it on our kitchen counter, saying she was happy she could help others and that my mother didn't need to thank her. I'd been just about table height then, and I was eye level to the chipped bowls, plates, and saucers she pulled out of her basket and placed on our counter.

My mother had told her there was no need to thank her because we wouldn't be keeping the china. The woman had gasped and sputtered, turning a strange shade of red. After she'd left—with the china packed back into her basket—my mother had bent down, put her hands on my shoulders and said, "We always have our dignity, Emmy. Always."

I'd allowed Madame Jolène to trot me out to the press. I'd smiled and nodded and eaten dry tea sandwiches at every luncheon, charity event, and dedication in Avon-upon-Kynt, even as my competition time was reduced to practically nothing. *I'd worn pink*, day in and day out. My sketches had been ruined and no one had even bothered to investigate; my brocade gown had been made without me even knowing. I'd fumed and fussed, but I'd gone on with my duties.

Because that's what I was supposed to do. That's what was supposed to get me a chance to win the Fashion House Interview.

"I know it's frustrating," Francesco said. "This isn't an easy life for anyone. Not for me, not for you, not even for Madame Jolène. Just be patient, and time will sort everything out."

"You don't understand. I need the money," I said. "I'm going to talk to Madame Jolène about it tomorrow."

Francesco sucked in his breath, making his cheeks puff out. He held up both his hands, as though trying to stop me, even though I hadn't moved a step since he'd arrived.

"I wouldn't suggest that. Madame Jolène is under a lot of pressure right now, and you should keep your head down. Just wait. Things will right themselves. They always do." He paused. "It's late. You should be getting your rest."

He brushed aside a stray strand of hair from my face. The gesture reminded me of my mother and made my throat compress. I knew I ought to thank him—he'd always been so kind to me—but, for the moment, I needed to get away.

I should have gone back to my chamber, but I didn't want to sit there on my vanity stool or lie in my bed, surrounded by Fashion House lavishness. I needed to walk. I needed to think. Grabbing up fistfuls of my pink skirts, I wanted to tear the dress off my body.

I went down the staircase and passed my floor. Then, halfway down to the lobby, I stopped and sank down onto the steps. In the darkness, it seemed as though the stairs went on forever in both directions.

Pulling my knees to my chest, I wrapped my arms around them, my back against the railing. The Fashion House paintings loomed above my head, dark shapes against the wall. I could barely make out the images, but I knew I was sitting below the painting of Princess Amelia's blue gown.

How things had changed since the first time I'd passed beneath the painting. I'd known Madame Jolène didn't want me at the Fashion House then—but I hadn't known all the ways I'd be excluded.

I sagged against the railing, its knobbiness hard against my shoulders. How could I stay here when I couldn't design—and now wouldn't even get paid? Yet how could I go anywhere else?

Even though I could only see hints of blue paint picked up by the bit of light from the last landing, I stared up at the painting. Before, I'd seen it as my future: making gowns that shaped fashion. Now I knew the truth behind it. That it was a gorgeous gown that had empowered one woman and ruined the life of another—the duchess.

If only there was another fashion house, one where I would be judged on my designs alone. But there wasn't . . .

If someone wore something new or if a collection started without funding from the bank, it could gain enough traction to evade Madame Jolène's reach.

. . . unless I made one.

Earlier, when I'd thought about creating a fashion house, I'd dismissed the idea. I'd been angry. Tired. Irrational.

But as I thought about it now, it seemed so bizarrely simple. Someone would need a well-known figure to wear their gown and get noticed by the press. They would have to start a collection without outside funding, and fast, before Madame Jolène knew about it.

And—I did know someone. Well, not directly. But Tristan did. He'd told me so. He'd told me he was going to interview Cynthia, the blacklisted duchess. Everyone talked about her. Granted, they didn't say very kind things, but attention was attention. If she wore an exquisite gown, something different, people would notice. And what had Tristan said? That the *Eagle* wasn't under the thumb of the Crown? It certainly wasn't a reputable paper, but *everyone* in Avon-upon-Kynt read it. He could write a story about Cynthia and feature her new gown. He said he always loved writing a breaking story, and this one was sure to fit the salacious nature of the *Eagle*. If they were resorting to writing about mermaids, then they would definitely want to write about real women with real feuds.

But how could I contact her? Would she even agree to wear a dress by a no-name Fashion House Interview contestant? And how would I pay for the fabric?

I violently shook my head. It was enough to dissipate the questions for the time being. One thing at a time. That's what my mother always said when she was short on the mortgage and the sink was dripping and the stove broken. No matter how many obstacles she faced while running her business, she would somehow figure it out.

I'd always thought that design was all I knew. But I'd spent my whole life watching my mother as she built her pub into a thriving establishment. Without realizing it, I'd seen firsthand what it took to create a business—and the freedom that came with it.

First thing: I had to contact Tristan. I knew he worked at the *Eagle*—that was where I would go. Tomorrow was Saturday. Everyone would spend the day working on their wedding gowns. I would go then and see what Tristan thought about my plan.

My plan. My racing mind settled around the thought, and I smiled into the darkness. Ever since arriving at the Fashion House, I'd been told where to go, what to do, and even what to wear—the architecture of my life plotted out by others. Yes, my plan was risky, but for once, I would answer to myself and my own will. Even though I was sitting completely still, my heart lifted in my chest, excited, breathless, skipping through its beats. The sensation rose through my body, the elated rush half dizzying lightheadedness, half intense focus.

I'd felt that way once before. Right after I'd gone back into Madame Jolène's tent at Evert and secured my spot at the Fashion House. It was the sort of feeling that only comes when great risks pay off. This plan hadn't paid off yet, not in a measurable way. But I was more myself than I'd been since arriving here—and that was all I needed.

PART II

CHAPTER TWELVE

I THOUGHT IT MIGHT BE hard to sneak out of the Fashion House, but it ended up being easier than I'd anticipated. I told Francesco I was coming down with a cold, and since I would be presented to the press at the gala, he told me to take a nap, saying, "Red noses don't go with pink dresses. To bed with you, little scarecrow dresser."

As soon as I got to my chamber, I put on one of Sophie's black capes, crept back down the stairs, and simply walked out the front door like a client leaving an appointment. Once outside, I pulled the cape tightly around me, trying to hide my obnoxiously pink skirt.

At some point, I really did need to talk to Francesco about getting a new wardrobe. All this pink was making me feel like a walking cupcake. I'd noticed the other girls found ways around Madame Jolène's fashion edicts. Sophie, after all, wore black day in and day out. But then again, Sophie wasn't a press pawn.

The Fashion House sat directly on the street, unsheltered by gates or barriers. Leafy green ivy was neatly cropped around the long windows and, of course, around the *FH* insignia.

Despite the dreary morning, the gold letters managed to pick up a few faltering rays of light. I'd never stood on the front steps of the Fashion House, or even on the sidewalk in front of it. When I attended events in the city, I was always picked up at the rear entrance. As I walked down the cobbled pathway toward the street, I wanted to pause and let the place seep into me through my feet, as though fashion magic ran through the ground. But shaking my head, I made myself walk briskly forward. I couldn't get caught up in emotions, especially when I was about to do something akin to Fashion House blasphemy: attempt to contact a blacklisted client.

"Do pardon me." As I stood on the sidewalk, a Fashion House customer brushed by me. She inclined her head toward me and gave a polite smile even as she looked me over, sizing me up, trying to figure out if I was above or below her on the social ladder. She thought I was a Fashion House customer as well, someone wealthy enough to purchase couture.

"Of course," I murmured, and quickly ducked away down the sidewalk. Elegant black hacks with gold trim glided along the street like enchanted fairy-tale carriages. Most of them had small red flags attached to their doorknobs, indicating they were reserved for the day by a well-to-do customer. I saw one without a flag and quickened my pace so I was nearly jogging alongside it. I'd never hailed a hack before, and I waved my hand uncertainly at it. The driver noticed me from his position up in the back and pulled on the reins, drawing the hack to a stop. Stepping down, he opened the door and took my hand to help me into the cab.

"Where to, miss?" He bowed at the waist, his gaze averted. Like the other woman, he thought I was someone of note.

"I need to go to the offices of the *Eagle*."

His eyebrows shot up and he straightened, lines of confusion spreading across his forehead.

"The *Eagle*, miss? Are you quite sure? That's in the Republic District."

"I'm sure." I tried to sound confident, but his reaction shook me. Maybe I didn't know what I was getting into. I involuntarily looked over my shoulder at the Fashion House.

"Very well. Do you have a companion?" A chaperone, he meant. Young single girls rarely traveled alone in the city.

"Not today." Without waiting for his response, I stepped into the cab and settled on its velvet bench. The driver worriedly rubbed his hand over his face and then scratched his head. I stared straight ahead, pulling myself upright and hoping I appeared somewhat commanding. Madame Jolène and Sophie kept their spines as straight as broomsticks and their faces as frozen as ice. I adopted a similar countenance, imagining I really was someone with important business to attend and money to wield.

"All right, miss." The driver shut the door and clambered up onto the back of the coach. It shifted with his weight, and he called to his horse. We started moving forward, and my hands shot out to grip the sides of the bench. I was really doing this. I really was being carried away from the Quarter District and to the underbelly of Avon-upon-Kynt.

"Miss!" the driver yelled to me through the window after

about thirty minutes. "We're about to leave the Quarter District. You're certain this is where you want to go?"

"Yes," I called back, placing a hand on the windowsill. The change in landscape was almost instantaneous as we entered the next district. Narrow brick buildings were crammed together, thin plumes of black smoke rising from smokestacks atop their roofs. Stalls made from splintery planks and stacked crates lined the streets, and vendors yelled out to the men and women bustling by in threadbare jackets, their shoulders bent against the chill.

In the Quarter District, nearly every business had a sign supporting a Fashion House Interview contestant. Here there were fewer, but if I looked, I could spot them. I noticed, with a rush of gratitude, that almost all of them were for me.

The clustered buildings and sewage in the streets were foreign to me. Shy was not a wealthy parish, but the people were proud. What little we had, we kept orderly. We didn't have the architectural feats found in Avon-upon-Kynt, but we had open fields and forests. When I was a girl, my mother would sometimes take me to the fields just past our pub. We would lie down on a blanket and watch the clouds inch their way across the blue bowl of sky, finding different types of flowers and leaves in their shapes. We'd see a black willow leaf here, an amaryllis blooming there. The air smelled clean—not like rotting garbage and acrid smoke.

"We're here, miss," the hack driver called after we'd pushed through the streets for nearly an hour. He stopped the horses and climbed down from his seat to open the door. I stepped out, shivering. The chilly air had a bite to it. "That's the office."

He pointed with one gloved finger at a brick building. A sign hung from a rail protruding from just underneath the roof: THE EAGLE. There was, in literal fashion, an eagle painted onto the sign just underneath the text. It held a folded newspaper in its beak, and a sun rose behind its outstretched wings. The grand image was ironic considering the paper's tendency to report on everything from extramarital affairs to ghosts.

"Be careful now. A fine girl like you has no business down here," the driver said anxiously.

"I'm sure I'll be all right." I tried to sound firm, but my voice was swept away by the wind whistling down the street. He was right. I didn't have any business down here. In fact, I was fairly certain I wasn't even safe. There were two vagrants right outside the *Eagle*'s door, and they staggered into each other, one of them holding a bottle and the other flailing for it. I hesitated, ready to get back into the hack and tell the man to take me back to the Fashion House.

"Miss?" the driver prompted.

"Here." I pressed a banknote into his hand, trying to make my movements assured. He climbed back on top of his hack, giving me one last apprehensive glance before snapping the reins over his horse's back.

I paused for a moment, collecting myself.

"Hey, girlie!" One of the vagrants squinted at me. "What's a fancy thing like you doing down here?"

"Come to see how the other half lives?" the other one asked, hiccupping violently and lifting the bottle up to take a sloppy drink.

Pulling my cloak tightly across my body, I walked toward

the door. The two men struggled to right themselves as I approached, as if I was coming for them. I almost hesitated, but there were plenty of people around, and I couldn't imagine they would try to hurt me in broad daylight.

"That's a pretty dress." Sticking his thick, dirty finger at my skirts, the first vagrant leered at me. The smell of stale sweat and alcohol emanated from him. The other one grabbed a fistful of my cloak, but I wrenched away from him.

"You think you're too good for us?"

"Stop!" I struggled to grab the knob. "Let go!"

A few people walking by slowed to watch, but no one tried to intervene. Just as I jerked my cloak free, his other hand landed on my shoulder. I gave a petrified shriek and tried to shake him off, but his fingernails dug into my skin through my dress and cloak. His companion laughed.

"How about a kiss?" The one holding my shoulder sneered. Without even thinking, my hand balled into a fist and I cocked my free arm back from my shoulder.

"Let me go!" My fist shot forward and connected with his nose. Bright, red blood spurted from his nostrils, and he wheeled backward. His hand was still clamped around my shoulder, and his fingernails slashed down my arm as he crumpled to the ground.

With one swift motion, I reached for the door and dashed to safety inside the office. Once the door slammed shut behind me, I leaned against it, my chest heaving up and down.

I was standing in a poorly lit room. Several heavy wooden desks covered in sheets of white paper sat to my left. Each one had a light with a green shade and gold base. All the desks faced a gigantic chalkboard set on what had to be the largest easel in Avon-upon-Kynt. It was scrawled over with messy writing—phrases like "LIFE ON MARS?" "PARLIAMENT MEMBER LORD WILLIAM COTTEL SPOTTED AT THE THEATER WITH A PAINTED LADY," and "MERMAID FOUND IN TYNE BREAKS HER SILENCE." The room led directly into another, where an enormous printing press went all the way up to the ceiling. It whirred and clicked, its gears rotating and pumping a long line of newspapers out its far side. It looked like a metal monster that had somehow gotten itself trapped in an office building.

A tall man wearing a visor with a translucent green bill stood behind one of the desks, his fingers and hands smeared with ink. Three other men with untidy hair, cotton shirts, and corduroy trousers were next to him. They had been poring over a notebook on the desk, but upon my panicked entrance, they straightened up and stared at me, their eyebrows rising with confusion.

"Emmy?" I heard my name called over the squeaks and shrills of the printing press. Tristan stood up from where he'd been hidden behind the far side of the easel. Like the other men, his hair was a mess, his collar undone, and his shirtsleeves rolled to the elbows. He was the most beautiful thing I'd seen all day.

"Are you all right?" He hurried over to me. "You're bleeding!"

I glanced down at my sleeve. Red droplets of blood stained the fabric of my dress right at my shoulder. That vagrant had gouged me with his fingernails. The thought of him—of his disgusting odor and gnarled hands—racked my body with a shudder.

"I had a run-in with a gentleman outside," I said, my voice quavering.

"With who?" Tristan's eyes instantly darkened until they were nearly a different color. "Is he still there?"

"No," I lied. "I'm"—I took a shaky breath—"I'm all right."

His hands tightened into fists, and an angry, blue vein rose to the surface of his arm.

"He's gone," I said quickly. The last thing I needed was for this to become any bigger than it already was. I had the fearful thought of seeing a new headline scrawled across the chalkboard: "MADAME JOLÈNE'S COUNTRY CONTESTANT ATTACKED IN THE CITY BY HOMELESS PIRATE." I wanted to make headlines, but in quite a different way.

"You're sure you're all right?"

"I'm sure."

"Well, let's get this taken care of. Are you here alone?"

I noticed the other men listening closely, their faces alert with interest. I could only imagine they were used to chasing every story possible. Worry edged out the panic from before. Yes, I needed the *Eagle* to make my plan succeed, but it would only work if everything was timed correctly. If they mentioned anywhere in the paper that I'd been seen down here, I'd be as homeless as the vagrants outside in two seconds flat.

"Don't worry about my shoulder. I need to talk to you. Can we go somewhere else?" I murmured.

Tristan nodded immediately. "Of course. There's a pub

nearby. It isn't nearly as nice as anything in the Quarter District, but it's decent enough. You're sure your shoulder is all right?"

"Yes. It's fine."

"I'll take a look at it once we get to the pub."

Just as he spoke, there was a rap on the door behind me. For a second, I thought it was the vagrant, trying to get in. The thought of seeing his leering face made my stomach turn. I quickly stepped aside as the knob turned and it swung open. I expected to see the vagrant's yellowed eyes and to be enveloped in his stink.

Instead, a well-dressed man stepped into the office. He was wearing an embossed black suit with a black overcoat, matching top hat, and neckerchief tied in a gigantic bow. As was the current style, he held a skinny black walking stick in one hand. Like me, he obviously did not belong in the Republic District. He strode to the middle of the room and surveyed the space, as though it and everything in it belonged to him. His attention landed on me, first focusing on my cloak, then my pink dress underneath, and lastly, my face. His lips twitched—in a way I'd seen before.

He was the man from the library dedication, the one who'd asked about Sophie. What was his name? Taylor. Mr. Alexander Taylor. I buried my hands in my cloak, remembering the sensation of oily lotion moistening my palms.

"Ah, the Fashion House's little country girl. You've been out and about lately—I was worried Madame Jolène would keep you locked up at the Fashion House, but she's done just what we asked." Gone was the look of boredom that he'd had the last time he saw me—though the arrogance remained. His gaze leisurely ran the length of my body. "So, tell me, have you spoken with Miss Sophie Sterling yet?"

A new sort of fear, this one somehow more insidious than the terror I'd felt outside the office, came swiftly over me. Mutely, I shook my head.

"Funny." He moved toward me, his steps as slinking and agile as a wolf's. The men in the office fell silent, watching us. "Considering she's your roommate."

The color left my face—I could feel it draining away. As he approached, his dark form seemed to block out everyone and everything else in the office with its expanse.

"You don't know how things work in the city," he said, "so it's best you learn this quickly: I brought you here, and I can just as easily have you sent away."

A hand closed around my upper arm, and I let out a yelp of terrified surprise, twisting around to see Tristan behind me.

"Emmy is none of your concern," he said, his eyes fixed on Mr. Taylor's face. Gently, he moved me aside so he could step in front of me. Tension radiated from him, creating taut lines down his neck, arms, and shoulders. Mr. Taylor was much taller than Tristan, and he smiled condescendingly down at him.

"Calm down, Grafton," he said. "I was just welcoming the country girl to the city. After all, she has the Reformists Party and me to thank for even being here. Now, I have business with you. Come, let's talk."

He moved off to the side of the room, away from the other

reporters. He didn't check to see if Tristan was following.

"This won't take long," Tristan said to me. "Do you mind waiting just a moment?"

I nodded, glad that Mr. Taylor's attention was now on him instead of me. Tristan walked over to where Mr. Taylor waited near the printing press.

"There's going to be a protest at the gala." Mr. Taylor didn't preface his news. He spoke quietly, but I could still hear him, just barely. "Nothing violent, of course. Just a few concerned Parliament members and some allies. But I thought you might want to come, considering you often cover such things."

I listened, startled enough to forget my unease. A protest at the gala? Certainly, things were tense between Parliament, the Crown, and the Fashion House, but a protest?

"Was this something you orchestrated?" Tristan asked. He crossed his arms across his chest and stared up at Mr. Taylor, undaunted by the bigger man. "Hardly seems like something a government official should be involved in."

"I care only about results, Grafton. How I get them is inconsequential."

Despite his obvious dislike of Mr. Taylor, a thoughtful look entered Tristan's eyes.

"You know the queen is close to Madame Jolène. In fact, she'll be an honored guest at the gala."

"This country has been ruled by the queen and her old ways long enough," Mr. Taylor said. His low tone was tense, passionate. "The Reformists Party is ruled by the future. The protest must happen."

Tristan nodded briskly, his hand diving into his pocket for a notepad. He quickly wrote something on it.

"All right." He returned to his previous posture, staring up at Mr. Taylor, shoulders and chest squared. "You've delivered your message. I think it's time to go."

Mr. Taylor considered Tristan for a long moment, and then, with a smooth movement, replaced his top hat and brandished his walking stick.

"Whatever our differences, you'll do well to align with me." He walked past Tristan, brushing hard against his shoulder as he moved into the center of the room. "You'll *all* do well to align with the Reformists Party," he said, speaking louder to address everyone in the office.

The reporters glanced up at him, perplexed by the sudden, impromptu announcement. Unperturbed, Mr. Taylor made his way to the door, stepping outside with fluid grace.

"I hope he gets pickpocketed," one of the reporters said as soon as the door closed behind him.

"It would serve him right, the way he walks around like he owns the place." Another reporter joined in.

"How about we get some air?" Tristan made his way over to me. I nodded.

Tristan gestured toward the back door, and, relieved to be heading in the opposite direction from Mr. Taylor and the vagrants, I followed him out of the office.

We headed up the narrow alleyway behind the *Eagle*. Tristan offered me the crook of his arm as we stepped around the broken cobblestones and puddles of sewage. His shirtsleeves were still rolled up, and his bare skin was hot, his muscles flexing underneath my fingers.

"Who exactly is that man? I met him before, at a library dedication."

"Mr. Taylor? He's a patron of the arts and a Parliament member—very wealthy but untitled. He's become the unofficial leader of the Reformists Party."

"I don't like him."

"I don't either," Tristan said grimly. We walked a few paces, both of us quiet. Then I said, "I got your postcard."

"Did you like it?" He glanced at me, his eyes nervous.

"I did."

That made him smile all the way to the end of the alley, where we turned left. A pub sat right on the corner. THE PRINCE REGENT, the sign read. Tristan held the door for me. I let go of his arm to step inside, but I held on for a few seconds longer than necessary.

Inside the pub, friendly sights, smells, and sounds arose from every corner.

Hello, old friend, I thought. Heavy-handled pint glasses clinked and clunked, and the sweet smell of beer filled my nose with every inhale. A burly man was working behind the bar, filling a pint with Guinness. His motions—the way he pulled the tap and tilted the glass so a perfect white foam built over the liquid—were second nature to me.

I could easily imagine my mother moving about this pub. Yes, it was much gloomier than the Moon on the Square, but I could see her tending the bar, chatting with the customers, coming up to relieve me so I could take a break in the back even though she never did.

"Here, sit down." Tristan motioned me to a booth built into the wall. I slid into it, glad to focus on something other than my mother. He sat down next to me. The bench was short, and our elbows brushed against each other. The warmth of his skin and the smell of his aftershave were intoxicating. "First things first."

He pulled a handkerchief out of his pocket and eased aside the black cape so he could see my shoulder. Carefully, he started to dab at the blood. Even though his movements were assured and deliberate, his touch was a whisper, soft and gentle.

"It's fine," I said. His breath lightly tickled my cheek.

"It looks like a cat mauled you," he said, his attention fixed on my shoulder. "That man ought to be arrested."

"Thank you for helping me."

Tristan raised his head then, and his blue eyes met mine, our faces impossibly close. I could just lean forward the tiniest bit and our lips would meet and—

Oh my. I looked away then. If I hadn't, I would've been lost to him—his blue eyes, his fingers gently moving about my shoulder. I forced myself to straighten up and move back so we weren't practically nose to nose.

"It's strange," I said, making my tone conversational. "There were so many people around me, but no one helped. That would never happen in Shy."

"That's the city for you." Tristan sighed and shook his head. "In one sense, it's nice because no one really cares about you, so you get to be and do whatever you want. But it's also terrible because, well—no one really cares about you."

The man from behind the bar came up to our table, his huge arms folded across his barrel chest and his dour gaze flitting from me to Tristan and back again.

"If you sit, you order," he growled.

"I know, Grayson," Tristan said. "Have I ever just sat without ordering? I'm your best customer!"

"My best customer who always orders a half pint of the cheapest beer available. Do you think that half pints pay for this place?"

"Be fair. Do you think a reporter's salary pays for such luxuries as full pints? But look. I've brought a pretty face with me this time. That automatically raises your stock, because . . ." Tristan winced and gestured to the dour-faced men gathered around the bar. Grayson didn't laugh, but he uncrossed his arms and nodded.

"So, what'll it be?"

"Two teas today. But Grayson, someday I'll break a huge story, and then I'll be back here and it'll be beers for everyone on me—full pints!"

"That'll be the day." Grayson walked away, grumbling under his breath.

Tristan turned back to me.

"So now you know," he sighed.

"What?"

"That I may be handsome, but wealthy . . . not so much."

"That's fine." I laughed. "You are exceptionally handsome, so it compensates quite well."

I almost bit my own tongue. Was I . . . flirting with him? I'd never tried to flirt with anyone before. Yet here I was, sitting next to a gorgeous boy from the city, saying things I should not be saying when I had other things to focus on. I hadn't even mentioned my plan. In fact, I was surprised he hadn't asked yet why I'd come.

"Why thank you, Emmy Watkins. You're quite lovely your-self."

"Do you say that to all the girls?" I couldn't help myself. I would ask that one question and then redirect everything to my plan. But he was so handsome, and the most charming things flowed right out of him.

"Only you, of course." He grinned and winked. "Well, maybe not. But I have to say . . ."

"What?" I pressed.

"Nothing. I've just never met a Fashion House contestant brave enough to come to the Republic District on her own." He spoke frankly, all signs of joking gone.

"They don't for good reason," I said, motioning to my shoul-der. "Remember, I was clawed by an inebriated man who smelled like a week's worth of sweat."

Grayson came up, holding a tray with two white handled cups and a small pot of tea. He placed the entire tray down on the table with a loud thud.

"Cream and sugar, Grayson?" Tristan asked. "You may think I'm a barbarian, but I'm with a lady, and she might desire some for her tea."

"It's all right," I interjected before Grayson could complain. "I actually take my tea black."

"Isn't that sweet. Just like you, Tristan." He scowled at me, but there wasn't any real malice in his expression. "I'll let you two lovebirds alone, but remember—a cup of tea buys you two hours in here, no more."

At the word *lovebirds*, my face flushed, and I almost protested. Grayson, though, had already turned away.

"I'm afraid I don't have any news for you." Tristan didn't seem to notice my embarrassment. He was busily distributing the cups and pouring tea into them, as adept as any maid. "I've been checking the employee records at the textile mills but haven't found your mother yet. I'll still need some more time."

"Oh, I'm not here for that. Though I do appreciate you checking."

"Really?" He cocked his head to the side. "Then what brings you here?"

I tried to take a steadying breath. Everything had made much more sense in the safety of my chamber at the Fashion House. "I—well, ever since coming here, I've been used for press events. I want to succeed at the Fashion House Interview, but I'm not sure that's a real possibility. I . . ." I didn't know if I could actually say it. I hadn't told my idea to a single soul. Saying it made it too real, too risky.

"What are you thinking?"

Instead of speaking, I picked up my teacup and took a small sip. When I returned the cup to the saucer, my hand trembled a little. If my plan didn't work—if it somehow got back to Madame Jolène—my dreams would be over. I wouldn't even have enough money to get home to Shy, and a disgraced Fashion

House Interview reject couldn't find another job in the city, that much was for sure. If I did manage to get home, who knew what my mother would say or do. I still hadn't heard a word from her.

"Are you all right?" Tristan asked quietly.

"Yes." I took up the teacup again, despite the fact that I'd just set it down. This time I forced my hand to stay steady. I took another drink, slower this time. As I did, I thought about my gown—not the brocade one, but the one I'd drawn for my mother to wear when she came to the city. It had poured out of me like my pencil was enchanted. The story that inspired the dress would never happen, but when I'd sketched it, I'd felt powerful, as though I could somehow will it into reality. "I'm going to make a gown."

"What?"

"I'm going to make a gown," I repeated.

"Isn't that what you do all the time?"

"Not for the Fashion House. For someone else. And I need your help."

"My help? With making a gown?" Tristan stared at me in shock. Who could blame him? I could still hardly believe the plan myself.

"You're still interviewing Duchess Sandringham, aren't you?"

"Well, yes . . . tomorrow."

"Could you give her a message for me? Could you tell her there is a new fashion label starting, and they want her to wear their first gown? Tell her it will be a special gown, one that will change everything. She can wear it to the Parliament

Exhibition, and then, after the opening speeches, she can come to a debut, where a whole new collection will be presented. Everyone will be there, including the Fashion House critics and reporters from the newspapers."

"They" was a bit of an exaggeration since, at the moment, I was a one-woman operation. Still, I needed to appear convincing and official. It worked. For a passing second, I felt like something bigger and stronger than what I was.

"A fashion label?" Tristan sputtered a little. "What label?"

"Um . . . the Emmy Watkins label." His reaction made me falter. I tried not to let it show, clinging to the idea that I could do this and do it well. Even so, my heart pounded in my ears.

"All right. All right." He raised his hands just above the tabletop and took a breath. "Let's start at the beginning. You want to create a dress for Duchess Cynthia Sandringham and, at the same time, start a new fashion line?"

"Yes." Somehow, I mustered enough strength to make my voice as firm as my face.

"To start a fashion label, you need a place to work, material, and access to the press." Tristan ticked the items off his fingers. "And you'd somehow have to get it off the ground without Madame Jolène hearing about it. She's an expert at squashing new fashion start-ups. And, even if you do get it running, there's no doubt she'll come after you. She has the favor of the Crown."

"I'm going to work at the Fashion House, after hours, and I do have access to the press." I skipped the issues of materials and Madame Jolène. "You."

"Well." Tristan tilted his cup toward me in a miniature toast before rubbing his hand over his face. "You want to make an entire collection and a custom gown in time for the Parliament Exhibition?"

"It's the only event that the aristocrats, press, Crown, and Parliament attend together. For it to work, *everyone* has to see her. Since she's a duchess, she'll be formally announced. And then we'll debut our line on the same night."

"That's next month. You can't do it on your own. There's no way. You'll need to find help." He formed a steeple with his fingers, a line of concentration appearing between his eyebrows. He puzzled in silence for a few minutes, and then a strange, elusive expression crossed his face. "Have you thought about asking someone to join you?"

"I'm not sure who I could ask . . ." Even as I spoke, a face flashed in my mind, the image rising faster than my words. Sophie. She was strong in so many ways—a quick sewer with a fierce imagination. As focused as she was on the competition, there was an independent streak in her, something that wasn't quite satisfied with the way things were at the Fashion House.

But . . . could I trust her?

"There is one girl."

"Who?"

"Sophie."

I watched him closely. He fiddled with the handle of his teacup, and when he spoke, his voice was tempered, cautious.

"She is a good choice. I thought she would be happy at the Fashion House, but that doesn't seem to be the case. I think she'd jump at the chance to do something like this."

"Do you think so?" I asked. "You would know better than I, given your"—I almost couldn't bring myself to say it—"past."

"You'd think so, but when I was with her, I didn't know what was up or down or left or right. It was like falling in love with a figment—she was never graspable. We've been apart for a year, and half that time I've wondered if she only saw me because she likes doing things her own way . . . especially if it causes a stir." He leaned forward, toward me. "Are you all right hearing this? I want to be open with you."

"Of course," I said quickly. But I couldn't deny it—though I was strangely riveted, I hated it. Even if they weren't still together, they had a history all their own, something I had no part in. Sophie and her past were like shadows creeping across the floor: terrifying and inevitable.

"She's a strange soul," Tristan continued. "I don't think I ever truly knew her, but I do know that she'd be perfect for the task. Aside from her skills, she has resources, which you'll need, and a lot of savvy."

"I have savvy," I found myself blurting out. I didn't want to be compared to the beautiful, mysterious, talented Sophie, even if he didn't love her.

"That's obvious," he said. "You came all the way down here, got attacked by a drunk, and are still on your feet. You've got gumption, as we say in the journalism world, and you have it by the boatload."

I picked up my teacup, glad it could hide my face so he wouldn't see how pleased and grateful I was.

"If I give this message to Cynthia, how will you meet her to discuss it?"

"At the gala next week. She said she was attending, correct? Maybe you can tell her to meet me somewhere. Have you been to the Charwell Palace?"

"I have, for last year's gala."

"Is there some discreet spot?"

"Well, there's a gazebo out back in the gardens. Would that work?"

"Perfect. Tell her to meet me there thirty minutes after the gala begins."

"Slow down now. This is a lot to ask of a poor journalist such as myself with no name or family to speak of." He sounded like his typical self—his voice brimming with humor. But then I saw it—a hesitancy that passed through his eyes. "I want to write for the *Avon-upon-Kynt Times* someday. That means staying on the good side of the Fashion House. If I break this story, I won't ever be able to do interviews at the Fashion House again."

"I know. It's a lot to ask. But if you break this, it'll be huge. And times are changing. I've heard people say that soon the *Times* won't answer to the queen." I spoke more confidently than I had the right to. "Besides, aren't there some editors at the *Times* who want to curry favor with the Reformists?"

"Yes . . ." He picked at some dried skin around his fingernail. For a moment, this uncharacteristic pensiveness made me question myself. What right did I have to ask him to do this? To endanger his career? And for what? A slim hope of something that might not even happen. He had a job and a place in this city—and I was asking him to risk both.

"How about this?" When I met his gaze, his eyes were bright again, and that bewitchingly sly smile was back, pulling at the left side of his mouth. "I'll tell Cynthia about the plan. And if you are successful and pull off an actual fashion show, I'll write the story."

"Really?" I smiled back at him, unable to hide my relief. "Thank you."

"Yes. Just promise me one thing."

"What?"

"That you'll be really careful and you won't get caught."

"Promise."

There was a sudden flash of lightning, and it made us both jump. Tristan glanced across the pub to one of the grimy windows. Dark clouds gathered in the gloomy sky, and thunder rumbled, low and growly.

"It's going to rain. You need to get back. Also, Grayson might have us wash dishes in the back if we stay."

He was right. I needed to go home.

Correction. I needed to get back to the Fashion House.

CHAPTER THIRTEEN

THAT NIGHT, SOPHIE WAS GONE as usual, so I had our chamber to myself. I was glad. I could think in the empty silence of our room. Think, and plan.

I got out my sketchbook and sat down at my vanity. To make a full collection, I would need at least eight pieces. Ten, if I wanted to appear like a real designer. Madame Jolène's collections always had at least twelve, but that was impossible. Eight would have to do, and I'd be lucky if I managed that.

The easiest part was deciding on a theme. My collection would tell the story of a girl who came to the city for a better life. The first dresses would be clean, asymmetrical factory shifts that would slowly transition into fantastical gowns, fit for the noblest woman in the city.

I closed my eyes, letting a fog of watercolors wash over me, holding my pencil over my sketchbook. Slowly, the fog turned into wispy forms, purply shadows of shadows. I pressed the pencil to the paper, and the shadows turned to shapes and the shapes to styles, streaming out of me. A hooded tunic over a long shift. A two-piece dress cut from plain cotton. A structured nude overcoat with a sheer slip underneath.

I stopped with the three, staring down at them. I loved them. But from a practical standpoint, they were difficult. It would take lots of time and effort to make even one. And I wasn't about to simplify them, not when I needed them to prove my skills and vision. There was no way I could do everything I needed on my own in the three weeks before the exhibition. And if this collection didn't astound the press, I wouldn't stand a chance at starting a new fashion house.

The unexpected desire to ask Kitty for her help came over me. I quickly banished it. There was no way I could trust her, even if I wanted to. We'd seen each other frequently these past two days, but we hadn't spoken since I'd discovered her letter.

Sophie, though, might just have everything I needed, including quickness. In addition to her skills and creativity, she never ran up against the clock with the challenges. With her at my side, I'd be unstoppable. I looked over to her always-changing side of the room. Her wardrobe door sat open, her black dresses hanging partway out of it. The burgundy dresses Madame Jolène wanted her to wear were pushed to the back, as though Sophie couldn't stand the sight of them.

When my mother was considering hiring a new vendor, she'd make them a pie and have them over so she could "look them in the eye and get a real feel for them."

I pushed my stool back from the vanity. Before our falling-out, Kitty had given me a velvet box of white chocolates and a small bottle of wine from the hamper her parents sent. I grabbed them. Now I just had to find Sophie.

She probably wasn't in the dining room. Maybe the sewing room or her fitting room. I was in my nightgown, and I put on the filmy blush retiring robe that hung on a hook by my bed each night. I would start with the fitting rooms.

Throughout the day, the stairway down to the fitting rooms was constantly filled with the contestants, the design board, Francesco, and Madame Jolène's servants, tramping up and down in a ceaseless march. But at night, it was completely empty and unlit. White moonlight filtered in through the windows high above my head, but the slender shafts didn't quite penetrate the murky darkness. The only sounds were the soft padding of my feet, muffled by the long Turkish runners covering the stairs and the low swish of my nightgown.

The doors to the hallway swung open on their well-oiled hinges. Peering down the hall, I glimpsed a sliver of light shining beneath the curtain to Sophie's room and heard the familiar whir of a sewing machine. No one else had a sewing machine in their room. She must have specially requested it.

I walked over to it and knocked on the doorframe before slipping inside. I had never been in her fitting room before.

Sophie sat on an upholstered bench running along the far wall. She was wearing a thin black satin romper with a sheer champagne robe tied over it. Half her hair was wrapped up into a knot on the very top of her head while the rest lay over her shoulders. White silk spilled across her lap. She was working on her wedding gown.

"Emmaline?"

"I . . ." I moved to stand in the center of the fitting room so we weren't so far apart. This room was clearly her domain, and I was an intruder. "Hello."

I tried to focus on her, but the surrounding details drew me in. Surreptitiously, I glanced around at the designer's dream-world that Sophie had created. Swatches of cloth arranged by color created a perfect rainbow better than anything seen in nature. It was hard to tell in the dim light, but it seemed that the swatches were also arranged by texture: thicker matte fabrics to the right, thinner ones on the left. I had never even considered such an arrangement.

Sketches covered the wall behind Sophie. Not just of gowns, but of the female form, with notes down the sides. One had a provocatively tight dress with a gigantic, sheer ball-gown skirt layered on top. On another: a high neck and long sleeves with an open back. The fabric was completely sheer, revealing the body beneath.

"What are you doing here?" Sophie placed the white silk down on the bench and glided to her feet with catlike grace.

"I . . . can we sit?"

Her heart-shaped chin dipped in a nod. I moved toward the bench and sat down on it, her eyes following me. Now I was sitting and she was standing. I'd thought she was going to sit down as well, but she remained as she was, hands in the pockets of her robe. Cool detachment emanated from her as strongly as her witch hazel–violet scent.

"Is this what you do down here all night?" I asked, futilely trying to start a lighthearted conversation.

She took one step closer until she was looking down her nose at me, ignoring my question. "What is it you want?"

"Oh, right. Sorry." Her presence made me fumble for the right thing to say. Her eyes, twin pools of darkness, stared at me. All I could see in them was the reflection of the candlelight and my own outline. "I—well, we are roommates, after all, and I thought we should get to know each other a little better." I held out the bottle of wine in one hand and the box of chocolates in the other. "Kitty gave me these. Would you like to share them?"

Sophie's gaze flicked from my face to the wine and chocolates and then back to my face again. I smiled weakly, feeling dumber than I had in all my life.

"Very well." She crossed her arms. "Did you bring a corkscrew?"

"A what?"

"A corkscrew. To open the wine."

"I . . . no . . . want some chocolates?" I set the bottle down and opened the lid of the box. The rich smell rose into the air. White chocolates in the shapes of mermaids and seashells lay on turquoise tissue paper. I held the box out to her and she stared down at its contents for a long moment before taking a mermaid, as though the decision was of the utmost importance.

"Are you feeling better?" she asked, delicately holding the chocolate between her pointer finger and thumb.

"Feeling better?"

"Yes. Don't you have a cold?"

My lie from earlier. I'd completely forgotten.

"Oh, yes, much better," I said, but I spoke too quickly, too nervously.

"You don't look very sick." She bit into the mermaid's tail, never once letting her gaze stray from me. Bloodlike raspberry filling oozed out of it. "Did you go somewhere today?"

"Go somewhere?" I tried to laugh. "No. Where on earth would I go?"

"I don't know," she replied. "But I noticed my cloak was missing from my wardrobe when I went to our chamber at break. And you were missing as well. Perhaps with my cloak?"

"I . . ." I started talking before I had a lie ready, my stomach twisting into so many knots I thought I might throw up.

"It's fine." Sophie held up a hand. "I don't really care where you went or why." She smiled smugly and I stared up at her, confused. Did she just want me to know she could tell I was lying?

This whole idea was a mistake. I would have to figure out how to make the collection on my own or with someone else, someone less calculating. I stood up, quickly replacing the lid on the chocolate box.

"What do you want, Emmaline?" Sophie asked, still standing in front of me. She held up the mermaid, which she had nearly nibbled into oblivion. "You came down here for a reason, and it isn't just chocolates and wine. What is it?"

For a second, I considered pushing past her and retreating to our chamber. But even if I hid the truth from her now, how would I make a full collection when she lived in the same room? She was already suspicious and, somehow, always seemed to be a step ahead of me. If I showed her I trusted her and needed her, I could turn this disastrous roommate get-together into a business partnership.

"I want to make a gown for a blacklisted client." I was glad I was standing. Sophie was taller than me, but not so tall that I couldn't look her right in the eye. "And create a fashion collection."

"Oh?" Sophie sounded surprisingly unmoved, considering what I'd just said.

I squinted hard at her, trying to interpret her lack of reaction. "I want—well, need—your help to make the gown and the collection."

She popped the mermaid's head into her mouth, slowly chewing and swallowing before speaking again.

"Were the chocolates and wine some kind of bribe?" Her tone was mocking and she neatly wiped raspberry filling off her fingers.

"No. I just wanted to . . . be nice when I asked."

She didn't seem to pick up on that lie. I'd wanted to wait before asking her, to see if I could trust her.

"Good. I can hardly be bought for such cheap sundries. Who is the gown for?" Even though her face was impassive, there was a note of intrigue in her tone.

"It's for Duchess Cynthia Sandringham. I want her to wear it to the Parliament Exhibition."

"And why are you asking me to help?"

"I . . . well, you are talented and quick and think for yourself. Also, Tristan Grafton thought it was a good idea." It was awkward to mention him. But Sophie didn't even seem to register his name.

"And the collection?" She was all business.

"I—" There wasn't a way to undo things now. I pushed aside my worries about Tristan. "I want to debut it just after Cynthia attends the exhibition."

"Debut it? To whom?"

"The *Eagle* and some members of the *Avon-upon-Kynt Times* who are loyal to the younger Parliament members. I'll send invitations just a few days before . . . I was thinking you'd know who'd be best to invite."

"And then?" Her questions came out agilely.

"Then hopefully we can start our own fashion house somewhere here in the city. We'll have to get funding outside of any banks. It'll be hard, but the city is divided, and this is the perfect time to strike." My hands were slick with sweat as they grasped the chocolate box, their moisture catching in the velvet. She played with the ends of her hair and twisted a single strand around her finger. Other than that small motion, she might as well have been made of stone. "What do you think?"

"I will consider it." Abruptly, she turned away. "You should go now. Don't forget the wine."

"Wait—what do you need to consider?" I sputtered. I'd assumed yes and no were the only two answers. This nonreply sent my head spinning.

She bent down, picked up the bottle of wine by its neck, and held it out to me. Slowly, I took it from her, and she walked briskly over to the entrance to her fitting room, drawing back the curtain with a sweep of her arm.

"Sophie," I entreated, clutching at the wine bottle and chocolate box. "At least tell me what you think."

"I think it's late," she said. "I will let you know."

"When? Tomorrow?"

"Soon."

There was sharpness in her tone. She stood by the entrance, waiting for me to leave. When I got to the entryway, she followed close behind me, her toes nearly clipping the backs of my ankles with each step, shooing me out. I stopped and turned around to face her one last time.

She'd come to a stop right behind me, and I found myself closer to her than I'd ever been before. The scent of her perfume filled my head with its heavy scent, and I could see every one of her black lashes, and the almost translucent nature of her fair skin. Though many things are distasteful up close, Sophie was stunning. She didn't seem unnerved by my proximity. Her unfathomable black eyes remained evenly on mine, and she regarded me calmly.

"You won't tell Madame Jolène, will you?" I hated how pleading and small I sounded.

"Of course not." As she spoke, she angled her chin up and planted her hands on her hips.

When I was little, my mother had read me *Paradise Lost*. I'd been mesmerized by the passages about Satan. He sounded like the most beautiful creature in the world: proud, unrelenting, an angel of light. If I ever drew him as a girl, Sophie would be the only inspiration I'd need.

"Thank you," I murmured. "Please let me know soon. I'm meeting Cynthia at the gazebo outside the gala. Will you let me know before?"

She didn't respond. She simply stepped back into her dressing room, whisking the curtain shut behind her.

I didn't see Sophie again until the next morning at breakfast. The dining hall was one of my favorite rooms. Three chandeliers in the shapes of swans hung from the ceiling, their wings extended and their necks stretched downward. The ceiling was painted varying shades of blue, making it feel like we were underwater, watching the swans dive for fish.

Sophie sat at an angle across from me, in between Alice and Ky. I tried to catch her eye, but she didn't seem to notice me as she stirred milk into her tea and remarked on Alice's new ribbon bracelet.

I swallowed a bite of crunchy toast and it caught in my throat. Coughing, I picked up my own tea to wash it down. It dislodged the toast, but my throat was still tight. Probably because the tightness didn't have anything to do with the toast. It had been that way since last night.

I stared at Sophie, still trying to make eye contact, desperately trying to read her thoughts. If she didn't agree to help me, I'd have to drastically rework my collection—and that was the last thing I wanted to do. I wasn't worried she'd tell Madame Jolène. That wasn't like her.

But as I sat there, I realized with a streak of panic that there was someone else she might tell. Mr. Taylor.

It seemed as though she hated him. That she wanted to be free of him. But I couldn't be sure—so the thought hung over me, as heavy and present in the room of my mind as the swan chandeliers overhead.

"Emmaline?" I twisted around in my chair to see Francesco

standing behind me. "You have a gentleman caller."

"Me?" I blurted out.

"Yes, a Mr. Tristan Grafton. We typically don't allow these types of personal visits here but"—his eyes softened as he stared down at me—"I can hardly see the harm. You'll only have a few minutes before you need to dress for the botanical garden lunch. He's in the second-story parlor."

I tucked my hair back, trying to make sure there weren't any errant wisps. My heart lifted for the first time since talking to Sophie last night. I hadn't expected to see him again so soon. At least my gown was a dark shade of pink instead of the sickeningly pastel pink most of my dresses were. In fact, in some lights it could even pass for a soft purple.

"You look beautiful," Francesco said, noticing my actions as he led me out of the dining room and up the stairs. "No need to be nervous."

"Thank you," I murmured, my hands still fussing with my hair. We reached the second story, and Francesco gestured for me to keep going.

"Have fun." He grinned, jiggling his eyebrows up and down.

I opened the door and stepped inside. Tristan was standing by the window, his back to me. The sight of his messy blond hair made my heart jump. At the sound of the door opening, he turned around.

"What are you doing here?" I asked. Maybe he'd slept on my proposal and decided he was backing out. If he did, the entire plan would crumble before it even began.

"Good morning to you too," he replied. "Shall we sit?"

We met in the middle of the room, and he stepped aside, offering me that atrocious orange-and-pink settee I'd sat on last time we'd been in this room.

"Thank you, but I think I'll take the chair." I sat down on a wingback upholstered with a light-gray fabric. Tristan took the settee, and I laughed nervously at the sight of him balanced on its edge. "The colors complement you."

"Do they? I'll remember next time I'm buying a suit—I'll get one in orange and pink."

"Is everything all right?" I asked. I didn't mean to be rude but I couldn't wait any longer.

"I'm not sure." He didn't seem to mind my abrupt change of subject. "Last night, I finally finished going over the textile factory employee lists."

Textile factory workers. My mother. Amid everything else, I'd forgotten Tristan had taken on this task for me.

Almost involuntarily, I glanced over at the small clock sitting on one of the side tables. Nine thirty-five, it said. Back in Shy, my mother would be checking the taps and getting the beer glasses ready for the day. The stew, which she always set to simmer overnight, would be filling the whole pub with the rich notes of steamed rabbit. I saw myself there, too, pulling out silverware for the noontime customers and folding an endless number of napkins. But that wasn't right. Only she was there, alone.

Guilt rose in my gut.

"You did?"

"Yes. But it was very strange—there was no record of her.

There were plenty of Ediths, but there was no Edith Watkins anywhere."

I blinked at him. "How is that possible?"

"I don't know. The records seemed thorough, but perhaps she slipped through the cracks somehow?" Thoughtfully, he tapped his fingers on the side of the settee, his gaze distant. "Or perhaps she worked somewhere else?"

For as long as I could remember, my mother had always said she worked at a textile factory in the city. That was where she'd met my father. That was why she hated the city so much. Yet . . .

She did keep things from me. She'd never told me who my father was. Never told me about the letters from the bank.

"No, she said it was a textile factory."

"Could be so," Tristan said, shrugging. "What did she tell you about it? Did she say anything specific about where it was or what she did there?"

"Yes, she . . ." I trailed off, realizing I didn't have anything to finish the sentence with. I thought hard, willing myself to recall something, anything. She must have said something I could remember and hold on to. But nothing came to mind—it had never seemed odd before. I always just thought she didn't like thinking about the past.

"I wouldn't worry about it too much." He placed his hand on my knee. I held still, wanting his hand to stay there forever. "She could've very easily worked there and never been recorded."

"Yes, but what if she never worked there?"

Since arriving at the Fashion House, I hadn't heard a word from her. I'd written her letters and sent her money, but I might as well have sent them into a black void. I'd never expected silence from her.

"If she didn't, then I'm sure she had a reason not to tell you," he said gently, soothingly. "Everyone has a right to their secrets. Sometimes they are the only things we truly possess."

A memory came to me. My fifth birthday. I went down the stairs to find my mother had baked a cake for me. Of course, I'd been expecting a cake. She made one every year for me and, occasionally, for our best patrons. They were always the same: a brown cake dusted with powdered sugar and topped with berries. That year, though, was different.

That cake was covered in the frothiest white frosting I'd ever seen and sprinkled with crumbled candies.

"It's extravagant, I know," she said, sounding uncharacteristically embarrassed. "Your grandfather would roll over in his grave if he saw this. But five is a very important age."

"It's so beautiful," I gasped, my eyes nearly as round as the cake.

"Do you think so?" She came to put her arms around me and lift me up so I could see it better. "It's as pretty as anything you'd see in the city."

As pretty as anything you'd see in the city.

Before, I'd never given the comment a second thought. But now, it didn't make any sense. Now, I'd been to the Republic District where the factories were located. I couldn't imagine anyone having a decadently frosted cake there. In fact, the only confectionery shop was located well within the Quarter District.

"Did your father ever say anything about her time in the city?" Tristan asked. "Maybe she told him more than she told you."

"I—no," I stammered. "Actually, I never knew him. He passed away when I was young."

"Really? So did mine. Never knew the bloke or my mother." He spoke casually, unconcerned.

"That must've been difficult," I said. His hand was still on my knee, his touch so warm I could feel it through my skirts. "You were an orphan?"

"Raised in the children's home in the Republic District. But it wasn't so bad. You don't miss what you don't know."

"I suppose . . ." Almost without thinking, I placed my hand over his. A startled expression crossed his face and, for a moment, his bravado was gone and it was just him, staring at me.

"Emmaline?" Francesco opened the door. "Sorry, darling, but it's time to go."

We both withdrew our hands. I took a deep breath, reordering the bits of myself that'd gone soft and loose under his touch.

"Thank you for checking," I said as I stood up. It was hard to sound professional, but I had to—Francesco was watching. I doubted he minded (in fact, he seemed to enjoy all affairs, romantic or otherwise), but I didn't want word getting to Madame Jolène that I fancied a reporter. "I appreciate it."

"Take care of yourself. You have big things to focus on." He meant my new collection and Cynthia's dress, the things that mattered in the here and now. I nodded, but my mind wasn't on my plan. Instead, it was filled with elaborate cakes, my mother's eager eyes, and the sensation of Tristan's hand on my knee.

CHAPTER FOURTEEN

THE DAYS LEADING UP TO the gala were torture. I felt disassembled, scattered. In the mornings I was sent off to press events, and in the afternoons I struggled to work on my wedding gown in the sewing room with the other girls. All the while, I had a hundred imaginary conversations. Most of them were with Cynthia. I would beg her to let me design a dress for her, but no matter how I tried to rewrite it in my head, she said no. The rest were with my mother, only I couldn't finish those. In my mind, I would ask her, *Did you really come to the city? What happened? You didn't work at the factory as you said, did you?* and she would stand there, biting her nails, staring at me with no response.

"It seems like your wedding gown is coming along," Kitty said as I bit off some thread. I lowered the floss. Kitty's sewing table was next to mine, but ever since I'd discovered her letter, we hadn't said much more than good morning to each other. I assumed she didn't mind. She fit in well enough with the other girls, and they never questioned the sweetness that I now knew was fake. But her hesitant tone made me wonder if maybe, just maybe, she missed our friendship.

"I suppose so." As usual, I was far behind the other girls. Everyone else already had their gowns on mannequins. "It is what it is."

I sounded stiff, but I couldn't help it. I couldn't let her in, not like before. Her face fell, and she turned back to her sewing table. I thought she'd get right back to work, but she stared at her mannequin without seeming to see it.

Her gown, as always, was well constructed but too traditional. Now, though, I knew she was intentionally making it classic. Elegant ruffles ran up a fitted bodice on an A-line skirt. It wouldn't win her the challenge, that was for sure. Of course, she didn't want it to. Currently, Sophie was at the top of the rankings, followed by Ky and Cordelia. Alice was always solidly in the middle. I, of course, wasn't even considered a real competitor, but according to my scores, I was just behind Ky. If I hadn't scored so low in the first challenge, I'd be somewhere equal to or higher than her.

"Your seaming is impressive," I said. If she'd told me the truth, the compliment would be reassuring. "It shows masterful technique."

Kitty's face instantly brightened, and she smiled at me. It wasn't the too-sweet smile that she dispensed to everyone else. It was grateful. Real. I quickly looked away. We couldn't be friends—not with that letter tucked away in my vanity upstairs—and I needed to remember that.

At my words, Ky looked up from her mannequin. She'd reined in her usual style for this challenge, but I could still see it just behind the clean lines of her gown.

"What do you think about Kitty's gown, Ky?"

I addressed her without thinking. All I wanted to do was push away the guilt from ignoring Kitty's smile.

Ky didn't reply to me, but she said loudly, "Cordelia, I just don't understand. This is a challenge, but *some people* think they should be helping each other."

Cordelia nodded, holding some lace trim in her hands. Her wedding gown had the look of a men's suit on top but with a soft tulle skirt on the bottom.

"If you are both so confident in your work, why does it matter if we help each other a little?" I asked, grateful I could redirect my attention from Kitty to Ky.

"I've been told to be one way and look one way my whole life," Ky countered. "My father wants my style to fit in with Britannia Secunda. But it doesn't. Because I'm half Britannia Secundan and half Japanese, and I wouldn't change that ever. I've had to fight for every bit of my style—for who I am—and I'm not going to risk losing the competition because you think I should be *nice*."

Her tone was sharp, defensive. I fiddled with my thread. It was easy to think of Ky as petty and cutthroat, but perhaps she was that way because she needed to be. The longer I was in the competition, the more I realized that the other girls had carried as many struggles here as I had.

"I—" I cut myself off because a flash of black skirt in the doorway caught my eye. It was Sophie, passing by. She still hadn't given me an answer and, these past few days, she'd seemed more elusive than ever. I only caught glimpses of her as she disappeared around corners or into different rooms. The few times I caught her alone in our chamber, she said she needed more time. If she didn't want to help me, I would have to find someone else or simplify my collection.

And, since this collection would introduce me to the fashion world, there was no way I could do that.

The night of the gala arrived with a sky full of dark clouds. Its ominous nature was fitting, I mused, as I walked down the stairs to the lobby. The staircase stretched on, making me feel like I was moving in place instead of forward and down. My breath came in short bursts, despite the fact that I traversed those stairs several times a day at a brisk pace, heels and all.

I gripped my clutch. There were sketches inside: two from my collection and another two of gowns I'd drawn specifically for Cynthia. Since she hadn't been in the society pages for a long while, it was impossible to gauge her style. Hopefully, the four sketches would capture her imagination—and her confidence in me.

Sophie needed to give me an answer tonight, and I needed it to be a *yes*. Her skills, her connections, and her understanding of the city were essential parts of my plan.

When we reached the lobby, I searched up and down the clusters of girls. Sophie was at the opposite end of the room, talking to Ky. It was easy to spot her. Even though the contestants wouldn't be formally introduced at the gala, Madame Jolène had assigned us our wardrobe, and Sophie's wine-colored mermaid gown contrasted sharply with the white marble floors. Black tulle spilled out from under the hem and coordinated with the black tulle wrapped over her neckline and around her shoulders.

We made eye contact, and I started to make my way over to her. This wasn't the most discreet place to ask if she was willing to join me in Fashion House blasphemy, but I wouldn't have any other opportunities.

"Ladies!"

I jerked to a stop as Francesco entered the lobby. He was dressed in a gold evening jacket with tails that dragged on the ground behind him. A glossy black headband sprouting long deer antlers rose through his coiffed hair, and his heeled shoes had cloven hooves attached to the fronts. With a wave of his hand, he got our attention.

"All of you shall be transported to the Charwell Palace, where you will mingle with guests until Madame Jolène's presentation." He walked forward, his gold tails gliding after him. "Now, where is Emmaline?"

The sound of my name made my heart spring up in my chest like a cornered jackrabbit. I stopped midstep, certain he'd uncovered my plan.

"There you are." Francesco smiled at me. "As Madame Jolène's country contestant, you will be introduced formally to the press right before her presentation. You won't have to say anything, but do make sure I can find you once we arrive."

Weakly, I nodded. A murmur wound its way around the lobby. The other girls, except for Sophie, stared at me, their faces darkening.

"She hardly even competes, but she gets all the press attention," Cordelia said to Ky. "For the next Fashion House Interview, remind me to come back as a country simpleton."

Ky gave a snort of laughter.

Oblivious to the reactions of the girls, Francesco opened the double doors leading to Madame Jolène's private staircase. And there she was, an entourage of attendants surrounding her and all five dogs prancing at her feet.

I gasped as she stepped into the foyer's light. She was like a figure from an Italian Renaissance painting. Hand-painted red, orange, and navy roses delicately outlined with an ivory thread spread out over her entire dress. A huge train spilled out from an intricate French bustle wrapped around the back of the skirt, and a giant black hair comb was attached around the side of her face and up into the air above her head.

The press wouldn't care about me at all. Not when she looked like *that*.

Irrationally, I wanted to applaud. Yes, she treated me unfairly, but she was so . . . so . . . *talented*. She was living art—fashion personified—and that's what I wanted to be someday.

Madame Jolène walked over to us, the elaborate layers of her gown swishing on the marble. I held my breath as she passed by me, somehow convinced she could sense my plans just from my face or the way I held my clutch. Her disinterested expression gave me a rush of relief. She had no clue. I was being paranoid, overreacting.

"You ladies look very nice," Madame Jolène abruptly announced. "You do justice to my gowns."

I took an unsteady breath and switched my incriminating clutch to my other hand. Easing my aching fingers, I ran them over the skirt of my dress to hide their shaking.

My gown had a rose-colored bodice that was fitted through the torso, hugging my hips. The bottom transitioned into tufted pieces of raw silk and flowers made from peau de soie and point d'esprit tulle. The effect was of a girl walking through a field of flowers. At the Fashion House, everyone saw me in terms of Shy's sprawling fields and untamed meadows, Madame Jolène most of all. She was spinning a story in her head about each of us, and I was cast as the farm girl. Madame Jolène didn't bother to acknowledge the truth: that I had grown up in a pub, not on a farm.

So the gown was beautiful. Of course, everything Madame Jolène made was beautiful. But I'd slowly come to realize that the things she made were stunning illusions. There was no truth behind them.

"I will give individual notes at the door. Each of you must embody a distinct look," Madame Jolène said.

We filed out one by one, pausing only for her final inspection. Sophie moved easily across the floor, unconcerned. For a second, I stared at her, bewildered. Did she even remember our conversation in her fitting room? My gown and clutch suddenly felt too heavy, as though they would pull me right through the floor to some terrible place beneath it.

"Try, Sophie," Madame Jolène said as Sophie stood in front of her, "to be less severe. You are always on the borderline of bitterness, and it's terribly unattractive. Mystery is your angle. Mystery."

Alice stepped up next, her blond hair shining against her lavender gown. Baby-blue crocheted lace covered the skirt in a delicate spiderweb pattern. Madame Jolène instructed her to be birdlike, wideeyed, and girlish. She told Ky, whose white gown was like folded origami, to be quirky and exotic. I listened, realizing I wasn't the only one Madame Jolène stereotyped. Cordelia, of course, was told to be strong and stern.

Kitty was next, and Madame Jolène ordered her to be friendly and sophisticated. That, at least, fit the image she'd cultivated. She was demure but elegant in a classic navy-blue dress with a long train and an ivory sash.

I tried to keep myself from cringing as Madame Jolène's eyes fastened onto mine. I could feel my cheeks turning hot and red, my guilt a second rouge.

"Emmaline," she said, "remember your posture."

Then she waved me on. Normally, I would've been stung by her dismissal. But now I hurried out into the courtyard, grateful to get away from her watchful eyes. I was safe. No one knew anything, at least for now.

Fat raindrops started to fall just as we arrived at Charwell Palace. The hacks unloaded their passengers beneath an awning that dipped from the weight of the rain. As I stepped onto the cobblestoned entryway, I wanted to reach out my hand and collect the drops. I hadn't felt rain since arriving at the Fashion House. Or wind. Or the warmth of the dwindling fall sunlight.

Every Sunday evening in Shy, I would walk to the bluffs overlooking the pond behind our pub. Rolling fields dotted with cottages would stretch out in front of me and, as the sun slipped down into the hills, it would suffuse everything in orangey-red light. No matter how many times I saw it, I was compelled to worshipfully raise my face to the last hot rays.

I let the cold wash over me. I couldn't be homesick. Not now, when I needed my wits about me.

"What on earth?" I heard Alice ask. She faced outward from the palace, squinting into the night. Then I heard it. Shouts and running footsteps. Pinpoints of light in the night emerged from the opposite end of the courtyard. Figures appeared out of the dark, carrying signs and lanterns. They formed a line just outside the awning.

"Come in, ladies!" a servant called to us, eyeing the protestors. The other girls ran inside, but I edged closer to see the gatherers. They wore old, torn clothes, and their hair hung in strings around their faces. Many of them held signs. It was hard to read them in the dark, but an occasional lantern splashed light over them, illuminating phrases written in harsh scrawl: FASHION FOR EVERYONE, NO MORE FUNDING FOR THE FASHION HOUSE, END THE CROWN'S RELA-TIONSHIP WITH JOLÈNE.

The coolness of the night vanished as my body broke out in a sweat. This was the protest Mr. Taylor had mentioned. Only there was nothing small about it.

"Emmaline!" Through the noise, I heard my name as a fig-ure detached from the group of protestors.

"Tristan?" He was holding a small pad of paper, but as I watched, it was knocked from his grasp.

"Lovely evening!" he shouted at me over the din. He didn't seem frightened, but his body was tense as he was jostled about. "You should probably get inside, Emmy."

"What about you?"

"Don't worry about me." He gave me a quick smile and then pointed to Charwell Palace. "Good luck tonight."

I nodded and bent down to pick up my skirts. I headed into the palace, hoping Tristan's luck would get me through the night. When I stepped into the Charwell Palace's foyer, I couldn't see any of the other girls. Only a few servants milled about, and one of them, seeing my uncertainty, gestured at two double doors.

"The party is through there, miss."

I stepped through the doors, and immediately all thoughts of the protestors and my plan evaporated. I was in an entirely different world. A huge glass dome designed as a peacock's tail arched over our heads. Stained glass in jewel tones of green, purple, blue, and gold made up the intricate tailpieces. Candles hung on wires from the dome's underside, small pricks of light against the glass. Panels of mirrored mercury glass lined every single wall. On the far side of the ballroom, there was a stage framed in blush velvet curtains. Its painted backdrop featured the distinctive *FH* insignia encircled by roses, fluffy white sheep in lace dresses, and white cuttleworms in tiny hats.

Couples danced in the center of the room while others chatted along the walls. Musicians played stringed instruments, and servants circulated with trays of champagne flutes. Slowly, sounds of lively conversation started to build.

I made my way to the edge of the room, grasping my clutch. A maid offered me a glass of champagne, and I took it. I leaned against one of the mercury-glass panels. The bubbles stung my throat as I drank it down, grateful for its coolness.

Even though I wasn't moving, the ballroom seemed to spin around me. Maybe it was the dancing partygoers. The women's skirts blended with the men's tails until they were nothing but a colorful blur. Hints of early fall had crept into the latest styles: warmer colors, thicker fabrics, and fuller skirts, even though it was clear that none of these people went outside. Their skin was as white and thin as pages from a Bible.

I drained my glass, the last few drops rolling over my tongue. My head was hot and pulsing, and I raised the chilled champagne flute and pressed it to my forehead. Would Cynthia even come? Across the ballroom, I saw the gazebo just outside a window that overlooked the gardens. It was empty, and the sight left me more panicky than the protestors had. Cynthia was the linchpin to my plan. Without a person of interest to wear one of my gowns, I'd have no way to garner any attention for my line. *My line.* I nearly laughed aloud.

That was a joke. I was a joke.

Sophie still hadn't given me an answer, and it seemed doubtful Cynthia would attend tonight. The throbbing in my head grew. I pushed myself away from the wall. The air was hot and stuffy, and light seemed to flash off every silver tray, mirror, and piece of crystal. I walked along the edge of the room until I reached a door. I didn't know where it led, but I stepped through it, needing to get *away* for a few moments.

I found myself in a long corridor and paused to let my eyes adjust. Floor-to-ceiling windows lined the hallway's right side while more mercury-glass mirrors lined the other. Rain pelted the glass, running down the panes in wavy lines. The sounds of the gala were muted, and drafty air cooled my skin. I breathed in and out, trying to gather my thoughts, trying to gather myself.

A door on the hall's far side was open, and long shadows—silhouettes—stained the walls. I heard someone speak and knew immediately who it was. The voice was as distinct as its owner. Walking over to the door, I peered inside to see Sophie and a dark-haired man standing in the center of the room. Neither of them seemed to notice me.

"It pains you, doesn't it?" the man asked. I could hear him clearly—Mr. Taylor. His shadow stretched up the wall and onto the ceiling. Sophie's shadow was much smaller, hovering close to her body, diminutive beside his.

"Doesn't it?" His voice dropped an octave, and he leaned forward, his shadow merging with hers. He was *tall*, much taller than Sophie. My skin was suddenly crawling, something stirring deep down, far under the surface.

"I don't know what you're talking about," Sophie said.

"You need me. No need to be coy about it." He brushed her cheek with his finger while his other hand grasped her arm, his fingers wrapping around her sleeve. "You're cursed, Sophie, just like your mother was. And I am, too, because I love you."

Mr. Taylor's hand constricted on her arm, tighter and tighter. Then, with a frustrated murmur, he released her with a shove.

Despite her high heels, Sophie kept her balance.

"Everything I do, Sophie, I do for you. Those protestors out there—I orchestrated them. They are just the beginning. Someday, you can have a fashion house of your own with the power of Parliament and the Crown behind you. After the elections, the Reformists Party will have the majority vote in parliament. Together, we will rule Avon-upon-Kynt as leaders—in fashion *and* politics."

My knees went weak, their strength obliterated. Sophie was in league with Mr. Taylor. She wasn't going to help me. In fact, she'd probably thought it ridiculous that I'd come to her. And now she knew about my plan. Feebly, I grabbed the doorjamb.

Sophie shut her eyes for a brief second, as though willing him to disappear, then reopened them. When she spoke, her voice wavered, but her eyes burned in the darkness.

"I am not yours to will." She lifted her chin, raising her face to his, her lips nearly brushing his chin. Mr. Taylor stared down at her, fixated by her sudden strength. He placed a hand on the skin of her chest, just above her bodice. His fingers extended upward until they closed around her neck. They didn't tighten, but they remained there.

"My love, you misunderstand. I do not 'will' you. *You* will *me.*"

Juxtaposed with the scene—with the way that he loomed over her, the way his hand rested on her chest, the way he stared down at her—his words rang empty.

"You don't understand." She placed her hand on top of his. Her hand spread out over his, her fingers lining up with his. "I don't need you."

"Why? Because you've had success at the Fashion House Interview? You know as well as I do that you don't belong there. You were made to be envied, to be followed—not to be one of Madame Jolène's mindless designers."

"I know. I know that."

"Then come home with me. We can leave right now, together."

"No."

No?

"No?" Mr. Taylor echoed my question. "You can't be happy there."

Sophie lifted her fingers from his and circled both hands around his wrist. She didn't try to pull his hand away, but she held it, as though she might at any moment.

"I'm not going to stay at the Fashion House."

"Then where will you go? What will you do?"

"I have a plan."

A plan. Did she mean with me? I listened, torn between wanting to hear her say that her plan was *my* plan and wanting to pull her away from Mr. Taylor.

"And what would that be?"

"The girl from the country. We are doing something that will change everything."

Surprised relief overcame me, restoring strength to my knees.

"The girl from the . . ." He didn't finish the sentence. His fingers started constricting around her long, thin neck. She tried to pull him off, but he was strong, much stronger than she. Sophie didn't make a sound as his grip became tighter and tighter.

"*Stop!*" I ran into the room. He wheeled around in surprise. Jigsaw shadows hollowed out his eyes and the sides of his nose. I threw my whole body against his, dropping my clutch in the process. Caught off guard, he took a few steps, but he didn't let go, dragging Sophie along. Her eyes started to flutter shut.

"Let go!" I grabbed onto his arm.

An inarticulate sound rose from his throat—something between a growl and laugh—and he released Sophie to face me. I tried to turn away, but a crawling fear immobilized me. It spread through my limbs like dye through muslin. But when he looked at me, he only made the same half-laughing sound.

"Little country girl," he said. "I should've known from the beginning you'd try to use Sophie to your advantage."

I couldn't speak. I stood between him and Sophie, desperately looking around for a fireplace poker or vase—anything that could serve as a weapon. But he didn't seem interested in attacking me.

"You aspire to too much, girl," he said. He almost sounded calm, conversational. "There are consequences for those who cross me."

With that, he turned, heading for the door.

Sophie folded to her knees, her crimson gown spreading out around her. Her hair had been shaken loose, and it fell around her shoulders, tumbling down her back.

"Are you all right? Should we get help?"

Without speaking, she shook her head.

"Are you sure?"

"He's gone." She choked and started coughing. She pulled

away from me as the hacking sounds racked her body. Impulsively, I took her hand and then released it, startled. It was freezing cold, as chilled as the body of a corpse.

When her coughs slowed and became smaller hiccups, I asked, "What was that, Sophie? Who is he to you?"

"He's my benefactor." She straightened up and wiped her eyes. Even though her shoulders shook a little, she started adjusting her dress and hair. Bit by bit, she put herself back together.

"Your benefactor?"

"When my parents died, their will appointed him as my guardian until I come of age. I lived with him until I got into the Fashion House."

"He seems . . . volatile." *To put it lightly.*

"Yes." She rose gracefully to her feet, brushing off her skirts. "Now, don't we need to meet Cynthia in the gazebo?"

I didn't know what to say. Moments ago she'd been choked by a man three times her size. Now she was talking as though nothing had happened.

"Do calm down, Emmaline." She let out a small laugh, even though coughs still shook her frame and her hands trembled. She must have read the uncertainty in my face. "Don't worry about Alexander. I know my way around him."

This sounded preposterous when I looked at the five finger marks on her white neck. In the dark light of the room, they loomed shadowy on her skin.

"You're certain you don't need more time to rest?" I wavered, and then asked, "You're certain Mr. Taylor won't complicate things? He's a member of Parliament!"

"As I said, I know my way around him." She pulled a small bottle of perfume out of her pocket and sprayed it onto herself. It sparkled on her chest, beading like dew or raindrops. Reaching down to her hem, she tore a narrow, long piece of tulle from its bottom. She wrapped it around her neck, tying it off in a dramatic bow that covered Mr. Taylor's marks and lay across the thin bones of her chest.

"Very well," I said, reaching for my clutch. It seemed like we were preparing for a leisurely stroll, as though the terrifying events from just moments before hadn't happened.

But even as we walked back to the hallway, the terror from earlier came with me, wove through me like thread being pulled through satin. No matter what I did, I couldn't get free of it.

CHAPTER FIFTEEN

I WAS GRATEFUL WHEN WE stepped back into the ballroom. The jarring sounds and bright lights of the gala filled my senses, overcoming my ability to think.

When I'd moved around the ballroom earlier, I'd stayed to its sides, but Sophie crossed right through its center, stepping around the couples dancing and the people gathered in conversation. I followed in her wake. Eyes trailed her as she moved. Her gait fell into a saunter, as though she knew she commanded the room, even though she kept her head erect and her gaze fixed straight ahead.

When we reached the two French doors that led out to the patio, I rubbed the foggy glass, clearing a patch to see out. I assumed the gazebo would be empty. Even without the protestors, it was doubtful that Cynthia would come. But as I squinted at the outline of the gazebo, I saw something move. Someone was there. My heart jumped excitedly at the sight and I smiled. It was nice to finally feel something other than stress or fear or guilt.

I stepped outside, Sophie close behind me. The atrium's

beautiful, controlled environment vanished as cold air and wind pulled at my hair and skirts, tugging them into disarray. Raindrops stung my cheeks, and goose bumps raced up and down my arms and legs.

Bending down, I gathered my skirts high above my ankles with one hand. There were so many layers to my gown that it took me a few tries to grab all of it. With the other hand, I shielded my hair with my clutch. Mud sucked away at my heels, pulling me down.

Glancing back over my shoulder, I saw the windows of Charwell Palace lit with warm light, silhouetting the people dancing inside. That was where I should be. Not out in the rain, trying to find a client I didn't know and wasn't supposed to be meeting in the first place.

That was the problem with my scheme. I couldn't tell if I was getting closer to or farther from my dreams.

"Hurry up," Sophie called into my ear, urging me on to the gazebo. We stepped inside and a sharp odor assaulted my nose. Alcohol. The scent mixed with sweetness, as though someone had tried to cover the smell by dousing themselves in jasmine perfume. My eyes watered.

"Who's there?" Swinging around, a woman listed toward me. She was done up in a hunter-green party dress with a luxurious fur-trimmed stole. Shades of green shimmered in the cloth, caught by the moonlight slipping through the rain clouds. Though the design was basic, the fabric and fur must have been exorbitantly expensive.

"Hello," she said in a childlike tone. "Are you the new

designer?" She took a tottering step forward and blinked at me with bright, round eyes. I'd never thought she would look so young.

"I am." I stepped aside so I was standing next to Sophie. "I mean, we both are designers for the new line."

"She's drunk." Sophie muttered under her breath. Cynthia was a duchess, but Sophie stared at her with annoyance. I understood the feeling. This woman was unstable, and we were about to trust her with our idea.

"You two? Designers? You're both babies." Her tone changed from giggly to suddenly sharp and aware. Perhaps she wasn't as drunk as I'd first thought. "The reporter told me this was an official line!"

"I appreciate you coming to meet with us tonight," I said, ignoring her protests. Light-headedness descended on me, and the gazebo started to swim, making me feel like I'd been the one nipping at whiskey, not Cynthia. Everything seemed like too much. Sophie and Mr. Taylor. Betraying Madame Jolène. I wasn't quite sure when or where it had happened, but my life was all undone ends, an unraveled mess.

"This is ridiculous," Cynthia said. "But then, I knew it would be. Why on earth would designers ask to meet me at a gala that I wasn't even invited to?"

She pressed two fingers against her forehead. Her hand was trembling, like Sophie's had been just a little while earlier. She fumbled her other hand within her brassiere, removing a small silver object. Unscrewing the top, she took a long drink from the flask, never once shuddering against its bite.

"Everyone thinks I'm a fool," she murmured, more to herself than to us. I glanced at Sophie. Her arms were crossed tightly across her chest, and her foot tapped impatiently against the ground.

"We aren't established yet, but we will be," I said. Treating her like a respected client was our best option. My mother always knew how to handle our difficult customers, and I had spent my whole life watching her. Hopefully, I could cut through Cynthia's drunkenness and help her focus. "The dress we make you will shape fashion in Avon-upon-Kynt."

"*You're* going to make me a dress?" Cynthia demanded. "How can *you* make any gown that could compare to Madame Jolène's gowns?"

I unsnapped my clutch, pulled out the sketches, and carefully unfolded them. Intentionally, I'd placed the sketches for her possible gowns on top. They weren't as couture or avant-garde as the designs for the collection. I'd put the more extravagant gowns last, so she'd see them after the more traditional pieces.

"Look at these. Keep in mind, they are only ideas. We can easily redo them with your preferences." I handed them to her, and she struggled to look at them in the darkness. I kept talking as she studied them. Some women couldn't envision a sketch as an actual gown—I wouldn't let that be the case with Cynthia. "Imagine being at the Parliament Exhibition in that first dress you're looking at," I said. "It's a dusty purple. The skirt is covered in lines of dark crystals. Those points you see dotting the skirt are crystals, and there, there is exposed boning in the bodice." I trailed off, and we stood in silence as the rain battered down around us. Despite the situation, I wanted to smile. I loved designing, even if it was just spinning images into the air in lieu of thread and fabric. "You'll feel different in it. Transformed. It's one of those dresses that makes you stand taller and stronger, even if you don't know why. It'll show everyone you aren't afraid to make your own choices."

"That sounds nice enough, but it isn't designed by Madame Jolène," Cynthia said, almost sulkily, lowering the sketches. "The whole point is the label. I don't care about anything else."

"We don't have the label, but you will be part of something new," I said. "You will have something that isn't defined yet. You've been wearing copies of fashions made by seamstresses. We will design you a dress no one has ever seen or worn before. Don't you want to change the way people see you?"

"You think it's that easy? That I can just wear a dress and everything will be undone?" Anger filled her eyes and flushed her face, making her look almost feverish.

Sophie cut in. "It was a dress that put you where you are today." The vulnerability that had shrouded her like a black cloud was gone, replaced by poise and, as always, a touch of impatience. "A dress can return you to where you once were."

"I can assure you that we will make you a gown of equal, if not superior, caliber to Madame Jolène's pieces," I said. "And, since our label is unknown, it will give you intrigue. It will have the magnificence of a couture dress, yet it will mystify. Times are changing. Didn't you see the protestors outside the gala?"

Ever so hesitantly, Cynthia nodded, and a surge of victory ran through me. It wasn't much, but she hadn't left in a huff.

Yet.

"This is interesting," Cynthia held the stack of sketches out to me. "I need to think about it."

Think about it? There was no time for her to think about it. If we wanted to make her gown and the entire collection in time for the exhibition, we needed to start *now*. I nearly said as much but stopped, biting the inside of my lip. The tinny taste of blood welled onto my tongue.

"What do you have to lose?" I asked. I didn't take the sketches back, letting Cynthia remain holding them out to me—a reversal of when I'd held my sketch out to Madame Jolène and she hadn't taken it. "As far as I see it, no one else is offering to design you a gown."

In Avon-upon-Kynt, there was no greater disgrace. Cynthia knew it. She dropped her arm, still holding the sketches, her owlish eyes blinking furiously at me.

"I have plenty to lose," she replied. "I could end up in a terrible dress and then people will be talking about me again—but for the wrong reasons. It'll be like the queen's jubilee all over again."

Taking a decisive step toward me, she shoved the sketches into my hands. I grappled at them, two of them drifting to the ground. Sophie made one of her annoyed, soft sounds under her breath, one that seemed to indicate I wasn't handling the situation very well. Frustration flickered through me—frustration at them both. As I bent down to pick them up, I closed my eyes for a moment. I needed to change tactics. I couldn't act like Madame Jolène right now, because I wasn't Madame Jolène.

Cynthia was right. I didn't have a real line behind my name, not yet.

"You have good taste, Cynthia," I said, straightening and trying to sound friendly. She adjusted her fur stole, a hint of pleasure in her eyes at my compliment. "If you see the gown and you don't like it, you don't have to wear it. But I promise you, that won't be the case."

"Your sketches are quite lovely—from what I could make out of them," Cynthia admitted.

"You should see them in good light," Sophie said. "And you should know that Madame Jolène recreated an entire gown from one of Emmaline's sketches."

"She did?" Cynthia sounded awed, as though that fact alone was much more impressive than the gown I'd described, or the sketches I'd shown her.

"Yes, she did," Sophie said. "Lady Townsley wore it to the Ladies' Annual Charity Ball, and there was a whole spread of it in the society pages."

Despite the tenseness of the moment, I was distracted. I'd avoided the latest society pages—I hadn't wanted to see my dress sketched out under the Fashion House label. Once a gown was featured in the society pages, there really was no way to remake it, and I hadn't wanted to face that reality. But now I knew who'd worn it, and I was glad I knew. Sophie might not realize it, but she'd given me something I would carry with me. I hadn't expected Sophie to care, but she'd remembered that the brocade was originally mine.

"A whole spread?" Cynthia sounded awed.

"A whole spread," Sophie repeated.

"Is that true?" Cynthia looked at me for confirmation. I nodded, swallowing down my bitterness, measuring it against the hope that it could convince her to trust us.

Cynthia fell silent and we waited. Then she said, "Is anything required from me?"

"We will need forty percent up front," I said, trying to maintain my calm. She was close to saying *yes*, so very close. "That will cover the costs of materials, and you can pay the rest upon receipt of the gown."

"Payment," Cynthia repeated. Money matters were always handled delicately at the Fashion House. The customers had private bills, and two secretaries handled the financial aspect of orders. No one discussed money during appointments, because it was much too uncouth. Cynthia's face pinched with distaste but she said simply, "Very well. Contact my house manager regarding the money. She will see to the details."

"Thank you. Thank you very much," I said. Cynthia extended her arm toward me.

Our first client. I didn't realize it until her fingers closed around mine and we shook. For the briefest second, pure, untainted excitement ran through me. There was a very long way to go, and many things could go wrong, but for the time being, I let myself feel nothing but bliss.

We left Cynthia in the gazebo and returned to the gala, making it inside just as the party reached fever pitch. The air was thick with the sweet scent of champagne as guests danced in uneven circles, their arms raised. Bursts of laughter and loud conversations filled the room, competing with the music. The cacophonous roar thundered through me, but it didn't disorient me like before. Instead, it felt like everyone was celebrating alongside us.

I snatched two flutes of champagne off a maid's tray and handed one to Sophie. Wordlessly, we clinked glasses. I drank, letting the woozy powers of the champagne overcome my senses. A servant appeared to hand us two more and take away our emptied flutes.

"Emmaline!" Francesco came rushing toward us. "Where have you been? You need to get backstage. The introductions are about to begin."

"I'm coming." My tongue was numbed by the champagne and I giggled. With a *tsk*, Francesco took the glass out of my grasp. I thought he was going to set it aside, but instead, he drained the very last few sips. Then he took my hand and led me to the opposite end of the room, grumbling about Fashion House Interview contestants and their champagne consumption, even as he plucked yet another flute off a nearby tray and drank it.

The stage was much larger up close. Its curtains seemed to reach the ceiling, and the backdrop of the stage—the intricate, floral-festooned *FH* insignia set against a light-gold background—was about twelve feet tall. We rounded the side of it, and Francesco pointed to a small set of stairs.

"When you hear your name, walk up those stairs. I'll introduce you. Just smile and wave and then move to the back. Until then, make sure you're out of sight behind the stage."

"I understand." I glanced around, wondering if a maid with another tray of champagne glasses might be nearby. No such luck.

Francesco hurried away. I made my way to the back of the stage, stepping around the supports propping up the backdrop. Then I saw her. Madame Jolène, standing between two humongous beams. Awkwardly, I came to a stop.

She was on a small platform with gears attached to the sides, the sort that could lift a performer onto a stage for a grand entrance. All the fuzziness from the champagne evaporated. Madame Jolène was one of the few people who could sober one up with her presence alone.

Her huge skirt was laid out perfectly around her. In the dim backstage light, the embroidery stood out even more against the dark fabric, giving it a stark appearance. I'd never seen her alone before, without so much as a tiny dog at her feet. Her typical aura of haughtiness was gone, replaced by a quiet stillness. With her hands down at her sides and her eyes closed, she took a long, slow breath in through her parted lips and then exhaled.

I stepped back, hidden by one of the beams. Her quiet was mesmerizing, intoxicating. Her posture was all strength—her back perfectly straight, as always—but her face was completely relaxed, open. I stared, unable to look away.

"Ladies and gentlemen!" Startled, I realized Francesco was on the stage. I couldn't see him, but his theatrical timbre rang out across the atrium. Immediately, the musicians stopped playing, and I heard the rustle of gowns and footsteps as everyone drew toward the stage en masse. "It's been quite the evening, but it's time to direct our attention to the one thing that draws us together: the Fashion House. In Britannia Secunda, we stand alone in the world. We are fed not by crops, but by beauty." I smiled a little. Francesco's speech was a tad exaggerated, but it captured what it meant to be from Britannia Secunda. "Our times are difficult, and I hope we remember what the Fashion House means to us all, whether we are rich or poor. So, with that in mind, it is my pleasure to introduce Emmaline Watkins, our contestant from the country. She represents the Fashion House's commitment to broadening its horizons and working with the Reformists Party."

I picked up my skirts and carefully stepped onto the stairs. My heels wobbled on the thin wooden steps. There was no handrail, and I focused hard, breathing a sigh of relief when I got to the top in one piece. Francesco gestured to me, and I moved out onto the platform. A sea of people stretched out in front of me. My limbs moved slowly, jerkily, like a poorly made marionette, and my mouth was as parched as Shy during the height of summertime. Where was I supposed to look? Hundreds of people stared at me and I tried not to shift awkwardly. Most of the faces were curious, peering at me as though I were a strange specimen. And to them, the wealthiest people in our country, I most likely was. A few of them smiled, but not in a kind or gracious way. Their lips twisted maliciously, and they whispered to each other behind gloved hands and fans, laughing at the girl from the country up on the Fashion House stage.

"I've personally enjoyed having Emmaline among our new

season's contestants." Francesco smiled warmly at me, and I weakly tried to smile back. I'd been so consumed with my scheme that I hadn't thought much about whether it was the right or wrong thing to do. Francesco had always been kind to me—and turning against Madame Jolène meant turning against him as well.

Francesco motioned for me to step aside, his face flushed with excitement.

"And now, the guest of honor, Madame Jolène Marchion!"

The whole stage vibrated, and the sounds of gears turning and grinding rose from underneath the stage. A small door opened in the floor, and Madame Jolène was lifted through it. Gasps erupted around the room and blended into a singular sound of awe. With effortless ease, she took one step forward to stand in the center of the stage.

"It is such a pleasure to see each of you here," Madame Jolène said, facing the guests. Normally her face was frozen, but tonight, she was *alive*, her eyes sparkling and her cheeks glowing with a rosiness I had never seen before. All the quiet from before was channeled into a magnetic energy. She raised her hands to the crowd, perhaps in offering or entreaty. Everyone fell silent, waiting beneath her outstretched arms. For the first time, I noticed a line of embroidery under the sleeve of each arm, running all the way to the cuffed wrists. It had been hidden before, a detail that only revealed itself with movement.

"I thank you for indulging my artistic fancies," Madame Jolène said, "and for journeying with me. I find, to my great surprise, that each collection is a maze with one path. I am always lost until I end up in the same place."

A shiver ran over my arms and legs. Not the terrifying shiver that Mr. Taylor elicited. This was completely different. This was warm and delicious. I wanted it to last forever.

Madame Jolène dropped her hands to her sides and lowered her voice to a near whisper. Everyone strained to hear.

"I am excited to announce the theme for my fall collection."

The crowd surged forward in a soundless charge, desperate to hear but trying to stay quiet. I was swept away into their eagerness, listening with every bit of my attention, the magic of the moment trilling through me.

"It is"—Madame Jolène paused, her hands clasped in front of her—"*Papillion Nue.*"

Applause erupted and echoed off the atrium's glass dome. The audience glanced at each other, nodding in approval and exclaiming in eagerness.

I knew from Madame Jolène's lyrical pronunciation that *papillion nue* was French.

"Francesco!" I shouted over the noise. He was clapping with all his might and didn't hear me. "Francesco! What does *papillion nue* mean?"

"Naked butterfly," he said over the noise.

I rested back onto my heels. *Naked butterfly.* I imagined gowns embroidered with the delicate membranes of a butterfly's wings and fabrics in both the bold and muted colors of monarchs and chrysalises. I imagined a skirt disintegrating into small butterflies and the raw, skeletal outline of a butterfly on a bodice. The name *papillion nue* itself provided the story. It was easy to fill it in with images.

As everyone cheered, Madame Jolène stood on the stage, her hands still raised and her chest dramatically rising and falling. I remembered her eyeglasses, the ones shaped like a butterfly's wings. She must have been thinking about the collection for the whole past year.

"*Papillion Nue,*" Madame Jolène repeated. Instantly, the crowd quieted, only this time it was an agitated, ripe silence, as though they might break into applause at any moment. "A butterfly is often a symbol of spring. However, I want to explore the vulnerable, weaker side of these creatures. So, I have incorporated the element of nakedness and put the butterflies' context in fall."

"Inspirational," Francesco said as he stepped forward. "I know I speak for us all when I say we cannot wait."

I kept clapping with everyone else, but suddenly the cold truth hit me. I wasn't part of this. I couldn't get excited about the collection or fantasize about helping to create it. This belonged to the other contestants—to Madame Jolène and the rest of Britannia Secunda. I was outside of it, and for once, it wasn't anyone else who was trying to keep me out.

I'd done that all on my own.

The Fashion House Interview competitors were the last to leave the gala. By the time the hacks came for us, the guests had left. We collapsed into the chairs and benches along the outskirts of the ballroom, watching as the servants put the room to rights again. There were remnants of the party everywhere—emptied

champagne flutes with lipstick marks set in the most surprising places, forgotten fans and dance cards strewn about, and
half-eaten appetizers scattered across silver trays and napkins.
I could almost recreate where the attendees had been and what
they had been doing.

My throat was sore and my hands stung from clapping. After
so many hours of wear, my dress had become an instrument of
pain. Its boning dug into my ribs, and I struggled to breathe
around its constriction. My head ached, but I didn't know if it
was from exhaustion or from the stress—and excitement—of
the evening.

"Ladies, your hacks are here," a servant called to us. We
slowly stood up, wincing from our too-tight dresses and too-
high heels, and made our way back to the main entry.

"Emmaline," someone called to me from a side room. I
turned, confused. Then I saw him.

"Tristan!"

He was standing in a small parlor right off the lobby. I hurried over to him, nearly tripping over my skirts. At the last
moment, I slowed and stopped a few feet away. I'd already seen
him outside, in the chaos of the protest, but I hadn't taken in
his appearance. His suit was obviously cheap yet classic, and his
hair was parted to the side, though some of the strands flopped
free onto his forehead.

"Were you here the whole time?" I asked, coming closer.
"I didn't see you at the gala."

"I spent most of the evening covering the protest. Then I
slipped in here so I could do a write-up on the new theme. I

arrived just in time to see you get presented."

"You saw me up on the stage?"

"Yes." He grasped my hands, pulling me farther into the parlor and, at the same time, nearer to him. Glancing around, he whispered, "Did you meet with Cynthia?"

"Yes," I whispered back. "It went well."

He nodded but kept holding my hands. We stood, facing each other, our hands bridging the space between us. I glanced from his face to our clasped fingers and then back to his face again. He quickly let go, mumbling, "Sorry."

"Oh!" I said at the same time. *It's fine*, I wanted to say. *I like holding your hands.* Nervously, I moved to tuck a strand of hair back from my face, but my hair, since it was so perfectly done, didn't have any loose pieces. I lowered my arm.

"I'm glad it went well," Tristan said, his voice clipped and formal. "I just—I wanted to make sure your plan was working."

He couldn't seem to keep his eyes on mine, and he shifted back and forth in front of me. I watched him, confused.

Suddenly, he let out a deep breath and said, "I'd like to see you. As your suitor."

As my suitor? My heart was suddenly a bubble racing to the top of a champagne glass, all light and air and lift.

"You would?"

I smiled, a huge, overly happy, too-big-for-my-mouth smile. The sound of the smile spilled into my voice and Tristan raised his head, his eyes flashing with hope.

"I would." He grinned too. "Do you—what do you think?"

"I'd love that." I heard myself answer him, and marveled at

how calm I sounded when, inside, my champagne-bubble heart was bursting into a thousand more champagne-bubble hearts. They swept me forward, to him. With a confidence I didn't know I possessed, I put my hands around his neck.

Though I was emboldened, he suddenly seemed shy. "I-I'm glad."

Slowly, almost cautiously, he placed both hands around my waist. There wasn't any music, but we swayed slightly, staring into each other's eyes. He leaned in, as though to kiss me, and then hesitated. I laced my fingers together behind his neck, closing the space between us even more.

There was another second of hesitation and we moved forward together. When he kissed me, it was nothing like Johnny Wells's kiss. This one was impetuous and free. I wanted to breathe it in like air or sunshine.

"The hacks are here!" someone called from the lobby. Though the shout was coming from right outside, it sounded miles away.

Tristan stepped back, releasing me except for the hand that interlaced my fingers with his.

"You need to get going." He sounded husky.

"I know," I said. Or thought I said. My words were almost gasps, exhales as gentle as his touch. "When will I see you again?"

"I'm not sure." His voice was still husky and slow. "It isn't like a tabloid journalist can hang about the Fashion House without official business. But I'll find a way to come see you, I promise."

He reached out his other hand and brushed my cheek with it. I leaned my face into his palm, closing my eyes for a moment. The giddy, golden sensation from the kiss expanded inside me.

"Let's go, ladies!" the same person called again. Without even realizing what I was doing, I leaned forward and kissed Tristan again. My body, it seemed, knew what I desired. "Ladies!"

"I'll come see you as soon as I can," he murmured into my ear.

I stepped away, grabbing up my skirts with one hand, but leaving the other still holding his. I held on for as long as I could, our hands stretching out between us before we had to let go.

"There." Tilda undid the last button on my gown with a crochet hook. Finally, it was *off*. I stepped out of my gown, instantly feeling a hundred pounds lighter. The dress was so stiff with boning and crinoline that it stood up on its own. Tilda helped me undo my corset and camisole. The corset and gown had left deep red marks around my stomach and ribs. By morning, they would turn into bruises.

"My back is so sore. You'd think I scrubbed an entire kitchen floor," I said, slipping into my thin silk robe. I kicked off my heels. They were higher than the ones I usually wore. The soles of my feet were blistered and my toes ached. I flexed them, trying to undo the damage.

"You've scrubbed a kitchen floor?" Tilda scoffed.

"I have. What do you think I did back home in Shy?" I sat down at my vanity and started to pull hairpins from my locks, leaving the dress upright in the middle of the room.

"What . . ." Tilda hesitated. "What was it like tonight? At the gala?"

Her question took me off guard. The gala was like a fever dream. The protest, Mr. Taylor and Sophie, Cynthia. Walking in the rain. Kissing Tristan. Butterflies. I was happy it was over—but some part of me knew it had been, in many ways, the most memorable night of my life.

"It was magical." I picked up a washcloth, dipped it into the basin of water on my vanity, and wiped my face. The face paint I'd been forced into stained the cloth. I gave my cheek a firm swipe and my old face emerged. It was less impressive without the paint, but I liked seeing myself again.

Sophie entered the chamber. Her hair swayed freely down her back. Her dark eye paint was smudged, as though she had rubbed it, but it only served to make her more mysterious. She was wearing an evening robe, and it flared open to reveal a black corset edged with crystals and embroidery. Sheer panels showed hints of the milky skin around her stomach, and it cinched tightly around her waist with black laces up the sides. A lover was meant to see that kind of corset. Aside from the finger marks still marring her neck, she looked perfect.

She made her way over to our chaise longue, kicking off her heels and sending them catapulting across the room.

"You're dismissed," she said to Tilda, without bothering to look at her. I winced. No matter how often I heard it, I couldn't get used to the haughty voice everyone used with the maids, much less use it myself. I tried to catch Tilda's eye, but she quickly left. It was just as well. There was much Sophie and I had to discuss.

"Well, there's lots to do," I said. "We need to get the money from Cynthia."

Sophie didn't respond, her fingers searching through her tousled hair, looking for lost hairpins. "Do you have a bank account?"

I certainly didn't. But a girl of pedigree, a girl like Sophie, would.

"I do." Sophie extracted a black hairpin from her hair and flicked it onto the marble. "Alexander used to put funds into it, but he hasn't since I left his manor."

"The telegraph office is just up the street," I said. "I'll say I'm sending my mother a wire and I'll message Cynthia's house manager to transfer the forty percent there. It'll be a lot of money. We can buy the finest fabrics, threads, and beads to create her piece."

Thoughts of sumptuous silks filled my head. My fingers thrummed with excitement as I imagined touching them and crafting them together to create something wondrous.

"I don't think that's a good idea." Sophie abandoned her search for hairpins and lay down on the chaise longue, stretching. With a soft sigh, she arched her back and pointed her toes. "We should use it to buy all the materials for our collection. Otherwise, how will we afford them?"

"But Cynthia thinks the money is going toward her gown." I chewed on my lower lip. "I suppose we could buy a midrange silk and just a few crystals."

"We should supplement them by scrounging the beads that

fall off the Fashion House gowns in the fitting rooms. Those always get thrown away, so no one will notice."

"Isn't that stealing?"

Sophie grimaced with annoyance and tapped her fingers on the chaise's one-sided armrest. "Who cares? They're going to get thrown out anyway. And we won't have any other way to fund the collection if we don't stretch the money to buy everything we need."

I didn't let myself consider the consequences. Stealing beads was the least of my crimes. I rubbed my forehead, the champagne from the night combining with my exhaustion and rising to my head. "We also need to start thinking about our collection. We'll each need to design at least four looks, and I'll create the pattern for Cynthia. Her client card should still be in the filing cabinet with the rest. I'll have the pattern done by Tuesday. How about we meet up in your fitting room?"

There was much to do. I tried not to think about how we would manage it, all the while sewing our weddings gowns for the challenge. No matter what, we needed to appear to devote plenty of time to Lady Harrison's bridal dress.

"Sounds fine."

I glanced at my bed. Tilda had turned down the covers (sloppily, of course) and the thick layers of sheets and puffy blankets beckoned me. I wanted to slip into it and ease my aching body. Still, I pressed on. "There's also the invitations to the press and members of Parliament who are interesting in currying favor from the queen. Since I'm doing the pattern, would you do those?"

"Yes." As she lay on the chaise, she gathered up her thick

hair and wound it into a topknot. "Alexander has mentioned several of their names to me."

"I suppose he would know who to ask . . . but let's try to keep his involvement to a minimum." I didn't want his help—I didn't want to ever see him again. But we needed him. From Sophie's account to his contacts, he was involved in our new line. "We also need to book a venue for the show."

"I can do that when I mail the invites," Sophie said. "I know where the exhibition is going to be held, so I'll find a place nearby."

I nodded. Things were coming together. Maybe—just maybe—we really would pull this off.

CHAPTER SIXTEEN

THE NEXT DAY WAS SATURDAY, typically one of the Fashion House's busiest days. However, since the gala had been the night before, we were closed until Monday. We hadn't had a single day off since the Fashion House Interview began, so work on our wedding gowns was prohibited to give us time to rest.

"Madame Jolène has interviews with the *Avon-upon-Kynt Times* and several other smaller papers today," Francesco informed us that morning at breakfast. His voice was a raspy whisper, and he winced anytime the morning light hit his eyes. In one hand, he held a mug of fragrant peppermint tea. He kept drinking it, but it didn't seem to be reviving him. "You ladies may enjoy the day. Just do stay out of the way, and please, no loud sounds."

Ky and Alice, who were sitting across from me, immediately grinned at each other.

"Paddington Park?" Alice whispered to Ky. Ky nodded vigorously. The main street winding through the Quarter District ended at Paddington Park, where several of Avon-upon-Kynt's eligible bachelors often played croquet and polo.

While they would chase after titled gentlemen and enjoy a day outside the Fashion House, I'd finally have uninterrupted time to sketch and work on the collection.

I pushed my chair back and started to leave the dining room to head to my chamber. Then I stopped. Francesco was still in the dining room, trying to cure his hangover. Everyone else was finishing up breakfast. This was the perfect opportunity to take Cynthia's measurements card from the filing cabinet.

I hurried down the stairs to the fitting-room hallway. The card cabinet sat right outside it. Francesco organized and maintained the cards and pulled the ones we needed for our appointments every morning. Thankfully, he never threw any of them out. His motto was, "Once a Fashion House customer, always a Fashion House customer." Supposedly, even the cards of deceased clients were still in there, filed right alongside the current ones.

And, luckily for me, blacklisted clients as well.

The large black cabinet had gold letters affixed to each drawer. Approaching it slowly, I listened for any footsteps. Aside from the soft breakfast sounds trickling out of the dining room and down the stairs, everything was silent. Quickly, I found the *S* drawer and pulled it open, revealing rows and rows of thin cards inside. I ran my finger over them, my panic subsiding a little. Each one belonged to a woman who had come to the Fashion House for a custom gown. I could only imagine how many stories and lives were represented in these rows. Almost reverently, I ran my fingers over the different names on the cards. Most were traditional English names, but there were others in languages I didn't recognize, along with a variety of titles: *Her Imperial Highness, Maharani, Czarina.*

And there, right in the middle of the *S* drawer, was Cynthia's card. I pulled it out and read it.

CLIENT PROFILE: CYNTHIA SANDRINGHAM, DUCHESS OF
   KREMWALL ESTATES
FIRST APPOINTMENT NOTES
CLIENT'S NEEDS: HIGH-END COUTURE, READY-TO-WEAR, CUSTOM, TRAVELING AND SEASONAL WARDROBES
MEASUREMENTS:
BUST: 35.5"
WAIST: 25"
HIPS: 37"
HOLLOW TO HEM: 56.5"
BEST COLORS: WINTERS—EARTHY BROWNS, DEEP GREENS, BURGUNDIES

Big, black letters covered the bottom.

CLIENT TERMINATED

There was no additional explanation. If the duchess lived anywhere else, such a thing wouldn't matter as much. But she didn't. She lived in Avon-upon-Kynt, and the Fashion House was the axis upon which the nation spun. Slowly, I tucked the card into my pocket and closed the drawer.

"What are you doing?"

I whirled around. There, standing behind me holding a

broom in one hand and a rag in the other, was Tilda. My heart jumped straight up into my throat. I could feel the card in my pocket, its edges digging into my skin through my dress, proof of my theft. Had she seen me take it?

"I was going for a stroll." Even to myself I sounded strange—too panicked, scared even.

"Down here by the fitting rooms?" Her beady eyes darted from me to the cabinet. "Is that drawer open?" She let the broom fall to the ground and jabbed a finger at the cabinet. I turned around to see the *S* drawer standing open a fraction of an inch.

"Francesco must have left it open," I said.

"I've been cleaning down here all morning. I didn't see him."

"Well, I don't know anything about it."

"I've been working here for three years now," Tilda said, drawing herself up. "I know this isn't right. I'm going to tell Madame Jolène I found you down by the client cabinet. I'm sure she'll be able to tell if anything is missing." Triumphantly, she turned for the stairs.

"No!" I lunged forward and managed to grab her wrist just in time, jerking her to a stop.

"Ow!" she yelped. "Let go of me!"

"Stay still!" Desperately, I spun her around to face me. "If you tell Madame Jolène you found me down here, I'll tell her you've been stealing beads off the dressing room floors and selling them." I didn't even think of the lie ahead of time. It slipped right out of me, surprising me as much as her.

"What?" The triumph in her face wavered, and she stopped struggling. "She would never believe that!"

"I overheard Francesco talking to Madame Jolène." Another lie. "He said he's had his eye on you."

"He did? Why?"

"Yes. He said you've been slacking—in fact, he asked me if I thought it was true, and I told him about how you keep leaving my room in disarray. Do you really want to get fired from the Fashion House? I don't think anyone else would hire someone with that on their record."

She yanked her wrist out of my grip, but she didn't run away or try to leave. She rubbed it, staring at me with big eyes. Shaking free of my cold gaze, she bent down and picked up the broom.

"Fine. I won't say anything."

"Good."

I sounded harsh. Cruel. I forced my face to remain rigid, but my stomach hurt—not just from the close call, but also from the awful way I'd treated her. Never in my life had I spoken to another person that way. Never had I grabbed them and stared into their eyes and threatened their livelihood.

Tilda stomped away without looking back. Once she was gone, I raced up to my chambers, as though someone was chasing me. Safe in my room, I leaned against the door and slowly slid down to the ground so I was sitting on the marble, my limbs limp.

It's fine, I told myself over and over again. I closed my hand around the measurements card in my pocket. I would copy it and return it, just in case anyone did check.

I pushed myself up to my feet and walked over to my vanity.

Only one thing would calm me. I pulled out a piece of sketch paper and pencil.

I took a breath in, let it out, and then started sketching Cynthia's gown.

By the time Tuesday came around, we had the plan in motion. The money had been transferred successfully, and Sophie had bought the fabric for Cynthia's dress while she was out on a date with an approved gentleman caller.

"I think it's the exact color you asked for," Sophie said. We were in her fitting room. It was after hours, but we closed the curtain and only lit one candle. She pulled out a bolt of purple fabric from behind the bench and unfolded it so we could spread it out. It spilled across the floor, tumbling over itself, its lightness catching the air before settling onto the ground.

After the encounter with Tilda last Saturday, I'd been a bundle of nerves. Everything seemed so complicated, gnarled, like a sewing thread with hundreds of tiny knots in it, impossible to undo.

"It will be difficult to sew," Sophie said, seemingly more to herself than to me. I bent down and touched the silk. The fabric was like liquid: soft, sinuous, reflective.

"I know." It had been my idea to get the slinky silk. "Madame Jolène prefers more structured fabrics because they can make bigger, more exaggerated silhouettes. But I want to do the opposite."

I started to take the pieces for Cynthia's pattern out of my sewing box. I'd stashed them there earlier that morning so I could smuggle them down to Sophie's sewing room without arousing suspicion.

There were ten different pieces, each one fitting into the next. Slowly, I pieced them together to create the outline of the gown. The white shapes were stark and flat, and it was odd to know that even the most beautiful gowns started from these dull, lifeless scraps of paper.

Hopefully, Cynthia's measurements were still the same. We wouldn't be able to tell until she had her first fitting.

"It's quite complicated," Sophie said. I handed her the sketch of the dress so she could see it in its entirety.

"I know," I sighed. "But it's our first dress, so it has to be magnificent. Do you like it?"

Sophie examined the sketch and then knelt by the pattern. She glanced back and forth between the two and then gave a small nod. Coming from her, the nod might as well have been a glowing front-page article in the *Avon-upon-Kynt Times*.

Suddenly, we heard a door open far down the hall.

"Are you expecting someone?" Sophie whispered.

Muffled footsteps sounded on the carpeted floor, moving toward us.

"Of course not!"

"Don't just stand there!" she hissed. She yanked the silk hard, sending the pattern pieces flying like leaves in the wind, and tried to stuff the fabric into her sewing cabinet. I jumped to help her, but the material slid through my fingers, spilling out onto the floor as we tried to crumple it into the drawer. It seemed to grow in length and density with each passing moment.

Sophie slammed the drawer shut just as the curtain flew open and the whole room flooded with light. Madame Jolène stood in the entryway, the brass oil lamp she was holding throwing its glow over us. I ducked my head. I could feel every secret written across my face.

"Good evening," Madame Jolène said.

She was wearing a red evening robe embroidered with Japanese characters. Her blond hair draped loosely across her shoulders. I'd only seen her hair down one other time, when I'd met her in Evert. I'd been scared then, but I hadn't felt the worst of it as I did now, standing before her with my heart thundering away inside my chest.

"What are you two doing up so late?" Madame Jolène set the lamp down on a nearby cutting table. For a moment, I had the irrational fear that she could see through the sewing cabinet drawer to its incriminating contents.

"We were looking at patterns," Sophie said.

"How sweet." Madame Jolène surveyed the fitting room, her eyes finally coming to rest on me. "I trust you are well tonight, Emmaline?"

"Yes." I had to force the word out. My hands were clammy and cold, but sweat pricked my forehead.

"What patterns were you looking at?"

"We were—" I faltered, realizing with a streak of white-hot panic that I didn't know how to finish the sentence.

"Emmaline was showing me her pattern for Lady Harrison's wedding gown," Sophie interjected.

"Is that so?" Madame Jolène spoke to Sophie, but she kept

staring at me. "I find it refreshing that you girls aren't letting the competition discourage your collaboration. Now, let's see this pattern. Lay it out for me."

Obediently, we knelt and started assembling the pattern. The thin paper shapes all looked the same to me. As we fitted shapes together, my breath grew shorter until it was almost audible. There it was, our whole plan, slowly assembling beneath Madame Jolène's eyes, a blueprint of our guilt.

"It looks more like an evening gown than a wedding gown, no?" Madame Jolène asked.

"I wanted to try something different," I said weakly.

"Emmaline was telling me that she wants to experiment with the idea of formal gowns versus informal gowns," Sophie said.

"I see. Well, it's quite something." Madame Jolène expertly assessed the pattern. She nodded, as though seeing it come together and understanding its nuances. "I'm impressed at your ingenuity and willingness to make something so difficult, Emmaline. But you've made an error."

She pointed down at the pattern pieces. Two black, chunky bracelets slid out from under her sleeve and down her wrist. Of course she wore jewelry during her retiring hours.

"The dimensions are slightly off. Lady Harrison is only five feet and three inches tall, if I recall."

"It was on purpose. Emmaline intended the gown to be quite full with lots of crinoline," Sophie said smoothly. I had rarely seen the two interact for any long length of time. They were both, in their own ways, fascinating to watch, equals in their cunning and confidence.

"Yes, but even with lots of crinoline, this won't work. Listen well, both of you. You should always know your client's measurements," Madame Jolène said. "It's your responsibility as a designer. If you don't know your client's measurements—her proportions—you will hardly know how to dress her." She raised one finger to her lips, contemplating. "This will be much too long for Lady Harrison. Hand me that bottom piece. The hemline."

I shook inside and was certain my fingers were shaking as well. I snatched up the piece and handed it to her, rising to my feet.

"Yes, this is all wrong." She pulled a pair of heavy sewing shears out of her robe. "Here."

With one swift motion, she sliced the pattern piece in two. I barely contained a gasp of horror as the paper split apart, my hard work severed in one crisp tear.

"There." Madame Jolène held out the now-halved pattern segment. I took the pieces from her hands, hardly believing what had happened.

"And those shoulder sections, Emmaline, hand them here." She motioned to the pattern's bodice. Numbly, I picked up the two pieces and handed them to her. My hands lingered longer than necessary, trying somehow to stop her.

"Lady Harrison will look broad in these sleeves." Madame Jolène cut the piece apart, and her eyes flashed with enjoyment. Bile rose on my tongue. I'd spent hours measuring and cutting the pattern. The sound of crinkling paper filled the fitting room as she crushed the sections. "Choose a different neckline and then remake the sleeves around that. It's hardly fair for me to advise you, but since Lady Harrison is our actual client, it's essential that you represent the Fashion House well."

I nodded, staring at the hard work that had just been snipped and severed into oblivion. Maybe I could try to press out the wrinkles and reassemble the pattern . . . but it was so intricate that the slightest variations would ruin the dress and we couldn't risk it. I would have to remeasure and recut the severed pieces.

"Don't stay down here too late." Madame Jolène picked up the lamp by its handle. "I expect fresh faces for my clients tomorrow. No circles under the eyes, understood?"

"Yes," Sophie and I chorused.

But she wasn't done, not quite yet. Holding the lamp aloft, she looked around the fitting room once more, as though its light would reveal our secrets. The lamp threw bizarre shadows on her face, darkening the spots just below her cheekbones and under her chin.

"Remember, girls," she said, her voice raw and strong. "I know everything that goes on in this house."

With that, she left us with our severed pattern piece and torn-apart sleeves. We listened as her footsteps retreated and the door closed at the end of the hallway. I stared down at the crumpled balls of paper that had once been our pattern pieces.

"Do you think she knows?" I asked. I took a long, shaky breath, trying to get my heart back down into my chest.

"I don't think so. But she's obviously suspicious." Sophie ran her hand through her hair again, twisting the ends of the strands around her fingers. "At least she only ruined three pieces. It'll be all right."

I breathed in. "You're right." It was odd to see Sophie trying to reassure me. Nice, but odd.

"Maybe we shouldn't work down here."

"We don't have much of a choice," I said. "But you should bring in some dresses from your customers in case Madame Jolène stops in again. We can pretend to be working on them."

"All right."

I wiped cold sweat from my forehead. "We just have to be really careful."

Sophie nodded, for once looking appropriately grave. "We will be. Try not to think about the risks. It only makes it worse."

"That's for sure," I agreed. I walked over to her bench and slid down on it. "Starting a secret business is very . . . stressful."

For the hundredth time, I wished I could talk to my mother. She knew how to start a business and make it successful. Granted, hers wasn't a secret, but it must have been frightening to start up without any help.

I appreciated that more than ever before. Before she purchased it, my mother had taken me to look at the Moon on the Square. I'd run around the empty building, poking at the cobwebs in the corner and twirling in circles around the bar. I'd never thought about how Mother had felt that day, how she must have realized the risks of starting a business on her own. All I remembered was her making a list—a list of problems.

The sinks are leaking. Three barstools are too tipsy to use. The stove is broken but functional. Will probably need to be replaced in six months.

"Of course it's stressful." Sophie cut into my thoughts. Impatiently, she tossed her head, making her hair fall over her shoulder. "Secrets always are."

"I suppose so." It came so easily to Sophie. But it wasn't the same way with me. I'd never kept a secret like this before. I forced the thought away. "Let's make the most of the night. Have you done any sketches?"

"I did this one." Sophie pulled a sketch out from underneath the small cabinet in the corner of her room and handed it to me. She picked up the single candle on her table and held it up so it cast light onto the page. "I think it will go perfectly with the girl-coming-to-the-city theme."

Sophie's lines were thick and slashing, bordering on abstract, but precise enough to understand. Layers of rigid organza formed lines down a full mermaid skirt topped with a military-inspired jacket. The skirt had a long train, and the neckline plunged all the way down to the navel. Sophie had pinned small swatches of fabric to the corners of the sketch, and I ran my fingers over the nude organza and navy corduroy. Goose bumps ran up and down my arms, and I shivered, unsure if I was excited or alarmed.

"Can people wear such things here?" I'd never heard of a fashion show where so much skin was exposed. Sophie raised a shoulder in a half shrug.

"Maybe. Maybe not. But it's beautiful, and it goes with the

look. If we are going to stand out, we have to do things that the Fashion House has never done before."

"I love it." The intricacy of the skirt and exaggerated lines of the military jacket were perfect—my girl, the one who came to the city, would wear it as she found her footing and her style.

"I also did this one."

True to Sophie's look, the second design was also edgy. The gown was made from dark gray lace on a nude lining. The lace had a wide, detailed pattern so that it appeared to climb up the model's body. The shoulders morphed into points arching above the wearer's head like black lace wings, showcasing the intricate fabric. I closed my eyes, picturing the piece. It was beautiful, but it could be . . . even more unexpected.

"What if we made a huge skirt out of netting to go over it?" I asked, my mind brimming with possibilities. "We can use a delicate netting. There won't actually be an underlay. We'll just layer hundreds of pieces of netting on top of each other, and eventually it will become opaque." The design appeared fully formed in my mind, as though it had been there all along, waiting for me to discover it.

"Yes!" Sophie smile grew even bigger. "It's perfect!" She started to draw over the sketch, creating a skirt over the slim silhouette.

As she sketched, the line of—concentration? Annoyance? Displeasure?—disappeared from between her brows. Since it was always present, I'd come to think of it as a beauty mark or freckle, something one couldn't be rid of.

"What do you think about while you design?"

"I think about . . ." She started and then stopped. I waited, listening to the scratch of her pencil across the paper. "My family, my parents. I draw . . . dark things."

"Why?" I whispered, almost scared to hear her reply. I didn't know much about her parents. Just what Kitty had told me long ago—that they were extravagant people who loved attention.

"There is a bad streak in my family, Emmaline, and it's inside me as well," she said. "But sometimes, if you name something or put it down on paper, it's not as powerful as before."

She held the sketch out to me. I looked down at it. In addition to adding the skirt, she had blotted out the figure's eyes, leaving dark holes that nearly took up the entire face. I shuddered and raised my head. In the dim light, Sophie's eyes seemed blacked out too.

CHAPTER SEVENTEEN

WE SKETCHED, CUT PATTERNS, and sewed every night for the rest of the week and into the next. We worked in Sophie's fitting room on her sewing machine during the night and then, because customers came to her room during the day, we brought the pieces up to our chamber and hid them under our beds. It seemed like we were always rushing up the stairs with the pieces stored in our sewing caddies, or back down to work on them in the fitting room, all while we prepared our wedding gowns for Lady Harrison's viewing.

Sometimes the stress and exhaustion made me want to scream. Other times, it seemed to be the only thing inspiring me to sew another stitch.

"You look tired, Sophie," I said. She was hemming the duchess's gown while I worked on a skirt for the collection. We'd brought both pieces up to hide before Tilda came in to tidy up, but decided to take a few more minutes to work before we put them under the bed. For once, Tilda's neglect of my side of the room worked in our favor.

Sophie's creative output seemed to have turned her inside

out. Her cheekbones were pronounced, and her eyes were blood-shot.

"I'm fine," she said. I paused to stretch my fingers. They were numb from sewing for hours, except for my thumb, which was raw from forcing needles through thread. I'd finally started wearing a thimble, but it only served to inflame my finger further.

I pulled the skirt I'd created for our collection over the head of a mannequin, painstakingly working it inch by inch to get it down over the shoulders. I handled the charcoal-gray charmeuse delicately, trying to maintain its sharp pleats. It had taken me hours to iron them one at a time with a lead iron and a measuring tape.

Carefully, I added the next part of my look: a leather corset. It was easy to put on the mannequin because it closed via a series of gray ribbons in the back. I tied it on and stepped back to look. It gleamed just like the tackle and saddles for the work-horses back in Shy.

"It's seven," Sophie said. We lifted our sore necks and aching heads from our work to look at the clock Sophie had brought into our chamber from her fitting room. Its hands were exaggerated curlicues, so it almost appeared that the time could be eight, seven, or nine. I peered hard. Seven. We'd worked through breakfast. Francesco had squeezed one final fitting in for me this morning before I'd have to change for my press duties—my first appointment in a while—so we'd both be needed downstairs. This was the second time we'd worked through breakfast, and I wondered if anyone had noticed our absence. Suspicion was the last thing we needed.

The thought of removing my gown from the dress form was almost too much, but I couldn't leave it out. I unlaced the corset and then gently eased the skirt off. I folded both items up, praying it wouldn't undo the pleats in the skirt, and slid them under my bed where they would rest next to the other finished and half-finished pieces.

I found a pair of heels beneath my vanity and slipped them on, even though the red flowers painted onto their toes clashed with my gown.

I peered into the mirror, trying to straighten my hair. I almost didn't recognize my reflection. Dark circles were forming underneath my eyes. My skin was ashy and thin, pulled tight over the bones underneath. I sighed and followed Sophie out of our chamber and down the stairs.

Later on today, we were scheduled to present our wedding gowns to Lady Harrison. We both had barely managed to finish our dresses. Before, I would've agonized over every decision, falling into a tizzy of stress about whether Lady Harrison would like it. But now I was consumed by my own collection and Cynthia's gown. Lady Harrison's dress was just a far-off thought, something I only saw in terms of maintaining the appearance of normality. The challenges that had held such power over me no longer did.

"I love it, don't you?" Sophie's voice was low in my ear as we joined the other contestants heading down the hallway.

"What?"

"All of this. Designing. Even the secrets." Her smile looked severe against her bloodshot eyes and pale skin. I almost grimaced at the sight.

"Well . . ." I trailed off. We'd been sewing so much. Everything was a blur: the fabric pieces I'd handled, the needles I'd threaded, and the sketches I'd redone over and over and over again. Every other part of my life seemed like a distant dream—even Tristan.

But my designs weren't just paper and plans anymore. They were real. *I'd* made them real. And, like a real established fashion line, we would have a famous client wear one of our looks, and the press would review our collection.

"I do." I couldn't lie. "I love it, too."

We walked the rest of the way down to the fitting rooms with heavy, fatigued steps. I passed by the schedule posted on the hallway, hardly bothering to glance at it. Francesco had told me yesterday that I had just the one final fitting, so I only gave it a cursory glance.

But as my eyes passed over it, my name leaped out at me. Usually my name was toward the end, alphabetized by my surname. This time it was at the top.

MADAME JOLÈNE:

6:00 A.M. APPOINTMENT: HRH AMELIA/WINTER COAT
PREVIEW—NO ASSISTANCE NEEDED

7:30 A.M. APPOINTMENT: PRIVATE CLIENT—ATTENDING
CONTESTANTS: SOPHIE STERLING AND EMMALINE
WATKINS

I blinked at the list. Just a week or so ago, seeing my name at the top of the schedule would have thrilled me. Now, my heart sank all the way down to those horrid red heels. Maybe I had made a huge mistake. Madame Jolène was giving me a chance after all.

"Well, let's go. We don't want to be late." Sophie was standing behind me, looking over my shoulder. She gestured toward the stairs at the opposite end of the hallway. They weren't the ones we'd just come down. Instead, they led to Madame Jolène's private fitting rooms.

The blue-and-green carpeted steps leading up to Madame Jolène's rooms stifled our footsteps. If it wasn't for the dread in my stomach, I would've felt like I was floating. "Sophie?"

"What?"

"Do you think what we are doing is . . . wrong?"

I could only see part of her profile. She started to climb the stairs a little faster, her hand gliding up the banister.

"Of course." She spoke without hesitation.

"What do you mean?"

"Well, it *is* wrong."

"Then why do you do it?"

"Have you ever seen one of those hedge mazes, Emmaline?" Sophie asked. "The really tall ones?"

"No. But I know what they are . . ."

"Well, some of those mazes are cut in such a way that no matter which turn you take, you will always end up in the middle. You can turn right. You can turn left. It doesn't change anything." She stopped on the stairs and turned to face me. A few steps above me, she towered over my head. Somehow, she no longer looked tired. "That's me, Emmaline. It doesn't matter which way I turn. I'll always be like this."

Our rector at church had always said that nothing was pre-determined. It was up to us, he said, to choose who we wanted to be. Grace was just as accessible to us as evil. Yet I understood Sophie. There was a strange streak in her . . . and it seemed like there was one in me, too, one I'd never known existed until now. I gripped the banister, suddenly wanting to undo everything I had done. Sophie held out a hand to me, seeming to sense my uneasiness.

"Come," she said. "Madame Jolène is waiting."

I took her hand. As always, it was icy cold.

Madame Jolène's private fitting rooms were on the highest floor, next to her personal chambers. Sophie was the only Fashion House Interview candidate who had seen them before, and she entered with practiced ease, immediately striding over to a dark-gray fainting couch and sitting down. I hesitated at the threshold before walking over to stand next to her.

"Where is Madame Jolène?"

"She'll come when she's ready," Sophie said. "She never waits for anyone. We always wait for her."

The walls were covered in dark wood panels. Floor-to-ceiling windows opened to views of the perfumery's fourth floor directly across the street. A row of gowns arranged in a gradient of length and formality hung on a gold rolling rack, and an army of mannequins stood nearby in an orderly line. While our rooms had cotton forms, the ones in Madame Jolène's were silk taffeta with mahogany bases.

There was only one mirror in the room, a bold choice.

Usually, customers demanded a trifold mirror and a large hand-held mirror to see the front, back, and sides of the gowns. It appeared Madame Jolène did not cater to that desire.

Everything was oriented around the dresses, aside from a table scape of gilded birdcages, the only decoration in the room. The cages were empty and the doors stood open.

"I was expecting more opulence." I thought about the Fashion House's lavish wallpapered and chandeliered lobby. "This is so bare."

"This way there is nothing to distract anyone," Sophie said. "The focus is on the gowns."

Madame Jolène, it seemed, let her art speak for itself.

"Good morning, girls." Madame Jolène swept in from the side room, bringing with her a spicy aroma of patchouli. She wore a navy-blue gown that had shiny jet buttons stretching in a long, ant-like line up the skirt to the bodice and wrapping all the way around the collar. Her measuring tape hung around her neck, her permanent replacement for a necklace.

She was carrying a standard Fashion House sketchbook and, just before she turned her attention to it, her eyes swept over both of us. The tiny muscles around her mouth tensed, and then released. It happened so fast I almost wondered if I'd imagined it. The sight, as brief as it was, made my stomach clench and twist.

"Good morning, Madame Jolène," Sophie said, rising from her spot on the fainting couch. If she was nervous, it didn't show.

"Good morning, Madame Jolène," I repeated.

"We will be having a forty-minute consultation today," she said, preoccupied with the sketchbook.

"Is it an initial consultation?" Sophie asked. I didn't understand how she was so calm, especially now with our secret collection well on its way to completion.

"Yes. We will take basic measurements and discuss the client's needs," Madame Jolène said. Typically, when she made her rounds of the fitting rooms or previewed our work in the sewing room, she was brisk and annoyed at our incompetence. But today in her own chambers she was animated; her tight brow lines of disapproval were gone, and her steps were light.

"Ah! Here she is now!" Madame Jolène set the sketchbook down as the doors to the fitting room swung open. I turned to see the client, a polite expression fixed on my face.

Cynthia?

Her name leaped to the tip of my tongue, and I barely stopped it from escaping. I was seeing things. A woman had entered, and I had transformed her face into Cynthia's. I was exhausted. That was the only explanation.

Next to me Sophie sucked in her breath sharply and didn't let it out.

"Cynthia, welcome," Madame Jolène said, extending her hand. I blinked, desperate to change reality, but *she* was still there. Cynthia. Our Cynthia, whose gown was the centerpiece to our new line.

"Thank you, Madame Jolène," she replied. "It has been too long."

She sashayed forward, reaching out to take Madame Jolène's

hand. As she did, she looked over at me, and a small smile quirked her lips.

"Please, sit." Madame Jolène motioned Cynthia toward two chairs opposite the fainting couch. They both settled onto the furniture, their skirts spreading out over the upholstery, their faces masked in courteous smiles.

On the surface, they epitomized their roles perfectly: wealthy Fashion House customer and powerful Fashion House owner meeting for an appointment. But things stood out to me—the way Madame Jolène had them take the chairs facing us, how Cynthia didn't seem surprised to see us—and the tightening in my stomach turned into churning.

Cold fingers suddenly curled around mine. Sophie. She raised a shoulder in an imperceptible shrug and shook her head.

Stop, she was saying. *Calm down.*

Her eyes were empty and her mouth was firm. I tried to mirror her expression and subdue the whirlpool of thoughts in my head. If I didn't, I'd say something that would give us away. Ever so slightly, I took a step back so I was standing shoulder to shoulder with Sophie. Whatever happened, I needed her by my side.

"It's been quite some time," Madame Jolène said. "Have you been well?"

"Yes, thank you." Cynthia's voice was clear, strong, and slightly smug.

I didn't even recognize her. In the morning light, she looked nothing like the drunken woman who had met us outside the gala in the rain. For the first time, I noticed her eyes were green, not brown. They were piercingly alert as she leaned forward on the edge of her chair, as though waiting for something.

"Who has been handling your fashion?" Madame Jolène asked. Even though Cynthia was a titled, affluent woman, Madame Jolène ran her eyes over her clothing as though she was no more significant than one of us contestants. A flicker of annoyance flashed over Cynthia's face, but she answered with poise.

"I have a private dressmaker."

"Ah," Madame Jolène said. "A seamstress. That makes sense."

"I beg your pardon?" Cynthia asked.

"Oh," Madame Jolène said insouciantly, "I was just noticing your outfit. It's very well made. In fact, I dare say it's perfect."

"Thank you," Cynthia said. This time, she faltered just a little and her brows furrowed, confused at the compliment. She glanced down at her cowl-neck, rose-print dress.

"It's so hard to find good seamstresses." Madame Jolène was not done. "Then again, I wouldn't know very much about that. I never hire experienced seamstresses here. Certainly, I hire girls who sew and train them in the art. I've discovered seamstresses are good for, well, *copying* outfits. They hardly have the imagination to design their own. But yours did a wonderful job replicating my gown."

Two red spots stained Cynthia's cheeks, and her hands, folded in her lap, shook just a little bit.

"Of course," Madame Jolène continued, "there are risks to hiring young girls. They are so . . . ambitious."

A gasp escaped from my throat, strangled and alarmed. She

knew. She had to know. Yet Madame Jolène's attention was fixed on Cynthia with such intensity that she didn't even seem to remember Sophie and I were there. Sophie's fingers touched mine again and I closed my eyes for a second, trying to collect myself even though I knew each passing second was bringing us toward disaster.

"Well, I did hire some of your former contestants to work for me," Cynthia said. Despite her gravelly, uncertain cadence, she went on. Unable to hold still, I fidgeted, lacing and unlacing my fingers. "Of course, they had plenty to say about you. But I hardly think it's fair—it's terribly hard for a woman to run a business and not be, well, a little *snippety*."

Madame Jolène's eyes hardened, and Cynthia straightened up, a gleeful smile coming to her mouth. I'd never seen anyone get under Madame Jolène's skin before. Weak as she seemed, Cynthia was surprisingly sly.

"Now, I understand you need a gown." Madame Jolène ignored Cynthia's insult, her eyes as cold as her voice. "Since this will be the first piece of mine that you've worn in quite some time, it will need to be special. Something fresh and fashion-forward, to commemorate our renewed relationship."

"I agree," Cynthia said. She matched Madame Jolène's stony tone. Their polite words contrasted with their taut faces and icy voices. "Something magnificent for the Parliament Exhibition."

I took a raggedy breath and my knees went weak. Step by step, they were inching toward the truth—the truth they both so obviously knew.

"I have some ideas," Madame Jolène said. "How about a dress like this?"

She picked up the sketchbook and flipped it open. There, right underneath the cover, was a loose piece of paper: my sketch for Cynthia's gown. The air in my lungs escaped out of me in one single breath, and a heady sense of disbelief rushed over me.

"It's lovely," Cynthia said. A satisfied smile settled onto her face. "It's exactly what I had in mind."

"That's what I thought. Cynthia, will you excuse us for a few moments?" Madame Jolène asked. With a breezy huff, Cynthia stood up and swept out of the room. Madame Jolène didn't say anything until the door closed.

"Where did you get that from?" I asked, stumbling but trying desperately not to sound like I was. "That's a sketch I was doing for fun."

"For *fun*?" Madame Jolène spoke in a slow measured pace. "So, was it just *for fun* when you contacted Cynthia and offered to make her a new gown under a different label? Your label?"

"I . . ." I glanced at Sophie, but she was still, her face as white as mine felt. "There's been a mistake."

"Cynthia came to me," Madame Jolène said. "She requested a custom gown in exchange for information about my Fashion House Interview candidates. And imagine my horror when I learned that you two had told her you were starting a new fashion line. I had Francesco ask around—it seems the *Eagle* and even the *Times* were invited to some sort of fashion debut. Even Tilda has been strangely jumpy—at the slightest questioning, she started babbling on about you, Emmaline, and how she didn't steal any beads. I had her look in your sketchbooks, and this is what she found."

Slowly, deliberately, she crumpled the sketch in her hands

and tossed it aside. It landed at my feet, rolling to a stop just a few inches from my red heels.

"I—I was just trying to design something beautiful," I said. "I wasn't trying to hurt anyone."

"So you betrayed the Fashion House? Aligned yourself with desperate social climbers? Even as the Fashion House clothed you and fed you?"

"What did you expect?" My voice was a strange echo of itself. I wasn't even sure what I was going to say, I just knew that I had to speak. "My whole life I've admired you. All I wanted was to come to the Fashion House and show you I could be one of your apprentices. But you never gave me the chance, even though you know I can design."

"*This is my Fashion House.*" Madame Jolène's tone dripped with passion I'd never heard before. "I create it and make it what I will, and I will not answer to anyone else. You understand things in your silly, dim way. You don't realize that your very existence here signifies that I've—" She stopped, and I saw her drawing her persona back to her in the way one puts on a garment, her face cloaking itself in coolness and control. "That things are changing."

"We are talented," Sophie cut in. Anger, unbridled and undisguised, flared in her face, distorting her beautiful features. "You know we are."

"You are two stupid little girls who think you can start a new fashion line based on talent alone. Your line is nothing more than a pesky fly that will be squashed."

"That's not true," I said. Telling her no, that she wasn't right after all this time, was almost like being underwater—for a moment, everything was still, weightless, suspended. "You're terrified of us. You're terrified of what we can do."

Madame Jolène laughed then. She laughed so hard that she tossed her head back, her lips peeling back to show her perfect teeth. My moment of conviction was gone. Instead of being held still underwater, I was tossed about by it, tumbling without stop, out of control. Both Sophie and I stood, watching her. Finally, her laughter subsided into small hiccups and then to nothing at all. She moved to stand near me and, for an alarming second, I thought she was going to hit me. Instead, she put her hands on both of my shoulders and pulled me close, so close that her lips were right by my ear. As she held me near, all I could see were the black buttons running up into her collar like dozens of eyes staring at me.

Madame Jolène lowered her voice to a whisper. "You, Emmaline," she said, "are terrified of yourself."

Her words struck me more than any blow could have. I raised a hand to my ear, right where her breath had warmed it. Madame Jolène smiled, satisfied, and then took a few steps back so she could see us both.

"Get. Out."

As though through a fog, I saw Sophie turn and walk toward the door. I followed her, dumbly.

I had come so far. What could I do now?

Sophie opened the door, and for the first time since Cynthia had entered the room, our eyes met. She touched my arm. I didn't know if she was trying to comfort me or herself.

We stepped onto the landing outside Madame Jolène's chambers. Cynthia stood there, hands on her hips, chin raised so high

I could see up her nose. As soon as we stepped out, she brushed by us, rushing to get back to Madame Jolène.

Then I heard Madame Jolène: "Leave here and never come back."

The sound of Cynthia's protestations cut through the air, but I barely heard them.

Francesco was waiting in our chamber, his head turned away as though he couldn't stand the sight of us.

"You, Emmaline?" he whispered, and for the first time, crippling guilt washed over me. No matter how cruel Madame Jolène was, Francesco had always been kind to me.

Out of everyone, I wanted him to understand.

"I'm—" I started to speak, but he raised a hand, silencing me.

"Get your things. Both of you!" He stared up at the ceiling, sniffing. "You are only to take what you brought with you. Anything you've made or acquired here is Fashion House property."

He left as we scrambled for our possessions.

"Do you have a place to go?" Sophie's voice cracked as she opened her vanity drawer.

"I'll have to get home somehow."

I pulled my old carpetbag out from behind my wardrobe and unlatched it. Almost everything I had belonged to the Fashion House. I sank beside the satchel, staring into its depths.

From where I sat, I could see a bit of my charmeuse skirt poking out from underneath the bed. *We had been so close.*

"Sophie." She gazed at me from where she stood by her vanity. "Sophie, we can still do it." I pushed myself up and stumbled on my skirts, almost falling to my knees again. I barely caught myself, hands outstretched for balance.

"What do you mean?" she asked, her voice as weak as mine.

"Is there someplace we can go to finish the collection? Just until the debut? It's our only hope. Otherwise . . ." I didn't dare finish. Probably because it was too frightening to contemplate. But if we didn't try, we would never design again.

"I . . ." She stopped, running her fingers agitatedly through her long black hair. Her movements were fast and sharp. "I can't go back to Alexander's manor. And we don't have enough money left to get a flat."

I took a breath, sucking air deep into my lungs so I sounded strong when I spoke. We couldn't both be afraid.

"Do we have enough for tickets to and from Shy?"

"Yes." She tossed her hair over her shoulder in a decisive swoop. "We do."

Shy. *Home.* Ever since arriving at the Fashion House, I'd fought those two words. They symbolized defeat—a return to who I was before.

And, more terrifying, a return to who I would have to be again.

A waitress in a pub, in a place that hated the thing I loved most. The whole time I'd been at the Fashion House, going back had meant becoming a cautionary tale, a repeat of my mother: a girl who went to the city and returned humiliated.

No.

I would go back. But on my own terms. My mother's story wasn't mine—and going home didn't have to be defeat. Not just yet.

"Will your mother let us finish everything there?" Sophie

asked. "Wasn't she upset that you came here?"

"Yes. She was." I still hadn't heard from her. Not a word. Her silence was stronger than any letter might be. "But we don't have any other choice."

She would understand. I would explain things to her. I would show her not so much in words but in garments; the garments spun out of my mind and into sheer skirts, leather bustiers, pleated gowns. My designs. When she saw them, she would have to understand.

"We need to take our collection."

I lay down on the marble by the bed, reaching underneath it and yanking out bolts of fabric and half-finished dresses. My movements seemed to spur Sophie to action, and she ran to her bed, sprawling forward on her stomach to pull pieces out.

I piled our collection up, as though it was nothing more than dirty laundry, and grabbed my carpetbag. I struggled to force the garments into it. It seemed like the more I stuffed, the more they poured out over the floor.

Sophie grabbed one of the several pillows piled in a soft mountain on her bed. She pulled the pillow out and tossed it aside, clutching the gold-tasseled pillowcase, and began stuffing our collection into it.

"What is going on here?" Francesco shouted from the doorway, his charcoal-darkened eyebrows raised high on his forehead and one finger pointed threateningly at us. "You are not to take *anything* that doesn't belong to you!"

I stopped, clasping the pillowcase and my carpetbag. Sophie

slowed, one gown draped over her shoulder and two held in her hands.

"Drop it," Francesco commanded. "Drop all of it right now."

Looking over at Sophie, I said, *"Run!"*

Sophie, holding two pillowcases full of our gowns, bolted toward the door. I ran after her, straight toward Francesco. He grabbed at me and his hand nearly closed around my carpetbag. I ducked past him at just the last moment.

We ran down the stairs, our feet slipping on the rug, the pillowcases and carpetbag bouncing against our sides and legs. We burst into the Fashion House lobby. Customers and a few of the candidates wheeled around to stare at us in shock. Kitty called out, "Emmaline!"

We charged through the front doors, leaving them swinging behind us, and raced into the courtyard, gravel spitting out from beneath our heels.

Sophie and I didn't stop running for two blocks. Then we collapsed against a brick wall, our chests heaving. Sweat poured down my forehead, gluing my hair to the back of my neck. My feet screamed from running in heels, and I gasped for air, bent at the waist, limply clutching the carpetbag. Still, we couldn't rest.

"We need to keep going," I said. "Come on."

We ran through the side alleys that threaded between the boutiques. As we rushed by maids and shop girls, they flattened against the walls to let us by, probably terrified we were thieves.

Finally, the clean, well-cobbled streets started to give way to the unpaved roads of the Republic District, and we slowed down to a brisk clip. I limped in my heels until we both came to a stop, panting.

"We need to call a hack," I said. "We have to get to the train station."

"I know," Sophie replied. "It should be safe now. None of the drivers in the Republic District will care who we are."

As we waved to the hacks passing by, I caught my reflection in a gritty windowpane. I was wearing a stylish gown from the Fashion House, my hair was mussed, and I had a carpetbag and two gold-tasseled pillowcases at my feet.

I let out a frantic, hysterical-sounding laugh. The sound was snatched away by the bustling street and gusting wind, but it didn't matter. I'd never felt like such a disaster in all my life.

PART III

CHAPTER EIGHTEEN

WE DIDN'T SAY MUCH ON the train ride. Probably because we both knew that if we did, we'd have to acknowledge what was happening to us. That we'd been kicked out of the most powerful fashion house in the world. That our chances for becoming designers were next to nothing. That if we could, we might just go back and do everything differently. It was easier to catch up on our sleep than to talk about—face—our uncertain futures.

I was relieved once we arrived in Evert. I wouldn't have to sit still with my anxious thoughts any longer. We stepped off the train, pillowcases in hand. Sophie peered about.

"Where on earth is the station?"

"This is it." I motioned to the simple wooden platform and small ticket booth. A handwritten sign was propped in the booth's window: *Back in twenty minutes.* "This is the station."

The familiar song of the country greeted me. The wind rattling in tall trees. The last of the summer beetles buzzing in the weeds. The far-off baaing of sheep. Gone was the ceaseless clatter of hacks on the streets, the shouts and calls of people, the sounds of business being done in quick order.

"Everyone says things are small outside of Avon-upon-Kynt. But my word, I didn't realize they'd be this small. Now, where are the hacks?"

Sophie looked this way and that, as though expecting to see Avon-upon-Kynt's black hacks gliding up and down the dirt street.

"There aren't any. We have to walk."

"Walk?" She gaped, as though I'd suggested we fly. "What do you mean?"

"Think of it as promenading." With a confidence I didn't possess, I lifted my carpetbag and one of the pillowcases and gestured to the dirt road leading from the platform. "We'll be there before you know it. Shy is only two miles south."

I led the way. I knew exactly where to go. It was a strange sensation, an old one. In the city, I was lost—in every sense of the word. But here, even though I didn't want to acknowledge it, I belonged.

We trudged along in silence, pausing here and there to rest. We hadn't changed clothes since the day before, and our heels were rickety in the dirt. Each step seemed harder and heavier than the one before it, especially when we reached the outskirts of Shy. What would my mother say when she saw me? When she heard what had happened and what our plans were? We'd always been inseparable. Yet just one argument followed by a month and a half of silence seemed to have changed all that. I'd never known our bond could be so easily broken.

"Emmy? Is that you?" A person emerged from around the

bend in the road that would lead us into Shy.

I squinted at the broad-shouldered figure. "Johnny?"

Johnny Wells came to a stop in front of us. His tall form blocked out the descending fall sun and threw a long shadow over us. I stared up at him, surprised by how comforting it was to see his familiar face.

"Are you . . . all right?" He looked from me to Sophie to the satin pillowcases in our hands. "Weren't you in that fancy competition in the city?"

"Yes. But I'm back now. Just for a short time."

"Ah." He nodded slowly. "Your mother said you weren't ever coming back."

"She did, did she?" My grip on the pillowcase and my carpet-bag loosened, and they dropped to the ground, black tulle and gray chiffon spilling out of the pillowcase's mouth. "Is she . . ." *Furious with me?* But I couldn't ask that. I didn't finish the sentence.

"Well, I'm glad you're back. You look so . . ." Now he trailed off. I thought he might be surprised by my gown. It was a Fashion House dress, after all, and nothing like the simple dresses worn in Shy, but he didn't look at it. His eyes were fixed on my face, as though the peculiarities of my appearance—my dirt-stained designer gown, my pillowcases, my undone hair—didn't matter to him. "You look nice."

Nice. He wasn't the most eloquent of speakers, but the simple compliment warmed my heart. No one in the city ever offered compliments so freely.

"Thank you." Next to me, Sophie gave an impatient sigh.

"Oh, this is Sophie Sterling."

"Nice to meet you, miss." Johnny pulled off his cap, revealing his sun-lightened brown hair. He didn't quite meet her gaze. Sophie gave a brisk nod. "Are you heading to the pub?" he asked, addressing me once more.

"We are."

"Here, let me help you." He took our pillowcases and easily swung them over his shoulders and picked up my carpetbag.

"Thank you." I didn't realize just how heavy they were until I wasn't holding them any longer. I rubbed my aching shoulders and neck. With long strides, Johnny started off down the road. We followed him, passing by flocks of sheep and the wooden boxes where the cuttleworms spun their silk. Soon, though, Shy's small buildings emerged from the land to line the main street. There weren't any signs for the Fashion House contestants. I wasn't surprised. Such flash and focus on fashion went against Shy's simple ways—even if one of their own was competing.

At the very end, toward the bluffs, was the pub. It was backlit by the setting sun, and warm light spilled out of the windows. Everything about it was cozy and inviting, but I was a bundle of nerves. Inside was my mother. Inside, I'd have to face everything—her anger, the reality that I'd been kicked out of the Fashion House Interview, the fact that I'd returned to the place I'd tried so hard to leave behind.

We walked through the main dining room to the kitchen. Johnny moved easily through the pub. He stepped around the few tables and nodded to the men sitting at the bar. I walked awkwardly, breaking out in a sweat, even though I wasn't lugging the pillowcases any longer.

I knew every corner of the pub so well. The curtains did their gentle dance in the windows and the floorboards creaked their familiar welcome. Nothing had changed. The pub, with its well-worn yet hospitable feeling, wrapped around me with the friendliness of a barn cat weaving around one's legs. Yet I couldn't relax into it. It beckoned me with its easy familiarity, but I remained rigid, refusing to surrender to it.

We stepped into the kitchen, Johnny leading the way. My mother's back was to us as she chopped carrots at our dining room table. Usually, that was my job, and I would sit while I did it. She stood. At the sound of our entrance, she turned around. Our eyes met.

"Emmy," she breathed. "You're back."

My mother took a few steps toward me but stopped before she reached me. Her gaze, which had been on my face, moved to the pillowcases in Johnny's arms, and then to Sophie.

"You're back?" It was now a question, not a statement. Her face, which had been soft, stiffened into creased forehead lines and taut mouth. "What's going on?"

"I—" I didn't know where to start.

"Where should I put these?" Johnny asked when I didn't continue. He held out the pillowcases and my carpetbag.

"What's in those?" my mother asked. "And who is she?"

"I'm Sophie Sterling," Sophie said. She made her way over to the kitchen table and sat down, relaxing into the straight-backed chair with a sigh. "I was in the Fashion House Interview with Emmaline."

"The—the competition wasn't quite what I thought it would be." I had the vague idea that we should sit down. There was too much space between us, and we were facing each other as though we were adversaries, not mother and daughter. But I didn't know how to suggest it, not when she stood there, waiting for an explanation. "I tried to start a new fashion house with Sophie, but Madame Jolène discovered it. We were kicked out yesterday."

"And you came home."

"Yes."

Her eyes sparked again, just like they had when she first saw me. I wanted to stop there and stand in the warmth of her gaze forever. But I couldn't. I had to dash her hopes. Again. Just like I had when I left the first time.

"I'm home for now."

My mother seemed to retract into herself, like a snail curling into its shell. Then she crossed her arms and lifted her chin. I knew this look of pride. I'd seen it over the years, but this was the first time it had been directed at me.

"I see. What is your plan?"

"To finish the collection and debut it after the Parliament Exhibition. We would like to stay here until then . . . if that's all right."

"Stay here?" my mother echoed me. Before I could respond, she abruptly turned and walked back to the dining room table. She picked up her knife. The sharp *chop* of the knife severing the carrots filled the room.

"Please, Mother," I said.

Chop.

Chop.

Chop.

Her only answer was the vigorous slice of her knife. One piece of carrot rolled off the cutting board, but she didn't stop to retrieve it. Johnny shifted and awkwardly set down the pillowcases next to the carpetbag.

"I should be going," he said. "I'll leave these here, if that's all right."

None of us said anything, and he backed out of the kitchen. The minute he got to the dining room he hurried to the front door, as if he couldn't leave fast enough.

"Well." Sophie stood up. "Is there a place I can wash up while you two . . . talk things out?"

I nodded, still looking at my mother. She set down the knife and, without a word, picked up the cutting board and dumped the carrots into a pot.

"I'll take you up to my bedroom, Sophie." I left my mother in the kitchen. After a few minutes, I heard the *chop, chop* of her knife start up once again.

We never did talk about it that night. In fact, my mother didn't say we could stay, as much as she didn't tell us to leave.

I woke the next morning, bewildered. I was in my old room, under my old quilt, but there was an elbow jabbing me in my back. Sophie's elbow. I sat up and rubbed my eyes.

There was a voice, too. It drifted up the staircase and

through my open bedroom door. One that I knew, but one that most definitely did not belong in Shy. It was a cold fingertip against my spine. I jumped out of my bed, quickly tore out of my nightgown and into one of my old work dresses, and hurried down to the kitchen.

A man stood in the middle of the room, talking to my mother. He wore a black suit with a dark red tie and matching cufflinks. Almost involuntarily, I wiped my hands on my skirt, as though they were covered in oily lotion.

"Ah, there you are," Mr. Taylor said. His eyes followed the lines of my plain work dress. "I've been looking for you."

"What are you doing here?"

My mother took one glance at my face and came to stand next to me. She put her arm protectively around me. I leaned into her, just a little.

"I heard that you and Sophie came here after getting kicked out of the Fashion House Interview," Mr. Taylor said. Leisurely, he walked in a slow circle around the kitchen, his eyes trailing over each dish, glass, and pot. "I came to see you."

"See me?" I figured he was looking for Sophie. The thought that he had business with me made the fine hairs on my arms and neck stand up.

"I understand that you're trying to start a new fashion house." He cut his circle short and turned sharply to face me. I shuddered, trying to shake the feeling of his silky palm off my fingers. "I can help you with that. The Reformists Party brought you to the Fashion House as a symbol of change. But now I realize we were shortsighted. The Fashion House is the way of the past—and the things of the past must be set aside." His eyes gleamed as he spoke, and he smiled, as though swept away by his own words. "You and Sophie can start a new fashion house. One funded and inspired by the Reformists Party."

Next to me, my mother let out a surprised exclamation and, despite myself, my mind began to race.

A fashion house.

There would be no struggle to finish our collection, no desperate need for a debut, no reliance on customers to fund the house. Our futures would be secure. *We'd be designers*, real designers.

I simply had to say yes. The word nearly jumped from my tongue.

But all I could see were the marks on Sophie's neck. The way her hands trembled after he'd attacked her. No matter what he offered us, nothing could undo the fact that, underneath his suave hair and stylish suit, he was a monster.

I had done a lot of things I never thought I would to become a designer. Kept secrets. Told lies. But there were lines, lines that should never be crossed, and this was one of them.

"I cannot accept," I said. "But thank you."

Dark lightning shot through his eyes. Slowly, methodically, he straightened his tie and his cuffs.

"I'm sure you want to reconsider." His voice was soft yet slithery. "You cannot be successful in fashion without power, and that power comes either from the Fashion House and the Crown or the Reformists Party. You've rejected the Fashion House, which means you've also rejected the Crown. You cannot reject the Reformists Party as well."

"I-I'm counting on a third power." My mother's hand was warm against my back and I focused on its firmness. "The power of the customers to purchase beautiful gowns."

There was a quiet noise—a soft gasp—and we looked to see Sophie frozen in the kitchen doorway.

"Sophie." A blissful smile crossed Mr. Taylor's lips and he held out a hand to her. "Come home with me. We will make a fashion house, together. We can find someone else to play the part of the stupid country girl."

I stared at Sophie, willing her to stand up for herself, trying to impart some sort of strength to her. A glazed, dead expression took over her face, as though she wasn't in the kitchen or even the pub. Her face had an otherworldly look, like she'd slipped through the cracks of time to a place long ago.

I said, "Leave her alone. She doesn't want anything to do with you."

"No." Mr. Taylor cut me off. "That isn't true."

We looked at Sophie. Both Mr. Taylor and I were trying to speak for her, but she needed to exert her own will. To free herself. Slowly, she turned her head in profile—not enough to face Mr. Taylor but enough to see him from the corners of her eyes.

"It's true." Her voice was a whisper, as thin as gossamer. "The fashion line is happening. I am going to work with Emmaline."

"You don't mean that."

"I do."

At that, Mr. Taylor took a ragged breath, his anger mounting with his intake of air. Quickly, my mother pushed her way past me to stand between us and him.

"You heard the girls," she said. "You need to leave. This is my pub, and you are not welcome here."

Mr. Taylor glared down at her, his veneer of flash and style gone, replaced by raw rage. Slowly, his hand tightened into a fist, and I cried out in fear, expecting him to hit her. Instead, he struck out to the side and knocked a vase off the kitchen counter.

Crash!

Glass shards exploded across the floorboards. I recoiled, more shaken by his violent action than the actual sound or sight of the vase smashing into smithereens.

My mother snatched up her rolling pin. Even though Mr. Taylor was twice her size, she shook it at him.

"Out!" Her face was red. "Get out right now!"

He pushed past her and out through the dining room. The door slammed hard behind him, so hard it rattled the glass in the windows. My mother lowered her rolling pin and turned around to where I was backed against the kitchen table. She asked, "Are you all right?"

I didn't trust myself to speak, so I bobbed my head up and down in a nod.

My mother's face was still red. "This is what happens when you go to the city. You get caught up in things much bigger than you and then . . ." She gestured to the shards of glass covering the floor.

"I-I'm sorry. I didn't think he would come here." Numbly, I

reached for the broom and dustpan. "I didn't mean to bring any trouble here."

My mother held out her hand for the broom.

"It's fine. I'll take care of this."

"No, I'll do it." I didn't want her to clean up the glass. Not when I was the one who'd brought Mr. Taylor there. Not when I was the one who kept hurting her.

"I'm sure you girls have things to do."

"She's right." Sophie spoke from the doorway. Her face was whiter than normal, but she sounded resolved. "We have a lot to do."

She turned and headed up the stairs to my bedroom. I didn't follow her. Not just yet. I grasped the broomstick; my hand stood just below my mother's hand, my eyes searching her face. I wasn't certain what I was looking for. Maybe some sort of forgiveness, or even just understanding. My mother gently placed her hand over mine, loosening my grip on the broom.

"Go on now."

"Mother—"

"It's all right, Emmy." Her fingers grazed my cheek as she tucked a strand of my hair back from my face. "Your friend is waiting."

"I really am sorry," I said, letting go of the broom handle. "I'm sorry for—" I cut myself off. *Everything*, I wanted to say. *I'm sorry for leaving you to run the pub alone; I'm sorry for wanting a life that's far away from here; I'm sorry for not being the daughter you need.*

But such openness and such words weren't my mother's way, so I swallowed them down.

Sophie and I started sewing in my bedroom, taking turns on my old decrepit sewing machine. I was glad to immerse myself in work. It eased the terror Mr. Taylor had brought to our pub.

"I'm surprised Mr. Taylor came here," I said. Sophie waved her hand glibly at me, her attention on a measuring tape she'd laid across a tulle skirt. Methodically, she pulled it through her hands, lips pursed.

My head ached. I frowned down at my stitching, as though ignoring the pain would make it go away. I watched Sophie as she smoothed out the gray tulle, her brow furrowed in concentration, her shoulders bent over the fabric.

Perhaps that was why she was so obsessed with designing. It was the only way to outrun the taint of Mr. Taylor in her life and lose herself in something beautiful.

"Did you ever try to leave Mr. Taylor's manor before going to the Fashion House?"

Sophie's fingers froze on the measuring tape and her foot tapped against the leg of her chair. It cast a jumpy shadow across the floor, one that sprang forward and back.

"No. I won't pretend to think you could ever understand. It's terrible to take help from someone who . . . hurts you."

I nodded, trying to indicate that I understood, but she was right. I didn't.

"Sometimes the demons in your head are so strong that you don't know how to fight the ones in real life." There were long pauses between her words, as though she was trying to fathom the unfathomable into speech. "I did have one plan to get away before going to the Fashion House. But it wasn't quite right, so I abandoned it."

"What was it?"

"It's not important. Going to the Fashion House was the best option, or so I thought at the time." She gathered up the measuring tape. "The funny thing is, I could have stayed in the competition. I could have become a designer. Madame Jolène told me several times. I didn't need to do this."

Though her tone was guarded, her eyes watered. Or, I thought they did. I couldn't conceive of her crying. The wateriness had to be something else, a reaction to the stuffy room or bleariness from her exhaustion. It had to be something— anything—other than tears.

"I don't just want to run from Alexander. I'm tired of being under other people's control, especially when they don't deserve it. That's why I'm glad we're designing our own collection. It's so different designing our own pieces here, free from the Fashion House. Don't you agree?"

Free. I wasn't sure what the word meant. We were free from the Fashion House, but now we were in Shy, far from the city, facing an uncertain future. Freedom, it seemed, was falling into darkness without knowing if we would be caught at the bottom.

"Well . . ."

Sophie waited expectantly.

"Yes," I said. "It's just right."

I'd been lying a lot lately, but this lie felt different. It felt more important than the truth.

We spent the entire day sewing, spreading the pieces of the collection across my bedroom floor and bed. The various gowns, overlays, skirts, and jackets were a little rough from their journey in the pillowcases. Snags marred some of the silks, a few small holes had appeared in the laces, and dirt stains dotted the fabrics. Even so, the pieces looked opulent and rich in my drab room.

"Do you think we'll have time to finish everything?" I rubbed my forehead. It was late, very late. I'd tracked the time throughout the day by the activity of the pub. The dinner customers had come and gone, and I'd heard my mother wash up the last of the dishes before heading to her room to sleep.

That had been the worst. I had wanted to go help her wash the dishes and set out the pint glasses and silverware for tomorrow, but I couldn't. Not when I needed to finish our collection.

"We can finish everything if we work nonstop," Sophie said. "But maybe we should take a break."

"I can stoke up the fire downstairs in the kitchen. We can have some stew."

"Might as well. If we don't stop to rest, we'll start making mistakes."

Down in the kitchen, I ladled stew into two bowls and I opened a bottle of cheap cooking wine. I devoured my mother's stew, letting its heartiness stave off my exhaustion. I'd never been so worn-out in all my life. Everything was piling up—the tiredness from the Fashion House schedule, the trip here, the encounter with Mr. Taylor, the day spent sewing without any breaks—everything ached, especially my fingers.

Knock, knock.

The sudden rap at the pub door made us both jump. It was much too late for anyone in Shy to be out and about. I met Sophie's eyes. We were both thinking the same thing.

Mr. Taylor. He was back.

"Emmy?" A voice came from behind the door, drifting from the dining room into the kitchen. I was so certain it was Mr. Taylor that it took me a moment to realize that the voice wasn't Mr. Taylor's at all. It was much too young, too energetic.

"Tristan," Sophie said.

I sat up straight, all fears and exhaustion forgotten. Then I noticed Sophie. She grabbed her glass and gulped at the wine as though it were water. Pushing her chair back from the table, she stood up, running her fingers through her hair and arranging it so it hung down on one side of her face in beautiful waves.

Was she primping for Tristan? My Tristan? I realized, with a jolt, that while Tristan no longer fancied Sophie, she might still fancy him.

As though the pub was hers and not mine, she crossed through the dining room and opened the door. I followed a few paces behind.

Tristan entered and Sophie threw her arms around his neck in a hug. In her heels she was his height, but she tucked herself against him, her entire body pressed into him so that she seemed small in his arms. A sharp pang—the sort one feels when running—contracted in the spot right behind my heart.

"What are you doing here?" she asked. "So far from the city!"

She pulled back her head and placed a kiss on his cheek. It was a quick kiss—nothing like the one Tristan and I shared at the gala—the sort one friend might give another. Still, a flash of embarrassed anger flared hot on my cheeks. Tristan didn't return the kiss, and his eyes found me, even as Sophie stood right by his side.

"I went to visit you at the Fashion House, and Francesco said you'd been fired and left with Sophie." He crossed the floor and came to stand next to me. Without hesitation, he hooked his arm around my waist, drawing me near. "I came to see if you were all right."

Tristan's back was to Sophie, but I could see her over his shoulder. She stared at us, her face somehow grimmer than usual. She saw me watching her, but she didn't glance away. Instead, she responded the way she had back at the showcase. She gave a small half smile and shrugged.

"Let's go to the kitchen. It's warm there," I said, awkwardly filling the silence. I was happy when Tristan's hand stayed around my waist as we made our way back to the kitchen. I wanted to melt into his arms, but I couldn't. Not with Sophie so closely observing our affection.

"What happened?"

"Madame Jolène found out about our plan. We got kicked out, so we came here to stay until the exhibition," I said. "But it seems everyone knows it. Mr. Taylor was here this morning."

At the name *Mr. Taylor*, Tristan's face paled to a shade similar to Sophie's.

"He's gone now," Sophie said, guessing the reason for

Tristan's pallor. She picked up her wineglass. Swirling it with one wrist, she sent the liquid spinning inside the goblet. It orbited dangerously close to the top but not quite close enough to spill over. "We'll be gone by the time he returns. Besides, Emmaline's mother scared him off."

Without making Tristan move his hands, I grabbed my wine and took a long drink. The purple liquid rolled over my tongue. Even after I swallowed, the bitter taste clung to the roof of my mouth.

"Emmy." Tristan spoke to me and me alone. "Maybe things are too dicey right now to start your own collection. I know I encouraged you to do it, but the city is in such a precarious state. I didn't realize starting your fashion house would put you in Mr. Taylor's sights."

I looked down into the red depths of my wine. I was still wearing an amethyst ring from the Fashion House. In the flurry of getting kicked out, I hadn't taken it off.

"This dream is everything to me, Tristan."

I didn't want to speak so openly around Sophie, but she stood there, unhurriedly sipping her wine, watching us like two players on a stage performing for her.

"Clothes? How can clothes be everything to you?"

"They were never just clothes to me."

And that was the truth.

"I just want you to be all right."

"I know."

Loudly, Sophie walked over to the cupboard and took another glass out. First, she poured more wine into her glass, and then filled the extra glass to the brim. She approached us and extended the glass to Tristan, making him step apart from me to take it. "Have some wine. It's red, your favorite."

I didn't know that he liked red wine. In fact, I didn't even know what his favorite beer was—or even his favorite food. All I knew was that he drank his tea black.

"Thank you," he said stiffly, taking the glass from her. I took another long drink of my wine, letting the liquid send a wave of warmth through my body, but the wine's astringency just tasted like my own bitterness. Why couldn't I simply enjoy Tristan's presence? Why did it feel like Sophie's obvious interest in him diminished what we had, especially when Tristan's hand was on my back and not hers?

"Look at you." Tristan raised his glass to me. "Seems like you've already moved up in the world. We have wine instead of tea this time."

His words were stronger than the wine. They were a sun-beam of warmth that cut through my wooziness. We didn't have as many memories as he and Sophie did . . . but I loved the ones we did have, from that first time we'd met under the mural to our first kiss at the gala.

"It's cooking wine, but it's fine enough," Sophie said.

"Is there anything I can do to help with the collection while I'm back in the city?"

"You can hire us some models." Sophie spoke smoothly, almost as though I wasn't there. "We need twelve. Factory girls will do."

"All right. I can do that." He glanced from me to Sophie and then back again to me. If he'd been feeling awkward before, this was the first sign of it. "Well . . . I should probably get going. There aren't any formal lodgings here, but the general store owner is letting me stay in one of his rooms for the night."

"You just got here," I protested. Even so, I knew he was right. Mr. Crowe wasn't likely to wait up long for Tristan. "You came from so far."

"It's all right. I needed to check on you." This time, he didn't say *you two*, and I smiled, happy he spoke just for me. He took a final drink of his wine and stepped away to set the glass down on the table. Coming back to me, he leaned forward and quickly kissed me on the lips. "I'll miss you."

"I'll miss you too."

He turned to Sophie.

"Have a good night."

"You too," Sophie responded. Thankfully, she didn't embrace him like she had when he'd entered. We watched him walk the length of the kitchen to the dining room. Hardly thinking, I hurried after him.

"Tristan!"

I burst into the dining room. My motions made the door between the kitchen and dining room swing closed, shutting Sophie away. He stopped in the middle of the room, his face lighting up as he turned toward me. I rushed to him and his arms opened to enclose me. We kissed, only this time there was nothing quick or proper about it. It was exactly what I'd been wanting since he'd first arrived.

His lips were strong and insistent, and the kiss built into

something that was fire and ice at the same time. It cut through the mist of the wine, awakening my senses into tingles that started at my lips and spread down through my body. His hands reached around to touch the back of my neck and they followed the pathway of my spine, tracing it through my shoulder blades and down, down, down before moving apart to settle on my hips.

Vaguely, I heard a door open. At first, I tried to ignore it, but the sound of heels on the floorboards rang out, and I knew she was there. Tristan didn't seem to notice, his shoulders, hands, and mouth pressing into me, a force of energy that I didn't want to stop. The footsteps moved to the outer side of the room. I pulled away from Tristan, my lips buzzing with the touch of his.

Sophie's form walked along the perimeter of the room.

"Don't mind me. I'm just looking for another bottle of wine," she said when my gaze fell on her. Despite her comment, she stopped still, one arm folding across her middle, the other extending out to hold her wineglass.

With hooded eyes, Tristan turned to see her. His hands remained low on my hips, his fingers pressing into me, each one strong and demanding.

"It is late, though." Sophie gave her wine another swirl. "There's lots to do tomorrow, Emmaline."

"I should go," Tristan muttered, but there was no conviction or will behind his words.

"I'll miss you," I said, even though I'd already said that back in the kitchen.

"I'll miss you," he echoed huskily. He stepped back slowly,

heavily, as if fighting the pull of something much stronger than he.

Sophie waited as he walked to the door, pretending to be more preoccupied with sipping her wine than interacting with us. Once the door closed behind him, she lowered her glass and said, "You didn't have to make him leave on my account."

I sighed at her ridiculous comment. After all, she'd obviously been trying to force him out. Disappointed as I was, the reverberations of the kiss stayed, enveloping me in feverish warmth.

"I know." I responded to her several moments after I should have. "Let's . . ." Giddiness descended on me, a mix of kisses and wine. "Let's put away the collection and get some sleep."

We headed toward the kitchen, falling in step with each other. The biting scent of red wine mixed acridly with her violet–witch hazel perfume. I should've been annoyed at her for interrupting my time with Tristan, but I could hardly think straight. Beside me, Sophie let out a high-pitched sigh.

"You know, Tristan proposed to me once," she said casually.

I fell back a few steps, my legs wobbly beneath me.

"What?"

"Oh, it was a while ago." She waved her free hand flippantly in the air. "But don't worry—it was no great matter."

No great matter? I knew they'd been together, but *marriage* . . . that was more than I ever imagined between them. Marriage was sacred, it was forever, and he'd wanted it with *her*.

"I asked him to." She turned her attention from me to her wineglass, running her finger around its rim, still unconcerned. "I wanted to get away from Alexander. But then I was accepted

338

into the Fashion House, and I figured that was a better plan. Tristan was a dear about it. Even bought me a little gold band."

"You . . . so you asked him to do it." I struggled to understand. All the elation from Tristan's kiss evaporated, replaced by the nighttime chill and this new information. "He—he was doing it to help you."

"Yes, exactly. That's how he is, you know. Always helping the people he cares about, no matter what."

"I know." I tried not to sound snappish, peeved.

"Of course you do. He is your beau, after all."

"Yes." Despite my efforts, I was speaking too quickly. I couldn't stop myself. "He is. He's with me."

And not you.

She inclined her head slowly, mysteriously elegant in her rumpled dress. Then she gave a fleeting smile, and proceeded up the stairs, one hand on the rail, the other still clutching her glass.

I watched her figure recede upward until it was swallowed by the darkness swathing the higher steps. Tremulously, I took a breath. I willed myself to lift a foot onto the first stair. I couldn't stay here all night. Not with so much to do and no time to do it in. But I stood there, one foot up on the stair, the other planted on the floor, suspended between up and down.

He'd been trying to help her. It hadn't meant anything to him. Or to her. What we had was special, different. Still, even as I told myself that, the emptiness in my chest contracted into one constant, steady ache behind my heart—the same one I'd felt earlier.

At some point, I started shivering, and my teeth chattered. I roused my chilled limbs into movement. Standing still never got me anywhere or made anything better. And the longer I stood there, the more hurt and confused I became.

The only thing to do was keep climbing.

CHAPTER NINETEEN

I WOKE EARLY THE NEXT morning and went downstairs, leaving Sophie asleep in my bed. My mother was already up—I heard her moving about the kitchen. Wordlessly, I joined her at the sink, where she was scrubbing potatoes. I picked up one of the grubby potatoes and a brush.

"Are you all right, Emmy?" my mother asked as I slowly scrubbed the brush over the potato's uneven slope.

"I . . ." I didn't know if I should tell her about Tristan. She might see him as she saw everything from the city: a bad influence drawing me away from her. "Things are just so complicated."

"Is this, by chance, about a young man?"

Still holding the gritty potato, I turned around from the sink so I could see my mother. There was a knowing look in her eyes.

"There were three wineglasses left out last night."

"Oh." My face burned bright. "There is . . . someone I met in the city. He came to see me last night. But he isn't like the people at the Fashion House. He's different."

"Then why do you seem so burdened?" My mother's voice

was gentle, and its softness was as comforting as a hug. At the Fashion House, I'd been so on edge. I'd been unable to trust anyone, and no one really cared about me. My mother loved me. After being away, I could truly appreciate it, even if her kind of love didn't have much room for my dreams.

"I found out he had a past with someone. Someone I know."

"I see." My mother inserted her paring knife into the skin of a potato. "In my experience, it's best to let go of the past. If you dwell on it for too long, you'll find yourself living there. And there's no life in the past. What's done is done."

I walked over to the kitchen table and put the potato I held into the stew pot. My mother motioned me over to the table and I sat down. There was a pot of tea sitting on a dishcloth and she put down her knife to pour me a cup.

"The blue china?"

"I thought it would be nice." She placed her hand on my shoulder for the briefest moment before returning to the pot and the potatoes.

"Mother . . ." I mulled over her words about the past. She tensed, sensing I was about to ask her something she might not want to answer. "What was it you did in the city? Did you really work at a textile factory?"

She slowly pushed aside the pot of potatoes. She took a deep breath. "No. I didn't. I worked at the Fashion House. I was a maid there."

I set down my teacup with a hard *clink*. My mother had been at the Fashion House? *She'd worked there?* My whole life, I'd talked about going to the Fashion House—and she never said a word. I tried to picture her as a girl my age, moving about the Fashion House, her hand gliding up the banister of the stairs, taking in the wallpapered lobby. But even as I imagined a small, girlish form passing through the fitting room hallway, she had the aged face of my mother, her veiny hands with bitten nails.

"Why didn't you tell me?"

"I've never had much in my life, Emmy." My mother spoke so quietly that the crackle of the morning fire nearly overpowered her voice. "But my past is mine to reckon with in my own way."

With that, she reached for the pot again. Her motions indicated that the conversation was over, that she'd let me in for just a peek, but that was all she was going to allow.

I watched her, uncertain about what to do with this new knowledge, unsure if it changed the way I saw her. A shaft of light fell over her, illuminating her features. I'd always seen her as plain-faced—dour, even. But suddenly I was able to see underneath the web of wrinkles and weathered skin. There, hidden by exhaustion and time, were elegant lines that rose and fell in all the right places. I'd never realized it, but my mother had been beautiful.

I cupped my teacup and let the warmth seep into my hands. I thought about Tilda, about how everyone talked right past her and through her. My mother would've been treated the same way, before she was forced to leave in disgrace because she was pregnant. I always knew her story was full of pain, but now I understood it—I'd seen, firsthand, the hard ways of the city.

"Is that why you never wrote me back? Because it was just too painful to think about the city?"

"I wrote to you. I wrote to you the very night you left. You didn't get my letters?"

"No. I didn't."

I didn't know if I was happy that she had written me all along—or stricken by the thought that someone must have stolen my letters. Was it the same someone who'd destroyed my sketches?

I didn't want to give her any more reasons to hate the city, so I tried to brush it off.

"Maybe they got lost in the mail."

My mother pursed her lips. The clock chimed, and she wiped her hands on her apron. It was time to unlock the front door. She left me sitting at the kitchen table, weighted by her past and the familiar sense that someone had been sabotaging my every move at the Fashion House.

"Emmy . . ." She walked back into the kitchen. "This was tucked into the doorjamb. A note."

"For me?" She held it out, and I instantly recognized Tristan's scrawl. The sight brought back our wine-stained kiss. "I'll be right back."

I could feel my mother's eyes following me as I left the kitchen. I didn't look at her. I didn't need to. I already knew her expression was full of frustration. Disappointment. She saw me following in the steps of her youth—going away to Avon-upon-Kynt, falling in love with a boy from the city—she didn't consider that maybe our endings could be different.

Halfway up the stairs, I stopped. Part of me wanted to tear into Tristan's letter right away, but another part of me wanted to savor it. Slowly, I opened the envelope and took the note out.

> *Emmy,*
>
> *It's been only one night since I've seen you, but somehow it feels like two years.*
>
> *—Tristan*
>
> *PS. I'm headed back to the city, but I'll be in the front row at the debut. Can't wait to see your creations!*

Underneath the note, he'd drawn two stick figures facing each other. One wore a long cape, and they both held teacups. A larger stick figure with fuzzy, scowling eyebrows and crossed arms stood off to the side. Us and Grayson. Our time at the pub, captured in his messy lines.

I closed my eyes, remembering that day at the Prince Regent, how steam had drifted up from my teacup, how the pub had reverberated with the sounds of content customers, how Tristan had sat so close to me. Slowly, eyes still closed, I refolded the note and pressed it to my heart, trying to hold on to the moment a little longer. Then I tucked it into my pocket, making sure it was deep inside so it couldn't fall out. Anytime I was overwhelmed today, I would remember it was there.

The debut was only four days away. Normally, the thought would have sent me into a panic, but now it meant I'd see Tristan soon.

I headed back to my bedroom. I heard Sophie moving about before I stepped inside. She stood in the middle of the room, looking at something small in her palm. The minute I entered, her hand snapped closed.

"What's that?"

She stared at me for a long moment, her eyes dark and hollow, the face of someone who'd woken from a nightmare. Without a word, she lifted her hand toward me, and the item in her palm caught the light and glinted yellow. A small band, a circlet of gold.

"What . . ." My mouth was dry, and I cleared it with effort. "What is that?"

"It's the ring Tristan gave me." Her face was tight and expressionless as I let out an audible breath. There it was, sitting in her hand. A relic of their past, as shiny as though it'd been purchased yesterday.

"You—you carry it around with you?" While her cheeks were pale, I could feel mine afire with flush. "I thought you weren't even sure where it was."

"Well, I happened to have it in my pocket." Her voice was a skeleton of itself, just bare words with no soul inside them. Carefully, like I'd done with Tristan's letter, she tucked the ring back into her dress.

"Are you sure you don't still love him?" I blurted out the question, my cheeks growing even hotter. She let out a careless laugh.

"Of course not." She placed her hand over her pocket, as though she could feel the ring inside it. "I keep all trinkets from my suitors. Rings, necklaces, notes. It's half the fun of it, don't you think?"

"I wouldn't know," I said. I'd only received a postcard and a note from Tristan, and Johnny Wells had never given me any rings or necklaces—much less love letters. "It seems odd to keep a ring from a proposal. If an engagement is broken here, the girl returns the ring."

I didn't know if it was true or not—I'd never known anyone with a broken engagement. In Shy, engagements were nearly as good as weddings. I watched her closely, waiting to see if her facade would slip.

She didn't even pause.

"Things are different in the city."

By Friday, I was so sore and stiff from bending over our garments that I thought I might never stand straight again.

Since the day was clear, we went for a walk and circled the pond behind the pub. We were supposed to take a leisurely stroll, but Sophie kept walking faster and faster. I followed her, my satin flats catching on the pebbles and grass. Eventually, she stopped, staring out over the small pond.

"Are you all right?" I asked. The wind played with our hair, blowing it into our faces, catching on our lips. I wasn't used to seeing Sophie outside. In fact, I still wasn't used to being outside. After living in the contained Fashion House, the sun seemed much brighter and the wind much cooler, in the best ways possible.

"Things feel so different here. Smaller. And bigger."

I watched her. As we'd worked together these past days, it had been hard to push aside the fact that she was the girl who'd had Tristan's heart before me. But, at the same time, she was my partner. She'd stepped into the unknown with me. Yes, she was all pointy ends, rough corners, and dark passages. But when

I was with Sophie, we created what we wanted. She couldn't offer me safety or even unconditional friendship. And that was fine—because what we had together was more important. The ability to design how we wanted, without conditions or limitations, even if there was that ring of gold in her pocket.

"I've been in so many cages. They were all quite pretty. Alexander's manor. The Fashion House." She sighed and squinted as the sun reflected off the pond's surface. "It's easy to see everything in terms of the walls around you. You're lucky, Emmaline."

"Lucky?"

"Your mother loves you, and even if you leave, you'll always bring this"—she held her hands out to the glimmering circle of water—"with you."

"Why did your parents appoint Mr. Taylor as your guardian?" I was treading on dangerous ground. Sophie, like my mother, guarded her past and kept it tucked away out of sight. But there was something open and free about her as she beheld Shy's beauty.

"Alexander was my father's best friend." She spoke slowly, as though measuring out each word before she said it. "They loved the same things: art, theology, politics. They both loved my mother. You'd think it would have driven them apart, but it only brought them closer. My father was an odd man. His philosophizing made him . . . strange. When my mother designed a manor for Alexander, my father called it her love letter to Alexander. It never bothered him." She trailed off, her brows drawing together. "They drowned, you know."

"Your parents?"

"They were drunk one night, and walking along the Tyne River. No one knows exactly what happened, but my mother always loved to balance on the siderail. I imagine she fell in and my father jumped in after her. They were both found the next morning, floating facedown, tangled in her skirts. I was ten at the time."

I shivered, but it wasn't from the cold wind. I could see her—a little girl of ten with big black eyes that nearly swallowed her face—standing in an opulent manor designed by her mother and built for Mr. Taylor. Her parents, the people who were supposed to protect her, had left her and given her to Mr. Taylor. And she'd stayed there, in his grip. No matter where she went, he wouldn't release her.

What did one say to such a story? To such a life? "Things will be different, Sophie. If our collection is successful, we won't be reliant on people like Mr. Taylor or Madame Jolène. It'll just be us. Friends, designing."

At the word *friends*, Sophie turned to face me, hair falling back from her face. She reached up to tuck it away, her movements thoughtful and calm. A slow smile spread across her mouth.

"I suppose we really are friends, aren't we?" There was a note of marvel in her voice. I laughed in spite of myself.

"Of course we are. What else would we be?"

"Oh . . ." She hesitated. "I don't know. Partners?"

"We *are* partners. But definitely friends too."

"That—" She stopped and started. Then she finally finished. "I wasn't expecting that."

CHAPTER TWENTY

THE NEXT MORNING, we woke long before dawn and packed up our collection. We had just enough money for one-way tickets from Shy and a room in the Republic District. The debut would be the day after our arrival, and there was much we still needed to accomplish, including fitting the models. Tristan had sent word that he'd recruited them and told them when to come for the fittings. This added yet another complication—we didn't know their exact sizes, so we'd have to adjust each garment depending on their figures.

As we packed, my mother hovered in the doorway for a few minutes, watching us. I sat back on my heels. I wanted to say something to her. Something to encapsulate the fact that I understood her better now, and that I thought she was brave for always moving forward, even when life tried to hold her back. But before I could speak, she made a sharp *tsk* sound under her breath and left, her heavy footsteps tromping down the stairs to the kitchen.

"Give her time." Sophie carefully folded a black leather skirt. "She only wants the best for you, even if you have different interpretations of what that is."

"I know . . ." But even so, I went after her. I found her at the sink, but she wasn't cleaning vegetables or washing dishes. "Mother?"

"You don't have much time if you want to catch the early train."

"I know." I walked up behind her and put my arms around her waist. She leaned her head back against my shoulder. Then she gently pulled free of me.

"I'll miss you." She briefly touched my cheek before turning away. "You should get going."

I wanted to say so much more, even though it wouldn't change anything. She wouldn't give me her blessing. The same pride that got her through the difficulties of life now held us apart.

"Emmy?" Johnny Wells stood in the kitchen door, his hat in his hands.

"I need to check the taps," my mother said. She left for the dining room, leaving me and Johnny together in the kitchen.

"You're heading back to the city?"

"Yes." I found myself drawn to his easy drawl. There was something so straightforward about him. So open and familiar. We came from the same place. Shy was woven through us, inextricable from us. And maybe that tied us to each other, in a way. He didn't have the complicated life of someone who lived in the city. He didn't have a past with anyone else. Not like Tristan.

"Will you come back?"

"I don't know. It depends on whether our fashion house succeeds."

"If you do come back . . . I-I'm always here." He shuffled and

A DRESS FOR THE WICKED

crushed his hat in his hands. "So just remember that. And while you're gone, I'll look in on your mother."

"Thank you, Johnny."

"I don't fully understand you, Emmy." He stared down at his hat. "But I've always been taken by you, ever since you started wearing those crazy dresses to church."

I laughed, remembering the reactions. "The church ladies weren't fans. They said I was a distraction."

"Yes, they did talk. But I liked the way you looked, even if I never told you as much. I put up a sign for you in the woodshop. Course, it's off the main road, so hardly anyone sees it. But it's there."

I stared at Johnny. I'd always seen him as the quiet boy sitting across from me at our kitchen table, nervously drinking tea, watching me but never saying much. I'd hated how the people in the city didn't understand me. Hated how they'd cast me as a simple country girl. Hated how they didn't bother to see that I was more.

But maybe I did the same to Johnny.

"I'll miss you, Johnny." I meant it. I would. "Maybe I'll see you sometime."

"Maybe," he said, but there wasn't any conviction in his voice. "I already know, though. Your new fashion house will be incredible."

I left him in the kitchen while I went to finish packing. We'd hastily sewn garment bags out of old sheets. As I folded up our various pieces, I realized with a start that Johnny was the very first person to say he truly believed in this new venture.

352

The room we rented in the city was small, about the size of my bedroom back in Shy, but it had a large window that let in light and overlooked the busy street below. With a contented sigh, Sophie said, "The country was refreshing, but I belong in the city. Where I can be seen."

Even though we'd spent a day and a half on a train, Sophie still managed to look stylish. Her abundant hair was swept into a knot high on the top of her head, and she wore a black coat and black boots with pointed toes.

She worked on the gray-and-nude finale gown, while I focused on my piece: a gray gown covered in hand-cut wisps of organza. I'd spent hours cutting out the wisps of fabric to sew onto the smoky-colored lining. The petals graduated from light gray to dark, giving the impression the wearer was decaying into darkness. My fingers lingered over the fabric. I was decaying too—into an exhausted shell of a person.

I set the dress aside to pull some thread out of our bags. At the bottom, a hint of lavender fabric caught my eye. It was Cynthia's gown, folded in a Z pattern to minimize creasing. It was almost finished—in fact, it only needed the hem laid and the embroidery stitched down—but now it never would be.

It was sad to know it'd been so close to completion. At first, it had been a symbol of our new way into the fashion world. Later, it had incriminated us. It shouldn't mean anything to us anymore—we didn't need it. But, suddenly, I was tired of dispensing with things just because they didn't suit their original purpose.

"What are you doing?" Sophie looked up from where she was sewing crystals onto the finale piece. The tiny, sparkly crystals filled a small box next to her. Even from my distance, I could see the tips of her fingers were red from picking up the shards.

"Just thinking about Cynthia's gown." I stared down at the visible part of the dress, letting its details distract me from the impossible amount of work hanging over us.

There was a quiet knock on our door.

"The modeling girls," Sophie said. She adjusted her gown in front of the long mirror propped against the wall.

I slipped into a pair of heels just as Sophie opened the door. Twelve girls in plain work shifts and aprons entered. They peered around curiously, huddling and whispering together.

"Girls!" I called, and they automatically formed a ragged line. They were all different from each other. Some were tall, others short. One had voluptuous curves, while another one had freckles all over her face, shoulders, and arms. I loved the variances. "We will fit you into your outfits to see what alterations we will need to make. Now, what is your name?"

I addressed the tallest girl first. Not only was she tall, but her torso was straight with hardly any indentation at the waist. Her arms and legs were disproportionately long, like twigs extending from her body.

"Anneke," she said, ducking her head a little bit.

"Hello," I said. "It's nice to meet you."

She linked her fingers together in front of her. The way she shifted awkwardly in front of me reminded me of someone. I frowned for a moment before I realized who it was. Me, when I'd first met Madame Jolène. I intimidated her, just as Madame Jolène had intimidated me. If I wanted to, I could cultivate a persona of aloofness and pride, something befitting an important designer.

Or not. I smiled at her and she shyly smiled back.

"Thank you for coming," I said. "Let me show you the dress you'll be wearing."

My piece was entirely completed and hanging on a dresser door. I took it off the hanger while Anneke slipped out of her work shift. Just as I'd thought, her torso was straight and her legs unusually long. The gown would hang flawlessly on her body.

"The closure is on the side." I lowered the dress to the floor so she could step into it. She did so gawkily, holding onto my shoulder. I carefully worked the gown up, inch by inch. It was a tight fit. It had to be—I'd designed it to mold to the body. I laced the side shut with black leather cord and stepped back to see the dress on a real girl for the first time.

The black leather bustier bodice transitioned perfectly into the pleated, charcoal-gray skirt. Dramatic Antwerp lace covered the bust cups and neckline, forming a high collar right at the neck, and cap sleeves, cut from the same lace, cupped Anneke's shoulders.

"You're beautiful." I whispered more to the dress than to Anneke. I motioned her over to the long mirror and stood beside her. She raised her hands to her mouth, gasping.

"I feel . . ." Her voice trailed off and she ran her hands over the pleated skirt. It shimmered underneath her fingers. "Powerful."

I knelt to pin the hem. Somehow, this dress had sprung from my heart to my fingertips to the world. Anneke kept running her hands over the skirt. Her motions reminded me of the way Shy's farmers would run their hands through waist-high wheat. The skirt moved at her touch, undulating like it was underwater.

I glanced over to see Sophie styling three girls in a tableau. She pointed and hustled them into position. One was standing, one was sitting, and the other one was lounging on the ground, each trying to stay perfectly still. It was a configuration borrowed from the Fashion House's debuts.

I turned back to Anneke. "Can you walk for me?"

"What?" She abruptly stopped, but the skirt continued to flow around her body.

"Just walk up and down the room."

There was only one small sliver of space where Anneke could walk, because the ground was covered in fabric pieces, patterns, sketch paper, pin holders, and halfway-finished dresses. As she crossed the floor and stepped around the mess, the dress took on a life of its own. While she was stiff and uncertain, the dress rippled around her, the skirt surging with her strides as light danced off the pleats.

I couldn't contain my awe any longer.

"Sophie," I breathed. "Look! The dress is alive."

It was like a spirit possessed the dress: the skirt sank, rose, fell, and twisted, sometimes wrapping tightly around Anneke's legs to show hints of her shape, other times billowing out to completely conceal her.

"That's stunning." Sophie watched from where she was looping a measuring tape around a model's waist. "It shows the dress in a completely different way."

"We should have them all walk." I spoke so fast that I nearly started stammering. I didn't care. I was too excited. "We'll see the gowns the way people see them in real life: in motion. When women wear dresses, they aren't simply standing still. They're walking or strolling or dancing. That's how we should present the gowns."

"Girls!" Sophie clapped her hands. "Everyone start walking like Anneke. Single file."

They fell into one moving line. I watched, holding my breath. They walked rigidly at first. Then their bodies surrendered to their natural gaits and the dresses glided with them, the skirts swinging forward and backward against their legs, their movements revealing all sides of the gowns. They drifted, a row of gray and champagne-colored figures. Each one led to the next in a dreamlike sequence that built to the finale dress, with its huge overlay skirt.

"It takes my breath away," Sophie said. We stood, Sophie on one side of the girls, I on the other, watching them for a few moments longer.

A thought burned in my mind: *We might just pull this off.*

By the time the girls left our fitting, the light had taken on an orangish twilight hue—we'd worked through the day. We continued into the night, long enough for the sun to start streaking the sky, and only went to bed for a few hours before the debut.

I lay down next to Sophie, my limbs so achy that relaxation was impossible. I thought she was asleep, but when I brushed against her, she stiffened.

"Sophie," I whispered, even though there was no need to be quiet. "Are you awake?"

"No," she whispered back.

"Do you think . . . ?" Slowly, I rolled from my side to my back. Even though I couldn't see anything in the darkness, I didn't shut my eyes. "Everything is much more complex than I thought it would be." I didn't know what I was saying. I tried to cling to the fierce moment of confidence I'd felt earlier. But now, on the cusp of the debut, a dark sense of doom settled over me. "Do you think . . . do you think it will all be worth it? Everything we've been through? Do you think our collection will be successful?"

I couldn't see her, but I felt the bed give beneath her as she rolled over to face me. Her hand found me in the dark, touching my shoulder and following it down to my arm, where her fingers closed around my wrist. She held it tightly, securely.

"I've never met anyone like you, Emmaline Watkins."

It wasn't much of a reassurance—she didn't say that we would succeed. But even if I didn't believe in myself, it seemed like she did. That alone abated my firestorm of worry.

She released my wrist and turned back over, the curve of her back against the length of my arm. A few seconds later, her breathing deepened as she fell asleep. I paced my breathing to hers. I didn't think I'd be able to sleep, but before I knew it, darkness—one much deeper than the darkness in the room—overcame me.

CHAPTER TWENTY-ONE

THE DAY OF THE FASHION debut began with a shower of rain and a clap of thunder. For the second time, we packed our collection into a hack. It was much smaller than the one that had taken us to the train station after we left the Fashion House, and there was no room for us in it. We had to follow behind in another hack, using the last of our money to pay for it. I watched Sophie count the bills out into the driver's hand, realizing that we had just enough to get to the debut but not enough to go anywhere afterward.

We sat next to each other in the hack, watching as we passed businesses with signs in their windows reading GONE TO THE EXHIBITION. Once we neared the exhibition square, the hack slowed to a crawl, caught in traffic. The exhibition was in full swing. A man holding a black umbrella was giving a speech on the steps of the parliament building, and a crowd had gathered around him. Farther back, behind the crowd and in the center of the square, street musicians played, and people danced while holding tankards of beer.

Slowly, the hack inched its way past the exhibition and came to a stop in an alley just a few blocks from the square. When I stepped out of the cab, a blast of cold wind greeted me. I twisted, trying to angle myself so my hair blew away from my face. I was hemmed in on both sides by brick buildings with sooty windows.

"This is it, Sophie?" I asked.

"We're in the back," Sophie said, stepping out of the hack.

I walked up to the unpainted door. Its doorknob was covered with grime. I twisted the knob and pushed, but the door didn't open. The hack driver noticed my struggle and motioned me aside. He grabbed the knob, leaned his shoulder into the door, and shoved hard. The door sprang open, squealing on rusted hinges.

"Glamorous," I muttered. Taking a breath, I stepped inside. I knew we didn't have endless funds to get a beautiful venue. But the building's drafty, brick-walled interior and musty smell made me cringe. A long narrow stage was built against one of the walls. Red curtains, their color dulled by dust and sun, hung limply on a rod. The curtains were supposed to cover the ladders on either side of the stage leading up to a suspended platform, but they didn't quite manage it. Old theater chairs were scattered haphazardly across the floor, cotton tufts bursting from their seams.

"Come help." Sophie pushed her way past me.

"It's . . . dismal," I said. I pictured Charwell Palace in my mind, how all its opulence accented Madame Jolène's vision.

"We didn't have any other choice," she responded, garment bags draped over her arm and partially dragging on the floor.

I took a deep breath and surveyed the wooden stage, battered theater chairs, and smudged windows once more. I pictured our gowns moving along the stage, lone silhouettes of beauty against the theater's drabness. The sight was more pleasing than I'd first thought. The building and collection would contrast each other—and it felt fitting for the setting to be so humble. I didn't come from much. This was part of the story our collection told.

Once our gowns were on that stage, our collection would create its own type of beauty.

We unpacked the garment bags in the cramped space on the side of the stage. Every time I pulled a dress from its bag, I almost knocked into Sophie. We had to hang the gowns awkwardly on a hook anchored to the stage wall, piling them one on top of another. The delicate laces and silks caught on the beadwork, and we struggled to protect them.

There were two unfinished gowns without buttons or corsets, so we would have to sew the models into them. Some seams were misaligned, and we hadn't had time to alter all the dresses to the models' proportions. Three hems were much too long, and one dress was puckering along the closure.

"Do you think everyone will notice the imperfections?" Sophie asked.

"Hopefully they'll see the vision behind the collection, and that will be enough." I tried to fold a garment bag and give the backstage area some sense of order. "We just need enough interest and private funding to get started."

The old door screeched open once again. The models trailed in, one after another, and gathered around the front row of the theater seats.

I climbed up the small staircase to stand on the stage. The whole theater spread out in front of me.

"Everyone," I called, and the models raised their faces to me. "Thank you for coming. Let's get dressed."

It wasn't a very inspirational speech—if it could even be called a speech—but anything I said would've been meaningless anyway. Our gowns would speak for us.

The girls obediently started to file back to our makeshiftd dressing area. I stayed for a second longer on the stage, trying to calm myself.

This was the second time in my life I'd been on a stage. The only other time had been at the gala, and I'd been a Fashion House Interview contestant then—or as much of a contestant as I could be. I'd never really been part of the competition.

Now, I was the designer. I pictured Madame Jolène. Not the Madame Jolène who'd stared at me with pure disdain. Not the Madame Jolène who'd stood on the stage at the gala, hands raised and face flashing with true joy, or even the Madame Jolène who walked the Fashion House hallways, overseeing fittings with brisk professionalism.

I saw the Madame Jolène waiting behind the stage, breathing in and out, eyes closed, still. I gave myself my own moment to catch my breath and savor this, then went over to the backstage area to help the girls slide out of their clothes and into ours. I was glad for the rush of activity. Soon, my motions pushed my worries to the back of my mind.

It was an awkward, rushed transition to transform the girls from factory workers into models. Their elbows gouged my sides and their hands clawed my arms as they struggled into their gowns. They wavered like colts taking their first steps as I helped them slip into the heels. Problems arose faster than solutions. Two dresses just weren't fitting right, and we'd forgotten an all-important champagne lining. One of the models could sew, so we put her to work stitching the last few crystals on the finale veil. Even though we hadn't moved beyond the small space, I was out of breath and sweaty, as though I'd been running for miles.

"The guests will arrive any moment," Sophie said to me as I tacked up a hem, stitching faster than I ever had in my life. "We need to light the stage lamps."

"I have to finish this." I pulled a needle through dark-gray fabric. "Hold still," I implored the model. My back, neck, and knees burned from bending down and standing up over and over again, and my voice was hoarse from talking over the models to Sophie.

"Come on," Sophie said. "I took some matches from the tenement building."

She tossed a packet to me.

"All right!" I didn't have the will to protest. I left the needle dangling on its thread from the dress and went out onto the stage.

It was much cooler out there than in the cramped backstage area. The rafters were high above my head and I had to lean backward to see the rickety platform hanging over the stage. I slid open the matchbox and struck one against the box. It blazed to life, one small pinprick of brightness in the gloomy room.

Each stage lamp had a kerosene glass base and a blackened wick. I wasn't sure if they would catch, but the minute I knelt down and held the match to the first wick, it burst into a bright blue-orange flame. The mirrored panel behind the lamp magnified its effect. I lit them one by one, until the stage was framed in a half circle of warm light.

"Emmy!" a warm, familiar voice rang out, and a blond head moved up the side of the theater.

"Tristan!" I leaped off the stage and ran to him. Sweaty though I was, I jumped into his arms.

"I've missed you," he murmured into my ear, his arms wrapped around me, his hands spreading across my back.

"I missed you too," I said. I buried my face into the side of his neck, staying still in his arms for one minute, two, three. For once, I was safe, held in his embrace. "It's been so busy."

"Anything I can help with?"

"Unless you've somehow learned to sew, I don't think so."

"I have something for you."

Tristan let me go and walked back to one of the theater seats and snatched something from it. He came back down the aisle, carrying a single rose. Its fluffy head was a brilliant red. "This is for you. To congratulate you on the show."

"I love it."

"I figured it was better than one of my chicken-scrawl sketches."

"Those are my favorite!"

"Glad to hear it." He seemed to notice my distraction. "Are you all right?"

"Yes. Yes, of course. Just worried about the show."

"That makes sense. You're taking a big leap, Emmy. Big leaps can elicit some pretty big emotions."

And so can old proposals.

"I need to get back. The show's going to start soon."

"I'll be right in the front row if you need me."

His hand went around to the back of my neck and pulled me into him. I let myself be pulled, my worries and fears disappearing as my lips found his.

Only a few people came. They trailed in, picking their way through the theater seats and settling into the most comfortable ones. I observed from behind the curtain. Sophie peered over my shoulder, and the models, standing on their toes behind us, watched too.

"I was hoping more people would come," I whispered.

"It's who they are that matters," Sophie said. "Look! There's a reporter from the *Avon-upon-Kynt Times*, and that's Ms. Walker from the *Ladies' Journal*. Those two alone are more valuable than a crowd of a hundred."

Four figures made their way over to us, the stage lights revealing their faces. Alice, Ky, Cordelia, and Kitty. They garnered attention as they moved, their styles differentiating them from the rest of the crowd.

"I didn't think any of you would come," I said. I bent down

on the stage so I was eye level with them. It was strange seeing them outside of the Fashion House.

"We wanted to see your show," Cordelia said. "It's all everyone's been talking about."

"Really?"

"Yes. Of course, Madame Jolène doesn't say anything, but the whole city has been abuzz."

"It's true." Kitty pushed forward. "From the maids to the customers, everyone is dying to see what will happen with your new collection."

"Kitty . . ." I'd pushed her to the back of my mind, especially since we left the Fashion House. I didn't know if she'd been the saboteur—that letter still implicated her. It could've easily been her. Or maybe one of the other girls.

But, as they gathered at the edge of the stage, staring up at me, it didn't seem to matter as much anymore.

"Do a good job." She reached up and caught my hand in hers. "For all of us."

The other girls nodded, their eyes suddenly flashing. It reminded me of that first night in the lobby at the Fashion House, how they'd all looked so determined and strong. We really weren't so different. They'd all come to the Fashion House Interview to escape, to find, to be. For them, like me, fashion put their futures into their own hands.

"I will," I said. "I promise."

They found their seats, and as I took one last glance out at the small gathering, my heart started to pound. Raw, nervous energy made me skittish. I wanted to run around or jump up and down, but there wasn't any room. I had to just stand there in the small space, feeling the heat radiating from the models and Sophie.

"Tristan's here," Sophie murmured, more to herself than to me. She hadn't seen him arrive earlier. I searched the audience for his outline. I found him right in front, like he'd said. He was nothing but a black silhouette against a bulky theater chair. We both stood quietly on the side of the stage, staring at him.

Then Sophie said, "Here, we only have a few minutes. We need to change."

"Change?"

I glanced down at myself. I was wearing one of her gowns: a black dress with tiny Swiss dots printed over the fabric. It was stylish but hardly memorable, and now it was stained with sweat marks and dried raindrops.

"There's something for you." Sophie pointed to a garment bag lying in the corner. I hadn't noticed it in the rush to get the models dressed. I pushed through the smothering, narrow backstage to get to it. As I undid the strings closing it, I caught a glimpse of purple silk through the bag's opening. *Cynthia's gown.* Sophie had brought it.

"You finished it?"

"No. I didn't."

"Then how . . . ?"

"Your mother finished it. I told her you wouldn't have anything to wear at our debut and she sewed down the embroidery and finished the hem. I told her I'd bring it for you."

I unlaced the garment-bag ties and stared at the dress. My

mother, who hadn't even wished me luck when I left, had finished the gown for me.

"Hurry up." Sophie cut into my thoughts. "I'll help you change."

I quickly unbuttoned my dress and slipped out of it, letting it fall to the ground. When I touched Cynthia's dress, I slowed. The gown's beauty and the fabric demanded reverence. It slipped onto my body as though it were dressing me, not the other way around. The silk clung to my frame and it seemed to seep into my skin, as much a part of me as my bones and marrow.

We didn't have a mirror behind the stage, so it was impossible for me to see myself. But it didn't matter. I understood the dress better than anything else. It was everything I imagined: couture beauty that transformed me as much as it would have transformed Cynthia.

The gown was all of that but also so much more. My mother's hands had finished it. She'd dressed me for the day, even if she didn't understand my dreams.

"It came out well," Sophie said, pulling her new dress up. She paused to examine me, her dress around her hips. She was like a mermaid, the dramatic lines of her lacy black gown emerging just below her navel, her long locks covering her chest, her arms drawn up in front of her.

Sophie pulled the rest of her dress on, and one of the girls buttoned her into it. Incremental rows of black lace created the skirt and built into a plunging V neckline. I thought she would wrap her hair into a topknot like she usually did, but instead she shook it out, letting it fall down her back.

"Should we start, misses?" one of the models asked.

I nodded and suddenly, after all the busyness, I didn't have anything to do. Everything dulled except for my throbbing pulse. Sophie stepped out and welcomed the guests, but I couldn't focus on her words. She returned backstage and I motioned to the first girl, Anna, and she walked forward into the stage light.

Everything was different on the stage. In the fitting rooms at the Fashion House and my bedroom in Shy, each design element had seemed so exaggerated. But as I watched from behind the curtain, Anna's ombre gown suddenly seemed slimmer to me, its details swallowed into a blur of fabric and flash of beads.

Anna walked the stage's length, back straight, hands at her sides, head erect. I heard the audience gasp collectively, and I smiled. There weren't many people, so the sound was almost a whisper, but I knew.

They saw it.

They *felt* it.

I was so enthralled with the ombre dress floating across the stage and the audience's response that I didn't notice Anneke until she walked past me.

My favorite look was going out.

Anneke moved casually, as though the stage was simply a cobbled city street. I fought the urge to run over to her and lay out the small train for the millionth time. She stepped out of the shadows and onto the flickering stage.

When I was young, my mother would read me the Bible verse "For he spake and it was done." For the first time, I understood the scripture. My gown was suddenly alive, ignited by the lights, the audience, and the stage. The smoky gray charmeuse rippled like water and waved like wind through grass. The leather bodice glistened, sleek and durable.

It embodied the best parts of Shy, the parts that would always be mine. Everything—the fear, the uncertainty, the heartache, the homesickness—had been for something much more meaningful and powerful than I could understand. I only wished my mother could be here to see it.

Anneke moved down toward the audience, but I saw only my gown, drifting like an untethered ghost across the stage. She was up there for an eternity and, at the same time, a split second.

Once she was back behind the curtains, everything sped up. I hurried the girls out one after another. It seemed like I only blinked before Sophie and I were stepping out onto the stage. Suddenly I was standing right in the stage lights, staring off into the blackness just beyond them.

The sound of applause started slowly, almost carefully, and then mounted faster and faster, louder and louder. There were only a few people, but they rose, dark silhouettes outside the lights. They clapped, stomped, and cheered. The acceleration of sound and excitement built inside me until I thought I would burst. Sophie held my hand and tried to say something, but everyone was still clapping, so she simply curtsied, pulling me down with her. We straightened together, leaning into each other.

We stood out there for a few moments longer and then

retreated to the backstage area. Our models surrounded us, smiling and cheering. I hugged Sophie and, as I did, a face came into view.

I drew back from Sophie.

"Tilda?"

CHAPTER TWENTY-TWO

THE APPLAUSE STILL RANG OUT in the theater, but all I saw was Tilda's pinched face. She wore a cape over her maid's uniform.

"What are you doing here? Why are you backstage?"

She stepped close to me so I could hear her. Her breath was hot against my skin. "Everything that was supposed to be mine—it's all yours."

"What?"

"I've always wanted to design. When the Reformists pressured Madame Jolène to include someone different, I asked Madame Jolène if it could be me. Do you know what she said?"

I could barely hear Tilda over the noise. Sophie was pulling on my arm, trying to draw me away. But Tilda's eyes fixed me in place.

"It was you," I said, all the pieces coming together in my head to form one horrifying whole. "You took my welcome letter and ruined my sketches. And my mother's letters. You stole them."

"That man—Mr. Taylor—he told Madame Jolène that the new candidate couldn't just be poor. She had to be from the country, too. So I was forced to stay a maid and serve you and watch you and—" She took a raggedy breath. "But it doesn't matter. I saw Mr. Taylor and he said I could be part of the Reformists movement. All I have to do is stop you."

"Stop me?"

"Yes. That's the thing about the city. People remember dresses, yes, but they remember scandals so much more."

With that, she launched at me. I hardly registered what was happening until I hit the ground. Her hands clawed at my beautiful dress and the sound of ripping fabric cut through the air. We landed out on the stage and, almost immediately, the clapping turned to gasps.

"Get off me!"

I kicked with all my might and struggled to free myself from her hands. We rolled to one side and the bright flash of the stage lights flared in my eyes. I heard glass breaking as we shattered the light and something hard punctured my ankle.

The models and Sophie rushed forward, pulling Tilda off me. Her nails sank into my skin before she was yanked away. I sat up. The air was hazy and thick. It swam in front of my eyes and circled around me. I smelled something acrid. Fire. Flames from the stage lights were licking across the stage and eating their way up the stage curtain. The red velvet curled beneath the fire's heat and little orange sparks speckled the fabric and danced through the air.

"Fire!" someone shouted. "Fire!"

I pushed myself onto my knees and then to my feet, tripping on my skirts. Dark shapes rushed past me. It was the models, running off the stage. Sophie came up behind me.

"We need to get out of here!"

The flames reached all the way up the curtain and fanned out across the top of the stage. Now there was crackling and hissing, sounds I heard often in Shy when my mother lit fires in our fireplace. It was the sound of flames fed by wood. The stage was on fire, not just the curtains.

There was only one place we could go: behind the stage. We plunged into the small space beyond the flame-engulfed curtains. It was filled with hot smoke that swirled as we moved through it. All I could see were flames above us and the gray shapes of garment bags around us.

I groped for the rickety wooden ladder nailed to the wall. It led up to the platform hanging over the stage. We could climb up the ladder, make our way across the boards, and get down by the other ladder on the far side of the platform.

It wasn't wise to climb it. The smoke was rising, billowing its way to the ceiling and forming a massive gray cloud against the roof. Fire engulfed the curtains hanging across the top of the stage and they were only a few feet from the platform.

"Climb!" I screamed into Sophie's ear. Smoke filled my mouth, searing my tongue and throat. We had to go up, up where it was hotter. I didn't know if I could do it. I didn't know if I could climb up into the smoke. But there wasn't any other choice.

Sophie started to climb up the ladder. Once she was far enough above me, I put my foot on the first rung. My heel slipped off. I grabbed the ladder with one hand and a handful of my gown in the other and started climbing. The heat increased until tears streamed down my face and my skin blistered against my dress.

Up. Up. Up.

I reached the platform and barely hauled myself over onto it. My muscles shook and cinders nipped at my face, hands, neck. I wanted to curl up and close it all out. But I had to keep moving. I got to my feet. Sophie stood next to me, staring over the edge of the platform.

"Sophie!" I croaked. "Come on."

She was frozen, staring down at the flames below. I grabbed her arm, jerking her hard across the moaning platform to the ladder on the other side where the fire hadn't yet reached. I held Sophie's hand as she swung her legs over the side and started down the ladder. Once she made it halfway down, I hoisted myself around the ladder and moved down, my skirts catching every few feet on the nails and wood. When my feet touched the bottom, my knees buckled beneath me.

All of a sudden, strong arms enveloped me, lifting me completely off the ground.

Tristan.

Outside the theater, rain poured down on me, soothing my blistering skin and smoke-filled eyes. I coughed and coughed, trying to expel the ashy stinging in my chest. But no matter how much I heaved, the awful pain just behind my heart remained.

Tristan held me tightly, his hand running through my hair, cinders flaking out of my locks.

"Are you all right? I was—" His voice caught, and it wasn't

from the smoke-filled air. He cleared his throat vigorously. "I was terrified I'd lost you."

"It would take more than a fire and an attack by a maid to stop me," I said, only I was coughing at the same time, and my joke came out choked. I turned my head so my cheek pressed against the muscles of his chest.

There was a loud rattling nearby, and I pulled my face away. A red fire wagon was parked in front of the building, and firemen scurried around, shouting to each other and unwinding a leather hose. Black smoke mingled with black rainclouds in the sky.

Our models milled around, their dresses—our hard work—torn and stained with soot. Nearly all our guests were gone. Tilda was nowhere to be seen. Sophie was on the far end of the street, talking to a man and Ms. Walker. They both scribbled something down in notebooks. I rose unsteadily to my feet.

"Are you all right?" Tristan placed a steadying hand on my elbow.

"Yes. I'll be right back."

There was a woman just beyond Sophie. Her arms were folded over her chest and she was wearing a dark blue coat with a beaded capelet. It wasn't the sort of attire to wear in the rain. Much too fashionable. A mink hat with a full brim was pulled low over her forehead. I made my way over to where she watched the smoke rise into the sky.

"Madame Jolène?" I asked.

She turned, clearly shocked I had recognized her. Her eyes predictably traveled from my shoes to my hair. Even though I'd just escaped the clutches of a furious maid and a fiery building, she still appraised me. For the first time, it didn't matter to me.

"Emmaline," she said. "I see you've found your color."

"What are you doing here?" I demanded.

"I wanted to see the collection," she said, shrugging slightly as though I'd asked a daft question.

She didn't mention the fire or ask if we were all right. Fashion was always her focus, and everything else, even life-and-death peril, were peripheral to it. "What did you think?"

She took in a slow breath, seeming to deliberate over what she wanted to say.

"It was beautiful. I loved it." She stared at me, unapologetic. "I knew it would be. You girls are talented. It's too bad it ended in such calamity. Perhaps some things—and some people—are simply ill-fated." She pulled the brim of her hat down farther, shadowing her face. I could still see her eyes, though, and their gaze intensified, as though a new thought had struck her. "It reminded me of debuting my first collection, over a decade ago. Back then, the Fashion House was run by a man, Lord Harold Spencer. He used the Fashion House for profit and fame and cared little for beauty." She paused. "You think you are doing something new, but you are merely reprising all the revolutions that have come before you."

She stuck her hands deep into her pockets. Her entire body was covered: her face by her hat, her body by her coat, and her hands by her pockets. It was impossible to see anything besides her clothing. When she spoke again, it sounded like she was talking to herself, not to me.

"If, despite the scandalous ending to your show, you manage to succeed, you will pave the way for the next generation, who will have some complaint about your style or your ethics or any other ridiculous thing. Fashion isn't linear. It's cyclical. Just as trends are, so are movements. Remember that, Emmaline, when you go wherever it is you will go after this."

She turned to leave.

"Wait!"

Madame Jolène paused for just a moment, but then kept going. It was just as well. I didn't know why I'd asked her to wait. Standing here, with soot in my throat and ashes in my hair, everything seemed so vivid—how I'd struggled so hard, how she'd always seen me as a pawn and not a person, how I'd done so many things that I'd never thought I'd do to get what I wanted. To get what I needed.

She moved across the street and I watched her go. Life had pushed us up against each other. *She* had pushed us up against each other. But maybe now I could understand. She was just trying to protect what was hers.

I woke up the next day with the scent of fire in my nose. The minute I slipped out of bed and stood up, my head swam, and I put a steadying hand on the headboard.

Yesterday, we'd walked back to our rented room. Even though we didn't have money to pay for another night, we slept there, crossing our fingers that the landlady wouldn't come to our door.

Sophie sat at the table, drinking milky tea and reading the morning paper.

"Good morning," she said as I approached. "How are you?"

"I'm not so sure. Last night was . . ." I trailed off. Awful? Electrifying?

I saw Tilda's eyes in my mind, how they'd flashed with hatred. It had been her all along, not Kitty. The revelation filled me with a strange mix of relief and regret. As soon as I could, I would apologize to Kitty for pushing her away when she'd never betrayed me.

"Last night was a success," Sophie said. "Look at this."

A SECOND FASHION HOUSE
FOR THE FIRST TIME IN AVON-UPON-KYNT?

Rumors have been swirling for the past week that two former Fashion House Interview contestants had created a small collection of gowns outside the Fashion House label.

Yesterday, this newspaper confirmed the rumors. Select press members, including the Avon-upon-Kynt Times, previewed the gowns at a small fashion debut held after the Parliament Exhibition. Of remarkable note is that the two contestants are Emmaline Watkins, country talent from the north, and Sophie Sterling, the last remaining member of the eccentric Sterling family.

After years of Fashion House styles, the collection was a breath of fresh air, featuring haunting outfits that stayed with this reporter long after the final bows. Of further interest, the designers had their models walk, showcasing the pieces' movements. It was an ingenious decision.

Tragically, a stage light caught the curtain on fire, ending the debut.

"On top of it all, it's in the *Times*," Sophie said. "A year ago, the paper wouldn't have dared write anything against the

Fashion House for fear of the Crown."

"What about Mr. Taylor? Will he try to stop us since we won't design for the Reformists Party?"

"He might. But everything is in upheaval right now. It works to our advantage. There's even an opinion piece in the front of the paper. It talks about how fashion should be free from the government—both the Crown *and* Parliament."

I sat back in my chair. I'd never pictured this moment. I'd been so caught up with getting things done that I hadn't realized what the other side of the hard work would be like, what it would feel like.

"I thought for sure that Tilda's fire would ruin our chances."

"Normally, it would have." Sophie shrugged. "Things really are shifting, though. Ms. Walker wrote about it in the gossip column and concluded that the Fashion House had sent Tilda to stop us. Which isn't true, of course, but it makes us seem sympathetic."

"What will happen to Tilda?"

"Well, it seems like she's aligned herself with the Reformists Party. She probably doesn't realize she's in the clutches of a madman."

I supposed I should be happy—Tilda had tried to ruin me at every turn. But I kept thinking about my mother, how she'd been a maid as well. It wasn't so easy, when the things one wanted were so far outside one's grasp.

We sat quietly for a few moments, reading the papers. The restfulness was temporary, I knew. Soon, reality would descend on us, and we would have to work and plan and figure out a way to stay ahead of Madame Jolène and Mr. Taylor. But—just for the morning—I would celebrate.

"I wanted to say thank you. For choosing me to join you in this crazy venture." Sophie placed her cold hand on top of mine. The gesture was strangely awkward, considering her usual grace. She seemed to realize it and pulled her hand away. "I—" She stumbled over her words. "I think you are the first real friend I've ever had, Emmy. It's terrifying."

Sophie's words filled my soul in a way nothing else could.

"And I have something to tell you," she said.

"What is it?"

"I told you about Tristan's proposal because I wanted to make you . . ." She stopped, struggling. She began again. "I pretend like he doesn't mean anything to me, but that ring he gave me—I didn't just keep it for fun."

I pictured the thin band sitting on Sophie's palm that day she'd showed it to me. She'd kept it. She hadn't really said yes to his proposal. Hadn't really said no. She'd held on to it . . . and, in some ways, him.

And maybe, even though I didn't want to think it, he'd always have something with her, even if it wasn't love. Perhaps that's how it worked with such things. Promises of promises. They knit people together, just like simple rings of gold did.

"I don't think I loved him the way you do. But when I was engaged to him, it was . . ." She seemed to be searching for a word. I waited, needing to hear it, even though I didn't want to. "I felt *safe* for the first time in a long while, and it was . . . comforting." With nervous motions, she picked up the nearby saucer and poured milk into her tea, even though she already had. The milk plumed across its surface, turning the liquid white.

I remembered the way she'd interrupted our kiss in the dining room, how she'd pretended to be heading through to her room but had stayed, watching us. All along, she'd been trying to drive us apart and for what? She didn't want him back.

And yet, she was apologizing. In her own way. She hadn't said *I'm sorry*, but she wasn't the sort of girl who ever would. Simply stating the truth was a lot for her.

"I understand," I said, and the grimness that created lines around her mouth and furrows across her brow dissipated. With a light touch, she picked up her milky tea and took a sip. I let us move on. "Can you believe that Madame Jolène was at the debut?"

"I thought I saw her there." She jumped on to the change of topic.

"I spoke with her."

"What did she say?"

"She said . . ." How could I describe our conversation? How she'd been threatening yet sad and vulnerable at the same time? "She said our collection was good."

"I'm surprised she could bring herself to admit it."

"I don't know. I think, above everything else, she loves beauty."

I stared down at the newspaper. In a few days it would reach Shy, and my mother would read it. She would know, then, that we'd succeeded. And she would know that I wasn't coming back anytime soon.

The thought dimmed my elation. The second we turned any profit, I would send it back to her. And, when I could, I would go see her. Getting our fashion house started was important, but certain things—certain people—were more important.

I poured myself a cup of tea and put my fingers over the mouth of the cup, letting its steam warm my hands.

"We have to figure out our next steps," I said. "We'll need to make some more gowns and start taking appointments. And we need to come up with a press plan. The more we're written up in the papers, the better."

We started to talk about our new pieces, crafting gowns in the air. Their shapes and details rose in my mind and winged upward like birds, birds whose feathers were made of blue-violet silk and twisting chiffon ribbons. My heart soared with them, borne on the knowledge that, for better or for worse, my future was no longer bound by where I'd come from, but rather, what I would create for myself—stitch by stitch.

AUTHOR'S NOTE

While writing this book, I was working as a stylist at an upscale bridal salon in Beverly Hills. It's simplest to say that I fell in love with the elaborate designs and exquisite construction of the red-carpet couture and wedding gowns. Never in my life had I imagined such beauty and, at the salon, I could see, touch, and feel it on a daily basis.

As I developed this story, I chose to place it in a fictional country that is most like Victorian London. I wanted to set Emmy's journey amid the Victorian sensibility for its beauty, its rigid class structures, and its etiquette. However, my imagination was and is captivated by modern-day couture and the continuous dialogue between fashion and the ways it borrows from different places and points in history. As you read, you will notice that the styles and some of the Fashion House's operations are not consistent with the Victorian period. This was intentional as this book, in many ways, is an exploration of the universality and the evolution of the clothes we wear and how they make us feel.

ACKNOWLEDGMENTS

If this story was an outfit, its early incarnations might've landed it on the Worst Dressed List. However, through the loving care and guidance of several people, it was styled from a *Don't* to a *Do*.

The first thanks belong to Jamie Campbell, Carlos Delgado, and Paul Buchanan. They read the first ten pages of this story and said *Yes, you should pursue writing.* Thank you also to Amanda Jenkins for echoing their words later on when I needed it most.

Thank you to Emilia Rhodes for bringing me into the Harper family, and to Elizabeth Lynch for guiding this book to its equivalent of a chic, perfectly tailored LBD. Thank you to Molly Fehr for designing such a beautiful book, and to Katie Rodgers for the exquisite illustration on my cover. I still can hardly believe that the artist who works with Louboutin, Gucci, and Elie Saab dressed my novel with her art. Thanks also to Maya Myers, Alexandra Rakaczki, and the rest of the Harper team.

Thank you to my agent, Susan Hawk. I am eternally grateful for your insights, support, notes, and general amazingness.

I truly couldn't have done any of this without you. Thank you also to Kelly Dyksterhouse—you inspire me in so many ways.

Just as you need to have friends who will tell you if an outfit isn't working, you also need them to lay down the truth about your novel, and I'm lucky enough to have five. Nikki, I'm so glad we're friends. You were always there for me, whether I needed a listening ear, some long-distance writing timing, or a writing-date buddy. Here's to many more years of friendship. Katie, WE DID IT! Ha-ha, you know what that means. I love you, my friend who understands my love of aesthetics and has her own killer style. Aimee, thank you for cheering me on (also: glitter baths!). Gwen, you pushed me to get out into the writing world, and who knows how long I would've waffled without your encouragement. You're the best. Jenn, what can I say? You guided me through this process—I honestly owe so much of this to you. Thank you for giving so selflessly to me.

A very important thank-you to the Night Owl in Fullerton, whose coffee fueled this novel. Thank you to Kathie for helping me with Juliet when I had so many deadlines.

Thank you, Momopawns and Dad! This is as much yours as it is mine. And, of course, to Kylee (the real Ky! Byeeeeeeeeeee! You always look on point, but you already know that) and Seth, my "twin."

To Juliet, the little dark-haired fairy who lives in my house, and to Mark, my everything. You've embraced me in every way, from giving me piggyback rides when my heels hurt to telling me I can do it when I don't think I can. What would I be without you? I love you.

Most important, thank you to God for blessing me and putting so many people in my life who have helped me achieve my dreams, and for creating a world with so many beautiful things in it.